Echoes of Atlantis
Crones, Templars and the Lost Continent

A Novel by
David S. Brody

Eyes That See Publishing

Echoes of Atlantis
Crones, Templars and the Lost Continent

Eyes That See Publishing
Westford, Massachusetts

ISBN 978-0-9907413-2-9

1st edition

This is a work of fiction. Names, characters and incidents are either a product of the author's imagination or are used fictitiously. Except as otherwise noted in the Author's Note, any resemblance to actual events or people, living or dead, is entirely coincidental.

Cover by Kimberly Scott and Renee Brody

Printed in USA

Praise for Books in this Series

To my daughters, Allie and Renee

May you find your own personal versions of Atlantis

About the Author

David S. Brody is a *Boston Globe* bestselling fiction writer named Boston's "Best Local Author" by the *Boston Phoenix* newspaper. A graduate of Tufts University and Georgetown Law School, he is a former Director of the New England Antiquities Research Association (NEARA) and is a dedicated researcher in the field of pre-Columbian exploration of America. He has appeared as a guest expert on documentaries airing on History Channel, Travel Channel, PBS, and Discovery Channel.

The first four books in his "Templars in America Series" are Amazon Kindle Top 10 Bestsellers.

Echoes of Atlantis is his ninth novel.

For more information, please visit
DavidBrodyBooks.com

Also by the Author

Unlawful Deeds

Blood of the Tribe

The Wrong Abraham

The "Templars in America" Series

Cabal of the Westford Knight: Templars at the Newport Tower (Book 1)

Thief on the Cross: Templar Secrets in America (Book 2)

Powdered Gold: Templars and the American Ark of the Covenant (Book 3)

The Oath of Nimrod: Giants, MK-Ultra and the Smithsonian Coverup (Book 4)

The Isaac Question: Templars and the Secret of the Old Testament (Book 5)

Preface

Is the lost continent of Atlantis a mere legend? I had always assumed so. But, as often happens, once I started digging around in the dusty corners of history, I found some pretty compelling evidence that some kind of advanced civilization existed—and then was lost—approximately 12,000 years ago. This evidence includes, but is not limited to:

- the writings of Plato
- ancient European cave art and ceramics
- the Gobekli Tepe site in Turkey
- breeding and migratory patterns of certain eels and butterflies
- fresh water fossils found underwater along the Mid-Atlantic Ridge
- the geology of the Azores Islands
- similar "Red Paint" burial sites found on both sides of the Atlantic
- ancient Sumerian, Indian and Egyptian writings
- erosion patterns on the famous Sphinx

Perhaps most noteworthy of all, however, was this simple drawing of a Native American "witch" found in eastern Mexico, dating back to before known European contact:

Why, I wondered, did the Native Americans portray their witches, or crones, with pointed black hats riding on brooms just as did their European counterparts?

It is the evidence bulleted above which comprises the bones of this story. Who were these ancient peoples? Where did they live? How did they perish? Did any survive?

Of course, none of my stories in this series is complete without a tie-in to the medieval Knights Templar. Did the Templars know of the secret history of Atlantis? Were they in some way Atlantis' caretakers or successors?

Readers of the first five books in the series will recognize the protagonists, Cameron and Amanda, and also young Astarte. Readers of my 2006 novel, *The Wrong Abraham*, may also note the return of the Abraham Gottlieb character. This story called for a complex villain like Abraham, and it was fun to bring him and his cohorts back for some more vigilantism.

As always, if an artifact, site or art object is pictured here, it exists in the real world. (See Author's Note at the end of this book for discussion regarding artifact authenticity.) To me, it is the historical artifacts and sites that are the true stars of these novels.

I remain fascinated by the hidden history of North America, including the possibility that an advanced civilization lived in the mid-Atlantic before recorded time. It is my hope that readers share this fascination.

David S. Brody, August, 2016
Westford, Massachusetts

Note to New Readers

1. The artifacts and sites pictured in this novel are real. While the story is fiction, the sites and artifacts used to tell it are authentic.

2. Though this is the sixth book in the series, it is a stand-alone story. Readers who have not read the first five should feel free to jump right in. The summary below provides some basic background for new readers:

Cameron Thorne is a forty-one-year-old attorney/historian whose passion is researching sites and artifacts that indicate the presence in America of European explorers prior to Columbus. His wife, Amanda Spencer-Gunn, is a former British museum curator who moved to the U.S. from London while in her mid-twenties and shares his research passion; she has a particular expertise in the history of the medieval Knights Templar. They reside in Westford, Massachusetts, a suburb northwest of Boston. Newly married, they are in the process of adopting an eleven-year-old orphan, Astarte. Cam and Amanda are part of a growing community of researchers investigating early exploration of North America.

The Book of Enoch*

Chapters 7-8 [excerpted]

"It happened after the sons of men had multiplied in those days, that daughters were born to them, elegant and beautiful. And when the Watchers, the sons of heaven, beheld them, they became enamored of them, saying to each other, let us select for ourselves wives from the progeny of men, and let us beget children. Their whole number was two hundred, who descended from the top of Mount Hermon. Then they took wives, teaching them sorcery, incantations, and the dividing of roots and trees. And the women conceiving brought forth giants. Moreover the Watchers taught men to make swords, knives, shields, breastplates, the fabrication of mirrors, and the workmanship of bracelets and ornaments, the use of paint, the beautifying of the eyebrows, the use of stones of every valuable and select kind, and all sorts of dyes. And there arose much godlessness, and they became corrupt in all their ways. The Watchers taught astronomy, astrology, meteorology and the motion of the moon, so that the world became altered."

*The Book of Enoch is an ancient Jewish religious text, accepted as canonical by the Ethiopian Orthodox and Eritrean Orthodox Churches.

"There occurred violent earthquakes and floods; and in a single day and night of misfortune the island of Atlantis disappeared in the depths of the sea."

—Plato, writing in 360 BCE

Chapter 1

Westford, Massachusetts
March, Present Day

Amanda Spencer-Gunn stood at her front door, snow swirling in the night sky as a March storm howled. The echo of Venus' angry bark rang in her ears yet there was nobody outside. She suppressed a shiver as the last vestiges of a New England winter bit at her exposed skin.

"What did you hear, girl?" The dog rarely made a commotion.

The tawny Labrador pushed past her, offered another sharp bark and nosed at a shoe-box-sized package tucked tight against the wall of the house. "That's odd," she said, bending to pick up the box. "Clearly that's what you heard." She scanned the street. Nothing. "And why no footprints?" The wind had turned the driveway and front yard into a desert landscape of undulating snow drifts. But no way could the storm have erased tracks that quickly.

She brushed snowflakes off the simple white label, revealing her name and her Massachusetts address typed in capital letters. No return address, no stamp, no delivery service label, no extraneous markings of any kind. She glanced outside again. "And no bloody footprints," she repeated.

Cam and Astarte appeared at the top of the basement stairs, ping pong paddles in hand. "Who was at the door?" Cam asked.

"Someone delivering this."

"It's late for a delivery."

She sat at the kitchen table and peered at the box. Glancing at Cam, she swallowed. "Should I open it?"

They had both heard stories of people sending crazy things like anthrax and bombs through the mail. And she and Cam were not without enemies. "You want me to?" he asked.

She shook her head. Watching Cam's lungs get eaten away by a pathogen hardly offered a tempting alternative. "No. But Astarte please take Venus and go to the living room." Holding the box to the light, she examined it, shaking it gently. It felt too light to be an explosive of any kind. "Bloody hell," she murmured.

Amanda found a pair of rubber gloves under the sink and a surgical mask left over from a painting project. She grabbed some scissors and carried the box into the bathroom. This was the point in the movie where she usually looked away. Holding the box away from her body, she steadied her hand. With a swallow she gently sliced open the edge and folded back the flap. Not breathing, she counted to three. Nothing.

Cam stood in the doorway. "Boom," he joked.

"Not funny." She folded back the second flap, revealing a blank, cream-colored envelope resting atop a black suede jewelry box. Her gut told her this was not some late wedding gift. "Beware footless Greeks bearing gifts," she murmured.

"What?"

"Nothing. Just inane babbling." She lifted the envelope from the box and again examined it in the light.

"See anything?" Cam asked.

"No. The paper is too thick." Her hand still shaking, she opened the envelope and peered inside. A single sheet of paper, also cream-colored. And no apparent powder. She shook the paper gently over the sink. Nothing.

She remembered finally to breathe. Removing the paper, she returned to the kitchen table and began to read aloud the typewritten message. *"I entrust you with this necklace. It has been in our family since time immemorial. It is both a blessing and a curse; with it you will soar, and under its weight you will stagger. Guard it carefully, as there are others who will try to take it from you. I had intended to deliver it personally, but circumstances changed quickly. Remember, the growth of understanding follows an ascending spiral rather than a straight line."* She looked up. What the hell did all that mean?

"That's it? No signature?"

"Nothing. Just what I read. No return address, not even a salutation."

Cam exhaled, smiled and took her hand. "Looks like we have ourselves another mystery," he said. He loved shit like this. She could do without the mysteries and family curses and ascending spirals. "What say we open the box?" he said.

"That's what Pandora said." Returning to the bathroom just to be safe, Amanda slowly lifted the lid of the hinged container. A gray metal spiral hanging from a silver chain stared back at her.

Cam leaned in. "I guess that explains the growth of understanding following an ascending spiral."

"Hardly," she snapped back. As Amanda moved her hand closer, the spiral seemed to change color, from gray to steel blue, as if in resonance with her body like one of those 1970s mood rings. And not only did the spiral change colors, it seemed to pulsate in concert with her breathing. "How odd," she said as they watched the necklace gently throb. She held her breath—the spiral stopped pulsating. "It's almost like it is synced to me."

"Sort of like a baby using its mother's breathing as a cue."

She nodded. But this was *inanimate*. She examined the spiral more closely. It wasn't just a traditional spiral—its outermost ring angled off and split into a pair of lines that escaped the orbit of the coil like the twin tentacles on the head of a snail. *An ascending spiral.*

They both knew the spiral was an ancient sign of the sacred feminine, or earth mother, of the old pagan religions. Someone was trying to tell her something. And according to the note people would be trying to take the necklace from her. Apparently the two were related. But that was pretty much all they knew. And that someone braved a nasty storm to make the delivery without leaving footprints.

She lifted the necklace from the box, the spiral cold against her skin. It was heavier than she expected, almost like lead.

"Any idea who could have sent this?" Cam asked. "The note referred to 'our family,' like you were part of it."

"No bloody clue." She barely knew her dad—he ran off when she was four or five. She turned it over, looking for markings. "My Mum would have pawned this decades ago if she had the chance."

"Other relatives?"

She shrugged. "An aunt who died back when I was young. Nobody else I really know."

"Well, it seems as if they know you."

"Apparently so." The spiral had resumed pulsating in concert with her breathing and had now turned light blue. If Amanda recalled correctly, that was the mood ring color for relaxed and at ease. She held the necklace in the palm of her hand, wondering if and why it felt soothed in her presence. The phone rang, interrupting her musings and drawing them out of the bathroom. As Amanda lifted the receiver, she glanced at the necklace. It had suddenly turned dark gray again.

Amanda took a deep breath. "Hello." The caller ID read unknown.

"Is this Amanda Spencer?" A woman's voice, cold and flat, the hint of a British accent.

"Yes."

The line went dead.

Astarte was used to getting called down to the principal's office. It usually happened on the last Wednesday of every month, but they didn't have school yesterday due to the storm. So she wasn't surprised when, after lunchtime recess on Thursday, Mrs. Wickard told her to put away her snow clothes and go to the office.

Blowing her hands warm (it being easier to make, and throw, good snowballs with your bare hands), she skipped down the familiar hallways. A fifth-grader, this was her third year at the Abbot School. She had known no other—before Amanda and Cam adopted her she had lived with her Uncle Jefferson and Aunt Eliza in Connecticut. Eliza home-schooled her. When Jefferson died she didn't want to live with Eliza anymore and asked to come live with Amanda and Cam. They let her go to a real school. The only sad thing was that she missed Uncle Jefferson sometimes. She kept a picture of him next to her bed, but it was becoming harder and harder to remember him. That was okay, she supposed. Amanda and Cam were her parents now. Not officially, yet. But soon. That was what these meetings every month with her social worker were for.

She smiled at the secretary, Mrs. Boisvert. They were friends. Mrs. Boisvert was part Algonquin so she knew what it was like to be Native American. "Hi, beautiful," the woman sang to her.

Astarte smiled. "Hi."

"Oh, that smile could light the darkest night," the woman laughed. "And those blue eyes! You're going to have to fight the boys off next year in middle school."

Astarte wasn't sure if she meant it literally. "That's okay. I can run faster than most of them."

The woman laughed. "Yes, I'm sure you can." She lowered her voice. "There's a new man to see you. From the state. I've never seen him before."

Astarte exhaled. "Not Mrs. Bean-Brown?" Every time the state sent a new social worker it meant Astarte had to answer a thousand dumb questions.

"Mrs. Bean-Brown is with him." She smiled. "It must mean you are doubly important."

She went into a side office where an older man with a blue blazer and bow tie sat next to the bird-like Mrs. Bean-Brown on one side of a round table. Mrs. Bean-Brown always seemed nervous, but especially so today. She waved meekly at Astarte, her four fingers barely moving, as the man stood and smiled widely, his crooked teeth matching his bow tie. "Are you Astarte?"

He pronounced it wrong, with the accent on the last syllable like escargot. She corrected him, placing the emphasis on the second syllable. "It's As-TAR-te." Her mother named her after the Phoenician goddess—family legend was that her line descended from an ancient Carthaginian travel party that had made its way up the Mississippi River from the Mediterranean and assimilated into the Mandan tribe almost two thousand years ago. Her uncle had collected artifacts from Illinois that proved the legend; Astarte kept many of them in her room.

"Well, it's nice to meet you. My name is Mr. Saint Paul."

For some reason she didn't like that name. Nobody should have the name 'saint' in their name.

He sat back down, as did she. She looked at Mrs. Bean-Brown, but the social worker kept her eyes averted. Astarte sensed trouble.

"I am here, Astarte," he pronounced it incorrectly again, "because I am a special friend of the governor of Massachusetts. He and I have taken a special interest in your case."

Astarte bit her lip. This was silly. Why should the governor care about her adoption? It was supposed to get finalized in a few months, now that Amanda and Cam were officially married.

He continued. "We, the governor and I, are concerned that Ms. Gunn and Mr. Thorne may be putting you in danger." He cleared his throat. "They seem always to be in the midst of some historical mystery, often involving significant risk of injury or even death. We are, frankly, concerned that this may not be a safe environment for you."

Astarte felt the wave of sadness wash over her even before the man finished speaking. He was no saint. He was going to ruin everything, going to take her away from her new parents. She bit her lip. *Where would she live?* The sadness turned to anger.

"No," she blurted. "It *is* safe. Nothing has ever happened to me."

"Well, perhaps not yet," he replied, his eyebrows rising over a pair of cold, blue, marble-like eyes. "Now, we have another family, they live in the western part of the state, they take in foster children. You'd have brothers and sisters to play with, and you'd be in a safe environment—"

"No," she interrupted, leaping to her feet. "I want to stay where I am. I'm happy there." She tried not to cry, but the tears came. First her mother had died, then her uncle. She moved in with Amanda and Cam, hardly knowing them. Now, finally, she felt loved again. "They *love* me. And I love them."

"Oh, dear," the man said, though it seemed to Astarte that he didn't seem all that sad. "I'm not sure what we can do about this. I suppose love *is* important."

"I'll do anything. Just tell me what. But please don't make me leave."

"Well, perhaps there is one way..."

Astarte knew she was just a kid, and that the adult world was complicated, but she had the strong sense the man was manipulating her. She also realized there was nothing she could do about it. Mrs. Bean-Brown clearly was not going to help. So whoever this man was, friends with the governor or not, he apparently had the power to do what he wanted. "What?" she asked, lifting her chin. Anything would be better than having to leave her family.

"I suppose if we knew you were safe, if we had a way to check on you, if there was a way to ensure that Mr. Thorne and Ms. Gunn were not engaging in dangerous activities…"

He let the words hang. She feared where this was going. But at least there might be a way she could stay. "I don't understand."

He shifted forward. "Let me put it this way. You have a cell phone, yes? There are times when you could speak privately?"

She nodded.

"Well, I think we might be persuaded to allow you to stay for a few more months if we had regular updates as to what your caregivers were up to."

She didn't like the term 'caregivers.' They were her parents. But he probably knew that. She swallowed. "I still don't understand."

Mrs. Bean-Brown finally looked up, her eyes moist and her shoulders slumped. "Astarte, darling, Mr. Saint Paul is saying you can stay with Cameron and Amanda, but only if you agree to spy on them." She swallowed. "And you must be very careful. They must not find out about it." She glanced at Mr. Saint Paul, who nodded at her. She took a deep breath. "If they do, or if you refuse to answer his questions, Mr. Saint Paul will make sure you never see them again."

2 Weeks Later

Cam blasted Springsteen as he cruised south toward Rhode Island, navigating his way through the last vestiges of Thursday rush-hour traffic. The nor'easter of two weeks ago had been largely erased by the April sun, with only a couple of inches of now-gray snow visible on the highway median. Cam had received a cryptic email from a guy named Donovan, claiming he had important information about the Newport Tower and asking to meet. Most researchers would have put it off, not wanting to invest five hours on a possible wild goose chase. But Cam had learned that meaningful historical discoveries came not just from within books or inside libraries but often from everyday encounters with everyday people who happened to have something tucked in a bottom drawer or stashed in an attic chest. Or, in the odd case of Amanda's spiral, from a mysterious delivery.

A hundred miles after leaving Westford, he navigated his way through the fading daylight past Touro Synagogue and the Viking Hotel to the highest point in Newport. He parked along the edge of snow-covered Touro Park. The round stone Romanesque tower stood illuminated near the center of the park.

Newport Tower, Newport, RI

"Hello, old friend," Cam said. He was especially pleased to see the star Venus hovering above the Tower, as if watching over it. The earliest record of the mysterious Tower dated back to the 1670s. He and Amanda, along with a growing list of historians, believed the structure was centuries older than that, built by the vestiges of the disbanded Knights Templar in the late 1300s. The architectural style screamed pre-Colonial, and there were a number of features of the Tower which tied its builders back to medieval monastic groups—including solar illuminations marking both the winter solstice and Easter, and similarities between this structure and other Templar-constructed edifices in Europe. Cam kicked the snow off his boots, sat on a bench and studied the enigmatic structure, content to wait for Donovan to arrive.

Twenty minutes passed, Cam beginning to think he had been stood up, when a man soundlessly took a seat on the bench next to him. "You Cameron Thorne?"

Startled, Cam nodded. His grandmother's voice popped into his head, repeating one of her favorite expressions: *Bad news goes about in clogs, good news in stocking feet.* Hopefully Donovan's stealthy arrival boded well. Cam stuck out his hand, studying the man as he did so. Slightly-built, eyeglasses askew, wearing a tattered green windbreaker and a pair of wrinkled khakis. "Nice to meet you," Cam offered.

The man offered a quick shake and grunted. "I've got some information on the Newport Tower," he said, his New York accent apparent. "I'm Donovan. Martin Donovan."

Donovan shifted, causing a sweetly sharp smell to waft over Cam. Like fruit salad that had gone bad. Cam recognized the smell from his childhood when his dying grandmother had lived with them.

Without ceremony, Donovan dropped a Ziploc bag on the bench between them. "Go on, pick it up."

Cam examined the bag. It contained a golf-ball-sized mass of gray-brown mortar, along with a guitar-pick-sized piece of seashell.

"From the Tower," Donovan explained. "I found it myself, in 2008, when I was helping out at an archeological dig." He pointed to one of the eight Tower pillars. "Right next to that pillar. My wife and I had a place here in Newport so we volunteered a few days." He lowered his head. "She's dead now, six years. But anyway, this piece of seashell—it looks like a clamshell to me—was attached to the mortar. So we had it carbon-dated." He sat back and paused.

"And?" Cam asked, his curiosity rising. He knew there had been a dig here back in the summer of 2008. And he knew that in ancient times seashells were often used when mixing mortar because they were a good source of lime. If the carbon-dating had indicated a date before Columbus, that would be a key piece of evidence proving the antiquity of the Tower.

Donovan pulled a fifth from his windbreaker pocket and swigged some vodka. He motioned to Cam. "You want some?"

"No thanks. But what about the date?"

Donovan took another swig, savoring his secret. "And," he said, "the date came back as 1450, plus or minus thirty. Before Columbus."

Cam exhaled, not realizing he had been holding his breath. "Who did the testing?"

"Woods Hole Oceanographic Institution, on Cape Cod. A guy I used to fish with worked there."

A world-renowned organization. Cam's pulse quickened. "How come you never told anyone about this before?"

Donovan coughed into a yellowed handkerchief. "We signed a non-disclosure agreement with the woman who ran the dig." He stuffed the cloth back into his pants pocket. "But I'm dying, so what's she going to do to me?" He eyed Cam. Everything about the man—his posture, his aroma, his breathing—screamed that death was near, yet his eyes gleamed with intensity. "Death is strangely liberating. I spent the day today at the casino. I had four strips of bacon and a Snickers bar for dinner. And I don't bother flossing anymore." He showed a set of yellowing teeth as if to prove his point. Or perhaps it was an attempt at a smile. "Last week I left a fifty dollar tip for a cup of coffee." He shrugged again. "It made me feel good, so why not, you know? And tomorrow I'm going to Yankee Stadium for opening day. Cost me six hundred bucks."

Cam nodded, impatient to get his guest back on topic.

"My doc says I shouldn't drink alcohol either, but like I said, I'm terminal anyway, so why not?" Donovan took another swig.

Cam shifted in his chair. "Then I guess the question is why didn't this woman, the one who organized the dig, announce anything back then?"

Donovan shrugged. "I heard she was trying to leverage the results into getting her own TV documentary. Maybe she still is. But I want to do the right thing. People should know about this."

Cam studied the mortar and shell. There was no way to prove it came from the Tower. But the original report would be difficult to refute, especially if it recounted that the sample had been submitted to the lab by a licensed archeologist. "Do you have a copy of the report?"

Reaching into his jacket pocket, Donovan extracted a thin document with an insignia of a blue sailing ship on the cover page. The dying man flipped open the report to the summary page and pointed to the 1450 date. "Pretty straight-forward. That seashell is almost 600 years old."

Cam was an attorney by training, and his analytical mind quickly honed in on the weakest aspect of the evidence. "Isn't it possible that someone built the Tower in, say, the mid-1600s and used a 200-year-old seashell to make the mortar?"

"Well, the shell still has color. Every shell I've seen that's been sitting on the beach for a long time has been bleached white. And I would think a 200-year-old shell would have been pummeled by the surf into sand." Shrugging, Donovan stood. "But I guess that's up to you to decide." He spoke over his shoulder as he shuffled across the park, the lights from the Tower casting a long shadow of his body. "I'm going back to the casino. There was a cocktail waitress there who caught my eye, and after doing this here good deed I'm feeling like maybe I should treat myself, you know?" He gestured toward the bench. "The mortar and shell are for you. Do with them what you want."

Mortar and shell. The meaning Donovan had ascribed to the words related to their use in constructing the Tower. For some reason a different image popped into Cam's head. Every time he began to study the Tower crazy things happened, dangerous things. His body tingled, as if sensing peril.

Mortar and a shell sat next to him. But in his mind Cam pictured instead a *mortar shell*, like something found unexploded on a beach near an old World War II battleground. Who knew when it might go off, and what damage it might do?

Cam sighed. He picked up the bag and traipsed back to his car. That was the problem with his obsession with rewriting history. He knew it could be dangerous. But he couldn't help himself.

Fighting a bad cold, and knowing she had a full day ahead of her, Amanda had resisted the urge to get out of bed when she heard Cam get home from Newport late last night. But when her alarm rang at five-thirty the next morning she got up, visited the bathroom and gently shook Cam awake.

Moaning softly, he smiled in his sleep and reached for her, his hand sliding under her nightshirt.

"Sorry, sailor," she said. "I'm still sick. And I need to run. But I wanted to hear how your meeting went."

Cam yawned and told her about the mortar sample. "I need to learn more about the seashell. You know the skeptics are going to argue the shell was already two hundred years old when it was used to make the mortar. Any idea how long it takes seashells to decompose?"

"I'm guessing it's the same as bones. It depends on the environment they're in." She leaned in and kissed him on the cheek. "I'll be back to say goodbye after I've had some breakfast and woken Astarte."

As she wandered into the kitchen her thoughts turned as they had often done recently to the spiral necklace. She had stashed it in her sock drawer, then spent the next two weeks researching spiral symbols and their meanings. Often used to symbolize life cycles and fertility, the spiral appeared in many ancient cultures around the world. Last week she and Cam had made the three-hour drive to the Catskill Mountains while Astarte was in school to examine a spiral carving on a boulder in the Neversink River. Called the Frost Valley petroglyph, the carving bore a striking resemblance to the necklace, though the 'snail tentacles' on the petroglyph were longer than on the necklace. She pulled up a photo of the carving on her phone, studying it as she spooned some yogurt.

Frost Valley Petroglyph, NY

According to her research, Native Americans in the area reported that the carving had already been in existence when their ancestors first arrived in the Catskills. And geologists opined that whoever inscribed it would have needed metal tools to penetrate the hard granite surface of the rock. The carving resembled spirals found at many Neolithic sites in the British Isles. It appeared to be yet another in a series of mysterious artifacts proving some kind of cross-Atlantic contact long before Columbus.

She returned to the bedroom to brush her teeth and say bye to Cam.

"You sure you feel up to it?"

"Actually, no. But I took some cold medicine. I should be there." She had volunteered to help organize the town-wide pancake breakfast before Westford's annual Apple Blossom parade. She and her team of volunteers planned to meet at seven this morning, before work, to buy the nonperishables for the breakfast. "The breakfast isn't for another three weeks, but you know how committees work." The parade—and accompanying carnival and community celebration—was the type of hokey, all-American tradition that had been absent in Amanda's life prior to moving to the States. The closest thing to a community-based activity in Amanda's youth had been when she and a group of other teenagers got arrested for drinking in a park. The arrest had actually been her salvation, the counselor assigned to her case insisting she join the gymnastics team as a condition of wiping her record clean.

"You sure you don't want me to drive you?" Cam asked. A diabetic, Cam was sitting on the bed checking his blood sugar levels.

"No, you get Astarte to the bus stop. I'll be fine. I took the non-drowsy stuff."

"Remember we drive on the right side here in the States."

She cuffed him playfully. "Barbarians."

Even after seven years in America, she still had to fight the urge to drive on the proper side of the road. But she managed the trip to the Town Common without incident and met her group of a half-dozen volunteers at the First Parish church. They split in half, some heading to a warehouse club in a neighboring community to buy bulk items and the rest, including Amanda, remaining in town at the Market Basket.

Amanda pushed her cart up and down the supermarket aisle as if in a fog, the cold medicine numbing not only her symptoms but her vitality as well. As she reached the end of an aisle, she nearly collided with an elderly woman rounding the corner.

"Oh, I'm sorry," Amanda sputtered. The woman wore her gray-streaked hair long and loose, like a schoolgirl, and sported a flowing blue and green layered dress that gave the impression of cascading water.

The woman looked up, her brilliant eyes matching the greens in her dress, and smiled kindly. "Did you do it on purpose?" She spoke with a foreign accent, not French but close to it.

"No," Amanda stammered, "of course not."

"Then there's nothing to be sorry for." She shook her head, the movement shifting her hair and dress and exposing her neckline—

Amanda gasped. A spiral necklace, identical to the one shipped to her two weeks earlier, pulsated gently against her fellow shopper's skin.

The woman must have seen Amanda's reaction to the necklace. Without hesitation she spun, moving with surprising alacrity for a woman her age, leaving her carriage behind.

"Wait," Amanda called. "Please, wait!"

She hesitated for a moment, not wanting to chase an elderly woman through the store. "Screw it," she whispered, realizing this might be her only chance to learn more about the mysterious necklace. And perhaps her family. Abandoning her cart, she rounded the corner of the aisle. No sight of her. The store was surprisingly crowded for so early in the morning, but even still the woman couldn't just disappear. Amanda glanced down a couple of aisles, her panic rising, before realizing her best bet was to try to catch the woman by the exit. Dodging shopping carts, she sprinted toward the front of the store, her eyes sweeping back and forth in search of the blue and green dress. But nothing.

"Damn it," she murmured. Keeping one eye on the exit doors, she walked along the front of the store, peering up each aisle. A swinging door in the back of the produce section caught her eye. Leaving her position at the front of the store, she pushed through. A college-aged boy loaded broccoli heads onto a cart. "Did a woman come through here, long hair and blue dress?"

He nodded. "Yeah, a couple of minutes ago." He looked at her oddly. "She said that someone would probably be looking for her. She said to tell them there's nothing to be sorry for."

Amanda stomped her foot, realizing she probably looked ridiculous. "Bloody hell." Now she might never learn more about the necklace, or her family.

Shoulders slumped, she returned to finish her shopping. Amanda and the other volunteers met at the check-out and loaded the food into an SUV. "Meet you all back at the church," she said, her mind still on the spiral necklace.

Hands in her jacket pockets to combat the cool April air, Amanda trudged down a row of parked cars toward her Subaru. She really wanted to go back to bed but knew she had a morning of stocking shelves ahead of her. A movement to her right, between two parked cars, startled her. Like a cat, the gray-haired woman leapt out and wedged a small handgun against Amanda's ribcage.

"Don't make a noise," the woman whispered, her French-accented voice calm and hard.

It took Amanda a second to realize what was happening. She nodded as a cold, paralyzing fear washed through her from the point of the gun.

"Slowly, take the keys from your purse." She kept her voice low. "Don't even think about reaching for the mace or whistle or whatever else you may have in there."

Amanda did as ordered. The woman had seemed so sweet and kind. Now she sounded like a trained operative.

"Good. Now push the unlock button. You will get in the front seat. I will get in behind you. No sudden movements."

Amanda nodded again. A minute later they were in the Subaru. "Start the car. You will drive with both hands on the wheel at all times." The highway onramp was only a block away. "Get on Route 495 heading north. Stay in the middle lane."

Robot-like, she did as told. They were on the highway before Amanda had a chance to formulate a plan. Perhaps she should have purposely crashed the car into a telephone pole, or jumped out at the traffic light. But now, cruising at sixty-five, any move like that would be too dangerous. "What do you want from me?" Amanda asked.

The woman shifted into the middle of the back seat, the two of them now able to look at each other in the rearview mirror. "Answers."

Amanda cringed. There was something ominous about the woman's calm. If all she wanted were answers, why the need for the disappearing act, not to mention the gun? "About what?"

"The necklace. Why did you react as you did?"

Amanda chewed her lip. The note with the necklace had warned others would try to take it from her. But this woman already had her own necklace; she didn't seem to be after Amanda's. She tried a vanilla response. "I've seen it before."

"Where?"

"I don't recall."

"You are lying. You reacted strongly, almost violently, when you saw it around my neck."

"Strongly, perhaps. The necklace has … family importance. That's why I reacted."

The woman held Amanda's eyes in the rearview mirror and lowered her voice. Her tone changed. "I know this is hard, with me back here holding a gun. But you need to trust me that if you just tell me the truth, this will end well for you."

Amanda fought to think clearly. Whatever the woman wanted, she wouldn't get it by shooting Amanda in the back of the head and sending the car careening off the highway. "How can I trust you? You have a gun pointed at me."

"Very well." She lowered the gun to her lap. "But you *must* answer my question." This time it was more a plea than a command.

There was something in the woman's voice, the same kindness Amanda had first sensed in the grocery store. Logic screamed that there was no reason to trust her, but Amanda allowed her intuition, which generally was spot on, to guide her. She took a deep breath. "Okay. I have a necklace just like it. It arrived in a package a few weeks ago. But that's all I know."

Amanda glanced into the mirror. The woman nodded. Her eyes pooled with tears and she let out a long, deep sigh. "My darling, we have so much to discuss."

Cam walked Astarte to the bus stop, glad to see her joining the other kids in sliding down what remained of a once-massive snow pile left by the plow. For the past couple of weeks she had not seemed her normal cheerful self.

After a three-mile run he showered and was at his real estate law office in the historic town center of Westford by eight-thirty. Twice a week he taught a course at Brandeis University on pre-Columbian exploration of America, while on the other three days he stayed in Westford to handle his law clients and do research. Not that he planned to spend long at the office today. It was one of the first warm days of spring and he hoped to spend most of his Friday at some beach, examining seashells.

He parked along the Town Common and unlocked the front door of a yellow and white Colonial-style home that had been converted to office use. He listened to voice messages and answered a few emails before picking up his phone. "Hey Fox," he said, using his friend's Native American name.

"Uh oh. I hate it when you call. I always end up either in pain or out of money. Usually both."

Cam chuckled. Last time they had gotten together for a day of skiing, Flying Fox had wrenched his knee and lost his wallet. "You working today?" Fox was a real estate broker on Cape Cod—he and Cam had met at a closing, after which their professional relationship budded into a friendship.

"Nothing until tonight. I'm just doing some paperwork."

Cam explained his meeting with Martin Donovan. "So I need a way to figure out how old this shell was when it went into the mortar."

"Hmm." Fox paused. "So let's make an assumption. If they were making mortar for a tower that size, they'd need a lot. So likely this shell would have been part of a large pile. A midden."

Cam knew that Native American tribes often piled their shells in a single location for hundreds or even thousands of years, a handful at a time, eventually creating sizeable mounds. "But what if there were no middens nearby?"

"I can pretty much guarantee you that around Newport there were plenty of middens. Still are, in fact."

"Okay. But how can we tell how old it is?"

"Have you looked at the shell? Can you still see the grooves?"

"Yeah," Cam replied. "They're faded, but you can still see them. And it still has a purplish tinge to it."

"Okay, I have an idea. I've been putting off going to the North Shore. This is a good excuse to get my ass up there." He gave Cam directions. "Meet me at eleven."

Cam worked for an hour, then threw on a pair of blue jeans and sneakers and headed northeast on Route 495. The highway tracked the Merrimack River toward the coast of the Atlantic—the river originated in the mountains of New Hampshire, but Cam was mostly interested in its importance as a major waterway used by ancient explorers to visit what was now northern Massachusetts. Along or near its path Cam had studied sites and artifacts such as the Westford Knight carving, the Tyngsboro Map Stone, America's Stonehenge and the Druid Hill Standing Stones. The fact that Fox had suggested they meet in Salisbury, at the mouth of the river, made Cam feel like he might be on the right track.

They met in front of a seafood restaurant, Fox joining Cam in his SUV. "Your shell, your gas. And you're buying lunch after." His handsome bronze face broke into a smile. Other than good-natured bantering, Cam had never heard Fox complain about anything. Not that he had much to complain about—in addition to being square-jawed and successful, he was the most self-reliant person Cam knew. Cam often joked that if society collapsed, he would use the last of his gas to drive to wherever Fox happened to be.

As Cam drove, Fox explained their destination. "There's a site at the mouth of the Merrimack where my grandfather used to take me fishing. It's a plateau between two brooks, overlooking the river, raised up maybe six feet. In pre-Industrial times, before the river was diverted upstream for the mills, the river was higher and this plateau was actually a tidal flat. My people, the Algonquin, used to gather shellfish there."

Cam understood where this was going. "That means there's a midden."

"Yes. And better yet, it hasn't been added to since the river level dropped. Probably 150 years ago."

"Brilliant," Cam replied, chuckling. He could compare his shell to the shells in the Salisbury midden. The climate in Massachusetts and Rhode Island was essentially the same, so if his shell looked less weathered and less sun-bleached than the shells in the midden, he would know it was less than 150 years old. "You're the best, Fox."

"You say that now. Hopefully the midden is still there. It's been quite a while since I've been here."

Cam parked at the end of a cul-de-sac and grabbed a folding shovel from his cargo hold. Fox led the way along a path through a thinly-wooded area. Here, closer to the warm ocean waters, the storm had been mostly rain; the ground was spongy rather than snow-covered. A few minutes into their hike Fox stopped, sniffing the wind. He turned to the west and pointed. "Storm clouds moving in."

All Cam smelled was the dankness of low tide. "That wasn't forecast."

Fox studied the sky. "No. No it wasn't." He began walking again, concern apparent on his normally imperturbable face.

They reached the plateau as the skies continued to darken. The smell of low tide was stronger here, close to where the river emptied into the Atlantic. After a few fits and starts Fox located a midden the size of golf cart on a small bluff perhaps a hundred feet from the banks of the river. "There," he said. "This used to be the shoreline." Reaching into his pocket, Fox pulled out a jar of chewing tobacco and stuffed it into the midden. He smiled. "An offering to the spirits, in exchange for the shells you are about to take." He sat on a boulder. "My work here is done. Now you get to shovel." He looked up. "But I'd hurry if I was you."

Cam studied the pile of shells. He had had the foresight to bring a few sandwich bags, and—just to be thorough in his approach—his plan was to take shells from the top, middle and bottom of the pile. He bagged one from the top then poked at the base of the pile; the shells here had solidified into a jagged mass. He dug in with the shovel, but the calcified mass resisted his efforts.

"Maybe go in from underneath," Fox suggested.

Cam nodded and dug into the ground along the edge of the midden, tossing aside the sandy soil as a soft rain began to fall. He went down a foot, then angled in. But before he could penetrate the soft interior of the pile a flash of lightening scorched the western sky. A thunderclap answered a heartbeat behind it and the rain intensified.

"Shit," said Fox. "That was close. Let's find some cover."

He sprinted for the wooded area, Cam at his heels. There was something instinctive about fleeing the storm, just as humans had been doing for tens of thousands of years. "I thought you weren't supposed to stand under a tree in a lightening storm," Cam yelled over the wind.

"You're not," Fox replied as another bolt of lightning flashed. "But anything is better than standing out in the open." He reached back. "And you might not want to carry that shovel up in the air like that." A third crash of thunder emphasized his words.

"Good point."

Hunched against the wind, Fox led them to the shelter of a small evergreen. "If you do stand under a tree, you don't want it to be a tall one," he explained. Not that it did much good—the rain fell almost horizontally in thick torrents, like waves crashing over a breakwall.

Ten minutes and perhaps twenty couplets of thunder and lightening later, the storm abated. The sun returned as quickly as it had disappeared. Cam took off his baseball cap and squeezed it like a sponge. "That came on fast. And angry," he said.

"Almost like someone didn't want you to dig," Fox replied.

Cam eyed his friend. Fox wasn't smiling.

Amanda found a diner off the highway where she and the mysterious woman settled into a booth in the back. The woman ordered tea and left her gun in her purse. Amanda thought about excusing herself for a bathroom run and bolting, but her curiosity won out. This might be her only chance to learn about the necklace. She ordered a fruit salad.

The woman studied her, almost lovingly, over the brim of her tea cup, her eyes matching the aquamarine coloring of her dress. "I should have seen it earlier, in the market."

"Seen what?"

"The family resemblance. *Our* family resemblance."

"What do you mean?"

"Fair skin, light hair, ovular face, those green eyes—"

Amanda interrupted. "I wasn't asking about my features, I was asking about my *family*." She saw her features every day in the mirror. She saw her family, well, practically never. "You said 'our family' as if we are related."

Abruptly the woman stood. "Ooh, I have made such a mess of this." She sighed. "I'm going to walk away and then return, as if this were our first meeting. This time I will not be such a ... witch." Blue and green dress cascading around her, she spun and floated toward the front of the restaurant, her movements almost liquid-like. Spinning again, she flowed back to the table.

She could have been anywhere between seventy and ninety. Her face glowed and the faint wrinkles and crowfeet around her eyes somehow served to frame and enhance her high cheekbones, giving her a kind of radiant, mature beauty. Other than a suede pouch hanging from a thick leather belt, and of course the spiral necklace, she was unadorned. She sat. A smile slowly formed. "You are exquisite, my dear. More so than I could ever have hoped. It is a delight to finally meet you."

"I still don't understand who you are."

"My best guess is that I am your great-aunt." She smiled again. "I will know for certain once you tell me your name."

This made no sense. "Wait, how can you say I am part of your family if you don't know who I am?"

"Because you have the necklace. The necklace is passed down generation after generation by the women in our family." She fingered the spiral as she spoke. It, like Amanda's, seemed to glow and pulsate in resonance with her body. "Actually, there are two identical necklaces, obviously."

"Okay. But I still don't know why you're here or why the need for the gun or why I have the necklace in the first place."

"Yes. Let me start from the beginning." She took a deep breath. "First, my name is Meryn."

"I am Amanda. Amanda Gunn." The woman looked at her blankly. Amanda swallowed. "Amanda *Spencer*-Gunn, to be precise."

"Aha." Meryn showed a row of even, white teeth even as a shadow crossed her face. "Then I am indeed your great-aunt. I am your mother's mother's youngest sister. I mean no insult by this, but you are not your mother's daughter."

Amanda rolled her eyes. "No. We are nothing alike." One of the reasons Amanda had moved to the States was to get away from her mother and her self-destructive lifestyle. And she had largely abandoned the use of her mother's Spencer surname.

"That is not completely true, actually. You have her green eyes. The green eyes of all the women of our family."

Amanda wasn't sure that was genetically possible, but she let it go. She sensed there were more important things to discuss.

Meryn—apparently Great-aunt Meryn—studied her for a few more seconds before continuing. "I sense you are strong. Your oracle chose wisely."

"My what?"

"Your oracle. The woman from our family who sent you the necklace."

"Who is she?"

Meryn angled her head. "I do not know."

None of this made sense. And Amanda's head was beginning to pound as her cold medicine wore off. She nibbled at the fruit salad she had ordered. "Well, then, how did you find me?"

Meryn covered Amanda's hand with her own, her skin warm and soft. "I am sorry for being so obtuse. As I said, there are two spiral necklaces in our family. Because they are so important and so valuable, which I will explain to you in due course, they are held by different oracles. I, of course, am one oracle. But the identity of the oracles is hidden, even from each other. The idea is that, in the event of some kind of calamity, at least one of the spirals will survive."

The talk of secrets and oracles, recounted to Amanda by the mysterious woman with the exotic accent, reminded Amanda of those rare times her mother read her bedtime stories. "Is that what happened here, some kind of calamity?"

Meryn nodded. "I believe so. What normally happens is, on her fiftieth birthday, an oracle begins to train her apprentice. That apprentice is chosen from all the women of our family who are of the next generation. Being well beyond fifty," she smiled. "I have already trained my apprentice. Upon my death or incapacity, she will inherit my necklace. Apparently what happened in your case is that your oracle, for reasons we may never know, saw the need to pass her spiral on to you before your training had begun." She spread her hands. "It therefore falls upon me to train you."

"Well, then, why the need for all the drama?"

"As I said, the identity of the oracles is kept hidden, even from each other." She explained that procedures were in place in the event of emergency to allow for communication between the oracles. "An intermediary informed me that a breach in the succession line had occurred. She was able to tell me that the apprentice, yourself, lived in Westford, Massachusetts. But that was all the information your oracle had been able to communicate. Just the town name." She sighed. "Again, we must assume some calamity befell her."

"You make this sound so ... nefarious, like someone killed her or something. Why would anyone care so much about these necklaces?"

"I will explain that later. Suffice it to say that some people would murder, and worse, to obtain the spirals." She said the words matter-of-factly, as if discussing the weather. "So I was faced with the task of trying to find you, while also staying on guard lest I meet the same fate as my sister oracle. I knew the town you lived in, but had no other way to locate or identify you. So for the past two weeks I have been loitering in the public areas of Westford, hoping you would come along and recognize the necklace but also fearing at every moment that our enemies would track me." She exhaled. "It has been a difficult two weeks, playing the dual roles of both hunter and prey."

The story was bizarre, but it at least began to explain things. Because Amanda did not use her Spencer surname, it had been impossible to track her.

Meryn continued. "I am quite pleased, finally, to have found you. Westford is a charming little town, but one can only spend so much time in its library, coffee shops and supermarkets before going a bit stir crazy." She smiled. "I have, by last count, seventy-three boxes of tea in my hotel room."

This, then, explained *how* Amanda ended up having breakfast with a woman who an hour earlier had pulled a gun on her. But the question of *why* still loomed. "I still have a thousand questions. But I'll start with, why did this oracle choose me, and what's so important about these spirals?"

"I cannot answer the first question, other than she must have believed you to be worthy. No doubt she has been observing you, studying you, for quite some time." She took a deep breath. "As to the second question, that will take some explaining. When I am done you will understand. Or at least begin to understand. Then you will have a decision to make."

"What kind of decision?"

"A decision the women of our family have been making for almost 500 generations."

Amanda's brow furrowed as she did the math in her head. "Wait, that's, like, 12,000 years."

Meryn leaned forward. "Yes. Yes it is."

Keith Magnuson glanced into his rearview mirror, adjusting it so it perfectly framed the angelic face of his six-year-old daughter seated in the backseat. "So," he said, smiling, "is your teacher going to tell me all the bad things you've been doing at school?"

She grinned, her finger curling a long strand of her golden hair. She knew he loved to tease her. "No," she sang. "I'm a good girl at school."

He laughed. "I'm sure you are. But what about at home?"

"Um," she said, titling her head. "Usually I'm good."

Laughing again, he said, "Usually?"

"Sometimes I'm ... horrid," she replied.

"I see." For the third time today he thanked the good Lord. Somehow a fucked-up kid like him—talk about horrid—had landed a great job, married a woman who was smoking hot and also put up with his shit, and fathered a little girl who kept him smiling all day. He truly was blessed. He patted the dash of his Lexus SUV—he never expected to find himself here, driving a luxury car and living in Derry, one of New Hampshire's most affluent towns. Hell, he had never even owned a suit before, and now he had a whole closet full of them.

And there was no way he was going to let anyone take it away.

"So, remember," he said, "don't get on the bus today. I'll pick you up after school." His job, in addition to paying well, allowed him to work occasionally at home. As long as the work got done, Admiral Warner often said, he didn't care where or when. The reality was that the kind of work Magnuson did rarely took place inside the sprawling corporate headquarters of Warner Industries. In fact, in some ways, the less time Magnuson spent there, the better. "Maybe we can go for an ice cream before heading home."

"Yeah!"

"But don't tell Mom, okay?"

"Last time she figured it out because you got chocolate sauce on your tie."

He grinned. He had never really wanted kids, but somehow this little ball of blond love had crashed ashore, washing away his former life and replacing it with sand castles and rainbows and starfish. What a dork he had become. But what could he do? He had known the heartache of being shunned by a parent and the agony of being tortured by the enemy and the shame of being homeless in the street. But the love he felt for Jocelyn dwarfed anything he had ever felt before. Her arrival had truly made him appreciate God. He touched his fingers to the red and black cross tattooed on his neck. "Thank you, Lord," he whispered yet again.

He braked as the car ahead slowed, careful to leave a safe distance between them. He was, after all, carrying precious cargo. And no way did he want to have to tell Admiral Warner he wrecked the company car. In fact, there was nothing this week that should put him in any compromising situations. But that could change, of course, at any time. It was what made the job so interesting. A Naval rear admiral decorated during Vietnam at a time when many of his country club contemporaries dodged service, Bartholomew Warner had taken over his family business and—using his Naval connections and also state-of-the-art Naval maps and charts of the Atlantic Ocean—built the company into one of the largest privately-held companies in the country. Warner Industries focused on energy, both producing and distributing it. The company was a global player in oil and gas exploration, power plants, wind farms and pipelines, focusing mainly on the Atlantic Ocean and eastern seaboard of North America. Admiral Warner had explained his business once to Magnuson: "It's actually pretty simple. In the beginning, there weren't many people and there was lots of oil and gas in the ground. Over time, the number of people keeps increasing, and the amount they want to take out of the ground also keeps increasing. I'd rather own the stuff in the ground than be one of the people trying to take it." And sometimes that meant putting people—enemies—*into* the ground. That's where Magnuson came in.

"All ashore that's going ashore," he sang as he pulled into the school's circular driveway. Jocelyn's matronly teacher greeted them. It was one of the nice things about private school—the teachers actually met the kids at the curb. When he was a kid, he was lucky if his teacher knew his name.

Magnuson chatted for a few seconds, lifted Jocelyn into his arms for a hug and kiss, touched his cross yet again and pulled back into traffic. He took a deep breath. Time to flick the switch.

Consulting the GPS on his phone, he passed under Route 93 into the neighboring town of Londonderry and snaked his way to a subdivision on a knoll overlooking the highway. It offered the chance for first-time home buyers to grab a small Colonial with a decent-size yard and maybe a pool. Exactly where he'd expect to find a guy making $55,000 as a procurement manager at Warner Industries. The brand new RV in the driveway, however, which Magnuson guessed went for just about the guy's yearly salary, didn't fit. Not with the wife staying home with the kid and not working. If people were going to steal from their companies, they should at least have the good sense not to flaunt it.

He drove around the block slowly, casing the home from all directions. He had confirmed that the manager was at work today, but there was no sense taking any chances. The single car in the driveway was registered to the wife. Magnuson parked on the street and walked up a path to the front door. He rang the bell and stepped back.

A thin woman breathing hard and wearing sweats and a t-shirt greeted him. Over her shoulder he saw a baby in a playpen and an exercise video playing on a large-screen television. "Mrs. Cheevers?" he asked.

"Yes, I'm Tina Cheevers."

"Sorry to bother you. I can see you're busy. I work for Warner Industries. I'm here to talk about your husband."

"Is he okay?"

Magnuson nodded slightly. "For now, yes." He let the comment linger.

"What do you want?"

The normal response would be to ask what he meant by, 'for now.' It was this kind of street smarts that made Magnuson so good at what he did. So the wife knew. That would make this easier. She pushed the hair back from her eyes, in what Magnuson guessed was a nervous reaction. He stood quietly for a few seconds, letting the tension build. "Nice RV in the driveway. Brand new. Did a rich uncle die?"

"No," she stammered. "We've been … saving."

"I see." He cleared his throat. "Perhaps you could give your husband a message. It would be best if he resigned his position, effective immediately, for personal reasons." Magnuson allowed his blue eyes to rest on hers. "And you might want to seriously consider parking the RV in the Warner Industries parking lot. Keys in glove box, title signed."

Her eyes widened. "What are you, crazy?"

He tilted his head and chewed his lip, as if mulling the question over. "Yes, I believe I am. At least I've been told so." Before Jocelyn was born, he competed in local Mixed Martial Arts bouts. Nobody wanted to face him because he was happy to accept five blows to get one good one in himself. Kamikaze Keith, they call him. He showed his teeth. "Remember, resignation letter and RV. Tomorrow. You have a good day."

Without waiting for a response, he turned and walked away. They could have called the manager into Human Resources office and confronted him with evidence of inflated invoices and suspected kickbacks, but Admiral Warner preferred to handle things differently. Identify the problem, remove it immediately, move on. A home visit from Magnuson, and involving the man's wife, made it clear that this could be done easy or this could be done hard.

But it would be done.

Amanda splashed water onto her face, gripping the edge of the sink as she eyed herself in the ladies' room mirror. She filled her lungs, then exhaled slowly. Addressing her reflection, she said, "Either Meryn's a daffy old bat, or…" Or what? If what Meryn said was true, Amanda's life had just changed forever.

She returned to their booth. Meryn smiled up at her over her second cup of tea and stood to greet her. She held out her arms. "May I be so bold as to ask for an embrace?"

Amanda felt strangely powerless in the woman's presence. Perhaps the second dose of cold medicine combined with the morning's strange events had made her a bit loopy. Plus a hug was better than a gun to the ribcage. She nodded and allowed herself to be enfolded in the woman's arms. The smell of flowers and musk and moss filled her nostrils, almost as if Mother Earth herself had embraced her. For some reason Amanda felt the urge to cry.

"I feel it as well, my dear," Meryn whispered in her ear, her accented English perfect. "I should have been part of your life. We are family."

After a few seconds they separated, Amanda surprised to see through moist eyes that her great-aunt was actually shorter than her. Amanda had had the sense of looking up at her all morning. The tears that wanted to flow, she realized, were rooted in the realization that this enchantress of a woman could have been the mother figure she never had. And had so often missed.

They sat, Meryn taking Amanda's hand, her eyes sparkling as she studied her grandniece in silence. Finally she spoke. "You are in a good place in your life, I sense."

Amanda nodded. "Yes. Finally." It had been a rough journey. But she did not want to spend more time wallowing in her past. "Aunt Meryn, would you mind repeating this ... story ... for me again." She pulled a small notepad and pen from her purse. "I'd like to write it down and make sure I've got it straight." *Because otherwise nobody is ever going to believe it.*

Meryn reached out and put a hand on Amanda's wrist, the gesture firm but kind. "No writing. Nothing ever must be written. Our story passes verbally, through the female line. It has always been thus, and must always be."

Amanda sighed and dropped the pen onto the table. "Very well. But I'd still fancy hearing it again." This time with a more critical ear.

"Of course, Cherie. I have not told this story for decades." She laughed lightly. "You have no idea what it's like keeping the world's biggest secret." Meryn spooned some yogurt into her mouth, peered out the booth to make sure they would not be overheard and focused her eyes on Amanda. She spoke as if reciting a script, as if she had memorized words that had been spoken to her and those before her for millennia. Amanda knew that some Native American tribes had passed their oral history down generation to generation for thousands of years in much the same way as Meryn was doing now, through recitations memorized by the female spiritual leader. Amanda wondered if she herself would someday repeat the words to Astarte.

"Mixed of blood but pure of spirit, we are the descendants of the peoples of Atala, the peoples of the lost continent, the peoples of untold calamity, the peoples who angered the gods. The great ocean gave birth to Atala and the great ocean swallowed it whole. In the thousands of years in-between, the people of Atala thrived, achieving greatness unrivaled in the ancient world…"

Meryn paused as the waitress, captivated by the sing-song cadence of her customer, turned to listen. Meryn waited for her to move on; when she resumed, she abandoned her script and spoke in a more conversational voice. "Atala, of course, is what you know today as Atlantis." She explained that the A-T-L roots connected the words linguistically. "Atala sat in the mid-Atlantic, a roundish landmass approximately the size of France, sitting atop what is now known as the Mid-Atlantic Ridge. Because of the Gulf Stream, Atala remained temperate even during the Ice Age, much as Iceland remains temperate today. As I said, our people lived on Atala for thousands of years, eventually developing a civilization far in advance of those on other continents."

Amanda interrupted. "You say we are the descendants, and talk about 'our people.' But after so many thousands of years, can we really be a distinct genetic group?"

Meryn nodded. "You make a valid point. That is why our history begins with the words, 'Mixed of blood but pure of spirit.' The reality is that you and I have not much more Atalan blood in us than does our waitress. When I say we are the descendants, I am speaking in a spiritual sense rather than a genetic one."

Satisfied, Amanda nodded.

Meryn pulled her thick, gray-streaked hair back and continued. "The Atalans became experts in agriculture, animal husbandry, alchemy, architecture and astronomy. This knowledge of the stars, and our sophisticated building skills, allowed us to navigate the seas and trade with other peoples. Through trade we became very wealthy, which allowed our citizens time to study science and culture. Our diet enabled us to grow, our men far exceeding six feet at a time when most humans were a foot shorter. Atala thrived, growing in both material and spiritual wealth."

Meryn paused to sip her tea, giving Amanda time for a question. "Didn't Plato write about Atlantis?"

"Yes. He wrote about it in 360 BCE. Obviously he was repeating earlier legends." She cleared her throat. "Approximately 12,000 years ago, 10,000 years before Plato, Atala was destroyed by a massive volcanic eruption following sharp tectonic movements. Some believe these tectonic movements were triggered by a meteorite or comet impacting the earth. In any event, the continent of Atala—or at least the vast majority of it—sank into the sea. The ensuing displacement of water and melting of the ice cap caused by the heat of the impact flooded the world, resulting in the flood narratives that are prevalent in ancient cultures worldwide. Only those Atalans who happened to have been stationed abroad at our outposts survived."

Amanda tried to imagine the terror of being on a continent as it erupted and then sank into the ocean, a massive wall of water washing away those who hadn't perished in the eruption. "How many people lived on Atala?"

Meryn swallowed. "Between two and three million people. Approximately 500 survived. Two-thirds of those survivors were living at outposts; the remaining were either in boats that somehow survived or in foreign lands on trading missions."

It all seemed plausible. None of the aliens or gods or super-beings that usually starred in the Atlantis sagas. Just a nation of humans a bit more civilized than others, living on a continent ravaged by natural disaster. "Can you explain these outposts?"

"Atala had long been plagued by volcanic eruptions, and our scientists and elders feared its existence might be threatened. It was decided that outposts would be established along the Atlantic rim, on lands surrounding Atala. Each outpost would be comprised of a dozen couples, twelve men and twelve women, all of child-bearing age. At least one person from each couple was an expert in their field—astronomy, navigation, alchemy, metallurgy, medicine, agriculture, animal husbandry, weaponry, architecture, botany, irrigation and ceramics. The belief was that if something cataclysmic happened to Atala, these colonies would survive. And Atala would survive with them."

"And that's what you're saying happened?"

"Yes, my dear. You and I are the descendants of the people of one of these colonies."

"Which one?" It somehow seemed important to Amanda. Until now she had known so little about her family.

"Our ancestors lived on the Iberian peninsula, near what are known today as the Pyrenees Mountains. The people who live there today are called the Basques. My surname, Eneko, is an ancient Basque name. The Basques are the descendants of this outpost."

"All of them?"

Meryn smiled. "No. Of course not. But that area of Europe has traditionally been isolated, so the Atalan blood runs thicker through Basque veins than almost anywhere else in the world." She shrugged. "But, even so, the bloodlines have been greatly diluted, as I said."

"Where were other outposts?"

"Concentrated around the Atlantic rim. Here, in New England, along the coast. Another in what is now eastern Mexico. The Orkney Islands in Scotland. The west coast of Ireland. Along the northwest coast of Africa in what is now Morocco. The Canary Islands off of Portugal. There was even an outpost in Lebanon, along the Mediterranean coast, where we had trade allies. Other outposts were wiped out in the flood, their locations unknown to us today."

Amanda shifted in her seat. "I'm sorry if I seem skeptical, but you said this goes back 500 generations. How can any family pass down a secret for so long? I mean, at some point there are no children or someone dies early or the secret is lost or people just don't care anymore."

"Precisely," Meryn replied. "That is what has happened. At the time of the devastation, there were twelve outposts of twenty-four Atalans each, 144 couples to carry on. Of those 144 lines, only eleven Crones survive today."

"Crones?"

Meryn smiled indulgently. "Earlier I used the title oracle, but Crone is more accurate. In pagan times a crone referred to a matriarch or priestess. It derives from the same root as 'crown,' referring to a leader. On Atala, women were the priestesses and controlled religious life. Society on Atala was not perfect by any means, but religion there served as a unifying force rather than a divisive one. But just before Atala fell, our society had turned aggressive, warlike. We had become dominated by our males." She angled her head. "We would have been better off following the Crones. Perhaps it is time to do so again."

"But the word crone has such a negative connotation today."

"It is just one of many examples of the Catholic Church marginalizing women. In the early days of Christianity, wise women who understood nature served as healers, doctors. Today we call these same women witches or crones. Women who healed with roots and herbs undermined the power of the Church—priests preached that only God could heal, and only through prayer." She shook her head. "That was the hardest time for us. The Church tried very hard to eradicate us."

The mention of the Church caused Amanda to think about the destruction of Atlantis in the context of the Biblical story of the flood. "So was Noah's flood the same flood that destroyed Atlantis?"

"Yes. As I said, around the world every ancient culture remembers the great flood. When so many disparate peoples share identical memories, how can one not conclude that those memories are grounded in fact?" Meryn fingered her spiral necklace. "Anyway, each of us—each oracle or Crone—wears one of these."

Amanda peered closer. The spiral was almost identical to hers, though Meryn hung hers on a golden chain rather than silver. "What is it made out of?"

"A substance that is not native to earth. Our legends tell us that many tens of thousands of years ago a meteorite struck earth. Early Atalans cherished the metal within it, believing it had been sent by the gods. Each female outpost resident was given one of these spiral necklaces, forged of that alien metal, both in recognition of their status and also as a way for us to identify one another in the event of cataclysm."

"So this necklace has been passed down 500 times?"

Meryn smiled, her green eyes misting. "Actually, 499 times for my spiral. You are the 500th for yours, my dear."

From a table in the corner, Xifeng Chang watched the encounter between the woman with the spiral necklace and her younger guest. Xifeng had been trained not to stare, but she had learned in her decade in America that it really did not matter. Nobody paid much attention to a short, plain-faced Asian woman in a dark blue business suit, and those that did notice her hardly felt threatened. She sipped her tea to hide her smile. If only they knew.

She was pleased to be doing something finally, even if it was nothing more than watching two people eat breakfast. She had been sent to the U.S. as a college student and, as was required of her, found a Chinese-American man to marry. Gerald was his name. He was no different than other men, happiest when scratching himself or farting or watching porn. But he didn't beat her, he didn't go snooping around her personal things and he didn't object when occasionally she disappeared for a few days for 'work' matters. As her name seemed to predestine—Xifeng meaning 'western phoenix' in Chinese—she had flown west and been reborn as an American. But that made her no less loyal to her homeland. In fact, just the opposite: She had grown to despise her adopted home, its people crude and boorish and unrefined. She would rejoice in whatever small role she might play in its downfall. Which until now had been precious little.

Shielding her phone behind her menu, she snapped pictures of both women. Her assignment was to see who Meryn Eneko was meeting and to learn what she could about her. She had already heard them discuss that the younger woman possessed a spiral of her own. This was a crucial development.

As was the tracking device hidden inside a Sharpie which Xifeng had slipped into the younger woman's pocketbook as she jostled against her entering the restroom.

Cam led the way back to the shell midden, Flying Fox strangely somber. "You okay?" Cam asked.

"Yeah, fine. Just that I've never seen a storm come on that fast. It sort of freaked me out."

Cam tried to lighten the mood. "Let me get those shells, then I'll buy you lunch. You can even have an ice cream—"

A movement behind a tree along the path ahead caught Cam's eye. A man in camouflage clothes and hat, crouching. Cam pointed, "You see that?"

Fox nodded. "Yeah. I figured we were alone out here."

"Hunter, maybe?"

"There's not much here to hunt."

Whoever he was, he must have sensed they were talking about him. He pushed away from the path, fighting his way through the underbrush, circling around them and back toward the main road. For the most part the camouflage hid him well. But for a split second a red and black tattoo, emblazoned on the man's neck beneath his ear, flashed into view.

Cam shrugged the incident away, and a few minutes later they approached the midden for a second time. Fox stopped short. "What's that?"

Cam followed his friend's eyes to the midden. A pool of red, blood-like liquid had filled the depression in the sand where Cam had been digging. He swallowed, his fingers tingling. It was as if the midden was bleeding from wounds caused by Cam's shovel.

Fox edged closer, Cam just behind him. Cam broke the silence. "That can't be blood, can it?" He thought about the man with the neck tattoo.

Fox took the shovel from Cam and, using the full length of the tool, poked at the area around the red, Frisbee-sized pool. He jumped back suddenly. "Holy shit."

"What?"

"I think there's a skull in the sand."

Cam took the shovel. This was his problem, not Fox's. Concentrating on keeping his hand steady, he probed the sand. "There's definitely something hard and round there." He pushed the dirt away. The top half of what looked like a human skull appeared. No hair or skin, just the skull. Cam's heart raced. Probing further, he uncovered what looked like the upper part of a ribcage. Again, just bone. "This makes no sense, Fox." Staring, he swallowed. "The flesh has completely decomposed. So how could there be fresh blood?"

The blood on the ground stood in stark contrast to the blood that had drained from Fox's face. "My grandfather used to tell me this area was haunted by the spirits of our ancestors."

"You believe that stuff?"

Fox shrugged. "Not really. At least not until now. My grandfather said the spirits have many strange powers. He would have said they did not want us digging here and that's why they sent the storm. Now they send the blood." He stepped back and stared at the pool. "He would have said we disturbed the souls of the unliving."

Cam frowned. There must be a more practical explanation. "So what should we do?"

"Well, I know what my grandpa would do." Fox reached to his belt and unclipped his hunting knife. Holding it with palms to the sky he crept forward and lowered the knife to the ground next to the skull.

"This is another offering to the spirits. A gift. Obviously the tobacco was not enough."

Cam pulled out his phone. The sudden storm and unexplainable blood and tattooed man had unnerved them. But spirits or not, a pile of human remains lay only a few feet away. He dialed 911.

Magnuson's second stop of his Friday morning had been a personal one. He had driven south on a special assignment for a fraternal group he had joined. Again, Admiral Warner didn't mind as long as his work got done—and in fact his boss had encouraged him to join the group in the first place. He told his wife the group was sort of like the Freemasons, which actually was partially true. Ninety minutes later he was back in the car, the air conditioner cranking to cool him after his exertions.

Stop number three would be more mundane, in Derry at the town's brick municipal building. Warner Industries employed two thousand people at its corporate headquarters in New Hampshire and additional tens of thousands worldwide. Admiral Warner didn't get that rich by being careless with whom he hired, though of course the occasional bad apple like the procurement manager slipped through. Part of Magnuson's job was to screen the job applicants at corporate headquarters, one of many tasks he carried out that only Admiral Warner knew about.

Armed with a list of applicants, Magnuson straightened his tie and strolled into the town clerk's office. "I'd like to see the voting registration list," he said politely. He had learned quickly how to harden his voice in such a way as to discourage questioning. The law allowed the public to view these records, and his tone indicated that he would not be denied that right.

One by one he checked the party affiliations of the job applicants. Admiral Warner had a strict policy for hiring at corporate headquarters. "I'd like to fill the whole place with Libertarians," he often bellowed. "But there aren't enough of us. So I'll settle for

Republicans. But no Independents." His eyes would twinkle. "And don't even think about letting a goddamn Democrat in the door, Magnuson, or it'll be your ass!"

When he finished in Derry, Magnuson drove to four surrounding towns and repeated his task before breaking for a sandwich. After a late lunch he drove to the public library in the state capital of Concord. Here he retrieved yearbooks from all the colleges in New Hampshire and, again working from his list of job applicants, cross-checked the potential employees against involvement in clubs and organizations that Admiral Warner believed to be, in his words, 'sinister.' "I suppose I could live with an occasional Democrat if I had to," he said, "but I'd rather close Warner Industries down than hire one of those liberal activists." It had taken Magnuson some time to learn which activities were sinister and which were not. Being gay, surprisingly, was perfectly fine. As was being Jewish. But no Muslims, and no Jehovah's Witnesses.

When Magnuson had—tentatively—questioned Admiral Warner on these seeming incongruities, the company founder had replied, "I don't give a damn what people do on their own time. What I give a damn about is when they try to tell *me* what I can and cannot do. I count two groups on that list—liberal busy-bodies, and religious fanatics. I think you understand what I mean by the religious fanatics." He had then handed Magnuson a copy of the novel, *Atlas Shrugged*, by Ayn Rand. "Read this. That'll give you an idea about the liberal busy-bodies." The novel glorified the ancient, lost continent of Atlantis as an ideal society in which man thrived by virtue of hard work and freedom from government constraint. Utopia/Atlantis collapsed, the book argued, when government regulation shackled the entrepreneurial spirit. Magnuson came to understand that it wasn't liberal ideals or lifestyle choices in the traditional sense that so frightened Admiral Warner. It was the type of liberal *activism* portrayed in the novel that he feared. Admiral Warner believed in absolute freedom from governmental constraint. And he wanted workers who believed the same.

Magnuson was not sure if Admiral Warner had begun to study Atlantis after reading *Atlas Shrugged*, or if his interest in the lost continent had led him to the novel, but there was no doubting the man's fascination with the Atlantean civilization. He had a large map of the continent, placed in the middle of the Atlantic Ocean where

Warner believed it to have been, on his office wall. "You know, Atlantis was the world's only true utopia," he often said. "When most humans were living in caves and grunting at each other, these people were developing an advanced civilization. That's what happens when humans are left alone, Magnuson. They thrive. We can learn a lot from Atlantis."

"So that's the decision I need to make?" Amanda asked. The diner, which had emptied as the morning hours passed, was beginning to fill for lunch.

"Yes," Aunt Meryn said. She fingered the spiral-shaped, pulsating metal that hung from a gold chain around her neck. "As I said, this necklace has been passed down for 12,000 years. Its wearer is imparted with the oral history of our family, of our people—I suppose one could say of the world."

Amanda still had a thousand questions. "I don't understand why all this has been kept secret."

Meryn smiled patiently. "It hasn't. You've heard of Atlantis. Many have studied it, written books about it, theorized as to its location. Let's not forget, an entire ocean is named after it." She shrugged. "The fact that historians do not accept it as a reality is a function of their close-mindedness, not of any attempt on our part to keep it secret."

Amanda guessed that wasn't entirely true. "But you haven't tried to set the record straight. For example, you could have your necklace tested. And you could do DNA testing with the other Atlantean descendants."

"Who's to say we haven't done those things?" Meryn turned her palms to the sky. "There is only so much I can tell you in one morning."

"Well, then that just makes my question more germane. If you have science to back up your story, why haven't you publicized it?"

Meryn stared into her tea cup for a few seconds, the spiral necklace seeming to darken to match her mood. "The short answer is, well, that we don't feel the world is ready to learn the truth yet. There are many who would use our existence to try to divide the world rather than unite it. To argue certain peoples or cultures are more 'advanced' or 'civilized' than others. We saw what happened when Hitler believed he was part of some master race." She smiled sadly. For the first time she looked elderly. "In fact, as a young man Hitler belonged to a group called the Thule Society. They believed that survivors of Atlantis could endow Thule initiates with esoteric powers and wisdom that could be used to create a master race. This was Hitler's first exposure to the idea of racial purity and superiority."

"But you can't blame Atlantis for what Hitler did."

"No. But you can see how dangerous the concept of a superior bloodline might be, when in the wrong hands. We do not feel the world is ready yet to learn about Atlantis. Perhaps your generation will see things differently."

It was a valid explanation. "You say 'we' as if others are part of this decision."

"Yes. As I said, there are eleven surviving families, most with two oracles like ours. We meet once every five years. But otherwise we have no contact with each other—in fact, often we do not even know each other's real names. That is why it was so difficult for me to find you when your oracle died. We feel that the less contact we have with each other, the more likely it is that at least some of us will survive." She smiled wistfully. "It is possible there are others, someplace in the world, unknown to us—we lost a family in the Holocaust that may have somehow survived. But even with social media and communication what it is today, we do not hold out much hope for finding others."

Something Meryn said earlier resonated. "You said the ancient Atlanteans possessed an advanced culture, and that the outpost families were supposed to carry on after the continent sank. So why did the human race not become, quote-unquote, civilized until many thousands of years later?"

"Good question. Let me put it to you this way: Do you have any hobbies?"

"Pottery. I have my own wheel and kiln."

Meryn nodded. "Imagine, if you would, that some massive calamity hit North America. You may be an accomplished potter, but what if you had no electricity to run your wheel and kiln? Would you be able to find your own clays in nature, or to formulate your own glazes, or to build a replacement wheel or kiln when yours eventually broke down? And even if so, would you have the time and inclination and ability to teach these skills to the next generation? I think what you would find is that some rudimentary form of pottery might be preserved, but that it would not approach the levels of expertise that existed before the calamity." She leaned back. "That is what happened with the outpost families. Some skills were preserved. But our numbers were too few and our infrastructure too fractured to allow our technology to survive."

Meryn paused, as if unsure whether to continue. "I should clarify that. Some of our technology survived." She smiled, her face young and vibrant again, the spiral lightening in concert with her. "As the expression goes, we still have a few tricks up our sleeves. That is another reason we choose to keep to ourselves. Some of this technology, if in the wrong hands, could be very destabilizing. Even today."

Amanda took a deep breath. Some—in fact, many—of her questions would have to wait. But it seemed like the one thing she needed to focus on was whether she wanted to get involved in this at all. "What happens next?"

"As I said, if you choose to accept the necklace you will be its five-hundredth wearer. I will then train and educate you, just as I was trained and educated. Decades from now you will do the same for the next generation."

"And if I decline?" Amanda was intrigued, obviously, by the fascinating history her great-aunt had shared. But was it all true? Amanda sensed that Meryn believed the story, but that didn't make it accurate. And even if the whole thing was true, there was something disquieting and almost cultish about keeping the true history of the world secret from its inhabitants.

"For one thing, I will be very disappointed. My instincts are that you possess a wise, generous spirit." Meryn shrugged. "But there are other candidates, other grandnieces and even more distant cousins."

For some reason Amanda's thoughts turned to Astarte. "I have an adopted daughter. Not officially yet, but soon. Must the necklace always pass to a blood relative?"

Meryn's face broke into a smile, Amanda realizing she had shown her hand with the question. Which she supposed was fine. "An adopted daughter is fine, provided she is worthy. As I said, ours is not a racial legacy but a spiritual one."

"What do you mean by spiritual?"

"Atala was not perfect, but it strived to be. People worked for the common good. Every citizen was valued and treated with respect. There was equality between the sexes. It has taken the world 12,000 years to even begin to re-approach these values. Not that we are there yet. But at least we are trying." She stared out the window. "Technologically, modern society has far surpassed what we ever had in Atala. But we are still behind today when it comes to our ideals."

This last exchange resonated with Amanda. She and Cam had long felt that Western society could use a kick-start when it came to questions of morality. And of course the behavior of extremists around the globe was nothing short of barbaric. Perhaps Atlantis could serve as a model. "Has anyone in our family ever said no, declined to take the necklace?"

Meryn smiled, her eyes shining. "We make it a point to ask only those we feel are qualified. And part of being qualified is a selflessness that makes one willing to serve. So, no, never. Nobody has ever declined the honor."

Amanda exhaled. "I had a feeling you'd say that."

Cam and Flying Fox met the police cruiser at the edge of the woods. A barrel-chested, middle-aged officer in uniform pulled himself from the car. "My name's Flanagan. You fellows say you found a body?"

Cam explained their morning, including their sighting of the man with the neck tattoo. "But it's weird." He shrugged, worried he sounded like a kook. "There's a pool of blood even though the bones look really old."

Flanagan grunted, grabbed some police tape and a shovel from his trunk and followed them to the midden. Crouching on one knee a few feet away from the shell pile, he studied the scene. With his shovel he poked gently at the skull. "Yup. Looks like it's been here awhile." Next he reached out and dipped his index finger into the pool of blood. He sniffed the liquid and grunted again. "Doesn't smell like blood." Edging closer, he extracted more liquid and rubbed it between his thumb and fingers. "Gritty." He stood. "I don't think that's blood."

That made no sense. Pools of red liquid didn't appear in nature on their own. "What is it then?" Cam asked.

Flanagan studied the shell pile for a few seconds. "I wonder," he said under his breath. He turned to Cam. "You said you started digging, then it began to rain, then you came back and found the red liquid?"

"Yeah."

He sniffed at the liquid a second time. "No smell at all." Speaking more to himself than to Cam and Fox, Flanagan muttered, "If that's the head, and that's the rib cage, then the legs should be down here." Using his shovel, he carefully scraped away the dirt two feet away from where Cam had uncovered the skull. Beneath the top layer of dirt, about ten inches down, the soil turned rust-colored.

"Wait, I think that's iron oxide," Fox said. He had been standing back but moved closer as Flanagan dug. "We use that to make red dye."

Bracing against the shovel, Flanagan pushed himself to a standing position. He chewed his lip, his brow furrowed. Another grunt. "I'm guessing what happened is the rain water mixed with this red soil here to give us that pool that looks like blood."

Something about this rang a bell for Cam. "Of course." He turned to Fox. "The Red Paint People," he said excitedly.

"Who?" Fox replied.

"Up in Maine and Canada." And apparently also here in Massachusetts. "Ancient people that covered their dead with red paint. They believed in reincarnation and wanted to make sure the bodies had enough blood to be reborn. So they painted them red."

"Wait, I've never heard of that," Fox said. "And this is Algonquin country. We didn't do that."

"That's the thing," Cam said, the details of the documentary he had watched coming back to him. "The Red Paint People lived here even before the Algonquin. We're talking maybe eight thousand years ago. They were long gone by the time the Algonquin started harvesting shellfish here. They liked to bury their dead near the shore, overlooking the sea."

"So these bones are eight thousand years old?" Flanagan asked.

"Or close to it," Cam said. His eyes settled on the midden. "Usually when they find these Red Paint burial sites the bones have decayed. I bet what happened here is the lime from the seashells preserved the bones. This might be a really important archeological find." And apparently it had nothing to do with the man with the neck tattoo. He clasped Fox on the shoulder. "I think your spirits sent the rain because they wanted us to find the body."

Fox seemed unsure. "Maybe. But you're still buying me lunch." As he turned to walk back to the car he called over his shoulder. "And also a new hunting knife."

Astarte raced in from recess, the wind whipping her hair as she flew past the other children. One boy, Nate, held a lead on her, his long legs covering huge distances as he loped along like a giraffe. But she pumped her arms harder, knowing her legs would keep up. "Zoom," she yelled, passing on his left and touching the tree next to the cafeteria door that marked the traditional finish line of the post-lunch race.

She grinned even as she sucked air, her hands on her hips. The boys hated it when she beat them. Lately she had not felt like racing, but today she had begun to feel like her old self. It had been fifteen days since the unsaintly Mr. Saint Paul had visited. Since then he had not contacted her again. Maybe he had forgotten about her. After all, how important could an eleven-year-old girl be to a man who was friends with the governor?

Ten minutes later she had her answer, the voice over the classroom intercom calling for her to come to the office. *No, no, no. Please don't let it be that man.* But in her heart she knew. She clenched her fists as she walked, her eyes down so nobody would see the moisture pooling. Passing a fire alarm, she had the sudden urge to pull it, to empty the school and send him on his busy way. She'd even happily serve detention. But she knew that would only postpone the inevitable.

This meeting mirrored the first, Mr. Saint Paul with his crooked bow tie and Mrs. Bean-Brown wringing her hands. "I have your first assignment, Astarte," he said, again pronouncing her name wrong. "I assume we still have a deal?"

She nodded. She had no choice.

"Today Ms. Gunn met with a woman. I want you to find out all you can about her." He handed her a slip of paper with a phone number. "Then I want you to call me and tell me what you've learned."

Astarte raised her chin. "My parents check my phone. They'll ask who I called."

"They are not yet your parents." He smiled condescendingly. "In any event, the recording will say you've reached a movie theater in Lowell. If you push 1, it will give you a list of show times. You will need to push 2—that will direct your call to me."

Deflated, she nodded.

He checked his watch, as if it would tell him how long she needed for this task. "I'll expect to hear from you by Sunday. That will give you two days." He showed his crooked teeth. "This will be a good test to see if I want our little arrangement to continue."

Cam scanned the audience in the library auditorium. He had taken Fox to lunch, gone home to shower and change, then driven toward Boston to the suburb of Lexington to address a group of amateur historians. For the most part the body language of the eighty or so people looked positive—bodies leaning forward, eyes on his, legs and arms uncrossed in an open and receiving position. But not the short-haired guy with the red and black tie sitting in the second row to Cam's right. Jaw clenched, body turned oblique to Cam, arms folded. His posture oozed enmity.

And that was fine. Not everyone bought what Cam was selling. Cam's research showed that remnants of the outlawed Knights Templar crossed the Atlantic and came to New England a century before Columbus. This, of course, went against accepted teaching. But Cam sensed that, for this guy, the disagreement transcended academics. It seemed almost visceral. Cam wasn't just some speaker, he was the enemy, his message somehow threatening. And there was something familiar about him...

Cam shrugged and glanced at his watch. He had given enough of these presentations to know that forty-five minutes was about as long as most audiences could focus. Especially on a Friday night after a long week. Time to wrap it up. "So, as you can see from the

artifacts, clearly someone was here. The evidence points to the
disbanded Knights Templar living in Scotland. Not to sound too
much like a lawyer, but they had motive, means and opportunity."
He held up one finger, summarizing the points he had made earlier.
"Motive. They needed to get themselves—and their treasures—out
of Europe before the Pope came after them again. They had a safe
haven in Scotland, but who knew when the English would invade
again and change that?" A second finger. "Means. Prince Henry
Sinclair had a fleet of ships and, being Norse on his mother's side,
likely had charts and maps used by the Vikings to make the
crossing." He moved to his third point. "Opportunity. Prince Henry
had solidified his rule in Scotland, and the Templars had ensured
their continued existence by reconstituting themselves as the
Freemasons. Scotland was at peace. The time was right." He paused
to emphasize his conclusion. "The year was 1398. I may have some
of the details wrong, but the artifacts don't lie. Someone was here."

He sipped from a bottle of water as the applause subsided. "I'd
be happy to take some questions."

A man in his twenties asked why Cam thought the Catholic
Church turned on the Templars, who for two hundred years had been
the army of the Pope. "I think two things were going on. First, the
Templars, while in Jerusalem, were exposed to a different version of
Christianity than what the Church was preaching, one that
emphasized the importance of women in religion and also embraced
many pagan beliefs. In addition, they were exposed to ancient
knowledge and culture that made them realize just how backward the
Church was in many of its beliefs—remember, Europe was just
coming out of the Dark Ages at that time. Stuff like the earth being
the center of the universe, and only priests being able to heal the sick,
must have seemed absurd to the Templars after what they had learned
in the Middle East. So when they got back to Europe, they began to
question the Church. I suppose you could call the Templars the first
to bring Enlightenment thinking to Europe. The Church,
understandably, saw all this radical thinking as a threat."

A tall, gaunt, elderly man in a gray suit raised his hand. A
numbered tattoo, which Cam recognized as a concentration camp
branding, adorned his right wrist. The man stood and cleared his
throat. His German accent did not surprise Cam. "Do you think it is
possible that one of the reasons the Catholic Church turned on the

Templars was because of the close relationship between the Templars and the Jews?"

Cam was not an expert in this field, but he had done some reading. "So just to give some background, the Templars and the Jews of France and Italy had a close relationship in the 12th and 13th centuries even though non-Christians were being persecuted by the Church in most of Europe. The reason for this was that the Templars were bringing documents back to Europe from the Holy Land and needed help translating and understanding the Hebrew and Aramaic." He sipped more water. "I don't think the Church leaders would have been too upset with this relationship per se. I think what upset them was what these documents said, what they revealed about the true origins of Christianity. After the Templars were disbanded, the Church eventually turned on the Jews and forced them to either flee Europe or convert as part of the Inquisition. But by then it was too late. The documents had been translated, the message delivered. Killing the messengers at that point didn't do much good."

The elderly Jew nodded, his gray eyes sharp and alert. "Thank you, Mr. Thorne."

The man in the red and black tie surprised Cam by raising his hand. As he did so he turned sideways to Cam and a red and black cross tattoo became visible on his neck. Cam froze. A second tattoo in a row. Was it the same one he had seen near the midden? Cam studied the man with renewed interest. Thirty-something, average height, fit—a slightly younger version of Cam, but with cold blue eyes and a military haircut. Cam wondered if the black and red tie was chosen because it matched the cross tattoo. "Yes," Cam said.

The man set his jaw; Cam imagined the cross pulsating beneath the shirt collar. "You say the Knights Templars adopted ancient pagan beliefs. That they questioned the Church. That they allied with the Jews. That they were, in essence, heretics. But I've done a lot of reading, and I see no evidence for any of this. The Church has, in fact, pardoned them of any sins." He slowly raised his arm and pointed at Cam, his forefinger steady as a marksman. "I think you need to be careful, Mr. Thorne, about defaming these holy warriors." Again, Cam felt the man's oozing hostility. "There are those who take these matters very seriously. There are those who carry on the glorious legacy of the Knights Templar even today."

His eyes locked on Cam. "You don't want to mess with us."

Chapter 2

Abraham Gottlieb studied himself in the van's passenger seat mirror. A man who had no time for vanity, he was surprised to see how old he looked. Someone had once told Abraham he reminded them of the emotionless Mr. Spock of the old *Star Trek* series, both in appearance and behavior. Well, Mr. Spock was looking old. Like a tree, his thin, aquiline face boasted a wrinkle for every one of its eighty-nine years. But his eyes, gray and large, remained alert and alive. Especially on nights like tonight.

Clevinsky drove, barely able to see over the steering wheel but still somehow adeptly maneuvering the van through the darkened Boston streets. "Are we close?" Abraham asked.

Clevinsky held up five fingers, then did so a second time. He had lost his tongue in the Holocaust, forced to suck on a hot coal by a sadistic concentration camp guard. But he had survived when so many others had perished, a young boy whom Abraham had taken under his wing at Dachau. Clevinsky wore a permanent smile on his face like a circus clown, as if in recognition that the last seventy years of his life had been an unexpected gift. Albeit one that required him to communicate with hand gestures and grunts with those who did not know sign language.

Abraham turned in his seat. The six other members of his team rode in silence. "Ten minutes," he said. "Is everyone ready?"

Solomon Massala spoke from the rear, his chestnut-colored skin barely visible in the dim light. "My men and I will go in through the rear door." An Ethiopian Jew, or Falasha, he had been airlifted out of Africa as a young boy in 1991 during a rescue mission by the Israeli government, but not before witnessing the rape and decapitation of his mother and older sister by a marauding band of Muslim Sudanese. Abraham did not know the two soldiers on either side of Solomon, but had no doubt that the former Israeli army tactical officer had chosen his men wisely. "Barnabus will stand guard."

Abraham addressed the bear-sized Hassid seated directly behind him. "Patience, Barnabus. Your work will begin when we get these animals into the van. Until then, no unnecessary noise."

Barnabus leered in the dark, his yellowed teeth wet with anticipation behind his dark beard and his *payos* swinging against his cheeks like a young girl's curls as the van bounced along. "You know I don't work on the Sabbath, Abraham. This is *play*."

Abraham allowed himself a rare smile. Men like Barnabus were necessary; Jews needed thugs to counter other thugs that would do them harm. Like the man with the cross tattoo and cold eyes at Cameron Thorne's lecture earlier tonight. Men like this did not listen to reason. They listened to a fist to the jaw.

"What about you, Dr. Walters?" Abraham asked.

Squished into the middle seat next to the hulking Barnabus, a thin man wearing a white button-down shirt and a yarmulke on his head nodded, the movement causing his thick eyeglasses to slide down his nose. He looked like a college student, a row of pimples lining his forehead where his bangs hit. He was in fact a respected anesthesiologist at Beth Israel Hospital, albeit one who still bore the emotional scars of being bullied by skinheads in high school. "It's going to be a little tight with two of them." The van was more like a delivery truck than a van, with a hospital bed bolted to the floor in the back behind the three rows of seats. "We'll need to restrain one while I have the other on the bed."

Abraham nodded. "I'm sure Barnabus can handle that. And you have enough sodium pentothal?"

"No. I'm using scopolamine instead. It is easier to administer, and just as effective."

"Very well." He turned to Madame Radminikov, the last member of their team. Short-haired and thick-necked from a lifetime of work as a butcher, she was second-in-command. Her father, and Barnabus' as well, had been with Abraham and Clevinsky at Dachau. "Madame, what have you to add?"

She took a deep breath. She brought a skeptic's point of view to the team, probing for unseen obstacles or developments that might derail an operation. "Remember, these are college students. College students don't always sleep where they are supposed to. They might have girls with them or friends drunk on the couch or maybe they didn't even come home tonight."

"If they are drunk, that will make our job easier," Solomon said, his voice even and cold. Abraham was considered emotionless, but Solomon made him look like a door-slamming teenager by comparison.

As they drove Abraham reflected on the Thorne lecture from earlier in the evening. The Knights Templar had long intrigued him. Though they were the fighting force of a fervently anti-Semitic Catholic Church, the Templars had somehow maintained cordial relations with the Jews during medieval times. It was rare for foreigners—much less foreign armies—to befriend his people. He sighed. Would that it could happen more often.

Clevinsky turned off of Commonwealth Avenue and snaked his way to Bay State Road, a quiet, tree-lined side street tucked between Boston University and Storrow Drive in Boston's Back Bay. The Aboof brothers lived in a first- and ground-floor brownstone duplex, its two bedrooms located on the ground floor.

Madame Radminikov spoke. "Make sure they are fully dressed and carrying their keys and wallets." They had been over the plan a half-dozen times. She pointed. "The building is dark. Now is the time."

Clevinsky turned into the alley and drove half a block. He grunted and pointed. Before he had the van in park Solomon and his men had jumped out the back. Barnabus lumbered out the side door and paced the alley.

"Here we are again, Madame Radminikov," Abraham said.

"We're getting too old for this," she replied. "All of us. We need more help. Younger help. Men and women willing to fight."

He nodded. Until recently his team had been focused on avenging attacks on Jewish citizens and desecration of cemeteries and synagogues. But the Boston Marathon bombings, and terrorist attacks in its wake, had convinced Abraham that they needed to move beyond vigilantism. They needed to anticipate attacks on Jewish targets and prevent them. But, as Madame Radminikov noted, that required manpower. "I may have a solution. If you are free, join me tomorrow evening—"

Their conversation was interrupted by Solomon and his men emerging from the back door of the brownstone, two young men in jeans and windbreakers in their custody. "That was fast," the doctor said, standing. With Barnabus' help, Solomon's men hoisted the two prisoners through the back door of the van. Careening down the alley, Clevinsky made a couple of sharp turns and was on Storrow Drive heading for the Massachusetts Turnpike within seconds.

Boston slept as the doctor began his work.

Seated together in an oversized chair looking out over the moonlit lake, sipping wine from the same glass, Cam and Amanda stayed up late into Saturday morning sharing their experiences from the day. She loved that their lives together were so filled with intrigue and adventure, though she could do without the gun stuck in her side.

He smiled at her and kissed her gently. "I don't think of you as a crone. Honest. Witch, maybe…"

She pushed him away playfully. "Watch it or I'll turn you into a toad."

He sighed. "Seriously, I come home with news about an eight-thousand-year-old grave site, and you trump it with something even older."

"I don't know, Cam. I mean, Atlantis? Really?"

"Why not? Nobody has trouble believing in the Bering land bridge, even though there's really no hard evidence for it." Most historians believed Native Americans originated in northern Asia and crossed a land bridge to Alaska about 20,000 years ago when sea levels were lower. "The land bridge supposedly disappeared about 12,000 years ago. So why not Atlantis also?"

"Atlantis just seems so … fairytale-ish. An old legend. Even Disney made a movie about it."

"You know the saying: *Legends are more historical than fact, because facts tell us about one person while legends tell us about a million.*"

He had a point. Before the written word, legend was the way ancient peoples preserved their history. Even some later cultures chose story-telling, figuring written records could be more easily destroyed than oral history. The Church proved them right, wiping away much of the collective knowledge of Europe during the Dark Ages.

Cam interrupted her musings. "Tell me more about this Meryn. Why don't you believe her?"

"I do believe her, in the sense I don't think she's lying to me. But, after 500 generations, who knows how accurate the story is."

"You said she hinted at DNA testing. Hard to fake that."

She knew he was playing devil's advocate, which was fine. "Yes and no. They say one in every 200 men alive today descends from Genghis Khan, and he lived only 700 years ago. If you go back 12,000 years, probably everyone has common ancestry." She shifted. "Besides, wouldn't there be more evidence of some ancient, advanced civilization?"

He shrugged. "Maybe there is, and we just haven't opened our eyes to it. Is it a coincidence that the Frost Valley Petroglyph looks just like your necklace? I mean, there has to be a reason someone added tentacles to the spiral. Think about all the artifacts in New England that people have been ignoring for centuries. History is always being rewritten. You know that."

She nodded. Many academic types refused to consider evidence that might challenge existing assumptions. "Yes, it is hard to learn what one already knows." The recent finds at Gobekli Tepe, in Turkey, had pushed back the date of the earliest civilized society—usually defined as a group that had moved beyond the hunter-gatherer stage to live together in a complicated social structure—from six thousand to twelve thousand years ago. Someone, somehow had organized a massive workforce together to build an elaborate, sprawling religious complex six thousand years before historians believed such a social structure was possible. So the experts had not just been wrong, but wrong by a factor of two.

Amanda sat up suddenly, splashing the wine. "That's it. Gobekli Tepe."

"What about it?" he asked as he licked wine off his forearm.

"It just appeared, out of nowhere. And at an incredibly complex and sophisticated level." She recalled one of her favorite Greek myths. "Poof. Like Athena springing full-grown from the brow of Zeus. Where was the build-up?"

He smiled. "Poof. Hard to argue with that." He turned serious. "You think Gobekli Tepe somehow connects to Atlantis?" He was good at following her reasoning.

"The dates are spot on. Twelve thousand years ago, just when Atlantis disappeared. I wonder…"

He nodded. "Well, there you go. The evidence might be there. We just need to look at it with fresh eyes."

They stared at the moonlit lake. He broke the silence. "So what are you going to tell Meryn?"

"I think I have to play this out. How often does someone come along and offer you the chance to look behind the curtain? Even if the chances are only one in a hundred that her story is true, I can't risk missing out."

He grinned. "If you don't want to do it, I'll put on a dress and some lipstick and take your place."

It made her feel good that he was so excited for her. But she knew he was anxious to talk about his day as well. "Before I ask you about your skeleton, were you able to get any shells?"

"Yes. This is an old midden pile, so of course all the shells on the top have been bleached white. But even the shells from inside the mound are white."

"That makes sense. At some point they would have been atop the pile."

"Right. And that's the point about the Newport Tower shell. Since it's still pink, it was not an old shell when it was put into the mortar. I'm going to have some experts look at it, and also look at the weathering of the shells I collected from the midden, but it looks promising."

"Which would have been a very big deal even if you hadn't also found that skeleton. You said it could be as old as eight thousand years old. Could it be older?"

"From what I've read nine thousand is about as far back as these Red Paint People go. But we really don't know much about them. So, yeah, sure."

She let her mind wander. Sometimes the best research had its roots in playing games of 'what-if' over a glass of wine. "I know how much you hate coincidences, but I'm just wondering if our two days might be connected. I mean, is it possible your Red Paint People were related to some of the Atlantis survivors?" If they were going to play connect-the-dots with sites like Gobekli Tepe, why not try a few more?

Cam shifted in the chair. "That's an interesting thought." She could see his mind racing. "One of the mysteries of the Red Paint People—the experts call them the Maritime Archaic culture—is that they were deep-sea fishermen. They went way out into the Atlantic to fish for giant swordfish and maybe even whales. And some of the harpoons and spears buried in their graves are really sophisticated."

"I thought your Native Americans in this area were not seafarers."

"They weren't. That's why this is strange. The Red Paint culture, even though it was older, was more advanced than the later Algonquin. That's not how things usually work." He smiled. "Sort of like what you said about Athena."

"How long do you think it will be before they have a date for those bones?" she asked.

"Probably a few weeks. This is a big find, so they'll get right on it. But they'll be careful with the dig. There might be more than one body, and if it's like other Red Paint burials there will be funerary items buried with it. They believed in reincarnation so they made sure the dead had lots of tools and weapons for their next life."

Amanda yawned. Her body seemed to have fought off her cold, but it had been a long day and it was now past three in the morning. "I don't suppose your bloke was wearing a spiral necklace?"

"Sorry, no. But I did notice something odd."

"What?"

"I'm not an expert, but the skull didn't look like a typical Native American. You know how when they found Kennewick Man some people said he looked European?"

She smiled. "Yes, like Captain Jean-Luc Picard from *Star Trek.*"

"Exactly. Well that's what this head looked like. It was long and thin. He looked European."

Leah Radminikov sighed. How in heaven's name had she ended up riding around in a retrofitted van in the middle of the night, second in command of a vigilante group holding two terrorists captive? Her friends—those that hadn't already moved to Florida—spent their time at her synagogue's Sisterhood, gossiping and bragging about their grandchildren. Many of them young adults the same age as the two boys bound in the rear of the van.

She turned her attention back to the activity in the van. Dr. Walters was skilled at his craft and, much to Barnabus' disappointment, the combination of fear and truth serum had quickly broken the Aboof brothers' resolve. Within an hour Leah had a list of names of their cohorts.

"Can we trust them?" Solomon, the tactical officer, asked.

The doctor replied. "They both gave pretty much the same answers." While one was being questioned, the other wore headphones with *Hatikva*, the Israeli national anthem, blaring.

Leah weighed in, her finger resting on the edge of the laptop keyboard. "And I've been cross-checking their story against known facts. Everything seems to check out."

She called to Abraham, still riding shotgun in the front seat with Mr. Clevinsky. "I think we are done here."

Abraham clasped his hands together. "Good. It will be light soon. And we still have … one more stop to make."

Leah understood the necessity of what they were about to do, but she hated it nonetheless. These boys were some woman's babies; the memory of them filled some woman's heart. Somehow they had wandered onto the path of evil. But to their mother they would always be her tousle-haired little boys. And now they sat, shivering in fear, blindfolded and bound and drugged in the rear of a dark van. Leah's heart ached for them almost as much as it did for their mother. Which is why, at her insistence, Abraham had spoken so euphemistically about having one more stop to make.

Leah rested one hand on each of the boys' knees and spoke soothingly. There was no reason to make the boys suffer. "You did well. Both of you. Very well. There is nothing more to fear. We are going to drop you off now—not at your house, as that would be too dangerous for us, but not far away. We will even give you money for a taxi." She paused. "But we know where you live. And of course we expect there will be no more … mischief from you."

The younger boy nodded. "Thank you," he breathed.

The older brother, who had been drugged first and now was less under its effects, was no quite so docile. "Others will take our place."

She shook the list at him and motioned for Solomon to gag them. "Yes, well, not as many others."

Clevinsky exited the highway and drove toward Boston's Allston neighborhood. He pulled the van into a narrow alley behind an auto body shop, perhaps a mile from the boys' apartment.

Abraham motioned Solomon and Leah forward. "You are certain the security cameras are disabled?" he asked.

Solomon nodded, the whites of his eyes bobbing in the dark. "I confirmed this with the owner myself."

"And there are no other possible witnesses?"

"The high wall separates us from the neighboring apartments."

Abraham nodded. "Very well. Proceed."

Solomon's soldiers leapt from the van and dragged the Aboof brothers after them, their legs wobbly. Leah called to them softly. "Remember, no more mischief."

She watched as the soldiers shoved the boys against the back wall of the building. Solomon dropped a small Ziploc bag of cocaine and a couple of twenty dollar bills on the ground between them, then stood back and nodded to his men. Without preamble, each soldier pulled a nine millimeter handgun with silencer from his waistband and fired a single shot into the back of his prisoner's head. The boys crumpled. Leah sobbed, bile rising in her throat, not wanting to watch but unable to turn away.

Dr. Walters checked for pulses while the soldiers removed the ropes, gags and blindfolds, doing so carefully to avoid leaving signs of bondage. Solomon surveyed the scene a final time. A drug deal gone bad. Nodding, he led the team back into the van.

Forcing herself to slow her breathing, Leah rubbed the tears from her eyes and tried to gather herself. As the van bounced through the streets of Boston, she said a quick prayer in Hebrew. *"Yit gadal v'yit kadash sh'mei raba..."*

"Amen," she sighed. They had done what needed to be done. Two with darkness in their hearts had died so dozens of innocents could live. No act could be more holy than this.

At least the boys had not known fear at the end. But still her heart ached.

Venus' low growl woke Cam from a deep sleep. His eyes shot open, adrenaline pumping through his body. His subconscious had heard the same noise that had alarmed Venus.

A hint of light seeped through the sliding glass door of their master bedroom. The sound had come from below, the creaking of the basement bulkhead door. Sometimes it blew open, but as he peered out over the lake he could see that the reflection of the moonbeam was unbroken by any lake turbulence. "Stay," he whispered to Venus. The bulkhead led to a utility room which in turn led to the finished part of the basement, separated by a door with a simple lock that any two-bit burglar could force open. Heart thumping, he swung his legs out of bed and grabbed a heavy flashlight he kept in a drawer in his night table.

Flashlight off, he padded into Astarte's room to check on her before tip-toeing down the stairs to the first floor. On the bottom step he froze, forcing himself to breathe, and allowed his eyes to adjust to the darkness of the curtain-drawn living area. A shadow moved near the top of the basement stairs. Or maybe his eyes were playing tricks on him.

"Cam," came Amanda's whisper from behind, startling him. "What's wrong?"

He cupped his mouth. "Venus heard a noise." He anticipated her thoughts. "I already checked on Astarte."

The shadow moved again, this time back toward the switchback stairwell leading to the finished basement. Cam flicked his light in time to catch the backside of a lithe, hooded, black-clad body leaping to the first landing. "Hey," he yelled, pursuing, every fiber of his being focused on protecting his family.

"I'll call 911," Amanda announced, reaching for the kitchen phone.

Cam raced after the intruder, punching at the light switch as he passed. He caught sight of the black form a second time—he had the sense it was a female body—but she slid through the door to the utility room and scurried up the bulkhead stairs before he could close the gap. He considered pursuing when Amanda's voice echoed down. "Cam, up here!"

Venus's sharp bark accentuated Amanda's call. Cam didn't hesitate, taking the stairs three at a time, the flashlight heavy and firm in his hand, cursing that they had left Astarte alone in her room. He raced through the living room and up the stairs to the sound of Venus's angry bark in the master bedroom, arriving just in time to see a second black-clad figure, again female, slip through the sliding glass door to the bedroom deck. Cam pursued. The figure leapt from the deck, grabbed the branch of a nearby tree and swung like a gymnast on a bar, landing effortlessly on the ground below before disappearing into the night.

He strode back into the master bedroom, the sounds of police sirens audible in the distance. Amanda held Venus; Astarte appeared, yawning. "Everyone okay?" Cam asked. He breathed for what seemed like the first time in an hour.

Amanda nodded. With her chin she motioned toward her dresser. "But look."

The second intruder had rummaged through her belongings, focused apparently on her jewelry box. Amanda flicked on a light and examined the mess. "Odd. Nothing is missing. They left some nice pieces."

Astarte spoke. "What about the spiral necklace?"

Amanda opened a drawer and pushed aside some socks. "Still here. On a whim, I hid it."

"I bet that's what they were after," Cam said.

She nodded. "They left everything else."

Cam considered it. The first intruder was probably a feint, used to lure them downstairs while the second intruder scaled the frame of their deck and broke into the master bedroom. "Good thing Venus was here. With more time they would definitely have found it."

Amanda sighed. "I'm almost wishing they had. I'm worried that necklace will turn out to be an albatross around my neck."

Meryn awoke with a jolt, her hands clenched and her heart racing as she fell, spinning, the roiling, cavernous vortex of fire that had been the land beneath her home ready to swallow her...

She exhaled. The nightmare again. Five hundred generations had passed yet the memories somehow still remained, imprinted in her subconscious. Someday Amanda would have the same horrible dreams. It was the price paid for wearing the necklace.

Climbing from bed, she pulled back the curtain of her hotel room window and watched as the clouds on the eastern horizon began to glow and Boston Harbor turned from black to gray. She touched her fingers to the glass, her eyes focusing on a spot far out to sea. It was one of her few indulgences, always staying in hotel rooms with views of the Atlantic.

She didn't wear a watch, instead determining time based on the sun and on her own internal clock. Five-thirty was late for her to rise. She made a cup of tea, propped herself up in bed and reviewed the notes she had made the night before. There was so much to teach Amanda, so many things Meryn needed to impart. She had had years to train her first apprentice. Now she had, what, a week? Maybe two? How to share with someone the memories of five hundred generations? And how to get her to hearken to the call of her ancestors, to commit to everything it meant to be a Crone?

The answer, she had come to realize, was obvious: Rather than telling her about Atlantis, Meryn would show her. She opened her laptop and sent a quick email to Amanda:

Remember when we talked about crones and witches? I thought you'd like this picture, an image of a witch on her broom wearing a black hat. Her name is Tlazolteotl. She is best understood as being an Aztec goddess who represents the regenerative powers of the earth. The fascinating thing about Tlazolteotl is that she comes from eastern Mexico, and dates back long before supposed European contact. How is it that both European and North American witches wear pointed black hats and ride brooms? The answer, of course, is that the witches, or crones, have a common origin. Atlantis.

Smiling, she attached the image and pressed send.

The Aztec Goddess, Tlazolteotl

Setting down her laptop, she dialed a number in Paris and spoke to a man in French. "I will be sending you a list of destinations. Make arrangements for private transportation, beginning Monday. Start with the eels. Oh, and there will be two of us."

After the police left Amanda tried to nap while Cam went for an early morning jog to try to purge the adrenaline from his system. He checked his blood sugar, showered and shared a quick breakfast with Astarte before the two of them climbed into his SUV, leaving the still-sick Amanda to try to go back to sleep.

"Will they let me help in the dig?" Astarte asked. Though only eleven, she projected an aura of seriousness and maturity. Her teacher jokingly referred to her as Siri, the know-everything iPhone personal assistant.

He wished he could have answered yes. She had come home from school yesterday back in her funk. "I don't think they will be digging too deep yet. I'm guessing they're just securing the site, making sure it doesn't get disturbed."

Her cobalt eyes danced with mischief in the rearview mirror. "Disturbed? You mean like somebody sticking a big metal shovel into the bones?"

"Yeah," he grinned. "Like that." Even in her funk she still liked to jab him.

Astarte had lived with Amanda and Cam for two-and-a-half years now. She took pride in her Native American heritage and Cam and Amanda often brought her to Native American gatherings and cultural events. He was glad for the excuse to get her out of the house today, away from memories of the break-in. "So, have you ever heard of these Red Paint People?" he asked as they merged onto the highway. "They painted the bodies of their dead red."

"No. But my people lived far away." The Mandan originally lived south of the Great Lakes before relocating to South Dakota. "I've never heard of any Red Paint People."

Cam thought the conversation had ended, but a few minutes later Astarte said, "But we have a ceremony where we paint someone all white."

"Really?"

Astarte was one of the last living Mandan, its culture and memories barely kept alive after the tribe was mostly wiped out by a smallpox epidemic in the 1830s. "It's called the *Okipa* ceremony. It happens every year. We build a tall wooden boat in the middle of the village and everyone dances around it. We call it the Big Canoe."

Cam looked sideways. "Do you know what it commemorates?"

"The arrival of the First Man. It helps us remember how we survived the Great Flood. The Mandan came to America in a boat during a flood. Just like Noah. The First Man—he represents our ancestors—had white skin. So we paint our strongest brave white. We send him away and then he returns, walking into the village from the east, which is the direction his boat came from. He tells the story of how he survived the Great Flood while everyone else drowned."

Cam reflected on her words. A ceremony featuring a Big Canoe used during the Great Flood, in which their brave white ancestor, called the First Man, is the only survivor. This didn't merely hint at an Atlantean origin, it screamed it. He made a quick decision to exit the highway, pulled into a gas station and tapped a Google search into his phone. He knew the Mandan had long been rumored to have fair skin and perhaps be the descendants of the twelfth-century Welsh prince, Madoc. But there was no Great Flood in the twelfth century. Maybe it went back further than that. Much further. He found an early 1800s painting of a Mandan woman. His eyes widened. He showed the picture to Astarte.

Mandan Girl (Princess Mink)

"That's Mink," Astarte said. "The chief's daughter."

"Do most Mandan look like her? I know you've seen a lot of pictures."

Astarte tilted her head. "Maybe not so ... serious. I think the photographer told her not to smile."

Cam studied Astarte's face. Not so unlike Mink, though Astarte had striking cobalt-colored eyes. "But otherwise? Their features?"

"I would say so, yes."

There was no doubting Mink's long nose, round eyes and aquiline face shape. Dressed differently, she could easily have passed as Greek.

Astarte interrupted his thoughts. "I can tell you what Mr. Catlin said about the way the Mandan looked."

"Yes, please." George Catlin was one of the first pioneers to encounter the Mandan. His writings and paintings remained the main source of information about the tribe. Astarte's uncle had given her a rare copy of his book describing his visit and, Siri-like, she had scanned relevant sections into her phone for easy access.

She cleared her throat and read: "*A stranger in the Mandan village is first struck with the different shades of complexion, and various colors of hair which he sees in a crowd about him; and it is at once almost disposed to exclaim that, 'These are not Indians.' There are a great many of these people whose complexions appear as light as half- breeds; and amongst the women particularly, there are many whose skins are almost white, with the most pleasing symmetry and proportion of features; with hazel, with grey, and with blue eyes...*"

She paused. "He's right. Most of the women in my family had blue eyes just like me."

Cam shook his head. The genes of an occasional fur trader bedding down for the winter would not manifest themselves so strongly throughout the entire tribe. There must be another explanation for their European features. "This First Man, the one they painted white—you said he came on a boat from the east?"

"Yes," Astarte declared. "He came from the Sunrise Sea."

Amanda appreciated Cam letting her try to go back to sleep. But even with the police circling the block the fresh memory of the intruders kept her awake. She had hidden the necklace inside a frozen turkey in their freezer; on Monday Cam would bring it to the safe deposit box. When she closed her eyes Meryn's words flooded her consciousness and called to her. She gave up on sleep, finally puttering into the kitchen, Venus at her side.

She had been fighting this cold for three days and today was the first day she felt human. So she gulped some orange juice, returned to her room to throw on her sweats and put her hair in a ponytail, made sure the doors were locked and descended to the basement to step onto the elliptical machine. She set the timer for forty minutes and found a hip-hop station on her smart phone. "Time to sweat this out of me once and for all," she murmured. With her mind racing, she knew the workout would pass in a flash.

In the brief two hours she had slept her subconscious had begun to sort through Meryn's tale, organizing and interconnecting the data. For one thing, Amanda wondered whether the name 'Meryn' was a random one. The name's root—'mer,' meaning 'sea'—tied the woman to the oceans. But it also perhaps tied Meryn and/or Atlantis to a line of French aristocrats Amanda had been studying, the Merovingians. The Merovingian dynasty ruled in France for three centuries during the Dark Ages. The family was most famous for being named as the carrier of the Jesus bloodline in the book, *Holy Blood, Holy Grail.* The name 'Merovingian,' of course, contained the same 'mer' root as Meryn. So, too, did the name Mary, as in Mary Magdalene. And, of course, Jesus was known as the Fisher King and his symbol was the sign of the fish. Perhaps it was just a coincidence, but everything seemed to tie back to the sea. Amanda let her mind wander: Was there some connection between the Jesus family bloodline and ancient Atlantis?

Stepping off the machine, she found a reference book on a bookshelf and, balancing the book on the elliptical's display consul, refreshed her memory on the history of the Merovingian origins. Merovech, the first of the line, was said to have been born in the fifth century of two fathers, the first being a descendant of Jesus. As to the second, the legend went that, while already pregnant, his mother went swimming in the ocean and was seduced by an unknown marine creature and impregnated a second time. Merovech was thus born with the blood of two different fathers running through him. By virtue of this dual blood Merovech purportedly possessed supernatural powers. In fact, he and his heirs were often associated with the British sorcerer, Merlin.

There was a lot to chew on here. First, the story of the sea monster fathering Merovech was obviously allegorical, meant to indicate that the family's origin was "from the sea," as their name indicated. Second, the comparison to Merlin caught her eye, as his name contained the same 'mer' root. So she had Meryn, Merlin, Merovech/Merovingian and Mary Magdalene with the same root. And third, from what she knew about Atlantis, it was said to have been first populated by the offspring of a human woman and the god Poseidon, himself an ocean dweller—the parallels between the Merovingian origins and the Atlantean were not exact, but they seemed close.

She was about to put the book down when, on a hunch, she opened to the index and checked for references to Atlantis. A single entry, the words jumping from the page: In some ancient cultures Atlantis was known by another name, *Meru*.

This was uneven ground, this landscape of legends and allegory. And she would need to be careful not to jump from such unsure footing to unfounded conclusions. But the question screamed at her, based on the confluence of so much otherwise unrelated information: Was it possible that Jesus and his bloodline were part of an even older royal family, one that had its origins 'from the sea'? Could Jesus have been a descendant of one of the Atlantis outpost families, perhaps possessing advanced Atlantean technology that allowed him to perform his so-called miracles? And if so, did the medieval Knights Templar, protectors of the Jesus bloodline, know of these Atlantean roots? The Templars, she and Cam had learned, seemed to play a part in almost every ancient mystery.

Forty-five minutes after leaving Westford, Cam parked his SUV and he and Astarte cut through the wooded area on an increasingly-worn path toward the Salisbury dig site. Recalling both the cold-eyed man in fatigues with the neck tattoo and the intruders from this morning, he kept Astarte close to him. Flying Fox had been spooked by the site; perhaps he should have left her home. As they passed through a particularly dark area of the woods, a flock of birds exploded in the brush next to them and Cam froze, wondering if they too had been spooked. But the trees hid whatever had alarmed the birds and Cam and Astarte arrived at the dig site without incident.

A half dozen people milled about, an assortment of ages and gender, all speaking in hushed excitement and moving about the site carefully and methodically as if a wrong step or even a raised voice might somehow cause the bones to crumble. Cam was glad to see the area had been staked and roped off, with a tent shielding the burial area. He was even more happy to see the Maine state archeologist, a man named Potvin, had made the trip and was standing near the midden. Cam's experience with his own state's archeologist was that she had more interest in being politically correct than historically correct. Hopefully, with Potvin and other professionals watching, the integrity of the site would be preserved even if the evidence it produced conflicted with accepted dogma. But Cam was getting ahead of himself. The first step would be to confirm that the burial was indeed a Red Paint People one.

Cam and the archeological community generally did not get along—mainstream archeologists did not accept his conclusions that waves of European explorers had journeyed to North America before Columbus. Cam angered many with his rhetoric, pointing out it was an accepted practice in the archeological community to throw away as "outliers" any artifacts that did not fit the accepted timeline. Likewise, archeologists often refused to look at evidence from other fields such as geology, cartography, genealogy, linguistics and astronomy. Essentially, their attitude was that if it didn't come from the ground, it wasn't good evidence. "How can you call it science," Cam would argue, "when you start with a conclusion and then ignore any evidence that doesn't support you? That's not the scientific method." During one exchange, when an archeologist was being particularly insistent that archeology was a hard science despite its treatment of outliers, Cam replied, "Uncle Fester on the old Addams Family TV show used to stick a light bulb in his mouth and make it glow. But that didn't make him a scientist." Amanda pointed out that Cam may have crossed the line with that comment.

The fact that Cam had recently been hired as a professor to teach a pair of courses in pre-Columbian history at a local university only exacerbated tensions. The Massachusetts State Archeologist acknowledged him with a curt nod. She couldn't very well kick him off the site—he was the one who discovered it, after all. Later he'd try to get some time with Potvin, who was at least civil.

Staying on the periphery with Astarte, he explained the site to her and described how the midden, which was now well inland, used to sit on the shore of a tidal flat. Eventually he wandered closer to get a sense of everyone's first impressions of the find. Even though he often disagreed with archeologists, he did recognize that, when dealing with sites like this, their work was essential. Through carbon-dating, they could establish with near-certainty the age of the burial. And any funerary items—tools, weapons, personal affects—buried with the body would speak volumes about how he or she lived. But it was the skull itself that Potvin and the archeologists were now focused on, still resting on its cheek where Cam had first unearthed it.

Red Paint People Skull, c. 8,000 BCE, Salisbury, MA

"Look at that cranium," Potvin said to two young women Cam guessed were college interns. A short wiry man in his forties who always seemed to be in motion, Potvin hopped from one foot to the other as he ran his hand through thinning brown hair. "It's massive. I'd say he was well over six feet tall. And I'll need to examine him more closely, but he looks Caucasian to me." He rubbed his forehead and closed his eyes, as if his conclusions were giving him a headache.

He lamented, "The skull shape is dolichocephalic, the zygomas are receded, the nasal apertures appear to be projecting and narrow—"

"What does that all mean?" Astarte whispered.

Cam pulled her away. "It means his face was long and thin, and so was his nose."

She nodded, immediately understanding the importance of the observation. "If he was Native American, he should have a rounder face with a flatter nose, like the Asians, right?"

"Exactly."

"So why does that archeologist look so sad?" She gestured with her chin.

Cam smiled. "Because if this skull is Caucasian, and it's as old as we think it is, it could change the entire history of North America. And some archeologists hate change."

As always, Pak Chol-su waited an hour after his supervisor had left for the day before cleaning his desk and shutting down his computer. Many things could get you in trouble in North Korea— questioning authority, being too flamboyant, doing poor work, even doing excellent work if by doing so those above you felt threatened. But putting in a short day was particularly unpardonable, even if that day was spent thousands of miles away from Pyongyang.

Someone, at some time, had made the curious decision to locate the North Korean embassy in Lebanon on the fifth floor of a modern, cubist-style building that housed—of all things—one of the Middle East's largest cosmetic surgery centers. For the Spartan North Koreans, nothing could be more decadently Western than the parade of pampered socialites jetting into Beirut for liposuction and facelifts. Perhaps the embassy was placed there as a stark reminder of what North Koreans should *not* aspire to.

In any event, Pak enjoyed the daily elevator rides, his eyes hidden behind sunglasses as he studied the would-be patients, trying to guess which imperfection they had targeted for repair. The game was made harder by the fact that many of the women for religious reasons covered their faces—why, he wondered, would these women go through the inconvenience and expense of these procedures when they could not even show their faces in public? Once in a while he'd get lucky and see the same woman a week later, after the procedure, and ascertain whether he had guessed correctly. He rarely did—the improvements all seemed arbitrary to him. Some women even intentionally had their lips enlarged, making them look like camels. He just couldn't grasp the Western concept of beauty.

Of course, he kept both the game and his insights to himself. He had learned early, as did all citizens in North Korea, that a single misstep could cost him not only his job but perhaps his life. A friend of his from the academy—Pak had been plucked from his village as a seven-year old to attend the prestigious National Academy because of his proclivity with languages —had recently been chosen to design a hotel and office complex in Pyongyang. Supreme Leader Kim Jong Un did not like the plans; he thought the design was too 'Western' in appearance. He fired Pak's architect friend, then had him executed by firing squad. A young man with a wife and small child. Not that Pak would ever question the sagacity of Supreme Leader. In fact, he had recently burned an American magazine which contained an article criticizing Supreme Leader, calling him a fat, bloodthirsty lunatic with a Fred Flintstone haircut (Pak was not sure what this was, but was afraid to look it up lest it be something obscene). The article claimed he was so powerful that not only were those closest to him afraid to criticize him, they were afraid even to *advise* him. Pak shuddered at what would have happened if the magazine had been found inside his apartment, vowing never to bring outside reading material home again.

Pak checked his watch as he exited the elevator. Just before seven o'clock on a Saturday evening. He felt like going to a bar, maybe dancing a bit. But he knew better, knew to assume he was always being watched and followed. Best to go straight home. Tomorrow, at least, he had an excuse to be out and about. A local religious leader, a member of the Druze community, had died overnight and Pak had volunteered to attend the funeral to pay respects on behalf of his government. It was the type of thing he often did and usually enjoyed. These types of public gatherings, where many congregated and emotions bubbled over, gave him valuable insights into the personalities of the Middle-Easterners. But he had a special reason for wanting to attend this particular funeral.

The Druze were an insular, quasi-Islamic sect who had lived in and around Lebanon for thousands of years. They were also a key component in a crazy, almost farcical, plan which Supreme Leader had hatched and which Pak, being one of the few people in North Korea fluent in Arabic, was supposed to carry out...

Pak slapped himself hard across the face, stopping the treasonous thought. He clenched his jaw, his cheek burning, and hissed out the words. "Supreme Leader is a brilliant military mind. Thus his plan must also be brilliant. The plan will succeed." He let out a long breath. "It is an honor he has chosen you."

He would need to be more careful, more disciplined. Under questioning, even his innermost thoughts could be revealed. The only safe course therefore was not to let these thoughts form in his mind.

"The plan will succeed," he repeated. And its success would ensure the long-term survival and prosperity of the Democratic People's Republic of Korea. Pak would be a hero, the smile of Supreme Leader directed at him...

Unless the plan failed. The brilliant plan. If it failed it would be because Pak had failed. No doubt he would then meet the same fate as his architect friend.

Pak's shoulders slumped. Maybe he'd go for one drink after all.

There were only so many times Xifeng could stroll past the house on the quiet street in the suburb northwest of Boston. At some point someone would notice the Asian woman snooping about on a breezy spring afternoon, especially after the botched break-in from last night. Not to mention it would be difficult to learn much from the end of the driveway. Sometimes it paid to be bold. Her handler had not been pleased that Xifeng had failed to retrieve the spiral.

Returning to her Volkswagen parked across the street from the lakefront home, Xifeng crouched down by the driver side front tire and, using her body as a shield, unscrewed the valve cap and deflated the tire. She then got back into her car and pulled her cell phone from her purse. She turned on the GPS program, opened up a half-dozen internet sites and downloaded a couple of videos, both of which she watched at full volume and with full brightness. As the time passed, she considered her mission. *Observe the Gunn woman.* Not a lot to go on. It would be nice if her handler had outlined the mission, given her a sense of what kind of things she should be *observing*. At least her orders to try to steal the spiral had been specific. But that was not the way of the East. She shrugged. It had worked for thousands of years, so who was she to question it. But it would be helpful to have an idea why these spirals were so important.

Within ten minutes her phone battery had drained to zero, ending her musings. She could have instead just turned the phone off, but draining it was the type of small detail she had been trained never to overlook.

"Hi," Xifeng said, now at the front door, her finger on the doorbell. "I'm so sorry to bother you, but I have a flat and my phone is dead." She held the phone up as evidence. "Can I borrow yours?"

The Gunn woman hesitated, scanning the yard and street, obviously skittish after the overnight incident. "I suppose so, yes." Xifeng did not usually find Westerners attractive, but the Gunn woman had the kind of beauty that transcended racial prejudices—fine features, emerald eyes, long strawberry-blond hair and porcelain skin. Even in a t-shirt and jeans she somehow looked elegant.

Xifeng called the number on her AAA card—she really did have a flat, after all—and arranged for assistance. While on the line she squatted and greeted the dog, allowing the animal to become familiar with her scent. When she hung up she addressed her hostess. "What a beautiful dog. I have a milk bone in my bag—may I give it to her?"

The Gunn woman chuckled. "Only if you want to make a friend for life. Her name is Venus." It had taken Xifeng years to be able to differentiate the different accents in America, but she clearly recognized this one as British.

Xifeng offered the snack, cooing and staying in contact with the animal to cement their new bond. And to allow her to clip a small listening device to the back side of her collar. People said dogs were good judges of character. In Xifeng's experience, dogs were no better judges of character than were people—they liked anyone who patted them on the head and gave them treats.

Amanda chopped zucchini in the kitchen while Cam fired up the grill on the rear deck and Astarte wrestled with Venus on the living room couch. They planned to have an early dinner, go out for ice cream and return to watch a family movie.

As she chopped, she forced her mind away from today's intrusion and focused instead on Atlantis. Was it really possible that, at a time when most historians believed humans were living in caves, grunting and hitting each other over the head with clubs, there was an advanced civilization living in the middle of the Atlantic? The reverse was true, she realized—today, isolated pockets of hunter-gatherers lived in straw huts in the jungles of South America and Indonesia, even as fellow humans traveled to outer space, lived with transplanted hearts and split the atom. One tribe, living on an island off of India, still did not know how to make fire...

Astarte burst in, interrupting her thoughts. "They're coming!"

"Who's coming?"

"The Jehovah's Witnesses. They're in the driveway."

Amanda sighed. She knew better then to let Cam see them. He would angrily confront them about the sexual abuse in their church, the years of cover-up and denial. He had been involved as a lawyer in the Catholic Church priest abuse cases and had seen firsthand the damage done to the children and their families. And, more to the point, a close childhood friend had committed suicide after being abused by a priest.

She met them at the door. "I'm sorry, we're not interested. We are comfortable with our religious beliefs."

The shorter of the two men, who with round face and small features looked like an adult version of Charlie Brown, smiled politely and pulled on his shirt collar. "With respect, are we really meant to be 'comfortable' with our relationship with God? Shouldn't he expect more from us?"

Amanda couldn't help herself. "He?"

The man's face flushed. "Yes, he. Our father. The Bible is clear on this."

"It seems just as clear to me that it is women who give life. So why would God not have the same form?" She didn't know what God looked like but was pretty sure it didn't involve beards or penises.

The man recovered quickly. "Yes, I see your point." He turned to his younger associate. "We see, yes."

He had been trained well. Amanda knew their strategy was to engage potential recruits in a conversation about religion, no matter what that conversation might entail. That was how they got their foot in the door, both figuratively and literally. "I don't believe you do. I don't mean to be rude, but there are some people in your church who have been covering up nasty, vile cases of child sex abuse. Perhaps you should get your own house in order before you come proselytizing at mine. Good day." She closed the door and flicked the deadbolt.

Feeling guilty for treating the men so impolitely, she explained to Astarte, "I was a trifle rude. We don't know those men are involved in the abuse or the coverup. But there's an old expression that says if you're not part of the solution then you're part of the problem. This has been going on for years. It needs to stop."

Astarte nodded. "I understand that it was wrong to be rude to them, but I don't think it's right when people knock on your door and tell you that your religion is wrong and theirs is better." She swallowed. "I mean, it would be better if people just let other people believe in whatever religion they want."

Amanda hugged the girl. She remembered what Meryn had said, about how on Atlantis the women were recognized as the spiritual leaders and religion served as a unifying force rather than a dividing one. There was no doubt in her mind—and Cam agreed with her on this—that the male domination of the Abrahamic religions had resulted in thousands of years of war, violence, torture and intolerance. Not to mention generations of young boys and girls permanently scarred by church-enabled sexual predators.

She recalled Meryn's exact words. Perhaps it was indeed again time to follow the Crones.

Abraham Gottlieb marched confidently into the hotel conference room, Madame Radminikov by his side. A dozen white-robed men and a handful of yellow-robed women sat in front of him, their eyes alert and cautious. He had left Solomon and his two operatives in the hotel lobby—his audience might think him weak if he required an armed escort.

Abraham walked with his chin up. He did not crave the spotlight, but also knew the benefits of commanding it. He was glad he wore a red tie with his gray suit—not just because the color matched the large red crosses emblazoned on the white and yellow robes, but because red was the power of blood and death. And that was the purpose of this meeting.

He leaned against the lectern and surveyed the room, making it a point to lock his gray eyes at least momentarily on each of the modern-day Templar Knights seated in front of him. Who would have thought that modern Christians would be so alarmed at the violence against Christians in the Middle East that they would reconstitute one of the world's most infamous fighting forces? These were not the Templars of various Masonic sects, focused on fellowship and ritual. These were men and women, some of them ex-military, who had taken a blood oath to defend Christianity here in America. But, as far as Abraham could tell, they were a fighting force without a battle field. Short of relocating to the Middle East, they had no way to identify, and therefore engage, their enemy. That's what this evening was about—a meeting between himself and the Templar senior officers.

"I am too old," he began, "to spend time on niceties. I have come to propose an alliance, a joint venture between our groups." His voice was strong, his accent German; many said he sounded like Henry Kissinger. "We have a common enemy—radical Muslim dogs who wish to destroy the Judeo-Christian world. You have seen the news: Elderly Christian women paraded naked through the streets, daughters raped, prisoners decapitated, children stolen from their homes, churches burned. My group has experience fighting animals like this, and significant funds to devote to such an effort." He paused. "And you have an army."

"What kind of experience?" asked a bearded man in the front row, his arms crossed at his chest. A gold silk collar draped over his robe identified him as the group's Commander.

"Experience forged at the fire of six million of our people murdered by the Nazis." Abraham scanned the crowd. "We call our group Kidon, after the Hebrew word for the sword David used to slay Goliath. We, too, will slay our enemies. To be more specific." He pushed a button on a remote and an image of a young man with a shaved head and blond goatee appeared on a projection screen behind him. Tattoos, a swastika prominent among them, covered the man's muscular arms and neck. "Though not his real name, we will call him Richard Neary. He is a neo-Nazi." Abraham flicked to the next image, a close-up of Neary's face. "Note the tattoo on Mr. Neary's forehead."

"Isn't that a Jewish Star?" the bearded leader asked.

"Yes. We placed it there after Mr. Neary desecrated a Jewish cemetery. Later, after a second attack, we captured him and castrated him." He paused. "I mean that in a literal sense—we surgically removed his testicles." He motioned toward the thick-necked Madame Radminikov seated at the far end of the front row. "In fact, Madame R herself assisted in the procedure." There was no need to use her full name.

"I took no joy in it," she replied, turning in her chair to address the Templars. "But it was necessary. Castration removes testosterone from the body, which we find can be an effective way to emasculate many of these angry young men."

"Did it work?" the Commander asked.

Abraham shook his head. "In this case, no. There was a third incident. Strike three, as they say. We had no choice but to eliminate Mr. Neary."

"Eliminate?" The question came from a clean-shaven man with a military haircut, a black and red cross tattooed on his neck and a cold hatred in his eyes. *The man from the Cameron Thorne lecture.* Abraham took a second to gather his thoughts. He knew the danger of an alliance like this. As the saying went, violence was often the last refuge of the incompetent—the misfits of society with sadistic tendencies had forever been attracted to the military's sanctioned violence. Barnabus was a perfect example of that. But Abraham had learned how to control the bearlike Hassid. He would have no such ability with these Christians.

Abraham nodded. "Yes, eliminate."

The questioner snapped his fingers. "Just like that."

"In this case Mr. Neary fell from a cruise ship in the Caribbean. Too much to drink, the authorities believed. His body was found the next morning. Or what was left of it after the sharks were finished. I will reiterate that we gave Mr. Neary three chances, which is three more than the ISIS vermin give Christians and Jews before beheading them."

Abraham clicked to the next image. A pair of swarthy young men sat on the metal floor of a passenger van, bound, blindfolded and gagged. "You may not care about men like Mr. Neary, but I'm guessing you will be interested in the story of these brothers from the Middle East. Students at a college in New England. They were planning to bomb the Hillel building, the Jewish student center. We stopped them and extracted confessions. Along with a list of accomplices."

"Then what?" The voice came from the side of the room, a gray-haired man wearing a priest's collar.

"They were shot in a drug deal that, I believe the expression is, went bad." He continued with a lie. "That was a year-and-a-half ago." No reason for anyone to look too closely into last night's events.

"Why didn't you just go to the authorities to begin with?" the priest asked.

"Because, frankly, the system is broken." Abraham shrugged. "We allow terrorists to enter the country, give them housing and welfare, then just assume they will become good Americans. That is naïve. Fatally so. And when our police do become suspicious, weak-kneed judges often refuse warrants to allow for searches or surveillance." He paused. "The recent atrocity in Orlando is a good example. The FBI questioned this monster twice. But they did nothing. Had they notified Kidon, fifty lives would have been saved. Just as the lives of the Hillel students were saved. Kidon is not constrained by the niceties of the law. Members of our law enforcement community understand this, and they look away while we do the dirty work. The necessary work."

The priest continued his questioning. "You're admitting this in public?"

Abraham shrugged. It was a calculated risk, a way to show his audience the power of Kidon. A group that could abduct and eliminate two terrorists, then brag about it openly without consequences, was a group to be reckoned with. Not that he had given enough details to tie Kidon definitively to anything. "I trust that none of you will go to the authorities over the death of these vermin." He paused. "And if you do, we have many in power who will protect us."

The bearded Commander spoke again. "Regarding these terrorists, what happened to three chances?"

Abraham lifted his chin. "Sometimes giving someone another chance is like giving them another bullet after they missed you the first time. We try to be compassionate. But we are not stupid."

The Commander spoke the obvious. "So you are a vigilante group."

"Yes, to a degree. But we also strive to prevent attacks before they occur, as was the case with the terrorist brothers." Abraham turned his palms up. "Unfortunately we are not prepared to deal with the size of the current threat. We are, as I said, well-funded. And we possess extraordinary intelligence-collecting capabilities, both here in Boston and in other major cities." He had built a network of thousands over the past seventy years, men and women in all walks of life—including many in law enforcement and the judicial system—willing to do what they could behind the scenes to help Kidon. "But we do not have the manpower we need. The truth is that few young Jewish men and women are drawn to groups like ours, and those that are go to Israel to join the fight there." He scanned the room. "You, on the other hand, seem to be looking for an opportunity to engage the enemy. You may not know this, but cooperation between the Templars and the Jews goes back to your order's earliest days, when Jewish scholars helped the Templars translate and interpret ancient texts found in the Middle East."

"The problem with vigilante groups is one of perspective," the Commander countered. "Who gets to decide what crimes to punish?"

Abraham raised his chin. "I do. I decide. And others like me."

The man spread his arms. "With all due respect, what gives you the right to do so?"

Abraham pushed his suit-coat sleeve up his left forearm and held his concentration camp tattoo aloft. *B9447.* He lowered his voice, speaking in little more than a whisper. "This does. This and the fact that six million of my people died while the world did nothing. Going forward, when the world does nothing, we will take action."

Silence filled the room, the whir of the projector the only sound. After a few seconds, during which nobody met Abraham's glance, the cold-eyed man cleared his throat and spoke. "When you say you have money, how much you talking?"

There was no reason for Abraham to demur. He was rolling the dice with this venture, revealing the secrets of Kidon to outsiders for the first time in seventy years. Hopefully the rewards would outweigh the risks. But none of it would happen without sufficient financial resources. "I am the sole owner of an insurance conglomerate with a market value of approximately six billion dollars. Even in our worst years we generate more than three hundred million in profit. These profits are earmarked to fund the efforts of Kidon."

"Just to be clear, you said three hundred million," the bearded Commander said, coughing over the words. "How much of that would be available to fund this joint venture you are proposing?"

Abraham locked eyes. "All of it. And more if necessary." Kidon's supporters had contributed more money than Abraham could ever spend.

The cold-eyed man leaned forward. "So how would this joint venture work? Who would run it? Who gets final say?"

Abraham showed his graying teeth. There was at least some interest, it appeared, in renewing the Templar-Jewish alliance of the 12th and 13th centuries. "Patience, please. You are like a man negotiating a prenuptial agreement on the first date. We have a long way to go, your group and mine. But I am pleased to see that both sides seem to be enjoying the flirtation."

Tracy "Trey" Blackwell sat in the middle of the hotel conference room listening to the strange Jewish guy. She wasn't quite sure what to make of him or his thick-necked companion. Were they serious? Had they really executed two terrorists? They looked like they should be in Florida playing mahjong and smuggling dinner rolls out of the early bird special.

Assuming their story checked out, she had to hand it to them. Not that she had an extra hand to give. She had lost two fingers on her left hand while serving in Iraq. The fact that it had happened while lighting a Roman candle on the Fourth of July was a part of the story she usually left out. The story always ended with something like: "In case you're wondering, I'm not named after my father and grandfather. The boys in my platoon started calling me Trey instead of Tracy after I lost the two fingers." That was her best skill, making people laugh. As a woman in a man's army, it was one of the few ways to feel like one of the guys.

Faced with a dishonorable discharge (the army frowning on its soldiers losing appendages while acting like idiots), she had quickly agreed to the only deal offered her: She'd return stateside with full accommodation and disability pay in return for agreeing to go undercover with Homeland Security. Almost a year ago they had assigned her to monitor the Templars, to make sure the Christian group's activities did not become a threat. She had recently been elevated to the Templar leadership team. It wasn't a bad gig for a girl in her mid-twenties with no particular career skills who couldn't hit the 'a' or 's' on a keyboard. But it sure was boring. Maybe tonight had changed things.

Trey studied the woman as the wolf-like old Jew spoke, watching her eyes and her breathing. The woman viewed Abraham almost reverently, leaning in, her entire body in rhythm with his. Trey shook the thought aside that they might be lovers. It was bad enough that she was going through a dry spell of her own. Trey wasn't bad looking in a tomboy kind of way—someone had once asked for her autograph, thinking she was the actress Sandra Bullock. And she worked hard to stay in shape. But for some reason the men she had been meeting since her discharge all seemed so … shallow. She was used to living on the edge, not knowing if her next breath might be her last. The guys she met stateside panicked at the thought that their next latte might be their last. Anyway, it would really suck if even these old geezers were getting some and she wasn't.

She shifted her gaze to her Templar comrades. Trey had done her best to feign enthusiasm and bond with the group. Knowing the number eight was sacred to the Templars, she had held up her eight fingers at their first meeting and declared, "I'm a natural." But the reality was that they were nothing more than a bunch of altar boys and girls playing dress-up. They had never seen battle, never heard the whistle of a bullet sizzle by their ear, never placed their hand over an open wound and felt their buddy's lifeblood gush out between their fingers. Actually, that was not entirely true. She sensed that the Commander had seen action. And the guy with the cold blue eyes and cross tattooed on his neck, Magnuson, had the look of someone who tortured cats as a boy and wanted to do more of it as a man. She could take care of herself, even down two fingers, yet she made it a point to stay clear of him. But the rest of them just liked the idea of telling their friends they were modern-day Crusaders, sworn to die for Christianity. It was an easy oath to make, thousands of miles from the enemy.

Yet this old Jew may have just changed things.

Leah did not have to be told what her job was. Abraham was not a schmoozer, not one for niceties and small talk. From the lectern he had excused himself and found refuge in the men's room, leaving her to continue their flirtation with the modern-day Templars. She took a deep breath and smiled. It's not like she had anything better to do on a Saturday night. And every woman, even a thick-necked, middle-aged widow, liked a good flirtation.

She rubbed her teeth clean with a forefinger and made her way toward the bearded man with the gold collar. He looked to be around sixty, gray dominating a dark beard which did a good job hiding his jowls. Twenty years and thirty pounds ago he had no doubt been unusually handsome; even today his command of the room and deep, dark eyes drew her to him. She wished she didn't look so much like a drill sergeant.

She held out her hand to him, hoping he wouldn't notice the calluses and scars accrued over decades handling a carving knife. "I am, as Abraham so eloquently put it, Madame R," she said, smiling.

He took her hand and, rather than shaking, covered it with both of his as he held her eyes. "A pleasure." His leathery cologne wafted over her. "Manuel de Real." He released her hand. "This Abraham— assuming that is his real name—is a fascinating man. And tells a fascinating story." A small crowd encircled them. "We are … intrigued by his offer. May I ask how you came to be involved in Kidon?"

She nodded. It was an obvious question, an obvious way for de Real to learn more about Kidon. And it was a story she was happy to share. "I have known Abraham since I was a baby. He and my father were in the concentration camp together. Dachau. I have heard the story so many times I feel I actually lived it."

She took a deep breath. "Well, Abraham was only a boy at the time, probably fourteen or so. My father was in his early twenties, but already he and the other prisoners looked to Abraham as their leader. They called him the Wolf. There was a ferocity about him that even life in the camps could not tame; some dogs are like that— they could live in your house for years without incident, then you leave the room for a minute and they attack the baby. Even the guards seemed to treat him a bit differently—they weren't exactly afraid of him, but they were careful not to turn their back on him."

The Templar Commander nodded, his dark eyes exuding sincerity. "I have known such men."

"The end of the war was growing near. The Allied troops were approaching. Hitler didn't want the prisoners to be liberated so he gave the order to kill them all before they could be freed. Abraham's plan was to approach the nastiest guard in the whole prison, Holtzman, to try to cut a deal. You will meet Clevinsky, perhaps—this animal Holtzman is the one who stuffed a hot coal in poor Clevinsky's mouth…"

She paused, took a deep breath and shook her head to clear the image from her mind and continued. "Anyway, the other prisoners argued with Abraham, tried to get him to approach one of the less brutal guards. But Abraham refused. 'Listen,' he said. 'Holtzman is cruel because all he cares about is Holtzman. His selfishness is the one thing we can rely on. These other guards are scared and desperate, which makes them irrational. But Holtzman's greed is constant. We can use it against him.'"

"A wise approach," de Real replied. "Greed has always been a powerful motivator."

"So he approached Holtzman and said he had a business proposition. The other prisoners thought that this was where Holtzman would laugh at him, maybe even shoot him. After all, he was a fourteen-year-old boy who had spent the war in a concentration camp, so what could he possibly have to offer? But Holtzman agreed to listen. Abraham said, 'Before the war, my father, who was a wealthy businessman, was able to fill a safe deposit box in Zurich with gold and jewels. To get into the box, you need the account number, a key, and a signature that matches the signature card.' Abraham then pulled out a piece of paper and a key that he had been able to hide from the Nazis. He said, 'Here is the key and the account number. Meet me at the Union Bank of Switzerland, in Zurich, in exactly one year, at noon. You cannot access the account without my father's signature, which I can replicate, and I cannot access it without the key and account number. So you will have to help me escape rather than kill me. If we both survive the war, we shall split the treasure equally. If we do not, the treasure will be lost to both of us.'"

"A brilliant plan," de Real said, nodding. "I doubt many men would have been able to come up with this under such trying circumstances."

Leah continued, pleased that the Commander appreciated Abraham's brilliance. She had told the story many times; it never failed to impress and captivate her audience. "The guard examined the key carefully—it was clearly authentic. And it seemed plausible that the poised and crafty boy standing in front of Holtzman came from a wealthy family. Since there was no way to steal Abraham's signature, he agreed, probably figuring he could steal Abraham's half from him after they emptied the box."

"So, did the plan work?"

"Wait," she smiled. "There is something more. Here is where Abraham became truly heroic. 'There is one more condition to our deal,' he declared. 'I will not abandon the other prisoners here. The war is over; the Allied troops are near; there is no gain for you if they all die. You must agree to let us all escape. When you are on duty tonight, let us run to the woods. The Americans are only a few miles away.' And that is what happened. A few of the prisoners were recaptured, but most made it safely to where the American troops were camped. Abraham saved close to forty lives that night. Including my father and Clevinsky. It is these people, and their descendents, who make up the core of Kidon."

Nobody said anything for a few seconds. A voice from behind her broke the silence. "So what happened to the safe deposit box?"

"As they agreed, Abraham met Holtzman at the bank one year later. And, just as Abraham expected, Holtzman insisted that Abraham wait in the lobby while he, Holtzman, went into the private area to retrieve the gold and jewels from the box."

Leah paused now, allowing de Real to ask the obvious. "Did Holtzman try to take the entire fortune?"

She grinned. "Oh, Holtzman got everything that was in the box, all right. Abraham had emptied the box out months before, using a second key his father had hidden in a graveyard near their home. He then booby-trapped the box with explosives. When Holtzman opened it, it blew up in his face."

"No need for Nuremberg trials for men like Holtzman," de Real observed. Leah was glad to hear it—it meant he had no problem with vigilantism. This was a risky alliance Abraham had proposed. Since its formation Kidon had always been insular and secretive. And wholly Jewish. Who knew if these Christians could be trusted?

She responded to de Real. "It seems to me that dying instantly from a bomb blast was a better fate than he deserved."

Out of the shadows Abraham appeared at her side. He often snuck up on her, wolf-like. "You must excuse Madame R taking some poetic license with this story. I was merely a boy trying to survive. Now, if you will excuse us, I am sure you have much to discuss."

As he led her into the lobby, he leaned closer and whispered, "I have never told you, Leah, that there was one thing in the safe deposit box which I did not sell."

She stiffened—he rarely called her Leah. And he almost never spoke of his Holocaust experiences. "What?" she breathed.

"It is almost time." He stopped and turned, holding her eyes. "Soon I will show you."

Amanda's suitcase lay open on their bed. She and Cam chatted as she packed. Venus helped also, though her idea of helping was to remove the clothes and hide them under an old comforter she sometimes slept on. Somehow the dog knew that if Amanda didn't have her clothes, she couldn't leave. The dog's playfulness helped soften the pall of the intruders having violated their space only half a day earlier.

"Did she give you an itinerary?" Cam asked.

There had been no doubt Amanda would comply with Meryn's request. And she knew Cam would support her decision—this ferreting around in the dark, dusty corners of history is what they did, both individually and as a couple. Plus, this time it was personal for Amanda. She had a chance to learn about and connect with her family. "No itinerary other than be at the airport early Monday morning," she replied. "She just said to bring my passport and pack enough clothes for four days. And that it would be a lot easier to show me the family history than to tell it."

"I'm jealous. Sounds like a fascinating trip."

She sighed. "I suppose so. I just wish it all didn't have to be so bloody mysterious. Just tell me where we're going and I'll be on my way." She tossed a pair of wool socks into the suitcase. "I'm going to end up looking like Mary Poppins, with nine different bags. How does one pack for Atlantis? I mean, what's the weather like in April at the bottom of the Atlantic?"

"Opposite of Arizona. Cold. But it's a wet cold. Dress for hypothermia."

She rolled her eyes at him as Astarte wandered in, wearing a blue nightgown and slippers after her shower. "Can we play a game tonight?"

"Sure, honey," Cam replied. "Venus can finish packing for Mom."

They followed Astarte to the kitchen table. As she set up the cribbage board Cam told Amanda about the Red Paint People skull, and Astarte explained the Mandan legend that they came to America across the Atlantic. "I know it's not politically correct to say so, but the head looked Caucasian," Cam said.

"Please," Amanda said dismissively. "You Americans need to grow thicker skins. Most Asians have slanted eyes. Most Africans have wider noses. Most Brits have bad teeth. You say 'politically correct' like it has anything to do with politics. It doesn't. It's science."

Cam smiled. "You have nice teeth."

She sighed. Her little rant had nothing to do with skulls; she was unsettled by the thought of jetting around the world for four days with a complete stranger and no itinerary. But Cam always seemed to know what to say to get her out of one of her funks. "Only because our landlady was a dental hygienist and took pity on me," she said, relaxing. "Otherwise I'd probably have little brown rat teeth."

"Well, like I said, this head looked Caucasian. We talked the other night about whether it was related to Atlantis. Seems one way to tell is to compare the DNA in the skull to your aunt Meryn." DNA testing could tell how long ago the skull and Meryn shared a common ancestor.

"And to me," Astarte piped in. "The Mandan came here from across the Sunrise Sea. Maybe I'm part of Atlantis also."

Amanda studied her blue eyes and Cleopatra-like features. Like many Native Americans, a good amount of European blood coursed through Astarte's veins. But there wasn't a single feature of the girl that looked Asiatic.

Magnuson remained seated as his fellow Templar brothers and sisters mingled with the thick-necked Jewess. He had nothing against Jews other than the small fact that they murdered Jesus. Even that could be forgiven, he supposed, given Jesus' unending and boundless compassion. That was between the Jews and Christ. What concerned Magnuson was the here and now: The Jews, through their aggression in the Middle East, had sparked the raging fire which had become ISIS and radical Islam. The Jews, in short, were the cause of the mess that America now found itself in.

He waited for the Jewess to leave and for Commander de Real to call their meeting to order. A few fellow Knights spoke in favor of the proposed alliance with Kidon. Magnuson remained silent, but de Real must have read his body language. "I sense you object, Brother Magnuson?"

He took a deep breath. He was relatively new to the Templars, drawn to the order by both his faith and his militarism. He had risen in its ranks through his dedication and hard work. And by keeping his mouth shut. But this time the words tumbled out before he could swallow them. "I do, Sir." He rubbed at his cross tattoo, which seemed to burn in support of his position. Knowing he was not an eloquent speaker, he kept his words simple. "A thousand years ago our predecessors fought the Crusades. Their goal was to take Jerusalem. For the Christians. Not for the Jews, for the Christians. I think our goal should be the same. By supporting the Jews, by supporting Israel, it seems to me that we are acting against our own best interests."

The priest, whom Magnuson knew only as Father Edward, replied. "But God promised Israel to the Jews."

Magnuson had been doing some reading about this. "Yes, to the Jews. But the present-day Israelis don't descend from Abraham." He explained how a Johns Hopkins geneticist had shown that most Jews today descended from a group of Central Europeans called the Khazars, who had converted to Judaism around 800 CE "So most Jews today aren't really Jews. The Palestinians have more of

Abraham's blood in them than the Jews—remember, the Arabs descend from Abraham's first son, Ishmael." He looked at the priest. "So I'm not sure that God's promise holds any more."

Father Edward rubbed his chin and nodded. "I'm familiar with this research and I'm not sure the science is as convincing as you say it is. But you make an interesting case. And it would be nice to have Christian control of the Holy Land again. As you said, that is why the Templar Order was first formed."

The meeting with the Templars ended around eight o'clock. Normally Leah would have insisted Abraham take some time for a proper dinner—he often forgot to eat, his body somehow able to function on what seemed a starvation diet. She guessed it was related to his years in the concentration camps, subsisting on watery soup and potato peels and even an occasional bug.

But tonight she was happy to skip the evening meal. Abraham, normally so stoic, seemed almost giddy at the secret he was about to share with her. With a flourish he opened the front door of his Tudor-style brick home tucked into a quiet Brookline neighborhood and ushered her to a door in the hallway under the main staircase. He flicked on a light and, almost bouncing, led Leah down a steep wooden staircase that creaked under their weight. The smell of heating oil wafted over her as her eyes adjusted to the dimly lit basement. They circled around behind the staircase, Abraham stopping in front of what looked like an antique bank vault door set into the building's concrete foundation. He spun a dial the size of a dinner plate back and forth and yanked the door open. "I had this vault built for safety reasons."

He flicked a light switch and she peered inside the prison cell-sized enclosure, the overhead fluorescent light contrasting with the antique, brass-colored metal walls. A rust-stained utility sink stood in the corner. The room was otherwise empty except for a workbench along a side wall, a stack of drawers wedged underneath it and a pair of fire extinguishers mounted on the back wall. Hardly the supplies one would expect in a safe room. "How long would you stay safe here without food?" she asked.

He grimaced. "You misunderstand. This room is not to keep *me* safe. It is to keep others safe *from* me."

By way of explanation Abraham opened one of the drawers and handed her a pair of goggles. Through them she studied the objects on the workbench: a gray, pinecone-sized chunk of rock along with a white, marble-like container the size of a large cigar box with its lid resting next to it.

Abraham pointed at the jagged rock. "This is bismuth. This piece is from Bolivia, but it is also prevalent in China and Australia. Bismuth is used predominantly in industrial usage as a replacement for lead. It sells for approximately one dollar per ounce."

From beneath the workbench he pulled out what looked like a car battery, except it had a thick electrical cord running from it to an electrical outlet recessed in the room's cement floor. Jumper cables protruded from the battery-like object; Abraham connected the cable teeth to a pair of metal rods protruding from each end of the marble box.

She had no idea what this was all about. And she sensed he was enjoying her perplexity. "All right, I'll bite. What is all this?"

"As I said, the rock is bismuth. Attached to the box are jumper cables. Inside the box is distilled water."

He was being purposefully obtuse. "And you are a pain in the ass. Now we've both stated the obvious."

In the shadows she thought his lips curled slightly upward. He pointed at the battery-like object. "That device is attached by its cord to the main electrical line running through this area of Brookline." She could imagine what kind of bribes he had to pay to tap into the power line. "Obviously, it channels electricity to the jumper cables."

"To what purpose?"

"Please close and latch the door." Theatrically, he loosened his tie and undid the top button of his dress shirt. From around his neck he pulled a silver chain, hanging from which was a black metallic spiral. She had never seen the necklace before, but then again she had rarely seen Abraham with his top button undone. She bit back the obvious question—why would a Jewish octogenarian be wearing a spiral necklace like some New Age spiritualist?

Abraham dropped the chunk of bismuth into the water-filled marble box. Onto a small, soap-dish-like shelf inside the box he placed the spiral. The spiral seemed to change color as he handled it, though that was probably just a trick of the light. He then covered the box with its lid.

Without preamble, as was his way, he finally explained. "You have heard how, before the Holocaust, my father took the precaution of stashing our family's most valuable jewels in a safe deposit box in Zurich. What I have not told you is this necklace and marble box were included among those valuables. The spiral has been in my family for twelve thousand years."

She blinked. "You mean twelve hundred years?" That would take them back to the Dark Ages, when Jews mostly lived in Eastern Europe.

"No, Madame. I mean what I said. Twelve thousand."

"Abraham," she stuttered, "how could that be?"

"I will explain all that later. For now, it is only important to know that this necklace was forged from a meteorite that impacted our planet tens of thousands of years ago. As the story has been passed down to me, *l'dor va'dor*, generation to generation, the necklace— again, forged from a piece of the meteorite—was by chance left atop a chunk of bismuth during a lightning storm. A lightning bolt struck the necklace and the stone, creating an astonishing result." He paused theatrically. "I will reproduce that event here. Stand back and observe."

He flicked a switch on the electrical device and, Frankenstein-like in his thick German accent, began counting loudly. At eight he snapped the switch a second time.

Leah had no idea what to expect. But she knew Abraham was not one for idle amusements—the man didn't even own a television. Grinning in a manner she had never seen in the decades she had known him, he pulled a pair of thick fireplace gloves from a drawer, put them on and carefully slid the lid off the box. Steam wafted out. Using a pair of fireplace tongs he also took from the drawer, Abraham reached in and removed the chunk of bismuth. He carried the sample to the sink and rinsed it under cold water.

Leah moved closer. The rock had turned copper-colored. "Was that some kind of chemical reaction?" she asked.

"Not chemical. Physical. The bismuth has been physically transformed at an atomic level, four of its protons literally sheared from its nucleus."

It had been forty years since she studied physics. "What does that mean?"

"It means, Madame Radminikov, that our chunk of bismuth has been transmuted." He bowed slightly, still grinning. "Into solid gold."

Trey peered through the dingy glass of the narrow basement window, watching as the two strange Jews emerged from what looked like a bank vault wearing goggles and thick gloves. She peered closer. It looked like Abraham was carrying a gold-colored rock in a thick glove. Odd. Her original plan had been to watch from the street, but when she saw the basement light go on she snuck through the shrubs surrounding the ivy-covered brick house and took the opportunity to observe.

She had no idea what they were doing, but she hoped when she was an old fart she'd be half as active as Abraham. Maybe something about surviving the Holocaust when practically everyone else you knew perished gave you the perspective that every day should be lived to—

She jumped back, her body reflexively recoiling into a defensive posture. The old man had seen her. Not just seen her. He had looked up and smiled at her. As if he had known she was there the whole time. *Time to get out of here.* She turned to run. But it was too late. The whites of a pair of large eyes shone in the night. "You may not be able to see it," a voice growled, "but I have a gun pointed at your chest. I suggest you not move."

Her eyes locked on his. The man was a pro—no fear, no anger, no panic. And also no doubt he would do what needed to be done. But there was something else as well. Kindness. Perhaps even sadness.

Leah did not recall following Abraham out of the vault and back up the basement stairs, but she must have because here they sat, at his kitchen table, a glass of cognac in her hand and her goggles hanging from her neck. And a chunk of gold on the table between them. She had a vague recollection of Abraham leaving the kitchen, and the voice of Solomon Massala in the foyer...

"How...," she began, but was not sure how to formulate an intelligent question. So she left it at that. "How?"

"Man has long known how to turn base metals such as lead and bismuth into gold. All it requires is a massive power source and—"

She interrupted. "Wait, then why don't we?"

"Because it is prohibitively expensive. Expense aside, the technology has existed for almost a century. In the 1970s the Soviets found that the lead shielding of a nuclear reactor had turned to gold during nuclear research testing. In the 1920s the Japanese turned mercury into gold using a nuclear reaction. And more recently scientists in California using a particle accelerator produced small amounts of gold from bismuth. All it takes, as I said, is an energy source strong enough to shear some protons from the base metal's nucleus."

She sipped the cognac. "Okay, but you did so using the town's electrical main. Hardly a massive power source."

He raised an index finger to emphasize his point. "The electrical main coupled with the spiral necklace. Apparently there is something in the alien metal which weakens the proton's bond to its nucleus. As I said, this was first discovered accidentally. Then, thousands of years ago, one of my ancestors built a stone box similar to the marble container you saw today. For hundreds of generations my family kept this secret, producing gold as needed. My mother was the first to use a source other than lightning. It took her quite a while to perfect the process—if the charge is too strong or too weak it will shear away too many or too few protons. The result will then be that the bismuth turns into mercury or lead or platinum or one of the other heavy metals. Obviously, gold is the desired byproduct, or perhaps platinum. It took me years of experimentation, and more than a few minor conflagrations, but eventually I succeeded in reproducing my mother's work."

That explained the need for the thick-walled bank vault and fire extinguishers. "Prior to your mother, your ancestors just left the box outside, hoping for a lightning strike?"

He nodded. "Lightning seems to be drawn to the spiral. And of course they would place the bismuth on a high point, away from trees. Eventually they learned about lightning rods, and this further increased their success rate. But, yes, for the most part they waited for nature to do its work."

"And this spiral, what is it about it that..." She waved her arms. "...that makes it work."

He shrugged. "Other than the metal being alien to this planet, I do not know. I could consult a physicist, but that would mean breaking my vow of secrecy. That I cannot do."

"But you are doing precisely that now."

"Yes." He smiled. "Perhaps you have not noticed, but I am an old man. This secret must not die with me."

She leaned forward. "You keep talking about hundreds of generations and thousands of years, Abraham. How could that be?"

He refilled her glass, his gray eyes locked on hers, and lowered his voice. "Have you heard, Leah, of the lost continent of Atlantis?"

"You may go," the dark-skinned man said without preamble as he untied the ropes that bound Trey to the dining room chair. In some ways she was disappointed—she had been listening to the two old Jews talk in the kitchen. She couldn't hear everything, but it seemed like the gold-colored rock in the basement had been exactly that, gold. And Abraham had somehow *produced* it down there using some spiral necklace made from an alien metal. Or perhaps she had heard wrong.

Her captor's warm breath tickled her neck as he untied her. He had patted her down—professionally, without copping a feel—and disarmed her, giving her a chance to study him at an almost intimate distance. Broad-shouldered, square-jawed and unsmiling, he looked like he belonged in the boxing ring. Clearly a pro—she had been naïve to think the house would not have extensive security. But his eyes, those eyes, they looked so sad...

"But first, Mr. Gottlieb has a message for Commander de Real." He spoke English fluently, articulating each consonant as new speakers of the language often did. "He says that he does not blame him for trying to spy on us. He would probably do the same. But he does wish his future partners were more skilled at it."

His lips hinted at a smile as he said this, as if to soften the insult which was so clearly directed at her.

This type of verbal repartee played to her strength. "Please tell Mr. Gottlieb that I will try to do better next time." She reached slowly into her back pocket. "And also please return his wallet to him. I lifted it from him after his speech."

The guard's eyes widened. "Truly? You took Mr. Gottlieb's wallet?"

She smiled. "No, no I didn't." She took her wallet back. "But please tell Mr. Gottlieb that Commander de Real does wish his future partners were not so gullible."

The black man glared at her, his nostrils flaring. Then, suddenly, he grinned. "Touché." He held out his hand. "My name is Solomon."

"I'm Trey." She flashed her best smile, holding his fingers in hers. "And I haven't had any dinner. Any chance you want to grab a bite?"

It wasn't until late Saturday night—perhaps in fact early Sunday morning—that Abraham had time to listen to the recording of what the Templars discussed in the conference room after he and Madame Radminikov departed. Solomon had handed him a disk before leaving for the night. "You may want to listen to this."

Listening while seated alone at his kitchen table, Abraham immediately recognized the voice of the man with the cross tattoo. This man, it seemed, was going to be a recurring problem. Abraham had suspected the Templars would eventually set their sites on Jerusalem, as they had a thousand years ago—one could hardly be a Templar, sworn to make Jerusalem safe for Christian pilgrimage, without yearning to control the Holy Land. It was a long-term problem at a time when the Jewish people did not have the luxury of thinking that far ahead. But it was distressing to hear his new allies already discussing plans to betray him. He shrugged. That was what contingency plans were for.

But this question of the Khazars was a more immediate problem, one that seemed to flare up periodically like a nasty virus. Or, more accurately, like a recurrence of cancer. If it could be proven that the modern-day Jews did not descend from Abraham and instead were merely late converts to the religion, as some research seemed to indicate, then Israel's claim to the Holy Land would be severely undermined. This was the type of research Abraham had paid millions over the years to suppress. And would need to continue to keep suppressed.

He sat back in the kitchen chair and exhaled. He was tired, perhaps ready to die even. But his people needed him. There were so many threats, so many enemies, so many scenarios in which the Jews could come under attack again. Many threats, like this Khazars revelation, were not even known by most people. He only knew of it because, as he had explained to Madame Radminikov, his mother's family traced its origins back to the original Atlantis colony of pre-history. What he had not told her was that his mother's family had lived for millennia in what was today known as southern Russia, in the Caucasus region near the border with Georgia. His mother's family had immigrated to Germany in the mid-1800s, but as a child Abraham and his sister had spent their summers along the western shore of the Black Sea with their cousins. With the descendants of the Khazars.

After the war, his immediate family all dead, Abraham had returned to his mother's homeland in an attempt to reconnect with her family. They, too, had perished. Decades later, still alone in the world but with means at his disposal, Abraham had returned yet again to learn what he could about his family. Finding the old family graveyard, he had conducted widespread DNA testing.

What he had learned he had kept secret. A secret he would take to his grave. But that was not to say others could not someday uncover it themselves. In fact a sect of Middle-Easterners living in Lebanon called the Druze had done so already.

Chapter 3

The chirping of his cell phone at eight o'clock on a Sunday morning surprised Cam. The night had passed uneventfully and he had just pounded out a half-hour on the Stairmaster in the basement and was about to shower. When he saw the name of the Maine state geologist, Potvin, on the caller ID, he jabbed at the answer button. "This is Cam."

Potvin didn't waste any time on preambles. "Can you come out to Salisbury?"

"Sure, when?"

"Like, now."

Cam rubbed the sweat from his forehead with the back of his sleeve. Hopefully nothing had happened to the site. "Is everything okay?"

"No. I don't know. Maybe not. But I need to talk to you."

Cam had hoped to spend the day with Amanda before she flew off on her adventure, but if he shot out to Salisbury now they'd still have the afternoon and evening together. "I'll be there in an hour."

Rushing through his shower and eating a breakfast bar and apple in the car, Cam arrived at the dig site just over an hour later. As he walked along the path he kept his eyes peeled, remembering the man with the cross tattooed on his neck. But he saw nothing until Potvin approached to greet him.

Actually, greet would be the wrong word. "You need to tell me right now if this is some kind of scam." The wiry archeologist looked like he hadn't slept—thinning hair disheveled, boots untied, eyes narrow and bloodshot. He wore a red and blue ski parka despite the spring temperatures; Cam guessed he had spent the night in it. The archeologist had always been a bit fidgety, but Cam had never seen him like this.

Cam took a step back. "What are you talking about?"

"This site. Those bones. Did you plant them?"

"Of course not. Why would I plant them?"

He gestured in the general direction of the Atlantic. "Because you want to prove explorers were here before Columbus."

There were many ways Cam could respond. Obviously the fact that Potvin was making the accusation indicated that he believed the skull was European, which pleased Cam. Cam took a deep breath, tried to stay rational. He didn't appreciate being accused of fraud, but he understood Potvin's world had been turned upside down and he was thrashing about, reaching for something to hold onto. "Look, my research focuses on the Templars and Prince Henry Sinclair. We're talking medieval times. This find is way earlier than that, by thousands of years. If I were going to plant something I'd plant something that proved my case." He shrugged. "I have no horse in this race."

Potvin eyed him, spittle on his bottom lip. "But something like this would help you get your foot in the door, show that ancient peoples really did cross the Atlantic."

"Look, give me more credit than that. If I were going to plant something, even something this old, I'd make it so someone else discovered it. I mean, how stupid would I have to be to plant something and then discover it myself?"

Potvin shifted, doubt in his eyes.

"And more to the point, I'm not qualified to do something this elaborate. Sure, I could find an old skull and bury it under a shell midden. But you're going to be meticulous in this dig, and you're going to be looking for any disturbances in the dirt or anything else that would call the find into question. I'm not an archeologist. No way could I fool you."

This, finally, seemed to resonate. "No, I suppose not." He rubbed his eyes with his knuckles before turning back to Cam. "But you could be working with someone, another archeologist."

Cam shook his head. "The next time I work with an archeologist will be my first. In case you hadn't noticed, people in your profession generally don't want anything to do with me."

Potvin turned back toward the dig and bowed his head as if in prayer. After ten seconds he straightened himself and took a deep breath. "Okay, okay." He did his best to force a smile. "I guess I should be thankful. This is the find of a lifetime. But all I can think about is that it's not possible."

"Why? Just because it's old?"

Potvin shook his head. "Not just old. Really old. Maybe ten thousand years old."

Cam nodded. That was even older than he had suspected.

"But that's not why I'm having issues with this." He turned. "Follow me, I'll show you."

As they approached the dig site Cam could see that Potvin and his team had made significant progress—the entire skeleton was now exposed, though it remained *in situ,* or unmoved, and in its original fetal position. Cam raised his camera to snap a shot. Potvin grabbed his arm. "You can't do that."

"Why not?"

"We made a deal with the Discovery Channel. They're funding the dig, but in return they get to control the information. Nobody's going to hear anything about this until it runs on Discovery. And that means no pictures except the ones I take."

Cam tried to modulate his voice. "For the record, I found this site. And I didn't sign anything with anybody." He stepped forward, blocking Potvin with his body and snapped a shot of the burial. "Sue me if you want."

Red Paint Skeleton, c. 8,000 BCE, Salisbury, MA

"Shit." Potvin rubbed his forehead and sighed. "All right. But please don't show anyone."

Cam nodded. "Fair enough." Together they stared at the body. "So?" Cam said.

Potvin sighed again. "I've been working nonstop," he said as he scratched at a bug bite on his neck. "I slept a couple of hours in the tent, but I haven't left. So my brain is totally fried. But nothing about this looks Algonquin to me."

"He looks tall," Cam observed.

"Yeah. Based on his femur, I'm guessing six-foot-five."

"Is that common for someone so old?"

"No. Native Americans of this era were about a foot shorter." Potvin brushed his hands through his hair. "Based on his height, and his skull shape, I think he was European." He practically choked over the words.

Cam smiled. "So that's why Discovery is paying for the dig."

Potvin didn't respond directly. "But that's not all." He led Cam back to the tent he had set up as a living area and dig headquarters. "Look at this." He opened a black metal chest resting on the ground just inside the tent entry and removed a plastic bag containing what looked like a barbed harpoon point. After putting on a pair of cloth gloves and instructing Cam to do the same, he extricated the weapon and handed it to Cam. "Normally I would have left these *in situ* with the bones, but I can't risk them disappearing—they're too valuable. Obviously the numbering is not done with a permanent marker." Cam set the point down gently and snapped a photo with his phone. Potvin acted like he didn't notice.

Salisbury, MA Red Paint Harpoon Point

Cam handled the barb carefully, awed by the thought that it might have been used ten thousand years ago. "Is it bone?"

"Yes."

"Very impressive. Obviously you showed it to me for a reason."

"Yes. Native Americans didn't start using barbed points until many thousands of years later. This is way too advanced for its time period. Also, this would have been used for deep sea fishing. Hunting swordfish, even whales. Native Americans didn't do that."

Cam handed the object back. "But we knew this already." He had had this exact conversation with Amanda. "That's one of the mysteries of the Red Paint People."

"No. Some people *suspected* the Red Paint People were some kind of advanced culture." He lifted the harpoon tip. "But we've never found anything this sophisticated associated with a burial this old. Like I said, based on the soil sediments, I think this burial goes back ten thousand years." He pursed his lips. "Maybe older. We'll know for certain when the DNA testing comes back. I've already sent a molar out for testing."

Potvin reached into the metal chest and removed another object, this one an arrow head. Again he handed it to Cam and again Cam snapped a photo, this time placing the object on a white background to increase visibility.

Salisbury, MA Red Paint Arrow Head (Serrated)

"Notice the serrated edges," Potvin said. "Again, these modifications don't appear until many thousands of years later. And also the symmetry and workmanship along the curved edges." He exhaled, alternately elated and defeated by the stone object in front of him. "The workmanship on this is far more advanced than it should be."

Cam couldn't resist the jab. "So does that mean it's an outlier?" Still holding the arrow head, Cam juggled it gently in the palm of his hand. "Should I just get rid of it for you?"

Potvin lunged, grabbing Cam's elbow. "Don't you dare!"

Cam smiled. Either Potvin didn't get the joke, or he didn't think it was funny.

Pak Chol-su walked to his car parked a block away at a tire repair center in the shadows of the bombed-out remains of a Beirut office building. Most of the city had been rebuilt after the 2006 war with Israel, but not all. The building in question had housed the headquarters of the terrorist group Hezbollah, which may explain why it had never been rebuilt. The fact that the neighborhood, which continued to house many Hezbollah members, would likely be the target of future Israeli bombing raids enabled Pak to afford a two-room flat and have enough money left over to keep gas in his twelve-year-old Nissan. He did not have a wife and children at home to support, though he did send money regularly back to his parents. Assuming he succeeded in his mission, he planned to return to Pyongyang and start a family. His stomach clenched. There were so many things that could go wrong with this plan, and the blame would likely fall on him. His pet hamster was probably as close as he would get to being a father.

A refreshing wind blew in off the Mediterranean, keeping Pak comfortable in his dark wool suit. The Nissan started on the second try and he drove into the hills south of Beirut, where the temperatures stayed cool even in the midday sun. The bright day and refreshing mountain air lifted his spirits; maybe he'd get lucky and the Chinese would veto the mission. When Supreme Leader had summoned Pak to his private island to explain the plan, a visit which had left Pak both awestruck and terrified, he had mentioned in passing that the Chinese were less than enthusiastic about the idea. "They think any plan based on legend is certain to fail." Pak knew that Supreme Leader, in his patient wisdom, usually did not oppose the wishes of his superpower neighbor. But, being infallible, Supreme Leader's judgment alone would determine North Korea's course of action, as it should. Pak repeated the thought aloud for emphasis. "As it should."

Traffic was light and a half hour later he pulled into a village set at the base of a steep slope. A dozen large, yellow brick structures with orange terracotta roofs encircled the town center, while smaller edifices of similar design climbed the slope of the hill. He parked, the village center strangely quiet. A distant loudspeaker pulled him down a curving, narrow street. Still alone, he ambled along without fear. Once known as the Paris of the Middle East, Beirut—even within insular villages like this—had long been a haven for foreigners. Children once in a while pointed at him, and adults were often surprised at his fluency in Arabic, but otherwise he was largely ignored. The people of Lebanon—Christian, Muslim, Druze—had known many enemies over the centuries. Koreans were not one of them.

Pak turned the corner, the sound from the loudspeaker now audible. A eulogy.

Ahead, hundreds of people had gathered in another village square, the black-garbed men wearing white fezzes with red tops and the women in black robes with white hijabs covering their face and hair. Many others stood on rooftops and balconies and hung out of windows surrounding the plaza. He pushed forward, politely but firmly, the afternoon sun creating long shadows. At the center of the square, on what looked to be a white marble table, rested a glass coffin. He did not need to see the body, nor hear the eulogy. Officially, it was enough that he was here—later he would find a guest book to sign. Unofficially, he strained to hear the words he had first heard many months ago at another funeral. Words that had set this crazy plan in motion.

Even as he listened intently, his eyes swept the crowd. Though technically Muslims themselves, the Druze had little in common with their Islamic cousins. They worshipped Jethro, Moses' father-in-law, more so than they did Mohammed; Jethro's tomb in northern Israel was their most revered shrine. Ethnically, other than their supposed descent from Jethro, their origins were a mystery—the people now known as the Druze seemed always to have occupied the mountains of southern Lebanon. Most strangely, they believed the messiah would be born, spontaneously, from a Druze man. Because of this the men all wore baggy pants to catch the newborn messiah before he tumbled to the ground. Even now, after almost a year in Lebanon, Pak couldn't help but glance down to see if the Druze men he met indeed wore trousers with low-hanging crotches.

The eulogizer paused, and a voice in the crowd called out. *"Niyyāl ahl al-Ṣīn sa'at waṣltak."* Pak cocked his head. A second voice echoed the first, the Arabic words clear and crisp. *"Happy will be the people of China at your arrival!"* A third voice joined the chorus, and soon the entire crowd chanted the words, their eyes on the coffin. Pak watched, fascinated. Unlike other Muslims, the Druze believed in reincarnation. Druze teachings held that the best of them—the smartest and most righteous—would be reborn in China, of all places. That's what they were shouting for—that the deceased would be transported to China for his next life. The Druze believed that in China these reincarnates would join a secretive group of other righteous Druze, led by their founder, Al-Hakim. A thousand years after his death, Al-Hakim was to lead an army of Druze across Asia to conquer the Middle East and install the Druze as the region's rulers. As to why Al-Hakim and other righteous Druze were believed to be hiding in China, unseen for the past thousand years, Pak had no idea. But Al-Hakim's death occurred in the year 1021, meaning its thousand-year-anniversary was fast approaching.

"Niyyāl ahl al-Ṣīn sa'at waṣltak," the crowd repeated, as if hoping the Druze of China could actually hear their call. *"Happy will be the people of China at your arrival!"*

As the wave of song swept over him, it occurred to Pak that Supreme Leader's crazy plan just might work.

Trey awoke to the sounds of birds chirping outside her apartment window. For the first time in years she felt like singing with them.

She checked the time—just before nine. Which meant late afternoon in the Middle East. She had been home for almost a year, but her internal clock still tracked time as if she were with her platoon. According to other veterans, it was a habit she would never break.

She had time for a shower and some breakfast before meeting Solomon at the Esplanade park along the Charles River. She had promised to teach him how to play Frisbee, something he had never learned as a child. She had made the promise just before they held hands for the first time on their late-night walk through the Back Bay. She had been careful to position herself so that if their hands happened to brush against each other he would find five fingers rather than three, only to have him dance around her a few minutes later and take her damaged hand. "None of us is whole," he had said simply in that deep voice of his.

She brought her hand to her nose, the scent of his body wash still lingering. "I do think you have a crush on the man," she said aloud in her best Southern accent as she swung her legs out of bed. The excitement of their date had almost made her forget about the episode with the gold. She would ask Solomon about it. But whatever ended up happening, it was nice to be back in the game. To feel giddy again. To wonder what it would be like to kiss someone, to share their bed.

She smiled at that last thought. Solomon had a gentleness about him that ran at cross-currents to his animal-like physicality. He was somehow both the summer breeze and the winter storm, the flower petal and the grizzly bear. She made the decision to clean her apartment and change her sheets. Who knew where a game of Frisbee might lead?

Astarte returned from Sunday school, finished her lunch and spent a half-hour helping Amanda pack. While she did so she asked about her upcoming trip and Great-aunt Meryn. She really was curious, but in her heart she knew she was only asking because she needed to tell Mr. Saint Paul about it. It wasn't really lying, but it made her stomach feel funny the same way a lie did.

"While you're away, is it okay if I go to the movies with my friends one day?" Another sort-of lie.

"Sure. As long as it's okay with Cameron." She smiled. "With your dad."

They were still figuring out the name thing. When Astarte had first moved in she called Amanda 'Mum' and Cam 'Dad-Cam'—not exactly Mom and Dad but partway to it. This past winter she had started calling them Mom and Dad. But it wasn't official yet. Maybe now it never would be. Astarte bit back the thought, staring out the window so Amanda wouldn't see her face. "It's a nice day. Maybe I'll take Venus for a walk."

"Good idea. Bring your phone. Dad will be back in a couple hours. We'll spend some time together as a family."

A family. How nice it sounded. She clenched her teeth. If she wanted it, she'd have to fight for it.

Ten minutes into her walk she flopped onto a bench at the community beach, looped Venus' leash around her ankle and pulled out her phone. It wasn't cold, but she shivered anyway. She dialed the number she had memorized.

"You have reached the number for the Showcase Cinemas in Lowell. Press '1' for a list of movie times..."

She pressed the number 2. After several rings a woman's voice answered. "May I help you?"

"I'd like to speak to Mr. Saint Paul."

"I'll connect you."

While waiting Astarte talked to Venus. "I'm going to tell him everything. About the necklace, about Mom's trip, about the Crones, about the burglars, about the Red Paint People skull, everything." Wrapping her arms around Venus' neck, she swallowed a sob, her words barely audible in the spring breeze. "Because if I don't tell him something, and he finds out about it later, he's going to take me away from you."

Pak remained on the periphery, respectful and somber. The singing had died down and much of the crowd had wandered off. He had no place else to be, and protocol demanded he not leave before paying his respects to the community's leaders. But that was not why he stuck around.

With a sigh and a smile, a heavy-set man with a bushy gray beard and moustache wearing a white turban disengaged from a second turbaned man Pak recognized as an Iranian diplomat. The heavy-set man approached. "Welcome, Mr. Pak," Wiyam Uddin said in Arabic, bowing.

Pak bowed his head. "I am here to pay respects on behalf of our Supreme Leader. The Democratic People's Republic of Korea mourns for your loss."

Uddin nodded his thanks. As one of the uqqal, or learned ones, he wore a black robe rather than the baggy pants worn by most Druze men. Apparently Uddin was the half-brother of a famous international lawyer who had recently married some Hollywood actor. He took Pak by the arm and walked him away from the small remaining crowd. "I would normally not discuss business at such a somber affair," he said. "But I feel it is appropriate, as our business directly involves matters that are spiritual in nature. Have you made any progress?"

Pak exhaled. He was glad Uddin broached the subject first. "Yes, I have. There is, indeed, an insular sect in the northern part of Korea who practice a religion very similar to yours," he lied. "They believe in reincarnation, they have seven guiding principals that are nearly identical to what I understand to be the seven pillars of your faith, and they hold their religious services on Thursday evenings, as I believe the Druze do."

Uddin raised an eyebrow. "Thursday, you say?"

"Yes." Pak expected this would intrigue the Druze leader. Few religions celebrated Thursday as the Sabbath.

"But you say this group lives in North Korea. Our belief is very specific on the point that Al-Hakim resides in China." He smiled and spread his arms. "We have a saying: 'The pen is in thy hands, write and fear not.' So, please explain this discrepancy."

They were at the crux of the matter. Pak nodded. "I shall try." He was not trained for this, not trained to lie and deceive. Uddin eyed him like a poker player who somehow knew what cards his opponent held. But Pak had no choice but to plow ahead. He swallowed. "As is the case here in the Middle East, the borders of Asia have changed many times over the centuries. For almost a hundred years, not long after Al-Hakim lived, much of what is now North Korea was part of the Yuan Dynasty of China." The dates were not exactly in line, but Pak had no choice but to stretch things a bit here. The pen was in his hands, and he was writing, but he did not do so without fear— hopefully Uddin did not notice how much the pen in his hand shook. "Your religious teachings are, of course, accurate—Al-Hakim was indeed reincarnated in China. But the political borders have now changed." He lifted his chin and forced his eyes to meet Uddin's. "It is our belief that Al-Hakim and his followers reside today not in China, but in North Korea."

Magnuson's cell phone rang as he spread grass seed on his lawn. When he saw it was Admiral Warner, he answered immediately. He wouldn't even have a lawn were it not for the old man. "Yes, sir," he said.

"Sorry to bother you on a Sunday, but I need you."

"I'll be right in." He wouldn't have asked if it weren't important.

Magnuson threw on some clean clothes, said goodbye to Jocelyn and his wife and rushed across town. As he drove, he reflected on Friday night's lecture. Magnuson was not quite sure what to think about Cameron Thorne. On the one hand his research glorified the Knights Templar. But on the other it distorted and denigrated them, portraying the warriors as a group of pansy liberals more concerned with getting in touch with their feminine sides than in fighting the Crusades and winning back Jerusalem from the Muslims. He touched his tattoo. It made Magnuson angry just thinking about it. For now he would simply gather information, per his orders. But when it came time to act, God would give the word.

Ten minutes later he sat across from his boss, dressed as always in a blue blazer with anchor-shaped brass buttons, pressed khakis and a yellow bow tie. He possessed the leathery skin of a man who had spent decades in the sun, but also the pasty fleshiness of a man who followed that up with decades sitting behind a desk. Normally Admiral Warner's blue eyes danced playfully as he spoke, but today there was a sadness in them that Magnuson had never seen. "Is everything okay, sir?"

Warner exhaled. As far as Magnuson knew, he had never been married. Other than to the company, that was. "I have had to make a difficult decision, Magnuson. A very difficult decision. As you know, one of my passions is the lost colony of Atlantis…"

He explained the details of an archeological discovery in Salisbury. "Normally I'd be thrilled. It looks like the site may help to prove the existence of a group of technologically advanced people living not long after the disappearance of Atlantis. These people had sophisticated tools and weapons and seafaring technology far in advance of what they should have possessed based on the historical orthodoxy. Essentially they are a missing link, tying man from ten thousand years ago back to the Atlanteans of twelve thousand years ago." He shook his head. "I have waited for such a find for decades."

"So what's the problem?" Magnuson asked tentatively.

He exhaled. "The problem is that I need to put Warner Industries in front of my personal feelings. And for the company, this type of find could be crippling."

"Crippling? I don't understand." Magnuson, though he reported directly to Admiral Warner and spent a decent amount of time with him, knew little about the specific business operations of the company. He knew *what* the company did—oil and gas exploration, mining, pipelines, wind farms—but the how and where and when it was all done was not something Magnuson was privy to.

Admiral Warner's shoulders slumped in a way that reminded Magnuson of a spoiled boy being told he must give up a favorite toy. "Have you ever heard of the United Nations Convention on the Protection of the Underwater Cultural Heritage?" Before Magnuson could answer his boss continued. "Of course you have not. Nobody has." He explained that it was an international treaty governing archeological sites under the world's oceans. The treaty was not approved by the United States or Great Britain and so was not binding within those countries' territorial waters. But the treaty had been approved by the U.N. as a whole and was therefore governing law in international waters. "The idea was to protect shipwrecks. But as usual, the bureaucrats overreached. Essentially the treaty makes it impossible to explore or drill or build a wind farm or lay a pipeline in areas where there is evidence of human activity more than a hundred years old. Not a big deal in most people's minds—we're talking the middle of the Atlantic Ocean. But I know better. I know what's out there. I know that almost half of the Mid-Atlantic Ridge was once above land and was home to a rich and advanced culture."

Magnuson wasn't sure how to respond. "Are you certain?"

"Oh yes. We have decades of drill boring results that make me more than certain. Beach sand. Fresh-water fossils. Pollen samples. Even a chunk of bronze, which obviously shows advanced metallurgy." He brightened. "The entire collection is kept in a vault at my estate. It is both my joy and my curse." A sigh followed. "I have proven the existence of Atlantis, yet this very proof could doom the company I have spent a lifetime building. Under the terms of the United Nations treaty, half the Atlantic would be closed to us. No more mining, no more pipelines, no more wind farms."

"So what are you going to do?" What he really meant was, what did he want Magnuson to do.

Admiral Warner shrugged before raising his jowly chin. "I have no choice. We have no choice." He removed a thick manila envelope from his desk drawer. "Here is $20,000. If you need more, let me know." He handed Magnuson a map of the archeological dig site in Salisbury. "Do what you have to do. We need this site to disappear. Including any pictures. And we need it done right away."

Solomon had willingly accepted Trey's invitation to return to her apartment in Brighton. They sat together on the couch, her legs over his, their lips and tongues tasting and exploring each other like a couple of teenagers in the back seat of a car. He smelled and tasted of their day together—dried sweat from Frisbee, pond water from when she had splashed him after their Swan Boat ride, chicken with cashew nuts, coffee ice cream. It all mixed together with his natural scent like an aphrodisiac. She drank, wanting more.

Turning her body to free her good hand, she reached down to caress his thigh. A sharp intake of breath told her he appreciated the gesture, but he did nothing to reciprocate. "Slowly," he breathed, between kisses.

Taking him literally, she moved her hand up his leg and slowly rubbed his crotch, rubbing and kneading like her grandmother used to when baking bread. *Not now, Grammy,* she thought. To clear her head she rubbed her breast against his shoulder, feeling her nipple harden. *Sweet Jesus, he tastes good.*

Praying that he would not think her a slut while at the same time not giving a damn, she lifted her arms and pulled her blouse over her head. He moaned but did not assist in any way. No doubt he was aroused. But it also was becoming apparent that he was letting her set the pace.

"Is everything okay?" she murmured.

He responded by framing her face between his palms and kissing her gently on the lips. "Heavenly," he breathed. "You are very beautiful. And my heart beats like a *kebero* drum. But it is not … my way … to be the aggressor." There was a sadness in his eyes as he said this, and Trey realized it likely related back to the story he had told, reluctantly, of watching his mother and sister being raped. It was not surprising that a man who witnessed such atrocities as a young boy would be careful not to force himself on a woman.

Emboldened by her newfound understanding of her lover, and in fact turned on by the poignancy of it, she pulled his shirt off, slithered her way out of her jeans and pushed him gently into a prone position on the couch. Her eyes locked on his, she unclipped his khakis and pushed them to his thighs. Resting atop him, their mouths together, she removed their undergarments. Time passed in a fog, his rock-hard body soft and supple beneath her.

Most men would have stormed the castle. Not Solomon. He stood at the gate, erect and ready, waiting patiently in the cold for her to reach for him and usher him inside to the warmth of her hearth.

Feeling every bit the princess, that was exactly what she did.

It didn't take Magnuson long to get his team together. He was paid to be ready to act on short notice.

He would have liked to have had more time to get a better sense of the layout of the site, how much security there was, whether the police were patrolling. But, again, he was paid to act on short notice.

For a job like this he didn't need a lot of help. And he knew he could trust Rejean and Yves, two French-Canadian brothers he grew up playing hockey with. They owned a towing company in New Hampshire, not a business for the weak or timid. He met them at ten o'clock at an all-night Mobil station off of Route 93 and handed them each $5,000 in cash as they climbed into his SUV. He explained their mission. "So we want this to look like Native Americans objecting to the dig, raising hell. No weapons, unless you really need them. And nobody gets hurt."

An hour later Magnuson edged the SUV off the road behind a dilapidated barn and parked. The three men dressed in black carried night vision goggles around their necks, heavy flashlights in their hands and hunting knives sheathed at their waists. Each shouldered a backpack with other supplies. They angled through the woods, Magnuson glad he had made a reconnaissance run earlier in the day as he followed his compass toward the mouth of the river. After a few fits and starts he spotted a tent in a clearing with police tape setting a rectangular boundary around it. "There it is," he hissed.

They crouched and studied the situation through their goggles. "I think I see a light on in the tent," Yves said, the smell of stale cigarette smoke wafting off him in the night breeze. Wiry with snake-like reflexes, Yves liked nothing better than to flirt with women in seedy bars and then beat up their jealous husbands.

Magnuson nodded. He had seen it also. And also movement inside the tent. A complication he had planned for but hoped to avoid. He took a deep breath. "Okay, follow me. Put your masks on, and try not to talk. And remember, nothing stupid."

Figuring the best approach was to lure out whoever was in the tent, Magnuson edged toward the site and approached the tent—a standard three-person camping model—from its rear. Unsheathing his knife, he sliced one of the guy lines. The tent sagged. He scurried to his right and sliced another. This time the entire rear of the tent collapsed.

"What the—?" came the response. A thin, middle-aged man in sweatpants and a winter jacket stumbled out the entrance. Probably the archeologist. Magnuson coiled, his senses honed, the flashlight in his right hand, waiting for his prey. Wheezing, the man turned the corner of the tent, his glasses askew. From the shadows Magnuson swung, delivering a measured blow to the back of the head. Grunting, the archeologist collapsed.

Magnuson bent to check his pulse, then nodded to his cohorts. As planned, the burly, black-bearded Rejean pulled out a can of red spray paint. He scrawled, *Respect Our Dead!* on the ground next to the tent and vandalized some of the equipment while Yves stood guard over the archeologist. Magnuson found the dig site and quickly collected the skeleton bones and stashed them in his pack—Admiral Warner had been clear that he wanted the bones and any funerary items for his own collection. Using a shovel resting against a nearby tree, Magnuson tore into the soil. A few minutes later the broad-shouldered Rejean joined him and together they quickly dug a grave-size pit, tossing soil into the surrounding shrubbery and stuffing other objects from the original burial into their pockets. After fifteen minutes, breathing heavily, Magnuson motioned to stop. The site had become neutered, archeologically worthless.

"You finish up here," he said to Rejean. "Dig down another foot just to make sure. But remember, don't do anything to desecrate the grave."

Returning to the tent, he searched the unconscious archeologist and found a cell phone in his jacket pocket. Scrolling, he found a series of dig photos and pocketed the phone. Inside the tent he found a camera and pocketed that as well. An oversized tool box on the floor by the entryway caught his eye—he unlatched it to find a stack of sealed plastic bags filled with dig artifacts. He lifted the box and handed it to Yves. Admiral Warner would no doubt enjoy having the artifacts in his collection.

He looked around. Was it possible there was another camera? Returning to the tent, he found a pad of paper and pen, plus a bottle of water. He scrawled on the pad, 'Are there pictures of the dig other than on your phone? Every wrong answer will cost you a finger.'

Still masked, Magnuson slid back through the door, unsheathed his hunting knife for a second time and splashed water in the archeologist's face. He moaned and blinked himself back to consciousness. Magnuson stuck the note in front of his eyes.

The archeologist took a deep breath, Magnuson's knife shining even in the dim light. Magnuson would know if he was lying since he had found the camera already. Swallowing, the man whispered, "I have a camera in the tent."

Magnuson nodded. With the pen, he wrote, "Any other pictures?"

The archeologist felt for the back of his head and sighed. "The guy who found the site was here today. He took some pictures. His name is Cameron Thorne."

Magnuson cursed, glad the mask muffled his reaction from his captive. He still didn't know what the hell Thorne was doing here. This had nothing to do with the Templars.

He took a deep breath and refocused. Whatever Thorne's interest in the site, the fact that he had pictures was a loose end. Admiral Warner would not be happy. Magnuson wrote a final note. "Leave our dead alone. Or you'll be joining them." Once he was sure the archeologist had read it, he pocketed the paper and motioned to Yves to watch their prisoner.

He returned to the dig area to inspect Rejean's work. "Good. Let's get out of here."

Before he left, Magnuson dropped a pouch of tobacco into the freshly-dug hole, an offering to the gods as payment for disturbing the dead. He had thought of it himself, a final clue that would leave little doubt that the vandals were Native American.

Chapter 4

The loudspeaker announced a departing flight. Meryn flowed toward Amanda, wearing a cascading blue-green sun dress that, again, conveyed the sense of water moving. She seemed to leave a sun-speckled mist in her wake. Amanda half-expected to hear seagulls cawing. Instead the flight announcement echoed a second time.

Meryn enveloped her in a hug, keeping Amanda's hand as they disengaged. Her spiral necklace, now amber-tinged, pulsed like a purring cat. "Do you want help with your bag?"

"No, I can pull it." It was twice the size it needed to be, but without knowing where they were going it was almost impossible to pack.

"Before I forget, do you have your passport?"

Amanda handed it over and Meryn scanned the first few pages with her phone. "It will make it easier when we land," she explained.

Meryn guided her through the small terminal at Hanscom Field, the suburban Boston airport that catered to private jets. "Flying privately is one of my few luxuries. I travel a great deal, and at some point in my life I just said, 'Enough.' So I bought a time share in a Gulfstream."

On the one hand it seemed like an extravagance. On the other, if even half of what Meryn said were true, Amanda could see the need to be able to jet around the world at will. "So where to first?"

"New Jersey."

Amanda stopped midstride. She expected to be visiting some of the ancient civilization sites such as Machu Picchu in Peru, or Yonaguni in Japan, or Gobekli Tepe in Turkey, or even the Sphinx and Pyramids in Egypt. "Why New Jersey?" she blurted.

Meryn smiled and took her arm. "Because that's where the baby eels are."

An hour later they landed in Atlantic City, where a car met them on the tarmac. A five minute drive southeast on Highway 30 brought them to a U-Haul center tucked between the road and a rail line. The driver parked on the edge of the lot and handed Meryn a fine-meshed fishing net. Meryn led Amanda down a shallow embankment to a brackish stream. "About a half mile east of here, this Abeson Creek empties into the Atlantic," she said. She removed her shoes, hiked up her dress and, moving around a rusted shopping cart, waded to her knees. She placed the net deep in the water, its mouth facing the Atlantic, and waited.

After thirty seconds she lifted the net from the water and dumped a translucent, snake-like animal into a Ziploc bag filled with water. She waded back and held the bag up to Amanda, who watched the three-inch long colorless creature slither around the bottom of the bag.

"This is a young eel, called a glass eel," Meryn explained. "Eventually it will change color to brown or black and grow to a couple of feet long. It will live most of its life upstream in a lake or pond."

Amanda asked the obvious. "So why are we looking at it?"

"Years from now, when the eel is an adult, it will swim back down to the ocean. If we were to come back here in October, we would find thousands of adult eels swimming past us in the other direction." She dumped the baby eel back into the stream. "The adult eels swim out to the continental shelf, then turn south. After a six-month swim they join millions of other fresh-water eels to spawn in a shallow area in the middle of the Atlantic called the Sargasso Sea."

"Isn't that odd, that a fresh-water creature would spawn in salt water?"

Meryn stood on a rock and kicked her feet dry. "Yes, quite odd. In fact, the mystery has baffled scientists for hundreds of years." She smiled. "But, as the expression goes, that is not the half of it." She paused dramatically. "As I said, eels from all over North America meet to spawn in the middle of the Atlantic. What is truly amazing is that millions of European freshwater eels do the same thing: They, too, swim down the rivers of Europe and cross the Atlantic to spawn with their American cousins."

Amanda mulled this over. How could two distinct groups, separated by a vast ocean, share the same instinctive spawning behavior? "The eels must, at some point, have had a common origin."

Meryn nodded. "I think that is undisputable. In fact, scientists have a word for it—nostophilia, meaning the instinct to return to a remote place of origin. And I think a strong argument can be made that that origin was near the Sargasso Sea."

Amanda understood immediately. "A landmass in the middle of the Atlantic. Atlantis. That's why they return there to spawn."

Meryn merely nodded. "Come." She took Amanda's hand as she stepped into her flats. "As I said, you will learn more from seeing than from me simply telling. And we have much more to see."

After securing the spiral necklace in their safe deposit box at a local bank, Cam spent the rest of Monday morning in his office getting ready for a real estate closing and fine-tuning tomorrow's lesson plan. But his mind raced with possibilities regarding the artifacts found at the Red Paint People burial site. Finally at lunch he had some time to focus on the Salisbury find.

Eating a sandwich at his desk, he surfed the internet, researching the legends of the lost continent of Atlantis and wondering— assuming the legends were true—if the Red Paint People were somehow related. Since the earliest reports of Atlantis began with Plato, he started there. Plato described Atlantis as a landmass located at "a distant point in the Atlantic Ocean" opposite the Pillars of Hercules (the ancient description of the Strait of Gibraltar). Cam pulled up a map—the Azores Islands fit the description perfectly, located roughly 900 miles west of Portugal in the middle of the Atlantic. Many other researchers had identified the Azores as the site of Atlantis, so Cam focused his research there.

Plato described Atlantis as an island having a large flat "plains" area in the south, surrounded by a ring of mountains on three sides. Cam found a bathymetric map of the Azores and the surrounding Atlantic ridge. From this map, someone had created a hypothetical version of Atlantis:

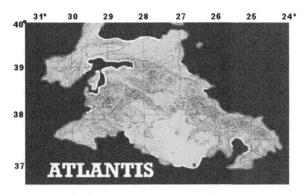

Hypothetical Atlantis

Cam studied the maps. The match wasn't perfect, but the bathymetric map did indeed show a landmass that was consistent with Plato's description, the "mountains" which rimmed the plains area on three sides being the Azores Islands of today. Using rough calculations, the hypothetical Atlantis landmass measured 500 by 600 miles. Plato did not describe the area of the entire continent, only stating that the plains area measured 2,000 by 3,000 stadia, or 230 by 340 miles, roughly the size of Kansas. Cam measured the plains area on the hypothetical map—not exact, but pretty close.

And the dates seemed to work also. Presumably Plato—living around 350 BCE—had no knowledge of the most recent Ice Age, or at least its exact date. But Plato stated that Atlantis disappeared into the sea 9,300 years before he lived. This was the exact date range, 11,600 years before present, which most scientists used to mark the end of the last Ice Age. As Amanda would say, "Spot on." Whatever cataclysmic event that caused the ice cap to melt apparently also sent Atlantis to its watery grave.

But did the entire Atlantis landmass sink in a single instant? Cam had long studied the Zeno map, a 1380 Venetian rendition of the North Atlantic that many historians believed help prove the Prince Henry Sinclair journey to North America in 1398. Other historians discredited the map, claiming the existence of a "phantom island" on the map—Frisland—proved the document was a 16th century hoax. Cam found a copy of the map and located Frisland south of Iceland (spelled 'Islanda') and Greenland ('Engronelant') along the Mid-Atlantic Ridge.

Zeno Map, 1380 (Frisland in Lower Left)

Cam knew that medieval European maps were often based on ancient maps and sailing charts discovered in the Middle East by the Knights Templar and their associates—during their nearly two centuries in the Holy Land the Templars were closely allied with Christians in and around Lebanon, many of whom descended from the seafaring Phoenician and Carthaginian cultures. In fact, Cam found a half-dozen other European maps from the 16th and 17th centuries, including one by the famous mapmaker Mercator, all showing the "phantom island" of Frisland.

Mercator Map of the North Pole, 1606 (magnified)
(Frisland toward Lower Left)

So apparently there was some historical basis for Frisland's existence—expert mapmakers like Mercator did not rise to the top of their fields by basing their work on mere legend. It seemed more likely to Cam that Frisland once existed, a vestige of some prehistoric land mass rising up along the Mid-Atlantic Ridge. Whether Frisland was Atlantis itself or merely Atlantis' neighbor, the conclusion was the same: Ancient lands now underwater apparently once crested above the waters of the mid-Atlantic.

Cam kept researching, returning his focus to the Azores, south of Frisland but along the same Mid-Atlantic Ridge. On the internet he found a U.S. Geological Survey of deep core soundings in the Mid-Atlantic Ridge showing that the ridge rose above sea level 10,000 to 20,000 years ago. Other scientists discovered fossils of fresh-water species along the ridge, indicating a fresh-water lake. Still other studies, including one from Woods Hole Oceanographic Institute, identified beach sand in drill samples along the ridge—beach sand could only be created above the surface, again establishing that areas along the ridge once protruded above the surface.

The reference to Woods Hole Oceanographic Institute reminded Cam of the carbon-dating the Institute had done on the Newport Tower mortar sample. In his mind the evidence was overwhelming in support of the Tower having a pre-Columbus origin. Would the mounting evidence in support of the existence of the lost colony of Atlantis build to something equally persuasive?

He turned back to the bathymetric map. The map showed that the land mass surrounding the Azores islands—the land that would have comprised the plains of Atlantis—currently sat at an underwater depth of approximately one mile. This was a problem, since sea levels had risen by far less than one mile since the last Ice Age. Was there another way to explain how and why the land had dropped so far? Cam found his answer in a phenomenon geologists referred to as isostatic rebound. The best way to think about it was to picture various interconnected land masses as seated on either end of a hemispheric seesaw. During the last Ice Age, North America was held down by the weight of the massive ice cap. When the cap melted, the unburdened North American landmass sprung up. But the seesaw effect meant that a connected land mass would correspondingly need to drop. In this case, that land mass was the Mid-Atlantic Ridge. This was not the sudden cataclysmic event that had already caused the destruction of Atlantis; rather, this was a slower, more gradual phenomenon that explained how and why the Mid-Atlantic Ridge came eventually to rest a mile or so beneath the ocean surface in modern times.

So did this match what Amanda was learning from Meryn? Meryn recounted how the entire landmass of Atlantis had been wiped out by a world-changing calamity. How could this be reconciled with the fact that a portion of the Azores landmass—its islands—remained even today above sea level? It was likely, Cam deduced, that the calamity which triggered the destruction of Atlantis also triggered massive tidal waves and/or tsunamis, effectively flooding the entire Azores landmass. The Great Flood, as it was known in ancient cultures. The waters eventually did recede, exposing the Azores islands. But there was nobody alive to witness it.

Cam sighed and checked his watch. He had killed an hour. He typed up a quick summary of his research and emailed it to Amanda—hopefully she would find it useful, wherever in the world she was.

Now it was time to get back to his real estate closing. His clients were buying an oceanfront vacation home. Hopefully for them Cape Cod was on the high side of the seesaw.

Solomon had left Trey's apartment before dawn, as he had warned her he must do in order to get to his job as a history teacher at an inner-city Boston high school. He had kissed her gently on the ear and, when she awoke, she found an intricately folded origami flower bathing in a sunbeam on the pillow next to her head— fashioned, apparently, from the red paper placemat he had pocketed as they left the Chinese restaurant. "Aw," she sighed. How had an Ethiopian Jew learned origami? She hoped there would be many more secrets to discover.

She lounged in bed for a half-hour, breathing in his scent on the sheets and pillows. One of the great things about her life as a Homeland Security agent was that, on many days, there was nothing she had to do. So she spent a lot of time at the gym, took advantage of Boston's many museums and even bought herself a used guitar which she taught herself to play with her eight fingers. But today would not be one for leisure. She needed to figure some things out.

No better way to think than on a long run along the river. She downed some cranberry juice, threw on sweats and cut down a side street toward the Charles River running path. As she found her rhythm and her breathing settled in, she focused on her situation. The military had ordered her to infiltrate the Knights Templar. The Templars, in turn, had assigned her to perform surveillance on Abraham Gottlieb and his Kidon group. While performing these duties she had not only seduced, but become infatuated with, one of Abraham's underlings. What could go wrong?

The answer to the 'what could go wrong' question proved too depressing, so instead Trey focused on how she could turn all this to her advantage. The last thing a female soldier wanted to do was gain a reputation as being easy—it brought the boys sniffing around like sharks to chum. So ideally she would keep this affair quiet. But she still hadn't figured out what Gottlieb and the old woman were doing in his basement with goggles and heavy gloves. Was it really possible they were making gold? It must have been important, else why would Solomon have been patrolling the grounds.

At the thought of him her cheeks flushed and her body tingled. It might be just the kind of thing she could learn during pillow talk. And even if not, it would be fun just trying.

Four hours after taking off from Atlantic City the Gulfstream jet landed in Georgetown, Guyana on the northern coast of South America just east of Venezuela. Again Amanda had expected something more exotic; she counted six fast food restaurants bordering the airport as they landed. But at least it wasn't New Jersey. The sun was still high in the sky as a customs agent waved them past and Meryn rushed them into a waiting SUV. "Are the butterflies flying?" Meryn asked the dreadlocked driver.

He responded in English, his accent reminding Amanda of Jamaica. "I believe so. They were this morning."

"Butterflies?" Amanda asked.

Meryn merely smiled.

They crossed the Demerara river on the west side of the city and angled north through a commercial district. Exiting the highway, they followed a single-lane dirt road north through the woods. Five minutes later they broke clear of the trees and parked on a ridge overlooking the ocean in the distance. "It is best to walk from here," the driver said. "The automobiles can confuse them."

The sun shone, and the temperatures were in the eighties with a refreshing sea breeze, so Amanda donned a straw hat and happily followed Meryn along a path toward the ocean. As they made a turn and emerged through some underbrush, Amanda froze and gasped. A wall of yellow—solid yet undulating—rose in front of them. As her eyes focused, she realized she was looking at thousands, perhaps tens of thousands, of butterflies. As one, they flew north, toward the open sea.

"Where are they going?" she asked, transfixed by the sight.

"To die," Meryn answered sadly.

"To die? I don't understand."

"Every year they do this. They fly due north, for hundreds and even thousands of miles, until they eventually drop into the sea from exhaustion."

"Do all butterflies do this?"

"No. Just these. This is a common species, the catopsilia. But the only ones who fly into the sea are the ones who live here along the northern coast of South America."

Amanda guessed where this was going. *Nostophilia.* "Could there be another explanation?"

Meryn shrugged. "When monarch butterflies migrate, they fly south from Canada to Mexico. Over Lake Superior they take a wide detour around what geologists say was once a high mountain. That goes back tens of thousands of years." She smiled. "Apparently monarch butterflies have long memories. As do these."

Amanda stared at the airborne mass of yellow. "Did anyone ever follow them?" She thought about Cam's email, making a compelling case for a massive land mass in the mid-Atlantic.

Meryn took Amanda's hand and turned her back to the path. "Yes. Many of them drop into the Sargasso Sea, where I imagine they make a tasty meal for our eel friends." She sighed. "Others continue even further northeast, toward the Mid-Atlantic Ridge." She eyed her grandniece, a teardrop balanced on her bottom eyelash. "But there is nothing for them there but death."

Pak Chol-su worked late into the night on Monday. His assignment was too important, and too secret, to work on in front of co-workers. He sighed. Working alone, in secret, was exactly the type of thing that could make his boss suspicious. For the thousandth time he wished he had been home sick the day the authorities did language testing at his elementary school.

For this whole convoluted plan to work, he needed to convince the uqqal religious leaders like Uddin that a group of reincarnated Druze, led by their founder al-Hakim, not only resided in North Korea but stood ready to march across Asia to join their cousins in Lebanon. Pak's head hurt when he imagined the logistics of staging a ruse like this. But Supreme Leader had apparently already rebuilt a village in the mountains using Lebanese architecture and had populated it with loyal, baggy-panted men and their families. Supreme Leader's mother had been enlisted to assist in the scheme and had agreed to relocate there, the implication of course being that the Korean ruler himself may have blood ties to the reincarnated Druze. Pak did not doubt that the villagers stood ready to march across Asia to Lebanon if so ordered. Such was the benefit of a totalitarian society—even the outlandish became possible. But what then?

Tonight Pak's research focused on the connections between the Druze and the medieval fighting force of the Catholic Church, the Knights Templar. Uddin claimed that the Druze and the Templars had, after an initial period of belligerence, grown to become close allies during the Crusades. He even hinted that Freemasonry, which many believed had its roots in the Templar order, was in fact modeled after Druze spiritual beliefs. The Supreme Leader had not shared all the details of his plan with Pak, but Pak did know that the Templars and Freemasons played a part in it. It would behoove Pak to learn as much as he could about the secret societies.

One thing in particular caught Pak's eye: According to some historians, the reason for the Templars' meteoric rise to power was their discovery of the so-called Philosopher's Stone. Pak spent a solid hour trying to translate and understand what exactly this Philosopher's Stone was: He eventually came to realize that it had nothing to do with philosophy, and in fact was not even a stone. It was, instead, an encoded way of referring to the scientific process by which base metals could be converted into gold. The discovery of this invaluable secret explained, so the argument went, how a small, obscure monastic order grew to become the most powerful force in all of Europe in just a few short decades. Pak sat back and thought about this. *The ability to change metal into gold.* Could anything, other perhaps than the Fountain of Youth, be more monumental? More to the point, was it possible that Supreme Leader had concocted a plan that might actually work? Until now Pak had been skeptical. But if the Templars really did have this power, and if they were as close to the Druze as Uddin claimed…

Pak spoke the words aloud. "The Supreme Leader is wise in all things." This time, he actually believed it might be true.

The Gulfstream took off from Guyana and headed northwest, Amanda wondering if their flight path would intersect that of the doomed butterflies. Meryn unpacked fruit salad, yogurt, cheese and a loaf of multi-grain bread for a late lunch. They sat across a small table from each other in beige leather bucket seats, Meryn with her back to the plane's cockpit. Music played softly in the background; Meryn hummed along to "Age of Aquarius" from the Broadway show, *Hair*. Amanda knew that many feminists believed that the new astrological era of Aquarius would mark the end of the patriarchy that had long ruled the earth. Perhaps that's what this was all really about.

"So, where to now?" Amanda asked, her mood still somber at the memory of the fatal flight of the butterflies.

Meryn sensed her gloom and reached across to pat her hand. "Tikal. It is a Mayan site in Guatemala."

"More animals?"

Meryn smiled. "No. Though I could show you migratory birds that fly from Europe out to the Mid-Atlantic Ridge in early winter, circling what they believe is a landmass until they, too, collapse into the ocean like the butterflies." She sighed. "But I think you get the point." She brightened. "We are going to see some Mayan ruins."

"Do the Mayans go back that far, back 12,000 years?"

"No. But they descend from people who do. And the memories of that time are recorded in their art and decorations. As I told you, some of the Atlantis survivors came to America."

"Speaking of which." Amanda pulled up the image of the Frost Valley Petroglyph on her phone and showed it to Meryn.

Frost Valley Petroglyph

"This carving is on a boulder sitting in a river in the Hudson Valley, north of New York City. To me it looks just like our spirals."

Meryn's eyes widened. "I've never seen this before. How old is it?"

Amanda was pleased to be able to contribute something new to the family's treasure trove of information. "The Native Americans say it has always been there."

Meryn grinned, her eyes shining. She squeezed Amanda's hand. "This is an amazing find. Another piece of evidence tying the Atlantis survivors to the Americas. Will you take me there?"

"Of course."

They sat in contented silence for a few seconds. "So, what are we going to see at these Mayan ruins?" Amanda asked.

Meryn smiled again and shook her head. "Like I said before, I'd rather show you than tell you. I don't want to spoil the surprise. But

I will remind you that the story of a cataclysmic flood as told in the Bible is prevalent worldwide, in almost every ancient culture. Including those in Central America."

Two hours later they landed in the lakeside city of Flores, 150 miles north of Guatemala City. From their descent, Amanda viewed red-roofed Colonial buildings and cobblestone streets clustered on an island in the middle of a sky-blue lake connected to the shore by a thin causeway. It looked like a great place to kill a long weekend with Cam and Astarte.

A Land Rover met them at the edge of the tarmac, Meryn again having arranged to bypass customs. Like the butterflies, the vehicle headed due north, driven by a twenty-something woman with a round face, an easy smile and a semi-automatic rifle over her shoulder. "Hello again, Señora Eneko," she said, eyeing her passengers in the rearview mirror.

"Hola, Consuela. It is nice to see you again." She turned to Amanda. "We are in good hands. This is a safe area, but once in a while bandits target the tourists. They know better than to bother Consuela."

Meryn pulled an image up on her phone. The same broom-riding witch with the pointed hat she had emailed to Amanda a couple of days ago. Or a lifetime ago, depending on what kind of scale one measured by. "Remember Tlazolteotl?"

The Aztec Goddess, Tlazolteotl

Amanda nodded. "On her broom, wearing a black hat."

"The reason for the broom, by the way, is that many of the ancient potions were hallucinogenic and give the sensation of flying.

Crones, after experimenting with these drugs, often insisted they had actually taken flight on their broom or staff or scepter." She smiled. "But I digress. Tlazolteotl was carved in some Aztec ruins not far from here, across the border into Mexico. The Mayans have similar depictions. As I asked in my email, how could it be that independent cultures across the Atlantic have virtually identical portrayals of their witch, or crone, figures? Could both cultures have independently settled on the broom to depict hallucinogenic flight?"

Amanda was ready for the question. "The answer, of course, is that they were not independent of one another."

Meryn beamed and squeezed her hand. "What a joy to find you so late in life, my dear." She looked out the window for a few seconds, apparently collecting her thoughts. "When the Spaniards arrived, they believed the Mayans were subhuman—I believe the exact term used was 'imps of the devil.' So they destroyed all their written history. But eventually they came to see the richness of the native culture and made some efforts to preserve what they could of the Mayan heritage. There were many accounts recorded, but they all agree on one thing: The Mayans claim they came to this land from across the eastern sea."

Amanda nodded. "I read a book recently written by a Smithsonian archeologist, Dennis Stanford. He believes the Americas were first settled by people from Europe, before the Asians crossed the Bering Sea. Apparently the oldest human activity is found in South America, not North America, which obviously means the first people did not come down through Alaska. He thinks they came here first, to the Gulf of Mexico area."

"I have read his work. It is good to see a mainstream archeologist with an open mind. I imagine his peers have made things difficult for him." She smiled. "He promotes something called the 'tiny boats' theory—because the ocean levels were lower during the Ice Age, ancient man could have crossed the oceans in small, animal-skin boats. His theory works even better with a large landmass in the middle of the Atlantic as a stopover point. Or perhaps even a starting point. I have often wondered if he secretly believes in the Atlantis legends."

For the hundredth time Amanda wished Cam were here to be part of this conversation, to share in this exploration. On a hunch, she asked, "Is there any evidence here of bodies painted with red paint?"

Meryn smiled knowingly. "Your instincts are sharp. At Chiapa de Corzo, a Mayan site just across the border into Mexico, two bodies were found painted from head to toe in red ochre. These people were rulers, buried in a pyramid."

"Were red paint burials an Atlantean custom?"

"I think you know the answer to that already," Meryn said pointedly. After a pause she continued, "There is a site not far from the Pyrenees, in northern Spain, called El Miròn Cave. A skeleton was found there, a woman covered in red ochre. This Lady in Red, as she has been named, was a priestess who lived during the end of the last Ice Age."

"The Age of Atlantis."

"Yes. This red paint burial custom can be found all along the Atlantic rim, most prominently in eastern Canada and the British Isles." Meryn shrugged. "Clearly this cannot be coincidence. How could so many ancient cultures, separated by thousands of miles, come up with the same burial practice on their own?"

They couldn't, obviously. Amanda returned to the main point. "So you think the Mayans descended from Atlanteans."

Meryn shrugged. "It does not matter what I think. When we arrive at our destination I will show you something and let you decide for yourself."

An hour into their drive they turned off the main highway at a sign marked, 'Tikal.' Five minutes later a pair of gray-stoned pyramids rose out of the jungle to greet them. One tall and lithe, the other shorter and squat, the pyramids faced off against each other separated by a green expanse, like two ancient gladiators ready to joust. "One is called Temple of the Jaguar, the other Temple of the Mask," Meryn explained. Amanda studied the amazing ruins, again wishing Cam and Astarte were here to witness the richness and grandeur of the Mayan culture with her. Meryn took her gently by the arm. "But this is not what I brought you here to see, and it is getting late."

Amanda allowed Meryn to lead her down a narrow path away from the central plaza area and into the jungle. The sounds of birds singing and monkeys screaming filled the thick, dank air pushing down on them from the canopy of green above. Meryn pulled a couple of bottles of water from her satchel and handed one to Amanda.

Three sips of water later Meryn stopped suddenly and pointed to a gray slab of wall barely visible behind a curtain of vines and undergrowth. As Amanda examined the wall closer she realized it was part of a larger pyramid structure, perhaps thirty feet in height. With sadness she realized that someday the jungle would swallow the site entirely. Meryn pointed up. "The lintel atop the pyramid was removed back in the early 1900s and shipped to a museum in Germany. It was lost during World War II. All we have left are photographs." She pulled a black and white glossy from her satchel. "This frieze was carved into the lintel."

Tikal Pyramid Carving, Guatemala

Amanda studied the carving, sensing immediately its importance. Her eyes first went to the bottom right quadrant, depicting a somber-faced man wearing Mayan garb rowing a boat. In the water next to the boat another man looked to be drowning. The upper left quadrant showed a volcano erupting, smoke and fire billowing out and buildings crumbling nearby as the volcano sank into the water. Between the volcano and the boat, a large 'C'-shaped wave bore down on the fleeing rower. There wasn't much doubt about the carving's meaning. "Wow," was all she could muster.

"Yes. I wanted you to see this in context, here in Tikal. As I've told you before, many cultures retain memories of the great flood. But this is more specific—this cataclysm, this flood, is clearly caused by an erupting volcano. Some fled, others died, but the land itself collapsed into the sea."

Meryn elected to fly out immediately from Guatemala rather than get a hotel room for the night. They could sleep in the air as they crossed the Atlantic. It would save time, plus it would allow her to maintain the pace of their whirlwind tour. Meryn needed Amanda to *feel* the connection to the family history. It was not enough simply to learn it and understand it on an intellectual level. That was the reason for the theatrics in the supermarket parking lot—the gun wasn't really necessary, but Meryn understood that touching someone on an emotional level, even negatively so, was far more impactful than a simple cerebral appeal. If Amanda was going to wear the necklace, she must connect with the Atlanteans on a spiritual level, must allow them to seep into her soul and their memories to become hers.

While her young apprentice slept in a cot in the rear of the cabin, Meryn made preparations for the next day's excursions and caught up on her emails. A couple of hours into their flight a wave of melancholy washed over her. They were flying over the Mid-Atlantic Ridge—she didn't need any map or chart to confirm what she knew to be true at a primordial level. The tug of her homeland pulled at her as it did at the eels and butterflies and migratory birds. A moan from Amanda interrupted Meryn's musings. She stood and peered toward the back of the plane. The young woman thrashed about under her blanket, calling out in her sleep, her fingers clawing at the air and her face damp with sweat. A nightmare. Atlantis called to her also.

Meryn smiled sadly but made no move to go offer comfort.

Chapter 5

Cam awoke in the middle of the night, jarring Venus out of a sound sleep beside him. "Of course," he said aloud. How had he missed this?

While he had slept his mind made the obvious connections. The Templars had found the maps in the Middle East which showed the ancient land mass of Atlantis. So, of course, they must have *known* about Atlantis themselves. This was an obvious, but crucial, revelation, one that shed light on Amanda's research regarding the Merovingians and the possible connection between the Jesus bloodline and the ancient Atlanteans. Why, he often had wondered, had the Templars agreed to serve as the protectors of the Merovingian descendants during medieval times? How had the Merovingians convinced the Templars that they were, indeed, the continuation of the Jesus bloodline? The answer Cam now understood was found in the Merovingian knowledge of and connection to ancient Atlantis. The secrets of Atlantis would have been passed down through the generations, knowledge of these secrets serving the same role as a secret handshake or codeword to prove membership to an exclusive and secretive group. Only the Merovingian families knew the true origins of the Jesus bloodline. And they knew this secret because it was theirs, and theirs alone, to hold and protect.

The Templars were therefore not merely the protectors of the Jesus bloodline. They were by extension the protectors of the Atlantis legacy as well.

Amanda awoke bathed in sweat, her mouth dry, the hum of the airplane reverberating not just in her ears but in her bones. She swallowed, trying to unplug her ears as she extricated her legs from the blanket twisted around them. She opened her eyes to see Meryn smiling down at her with a cup of tea in hand.

"Drink this, dear," she said. "The air can get very dry in these planes."

Amanda sat up and accepted the cup and saucer. She fought to clear her head of the dark dreams that had haunted her sleep. "Thanks," she murmured.

"We land in an hour." Meryn clapped lightly. "Once you feel up to it, I have a question for you."

Amanda took a second sip. "I'm fine, what is it?"

"What do you know of Lilith?"

She blinked and tried to focus. "Wasn't she Adam's first wife, before Eve?"

"Yes, exactly. As the story goes, she refused to be subservient to Adam, so he asked God for a replacement. Apparently she had the nerve to insist on being on top sometimes." Meryn smiled. "She was the first woman to demand sexual equality. Imagine the temerity."

Amanda had little patience for Bible stories, especially now, after her tortured sleep. "The Bible is a monument to misogyny," she declared. She worked to keep the anger from her voice. "Lot, Abraham's nephew, offered up his daughters to be gang-raped and then later impregnated them himself. A pig. But it was his wife who was punished—turned into a pillar of salt—because she had the nerve to look back at her burning home as she fled. And these are the men we glorify?"

Meryn laughed gaily. "Well, you may be interested to learn that Lilith was your ancestor, one of our family Crones."

"Wait, what?"

"She was one of the outpost survivors."

"But the characters in the Bible are not *real*." At least Amanda did not believe them to be so. "The Bible is legend, a compilation of oral history and myth and even gossip."

Meryn nodded. "I agree. But most legends sprout from a seed of truth. And the Lilith of the Bible is based on a real Lilith who lived twelve thousand years ago." Meryn sat in the seat facing Amanda. "Listen carefully. This is an ancient Sumerian legend." Amanda knew that the Sumerians were, according to the mainstream version of world history, the first human civilization, living in what is now Iraq approximately 3,500 BCE:

"Before the stars were born,
Before people built great cities,
The great mountain Atlen shook
And bled fiery blood
As it gave birth to Lilitu.
The land all around burned,
Many animals and people died."

Meryn voiced the words staring out in the distance, as if in a trance. When she finished her chin dropped and her eyes closed. A few seconds passed before she blinked rapidly and shook her head clear. "Did you notice any familiar names?"

"I assume Atlen is the Sumerian name for Atlantis?" Again, the A-T-L root.

"Yes."

"And of course Lilitu is the name for Lilith."

"Yes. Nabokov took the name for his *Lolita* character from Lilitu. The temptress."

Amanda nodded. She had never made that connection. She sipped her tea, finally awake. "The legend says Atlen shook and bled and burned and gave birth to Lilitu. I'm guessing the shaking and bleeding and burning and dying refers to the volcanic destruction of Atlantis. So the description of the birth is allegorical—Lilitu appeared out of the ruins. But Lilitu was real."

"Precisely. After Atlantis was destroyed, the outpost survivors realized there were not enough of them to rebuild a society. They knew they needed to take spouses from the local populations." Meryn smiled. "Apparently Lilith was a bit more aggressive sexually—and probably in other ways as well—than was the custom of the times. So much so that she became immortalized in the Old Testament as the world's first seductress."

The story interested Amanda, but even more interesting was the fact that the Sumerians, the earliest of all known cultures excepting Atlantis, possessed a legend recalling the Atlantis destruction. "Did other ancient cultures remember Atlantis?"

Meryn nodded. "The Egyptians. And there are also Sanskrit writings from ancient India that talk about a large island called 'Atala' off the western shore of Africa that had many cities and an advanced civilization. It burned and sank to the bottom of the Atlantic."

Amanda stared out the window at the orange glow of morning dawning over Europe. She assumed Meryn wasn't just making up these Sumerian legends and Sanskrit writings. And she had seen with her own eyes the eels and butterflies and Mayan carvings. So why did so many historians doubt Atlantis? Some went so far as to say Plato—perhaps the most rigorous thinker in world history—was simply repeating old wives' tales when he recounted the history of Atlantis. Never mind that he happened to be spot on with his dates, the collapse coinciding exactly with whatever natural disaster ended the last Ice Age.

She and Cam had run across this often in their research. Truths were hidden in plain sight, waiting for people with eyes that see to come along and reveal them. She had the sudden urge to phone him, the roaming charges be damned. She was still tormented by her nightmares, and she ached to share with him what she had learned. To her dismay, her phone did not have service on the plane.

Cam taught his nine o'clock class at Brandeis, then returned to his office in Westford late morning. Just before lunch his secretary announced he had an unscheduled visitor, a Mr. Smith looking for help on a real estate closing. Normally clients phoned first, but Cam shrugged and ambled down the hall to the reception area. He froze midstride as his eyes settled on the black and red cross-shaped tattoo on the man's neck.

Smith, obviously not his real name, stood and smiled, his hard blue eyes holding Cam's. He did not offer a hand. "I need ten minutes of your time." He wore a business suit, but Cam sensed this was a different kind of business.

Cam nodded and led him to his office, shutting the door behind them. Smith leaned jauntily against a bookcase, his muscular frame apparent even beneath the suit. Cam remained standing, circling to put his desk between them. Cam could take care of himself, but there was an animal ferocity about his visitor that Cam could not ignore. "I get the sense this is not about real estate."

"In a way it is, actually. Real estate in Salisbury, down by the river."

Cam had not expected this. "You're going to need to be more specific."

Smith nodded. "Okay. So here's the deal. I'm going to ask you one question. It's a simple one. But if you lie to me, I'll know it, I'll sense it, I'll *smell* it." He leered. "Everyone is good at something, and this is my thing. I'm guessing you're pretty good at it also, so you know I'm not bullshitting you."

Cam didn't doubt the man. Whether it was instincts or street smarts or just a hyper-ability to read body language, Smith oozed aptitude. "What's your question?" Cam asked.

Smith held up one finger. "Wait, let me finish. I have two guys across town now, waiting for young Astarte to get off the school bus." He paused. "Yes, I know it's a half-day and she gets home at 11:30." His eyes fired into Cam's. "Like I said, I'll know if you're lying."

Cam steadied himself against the desk as a wave of cold fear pumped through his core. Involuntarily, he checked his watch. Astarte would be getting off the bus in five minutes, going to a neighborhood friend's house for a few hours as she usually did on early release days. No way would the friend's mother be able to fight off two trained men. And no way could Cam make it across town. But who was this asshole threatening him? He clenched his fists. "I swear, if anything—"

Smith held up his hand. "Easy, counselor. Don't turn all Rambo on me. Like I said, if you just answer my question everything will be fine."

Cam clenched his teeth. "What then?"

"I know you took pictures at the dig in Salisbury. I need them. So, my question is, are they all on your phone or did you transfer them to your computer?"

Again, this was not what Cam expected. Obviously the guy came for the pictures. And it seemed the easiest way to get rid of him would be to hand over his cell. No way did he want this cretin to follow him home to his home computer. Cam pulled his phone from his breast pocket and tossed it across the desk. "Images are on there. I haven't downloaded them yet. Take it and get the fuck out of my life."

Smith scrolled through, found a dozen images of the dig site and deleted them, making sure also to empty the trash. "You say you didn't download them, right?"

"Right."

He tilted his head, half-smiling as he studied Cam. Cam forced himself to breathe, his eyes steady. "Not bad," Smith said after a few seconds delay. "I wouldn't want to play poker with you. But I still think you're lying." Smith shrugged, stepped toward the desk and tossed the phone back to Cam. As Cam leaned forward to catch it, Smith swung his right fist, nailing Cam square in the jaw. Cam collapsed onto his keyboard and slid to the floor, the room spinning around him.

From far away Cam heard Smith's voice, presumably speaking into his own phone. "Take the girl," he said.

Dazed, Cam tried to push himself to his feet, raising himself just enough to see Smith stride from the room. He punched out 9-1-1 on his cell, working his jaw to be ready to speak. But in his gut he feared it was too late.

By the time they landed in Santander on the northern coast of Spain a storm had moved in with full fury. Meryn's plan had been to drive to the cave site this morning to view the ancient artwork. But the road had become impassable. Even an advanced civilization was slave to the weather.

She and Amanda were holed up at the elegant downtown Gran Hotel with the requisite room looking over the Atlantic, waiting for the storm to pass. Swirling rain assaulted the thick-glassed windows, the frothing ocean barely visible in the gloom. This was as good an opportunity as any to have 'the talk' with Amanda. She had the sense it would not go well. But it was crucial to Meryn's plan.

"How close are you and Cameron?" she asked, walking into the living area of their suite with a couple of cups of tea. Amanda, unkempt after a restless night on the plane but still radiant, sat in a leather desk chair checking emails on her phone, one foot propped on the frame of the desk.

Amanda tilted her head. "I suppose just about as close as possible." She shrugged. "But I imagine almost all newlyweds feel that way."

"Could you envision life without him?"

The foot came down. "Should I?"

Meryn tried her best smile. "I didn't say should, I said could."

Amanda sighed. "Sorry, I'm not going to play games with you. I'm here. I dropped everything to join you on this excursion, despite that you've been less than forthcoming with me. But I'll not answer hypothetical questions like that."

Meryn looked out the window, the Pyrenees barely distinguishable in the distance through the curtain of rain. Those mountains had been her family's home for almost 500 generations, 30 times longer than the Pilgrim families could trace their ancestry in America. Yet Amanda's comment was a valid one. She took a deep breath. "I received an email this morning. Your oracle's death was not random. Her husband killed her."

Amanda rocked in the desk chair. "I'm sorry to hear that," she said noncommittally.

Meryn believed Crones should not marry. A Crone needed to be strong, independent. Most men fought against that, and even those who didn't became a distraction. Lovers were fine, but spouses complicated an already difficult job. And men were the worst kind of spouses—violent, temperamental, slow to forgive. Many, including herself, believed Atlantis fell as punishment from gods angry that it had turned its back on its noble values and had become in its final century a warlike, male-dominated society. At a minimum, Atlantis' focus on war had made its leaders blind to the clear signs from Mother Earth that change was coming; instead of preparing for the pending calamity resources were diverted toward war-making and conquest. Much as was happening today. "Many think Crones should not marry," she said aloud, explaining the reasoning. "Men are too temperamental, too volatile."

Amanda's eyes darkened. "Well, it's too late. I'm already hitched."

Meryn nodded. She decided not to push it yet. "Of course, dear. I just thought you should know."

Cam raced home, his heart pounding in his ears like a buffalo stampede. He dialed Astarte's cell but no answer. He imagined her bound, blindfolded, in a trunk. And scared. So scared. An innocent little girl skipping off the school bus, thoughts of jump rope and hopscotch and slobbery kisses from her dog. Horn blaring, he accelerated through a stop sign.

He had called 911 and the police had sent a car immediately to his house. From there they would begin the search, interviewing the neighbor's mother and whatever other parents may have been around. He checked his watch. Twelve minutes since Smith had left his office, six minutes since Astarte usually got off the bus. But in six minutes they could be on the highway already, speeding north into New Hampshire or south toward Boston.

He careened onto his lakeside street, tires screeching. Blue lights flashed ahead, the cruiser parked in front of his house a stark reminder that this was not just some horrific daydream. Hopefully they had something to go on, had already sent out a statewide missing child alert. He swallowed, the ache in his chest almost paralyzing in its intensity. His brain told him Smith had no reason to hurt the girl, but he knew better than to assume animals like Smith could be counted on to behave rationally.

Tears filled his eyes as he swung into the driveway. His girl was missing. Petrified, alone and in danger.

And it was his fault.

Leah Radminikov wiped down the countertop of her Brookline butcher shop, content to be alone with her thoughts on a quiet Tuesday afternoon. As had so often been the case over the past couple of days, those thoughts returned to Abraham transforming that lump of rock into gold. She guessed it weighed five pounds; even if impure, it had a value of over $50,000. And it had only taken him five minutes. No wonder he spent money so mindlessly.

With a thousand questions to ask, she had insisted he come in for a late lunch today. She would make him his favorite—corned beef and Swiss cheese on rye—and he would eat it slowly, a full sixty seconds between bites, savoring every mouthful like a man who had once known starvation. So unlike her husband, who used to wolf his food down with barely a chew. No wonder he died early.

She checked her watch, removed her apron and straightened her blouse with her hand. Abraham would, she knew, be punctual. But whether he would answer her questions was beyond her ability to foresee.

He ambled in a few minutes later in his gray suit and stood in front of the counter, his angular features further elongated in the reflection of the curved glass. As was his custom, he did not offer any kind of greeting. "You said you have questions, Madame?"

"Would you like a sandwich while we talk?"

His head tilted as he considered the question. "I don't believe I have eaten today, but even so, I am fine."

"Nothing?"

"Perhaps a glass of water."

She knew better than to have this argument again. "Go sit down." She waved him away. "Go. You have to eat."

Sandwich made, she joined him at a small round linoleum table in the corner next to a gum ball machine. "I want to know more about this gold. How much of it do you make?"

"As much as is needed," he said between chews of his first bite.

"That's not very specific."

He shrugged. "There are times when business is not good, or when the needs of Kidon are especially demanding, or when some other extraordinary circumstance arises. So, as I said, I make the gold as needed. The problem is more of how to convert it into cash—one cannot simply walk into a jeweler in Boston and sell him a chunk of gold. I solved that problem decades ago by purchasing a gold mine in Nevada." He waved away the details with a bony hand.

He had begun to transition control of Kidon to her. But obviously there were certain things he still kept secret. "You say extraordinary circumstances. Such as?"

He took a second bite. "The Druze, for example."

"The Druze?"

"They are a people of the Middle East—"

"I know who they are. But what do they have to do with this gold?"

He set his sandwich down and sipped from a glass of ginger ale. "Many years ago, in the early 1970s, I forged a strategic alliance with the Druze community in Israel and Lebanon. In exchange for my assistance, they serve as our eyes and ears in areas where Jews are not welcome."

"They spy for us?"

He shrugged. "Spy. Inform. Provide information. As you know, we are a small people, an isolated people. We need friends."

"So we give them gold?"

"I did not say that. I said I provide assistance." He took another bite of his sandwich, chewing slowly, his gray eyes on his food.

With Abraham, she knew she needed to be very literal. "Abraham, if you want Kidon to survive after you ... are gone ... then you need to give me more details. What do you mean by assistance?"

He swallowed. "The Druze, as it turns out, possess a spiral necklace identical to mine. Apparently they, too, descend from Atlantis and they, too, have passed down this spiral." He said it matter-of-factly, as if everyone knew someone who descended from an ancient advanced civilization. "I learned of this while visiting Israel, after years of doing business with the Druze and gaining their trust." Again he waved away the details as unimportant. "But they had lost the knowledge of how to utilize the spiral, or even what it was. All they knew was that it had been passed down for twelve thousand years and that, according to their legends, somehow it could be used to produce gold."

"So you showed them how."

He allowed himself a rare smile. "You know the famous proverb: *Give a man a fish and he eats for a day; teach a man how to fish and he eats for a lifetime.* Well, in business it is sometimes better not to teach a man to fish. So no, I did not. At least not initially. But as the years passed, and they proved their value as allies in the region, I eventually did—as the expression goes—begin to teach them how to fish. I have allowed them to witness what you witnessed Saturday evening."

"And you're certain they can be trusted with this secret?" There was something he wasn't telling her, something that was bothering him about his relationship with the Druze. She could tell by the way the muscles in his jaw tightened when he discussed them.

"Madame, the Druze are perhaps the most secretive, insular group in the world. Much like us Jews, they have always been strangers in a strange land. They are savvy and shrewd. They have needed to be to survive."

It occurred to her that he specifically had *not* answered that he could trust them. And it also occurred to her that gold was valuable because it was rare. If people other than Abraham could produce it in their basements, how rare in fact was it? But she assumed he had considered this before sharing his secret with the Druze. He was nothing if not thorough.

He chewed the last of his sandwich and stood. Almost as an afterthought he said, "I may have been mistaken, it turns out, in sharing this technology with the Druze. I thank you for the sandwich."

Without giving her time to question him further he walked out the door. But she grinned at his back. Her intuition had been correct about not trusting the Druze.

Amanda took advantage of the storm to pound out four miles on the hotel treadmill and do some crunches. After a long, hot shower she stepped into the common room of their hotel suite in a pair of jeans and blouse to see Meryn waiting for her. As usual, her great-aunt wore a flowing blue-green dress.

"Come," Meryn said, taking Amanda's hand.

"Where to?"

"To talk to some of the Basque natives."

"I won't be doing much speaking. I hardly speak Spanish, much less Basque."

"And I found some who do not speak English." Meryn smiled. "So perhaps we will listen more than we talk."

Somehow Meryn had arranged for three hotel chambermaids to meet with them in a small conference room. The women, all uniformed and all middle-aged, fidgeted in their chairs on one side of the conference room table. Meryn smiled at them and marched in. "No, no, this will not do." Speaking a language Amanda assumed was Basque, she directed the women to shove the table against one wall and arrange the chairs in a large circle in one corner. She poured coffee for everyone, played some Basque music on her phone and invited Amanda to join them.

"I have asked the women to relax, to talk, to gossip. Essentially to act as they normally would while on a break. The one thing I have requested is that they speak Euskara, which is another name for the Basque language, and to speak slowly. I would like you to listen."

Meryn broke the ice by asking questions of the women, who soon filled the room with chatter and laughter. Amanda listened. She had taken a couple of years of Spanish in high school, and she detected a few words that sounded familiar. But most of the words were unfamiliar to her. The accent, however, touched her at a primordial level, thick and buttery and reminiscent of the way she imagined peasant women spoke in the villages of Russia.

Meryn leaned in. "Does it sound familiar?"

"A few words, maybe. But mostly no."

"That is because Euskara is of ancient origin. It is unrelated to any other known language. It was present in Europe long before the arrival of the Indo-European family of languages spoken today. The few words you recognized have been imported, but for the most part the language is a mystery."

Obviously Meryn had a point to make. She continued. "I said the language was ancient. By that I mean Stone Age."

"How can you possibly know that?"

Meryn smiled. "Because of some obvious clues. The word for knife, for example, literally means 'stone that cuts.' And the word for ceiling literally means 'top of the cave.'"

Amanda understood immediately. Obviously these words originated at a time when man used stones to cut and lived in caves.

Meryn continued. "Euskara is an ancient language, the language of Atlantis. It lived among the outpost families and eventually spread. And it lives today."

"But you said Atlantis was an advanced culture. Why would they call a knife a stone that cuts?"

"They were advanced twelve thousand years ago, yes. And even long before. But like all humans, they were once cave dwellers. They simply developed more quickly than other groups. But they kept their ancient language." She paused as they listened to the women chatter, the sounds at once both exotic and haunting. "If you listen carefully, the story of the world is being told."

Cam sprinted from the car, toward their lake house's open front door. *Why was it open?* Venus bounded out to meet him, her tail wagging. He brushed by her, too panicked to even feel bad about it. A uniformed police officer stood in the kitchen, leaning nonchalantly against the counter, his attention directed toward the breakfast nook.

Cam rushed past him. Astarte sat at the table, chewing on a Granola Bar. She smiled up at Cam. "I got an 'A' on my math test," she announced.

He froze for a second, then rushed toward her, dropped to his knees by her chair and pulled her to him.

"Dad, don't squeeze so hard. What's wrong?"

A dozen emotions cascaded around inside Cam's head, confusion and relief paramount among them. But mostly he just felt love. Absolute adoration for this little girl they had welcomed into their lives. For some reason something he had read popped into his head: *Love is the angry bear that feeds you honey with its claws.* He had felt such anguish when he thought her to be in danger. And now such sweetness in knowing she was safe. He took a deep breath. "Nothing. I just thought something had happened to you."

"What?"

He kissed her on the cheek and disengaged, the movement jarring his jaw. Hopefully it wasn't broken. "It doesn't matter. I'm just glad you're okay."

Cam looked up at the policeman, who smiled and shrugged. About Cam's age, but husky with a round, pink-skinned face. "When I drove up she was walking home with your neighbor and her daughter. I told the neighbor I'd wait here with her until you got home."

Cam stood and thanked the patrolman. He exhaled. "Sorry for the false alarm."

The officer smiled again. "I'm not." He turned. "I'm a new dad myself. I can imagine what you were going through. I hope all these kinds of calls end up being false alarms."

Magnuson cursed as he cruised down the middle lane of Interstate 495. He had hoped Thorne would make this easier. Last thing he wanted was to involve a little girl in all this. Actually, that was not true—last thing he wanted was to tell Admiral Warner he had failed in his mission.

Which, so far, he had. He had deleted Thorne's cell phone pictures but was pretty sure they had been downloaded elsewhere, probably to Thorne's home computer. By now Thorne would have figured out that the whole abduction thing had been a ruse and that Astarte was perfectly safe. But hopefully the cold fear Thorne had felt at the thought of losing his daughter would stay with him—it should make their next encounter more productive. Magnuson had not kidnapped Thorne's daughter. Not this time. But Thorne knew he could. Knew he would.

He dialed Thorne's cell and spoke without preamble. "Hope you had a nice reunion with your daughter. But I want those pictures." He paused. "Listen carefully. Go upstairs or downstairs or wherever it is that you keep your computer. Disconnect it. Put it in your car and drive to the Ace Hardware on Route 40. Leave the computer in a garbage bag in the back parking lot next to the light stanchion. You have five minutes. And those pictures better be on that computer. Got it?"

Thorne exhaled into the phone. "Got it. I'm on my way."

He pictured Thorne climbing stairs. "Apple or PC?"

"PC."

"Good." If it was an Apple, the pictures would have uploaded automatically to the Cloud.

No doubt Thorne was wondering if in five minutes there was enough time to download the pictures. "You've already lost fifteen seconds," Magnuson remarked coldly. Magnuson guessed that his daughter meant way more to him than any dig photos. "And Thorne, don't screw around." An icy pause. "I know where you live."

Late in the afternoon the rain finally let up. Amanda mistakenly assumed it was too late to drive out to see the cave art Meryn wanted to show her.

"We are going into a cave," Meryn said. "It matters not whether it is day or night."

A Land Cruiser sat idling, waiting for them outside the hotel front door. The storm had passed, but a light rain and cool breezed remained. "Here in the mountains, close to the coast, the weather can be temperamental," Meryn said.

"Like men." Amanda wasn't sure why Meryn had brought up the issue of her being married to Cam. This was a chance to reopen the conversation.

"Yes," was all she got in reply.

Shrugging off the snub, Amanda pulled up a couple of images of cave art she had downloaded on her phone. Earlier in the day, while waiting for the storm to pass, Meryn had shared with her pictures of Stone Age paintings from Lascaux in France. Amanda had been amazed to see that some of the ancient art conveyed movement and scale and even a sense of abstract.

Cave Art, Lascaux, France

Cave Art, Lascaux, France

Amanda had done some painting. She shook her head, marveling at the skill of these artists. Could primitive man produce art like this? Or, as Meryn claimed, was there something else going on here? She looked forward to being able to see the paintings in person, to study them at an intimate level. Perhaps they would speak to her.

Twenty minutes into their drive they exited the main road and began climbing, the Land Cruiser fighting through potholes and over gullies. Occasionally the driver got out to remove a branch or other debris blocking the road. Their route hugged the coastline, but even so, snow-capped mountains loomed on the horizon. "We are going to a place called Altamira. It means 'high view,'" Meryn explained.

Abruptly the Land Cruiser stopped in front of what looked to Amanda to be a country farm. A uniformed man leaned out of a guard house and waved them forward. They parked on the shoulder of the dirt road; from the back of the vehicle Meryn removed two pair of rubber boots. "No doubt the cave will be muddy, if not flooded," Meryn explained. "Follow me."

They walked up a grassy slope. Between a pair of gnarled trees a square opening cut out of the hillside beckoned to them. Amanda had been expecting a cave cut into a cliffside. This was more like an underground passage.

"Normally there is a three-year wait to get in," Meryn said. "And even then the authorities limit visitors. The carbon monoxide from people breathing in the cave was ruining the artwork."

She clicked a torchlight and led Amanda inside, the narrow entry opening quickly to a height of almost twenty feet. "The cave was discovered in the late 1800s by a farmer and his dog. At first nobody could believe it." She cast her torchlight on the cave walls, illuminating dozens of painted images as they wandered slowly through the maze-like chamber, their boots squeaking and sloshing. "These paintings are 15,000 to 20,000 years old, some even older. Primitive man was thought to be incapable of this level of sophisticated artwork."

Amanda could see why. Some images even incorporated the contours of the cave walls into the art. They were as impressive as the French cave images she had been studying on her phone.

Meryn spoke as Amanda studied a bison. "Many of these were done through airbrushing. The artist blew paint onto the wall through a hollow bone."

Altamira (Spain) Cave Painting

Amanda turned. "Wait, really? They blew the paint?" Would ancient cave dwellers really have been that sophisticated? Of course not. That was Meryn's whole point of this excursion. Altamira was located in northern Spain, near the Pyrenees, near the Atlantean outpost. And the French caves, in Lascaux, were just on the other side of the Pyrenees, again not far from the Atlantean outpost. "So you think these were drawn by Atlanteans."

Meryn waved a hand at the bison image. "The bull was holy in Atlantis. And, again, look at the level of sophistication displayed. The evidence speaks for itself."

Point made, Meryn led them out of the cave and back to the Land Cruiser. Darkness had now fallen, but rather than return to the hotel Meryn instructed the driver to head straight to the airport. "We lost half a day today," she explained. "I'd like to make it up."

"So where to next?"

"The Czech Republic. You're a potter. You'll appreciate our next stop."

The jet engine was running and their bags waiting when they arrived at the airport. Two hours later they landed in Brno, the second largest Czech city. Even though it was approaching bedtime on a Tuesday night, the driver who met them on the tarmac whisked them downtown to what Meryn explained was formally the palace home of a Catholic cardinal. It now housed the Moravian Museum. The massive building appeared dark, but a side door opened and a frowning, middle-aged woman in a blue business suit ushered them in with a nod. Amanda wondered how Meryn seemed to have VIP status at all these sites. "This way," the woman said curtly.

The curator led them down a hallway and flicked on a light. Displayed in a glass case in the middle of what looked like the palace's opulent sitting room stood a soda can-sized dark gray statuette. A goddess figure. Wide-hipped and large-breasted, the figure depicted traditional fertility attributes.

Venus of Dolni

"Meet the Venus of Dolni," Meryn said, almost reverently. "She was found not far from here, along with hundreds of other figurines. They date back to almost thirty thousand years ago. They are the oldest known ceramic objects in the world."

"I didn't realize goddess figures go back that far."

"For tens of thousands of years humankind has worshiped the female, the giver of life. Only in the past few millennia have things been turned on their head."

Amanda studied the object. The work was fairly rudimentary, though of course impressive for a Stone Age culture. If that's what it was. But something Meryn said resonated. "You said this is among the oldest ceramic objects ever found?"

Meryn smiled. "I did."

Amanda did not want to get too technical, but the term 'ceramic' implied that some kind of process to cure the clay had been used. "Are you saying this was fired?"

Meryn nodded.

Amanda titled her head. That was not possible. "As in a kiln?"

"Yes. Based on the temperature at which the clay was fired, some kind of kiln was used. The science is undisputable."

It was one thing to fashion rudimentary objects from clay, and even to cure them over a campfire. But the act of firing them in a kiln should have been well beyond Stone Age technology. "You're certain?"

"Quite." Meryn smiled again. "You are right to be astounded. It would be at least another twenty thousand years before the people of Europe learned ceramic arts. Or should I say, relearned."

Amanda stared at the statuette. *Thirty thousand years old.* How could such a primitive culture have developed such an advanced technology?

The answer, of course, was that the culture was not so primitive after all.

Chapter 6

Pak Chol-su flipped his pillow and exhaled. He had not slept. The handwritten note tucked under his windshield wiper sent his mind racing. He had discovered the note when he left his office late on Tuesday night. Its simplicity raised more questions that it answered: "Meet for breakfast 7:00 usual spot. Urgent."

He recognized Uddin's handwriting. But why the note rather than a phone call? Were they ready to accept the deal? Or, worse, had they decided to opt out? If so, what would he tell Supreme Leader? These were the questions that kept him from sleep.

After watching the sun rise Pak walked to a nearby park and did some calisthenics before returning to his apartment to shower. A half hour later he sat atop a bench decorated with butter pad-sized blue, green and white ceramic tiles on the Corniche, a seaside promenade running through Beirut's fashionable central district. Normally he enjoyed the bookend views of the Mediterranean to the west and snow-peaked Mount Lebanon to the east, not to mention the people-watching opportunity the busy walkway offered. But today he was too anxious to do anything but suck on a cigarette and stare at the bullet-pocked palm trees around him, grim reminders of the 1980s Lebanese civil war that killed hundreds of thousands. No doubt Uddin would insist on coffee and pastry from a nearby push cart. Perhaps Pak could choke something down once he knew the reason for their meeting.

The heavy-set, black-robed Uddin ambled down the promenade just before 7:30, his tardiness only adding to Pak's distress. Pak took a deep breath, flicked his cigarette aside and forced a smile onto his face. "Good morning," he offered. He was in over his head here. He was a linguist, not a businessman or diplomat. Yet he was supposed to negotiate a crucial deal with a descendant of the Phoenician trading empire, a man who had probably been trained in deal-making since before he outgrew his diaper and put on his first pair of baggy pants.

Thankfully Uddin did not insist on the Arab custom of multiple cheek kisses upon meeting—Pak was not sure how deep he would want to dive into the Druze's bushy gray beard. They shook hands in the Western way and sat on either end of the colorful bench as was their custom when meeting in Beirut. As always, Uddin began with small talk. Eventually he rounded toward the point of their meeting. "Later today I will be meeting with the Iranians. I will leave my watch at home."

Pak thought this a commentary on how nobody seemed to keep to appointed time in the Middle East. "Because you will not need it?"

Uddin chuckled. "No. Because with the Iranians, they will steal your watch and then try to sell it back to you later." He shook his head. "At an outrageous price." He eyed Pak. "You should know this. Be careful of the Iranians."

Pak smiled politely, wondering if the Iranians somehow factored in to Supreme Leader's plan. If they did, he was not privy to how.

Uddin shifted his bulk on the bench. "As they say in the West, I have good news and I have bad news. Which would you like to hear first?"

Given his mood, the answer was easy. "The bad news, if you please," Pak replied in Arabic.

Uddin grinned, his gray teeth barely visible behind the thick hairs that surrounded his mouth like a barbed-wire fence. He raised a forefinger. "Actually, I will give you the good news first. We have decided to accept your proposal."

Pak exhaled and bowed his head in thanks. He took a moment to catch his breath. "That indeed is good news. Very good news. Supreme Leader will be pleased." He took a deep breath. "And the bad news?"

Uddin looked down. "The technology is not as … perfected … as I may have led you to believe."

"What do you mean?" Pak had never really gotten a good sense of the man, despite their multiple encounters. Uddin liked to eat, and his eyes often tracked the many women strolling along the Corniche, but he was also careful not to share much about his personal life. As Pak understood it, the Druze rarely opened up to outsiders, behavior shaped by thousands of years of living in the minority. People in North Korea tended to act the same way, wary to trust anyone not in their immediate family.

"Meaning," Uddin said with a sad smile, "that you and I are going need to fly to Boston."

Twin terracotta spires rose on either side of a massive domed mosque, the early morning heat rising from the sleeping city making them appear to undulate slightly like insect antennae twitching in the breeze. From her vantage point, a thousand feet in the air as their plane swept in on its approach, Amanda studied the Turkish metropolis. Sanliurfa. More commonly known as Urfa, the birthplace of the Biblical Abraham. Today it was largely inhabited by Kurds, many of them fleeing war-torn Syria a day's walk to the south. Out of this dusty plain, in what schoolchildren knew as the Fertile Crescent, civilization supposedly first took root in the form of the ancient Sumerians.

But unlike what Amanda had learned in school, civilization did not originate six thousand years ago. Rather, the discovery of the Gobekli Tepe site, only ten miles away, pushed that date back twice as far, to twelve thousand years ago. Obviously that was why they were here.

Meryn, whom Amanda thought was still sleeping, must have sensed her musings. "Hard to believe this was once the cradle of civilization." There was no sleep in her voice; perhaps she had been awake the whole time. Amanda was beginning to wonder if her great-aunt needed sleep and food like other people. "Today we think of the Middle East as backwards. But don't forget what Europe was like in the Dark Ages. Were it not for the knowledge retained in the Middle East, we might still be living as illiterate vassals, surviving in mud huts and treating disease through prayer."

Amanda asked the obvious question. "So is Gobekli Tepe connected to Atlantis?"

Rather than giving one of her evasive answers, Meryn said, "Yes. Very much so. After Atlantis fell the surviving families tried to maintain our technology, our arts, our culture. In the end we failed. There simply were not enough of us—it was like one master pianist trying to teach a thousand children to appreciate classical music." She smiled sadly. "And to do so without her piano."

Amanda knew the routine. A car would meet them at the tarmac and a local guide would whisk them through border control. Obviously Meryn had made these globetrotting sightseeing tours before.

A twenty minute drive northeast along a surprisingly good road through a barren desert-like landscape brought them to the base of a small mountain range dotted with a series of gently sloped hills. A handful of hearty shrubs had taken root in the arid soil near the tops of the ridge and a few of the slopes showed evidence of having been farmed. One hill in particular stood out, its slope covered with a series of corrugated metal roofs that reminded Amanda of a shantytown she had visited once in Caracas. Surrounding the metal roofs, the slope's rocky face was pocked with cavities and crisscrossed with narrow wooden walkways. Amanda got out of their car and walked closer, now able to see a series of stone structures protruding upright from the debris. No security, no fence. She snapped a picture. This was Gobekli Tepe, "Belly Hill," the modest, hardscrabble knoll that had doubled the age of human civilization. Twelve thousand years ago, when humans were supposed to be nomadic hunter-gatherers living in caves and mud huts, a village had taken root here, its residents joining together in a cooperative effort to build a massive temple complex dedicated to a pantheon of ancient gods.

Gobekli Tepe, Turkey

Meryn gave her a few minutes alone before appearing at her elbow. "It's hard to get a sense of the site from down here on the ground." She pulled up an image on her phone. "Look at this illustration. Remember, as far as we know, before this the most elaborate structure that man had built was a hut. And also remember that the date for this, 11,600 years ago, is exactly the date firmly established as the destruction of Atlantis."

Gobekli Tepe Illustration

Amanda studied the drawing. T-shaped megaliths stood in the center of three walled, circular, ceremonial areas. The illustration also hinted at additional temple structures nearby. "Why the need for so many temples?" she asked.

"Apparently each temple was dedicated to a different animal—snake, lion, fox, boar. When they built a new temple they buried the old one." She shrugged. "Nobody knows for certain why."

"And what are the T-shaped megaliths in the center?"

"The pillars appear to be anthropomorphic; that is, in a human form. Carved arms angle from the shoulders of some pillars, with hands covering their bellies. And they are wearing loincloths."

Amanda looked from the illustration to the real thing in front of her. "This must have been a monumental task."

"Yes. There are close to two dozen temples. Each would have required hundreds if not thousands of workers. Massive stones were quarried and dragged from a quarter-mile away. Even the closest drinking water source was a three-mile walk." She paused. "This was all supposedly done before metal tools, before writing. Even before the *wheel* had been invented."

"Obviously you think otherwise," Amanda said.

"Obviously. Follow me."

Meryn led her along a wooden walkway toward the roofed areas. A sleepy-eyed man peeked out from behind a wall, smiled at Meryn and waved them on, but otherwise they moved through the complex alone. She stopped in front of an intricately carved T-shaped pillar similar to the ones depicted in the illustrations. "Note the detailed carvings," she said. "And the fine craftsmanship."

Gobekli Tepe Pillar, Early Years

Amanda studied the pillar, clearly able to make out the carved figures of a scorpion and a dodo bird amongst other creatures. "Impressive," she declared.

They continued on, winding their way toward another temple circle. "Now notice these pillars. They are much plainer. The workmanship is clearly inferior."

Gobekli Tepe Pillar, Later Years

Meryn paused for effect, allowing Amanda to study the effort. The pillars themselves were smaller and less skillfully carved, uneven and partly askew. And absent of any decorative carvings.

Meryn explained. "These plainer pillars are younger by hundreds of years—we know this from the archeology." She gestured outward toward the dig area extending over hundreds of yards. "The pattern continues. The older the temple, the more advanced and intricate is the work. It is as if some kind of *regression* is occurring, with skills and techniques devolving over the generations. That is not the way society normally functions."

Amanda understood the point immediately. "Your example of the classical pianist, unable to pass along her expertise." She considered the possibility of Atlantean survivors overseeing the original temple work. "It is as if the first temples were built and supervised by the Atlantean survivors, who retained the skills needed to do fine work. But there were not enough of them to be able to pass this skill on to future generations. Either they weren't skilled enough themselves, or they were not good enough teachers, or they didn't know how to repair the tools that broke, or their students simply were not advanced enough in basic skills to absorb everything their teachers needed to teach. Whatever the case, things got worse rather than better over time."

Meryn nodded. "And remember, it all began exactly 11,600 years ago. Precisely when Atlantis fell. Somehow man went from building mud huts to constructing these massive stone temples. And then, almost as quickly, the skill was lost. Civilization disappeared for another six thousand years." She shrugged. "I suppose one explanation is that aliens arrived to supervise the work. But I think there is a better explanation. One that doesn't require us to believe in extra-terrestrials."

Amanda turned and surveyed the massive complex. Her words to Cam from last week about Athena emerging fully formed from the head of Zeus popped into her mind. This was even more dramatic. Somehow a society that had not yet invented the wheel and that had never built anything more complex than a simple hut had managed to engineer this sprawling masterpiece. She flopped onto a stone bench. *How was it that historians had not yet connected the dots?*

After seeing Astarte safely onto the morning school bus, Cam drove north to a local mall to buy a new computer. It sucked to lose many of his personal files and photos, and he had better ways to spend $1,500. But it was a small price to pay for Astarte's safety. And for peace of mind.

His jaw sore but not fractured, he had filed a police report after dumping his computer in the parking lot as Smith demanded. But he didn't hold out much hope of anything coming of it. With Astarte safe, the only crime committed had been the punch thrown, hardly a top priority for law enforcement. But Cam had met with a sketch artist and the lieutenant promised he would circulate the drawing to the patrol officers. Maybe someone would recognize the black and red cross tattoo.

From the mall Cam drove toward his Westford office, mulling over why Smith would care so much about the photos of the dig. Unable to come up with an explanation, he found Potvin's cell number in his phone log and called him as he navigated the vestiges of the morning rush hour. "Hi, it's Cameron Thorne. How's the dig going?"

"It's not."

"I'm sorry, what?"

Potvin explained how a gang of Native Americans had vandalized the site a few nights earlier. "They destroyed everything.

Even took all my photos." He paused and lowered his voice. "Is that why you're calling?"

"As a matter of fact, yes."

Potvin exhaled. "I should have warned you. In all the commotion I just forgot. They asked me who else had pictures of the dig and I gave them your name."

That explained things, at least. "So that's it? Dig is over?"

"There's nothing left to dig," he said listlessly. "Plus nobody wants to antagonize the Native Americans by desecrating their burial sites."

"They've been okay with it before, right?"

"Yeah, well, they're not okay with it now. I've got a lump on my head to prove it."

Cam hung up and reflected on the conversation. Something didn't feel right. And Smith, or whoever he was, definitely did not seem Native American. He dialed his friend Flying Fox.

Fox answered with the same bantering he always did. "Uh oh. Here it comes again. I'm going to be either in pain or out money. The only question is which."

Cam laughed despite his mood. "Can I run something by you?" He told the story in chronological order, beginning with Sunday night's vandalism at the dig site and ending with Tuesday's encounter with Smith and the loss of his computer. "I think it's the same guy we saw that day in the woods, wearing fatigues. With the cross tattoo. Son-of-a-bitch throws a mean right hook."

Fox did not hesitate. "Something's not right. Usually if shit goes on I'm in the middle of it. But I didn't hear jack about this. And we don't have many blue-eyed Algonquin. Let me make a couple of calls."

Five minutes later Cam's cell rang. "Not us. I can guarantee it. That dude with the tattoo is not Native American."

"Okay, thanks Fox."

So what was going on? Smith first showed up in Salisbury, but that was before it was even a dig site. So why was he even there? Then he popped into Cam's lecture that night, warning Cam about defaming the Knights Templar. Then yesterday, the whole business with the pictures. And if Fox was right, it was probably Smith who wrecked the site a few nights ago. Obviously Smith didn't want people to know about the dig. But why?

A handwritten note on a yellow sticky greeted Magnuson when he arrived at his desk Wednesday morning at eight o'clock. From Admiral Warner, it read simply, "Come see me ASAP." Magnuson dropped his saddle bag, grabbed a pen and pad of paper and jogged down the hall to his boss's office. One of Admiral Warner's secretaries ushered him in without a wait.

Admiral Warner, again, seemed upset. And that, in turn, troubled Magnuson. It wasn't exactly as if he had any real affection for his boss. It was more that if Admiral Warner was upset, that usually meant the company was suffering, and that meant Magnuson's newfound idyllic lifestyle might be in jeopardy. His uncle had said to him on his wedding night, "Remember, Keith—happy wife means happy life." It was sort of like that: "Happy boss means suffer no loss." He shrugged. Good thing he wasn't paid to write poetry. All this passed through his head as he sat down.

Admiral Warner waited for the door to close behind his secretary. "Nice work on the Salisbury dig site. We have effectively shut down the dig." He waved the report Magnuson had written in the air. "But we may have a bigger problem. What do you know about this Cameron Thorne?"

"He's an expert on the Templars. Claims they came to America before Columbus. I saw him speak last week. He's teaches a class at Brandeis University."

"What was he doing at the Salisbury dig? This has nothing to do with the Templars."

Magnuson shrugged. "I was surprised he was there also."

"Well, I think I may have found a connection. I got a call early this morning from Turkey. Thorne's wife visited the Gobekli Tepe site." Magnuson nodded, though he had no idea what his boss was talking about. "And from what I can gather she has been visiting other sites around the world as well." He focused his tired blue eyes on Magnuson, the dark circles reflective of a man who had not slept. "These are the sites one would visit if trying to prove the authenticity of Atlantis. Thorne and his wife are hot on the trail."

Now Magnuson understood. "And we don't want that."

"It's not a question of want or not. It's a question of the survival of Warner Industries." He shook his head and gestured to a thick bound report on his desk. "In this report is a list of our current and future projects, worldwide. Pipelines. Mineral exploration. Fiber optics. Mining operations." He let his hand drop to the desk with a thud. "A full sixty percent of them are located along the Mid-Atlantic Ridge. That means many of our current projects and most of our future projects would either be curtailed or severely restricted under the United Nations treaty if it is established that Atlantis rests on the ocean floor where I think it does. Where I *know* it does." He shook his head. "We are a large company, with healthy cash reserves. But we've invested billions in the Atlantic. No company can survive a loss like that."

Magnuson didn't know what to say. He hadn't realized things were so precarious. And all because of a couple of nosy historians and some stupid United Nations treaty designed to protect shipwrecks.

Admiral Warner looked as dejected as Magnuson had ever seen him. "I have spent my life studying Atlantis. And now it may be the thing that brings down my life's work."

Magnuson leaned forward in his chair. "Just tell me what to do."

Pak had been trained to be ready to travel on short notice. But he had never actually done it. Not that it was that difficult. He threw some clothes and toiletries in a small suitcase, made sure he had a charger for his phone and pulled his passport out of his sock drawer.

Actually, it was not technically his passport. For years North Koreans officials and members of the ruling family had been using fake passports issued by China. North Korea was a pariah in the world community and it was simply easier to move about posing as Chinese citizens. Not that there hadn't been glitches along the way— the Supreme Leader's older brother was arrested using a fake passport while trying to visit Disney Land in Japan. But that was because the Japanese recognized the difference between the Chinese and the Koreans. To most of the world one Asian was the same as the next. To be safe, Pak spent fifteen minutes re-memorizing his

Chinese name and other pertinent information before tucking the passport into his bag.

The hardest thing about arranging the trip was explaining to his boss why he needed to go. Pak had spent an uncomfortable half hour being questioned before he was rescued by a phone call from Pyongyang. His boss listened, hung up, studied Pak and finally nodded. "Perhaps I have underestimated you."

An hour later he hailed a taxi for the Beirut airport. As the car door closed he finally allowed himself to grin. He had never been to America, in fact never been anywhere other than North Korea, China and countries around Lebanon. This was a crucial mission, personally overseen by Supreme Leader himself. Maybe there'd even be some time for Pak to visit Fenway Park and try a hot dog.

The mystery of Gobekli Tepe still occupying her thoughts, Amanda barely noticed they had entered the airport tarmac. The Gulfstream, engines running, awaited. This time, Meryn announced, their destination was Cairo, due south a thousand miles.

They readied for takeoff as the late afternoon sun cast long, angled shadows over the jet, distorting its tail and nose and wing flaps to make it look like some misshapen flying dinosaur. History was like that, Amanda realized. One's perception of something often depended on just how the light hit it.

Meryn hadn't told her what they would be seeing in Egypt, but Amanda guessed it would be either the pyramids or the Sphinx. Perhaps both. In anticipation, she Googled the terms Atlantis and Egypt and quickly downloaded a few articles onto her phone before she lost her internet connection as the plane began to climb. Reclined in her seat, she dove in.

It took her a solid hour to distill things. Information was convoluted, and the dates didn't always work, but the possibility existed that the earliest Egyptian rulers were in fact refugees from the Atlantean cataclysm. Using one of Cam's legal pads she had stuffed in her bag, she outlined the argument connecting Egypt to Atlantis:

1. Egyptian tradition stated there were ten so-called "god-kings" who ruled Egypt prior to the reign of the pharaohs.
2. These gods came from a foreign land.
3. The Egyptian historian-priest Manetho, writing in 250 BCE, referred to these foreign kings as 'Auretians.' Given the common linguistic confusion between the l/r sounds, this could easily be read as 'Auletians,' not far from 'Atlanteans.'
4. In fact, the Phoenician historian Sanchuniathon, writing in 1193 BCE, called these very same kings 'Aleteans.'

It was hardly a smoking gun, but it was another piece of evidence—like the Sanskrit writings of India and the ancient Sumerian legends—that indicated the Atlanteans played a part in the history of ancient cultures. And if they played a part, they obviously were, well, real.

Amanda set her work down as the flight attendant brought a hot dinner resembling ravioli. Meryn called across the aisle. "It is *manti*, Turkish. Lamb meat steamed in a dumpling, served with yogurt. I generally do not eat meat, but this I cannot resist."

They made small talk as they ate, Meryn asking about Astarte and life in Westford. Amanda sensed she was leading up to something, and as they finished their meals Meryn smiled and said, "There is one more thing I wanted to discuss with you. I hope you understand the need for me to be both diligent and vigilant."

Amanda nodded.

"So I have conducted a background check not only on you but on Cameron as well."

Amanda nodded again. She had figured as much.

"I'm a bit concerned about his ... fixation ... on the Knights Templar. As you know, they were a male-dominated, patriarchal group. Even worse, they were the fighting force for one of the most misogynistic institutions in the history of the world—the medieval Church." She reached over and squeezed Amanda's hand. "I trust your Cameron doesn't share the Templars' patriarchal tendencies?"

Amanda resisted snapping back a response. This type of simplistic analysis was both insulting and intellectually lazy. The reality was that Cam was the least chauvinistic man she had ever met. She said so, then added, "Look, just because he *studies* the Templars doesn't mean he *is* one. I study them also. They were an important part of history."

"So he doesn't glorify them?"

She turned in her seat. "He glorifies their accomplishments, yes. They did some amazing things. But that doesn't mean he shares their beliefs."

Meryn smiled disarmingly. "Very well. I apologize for jumping to conclusions. It is just that we Crones are very sensitive to the dangers of patriarchy. It ruined Atlantean society, just before its destruction. As I told you, many old families believe the gods were punishing Atlantis for turning warlike and voracious." She shrugged. "Whatever the truth, we shall not allow it to happen again. Now, I'll let you get back to your research. I'm thrilled to see how engaged you are in all this."

Amanda moved on to another article. This one she found more compelling. In it the author began by making the observation that the Great Pyramid of Giza (also known as the Pyramid of Khufu or the Pyramid of Cheops) was the oldest of the three pyramids of the Giza complex, built approximately 2,500 to 3,000 BCE. And it was clearly the most impressive, slightly larger and far superior in quality and workmanship to its two younger neighbors. Why, the author wondered, would the builders have reverted back to building inferior versions once they had mastered the skills needed to build to a higher standard? Would a pharaoh really order a pyramid be built for himself which was *less* imposing than that of his predecessor? Based on this reasoning, the author theorized that the Great Pyramid was not just marginally older than the others, but so much older that the technology had been lost. In fact, he argued for a construction date of approximately twelve thousand years ago—that was the date a covered causeway leading from the pyramid would have led directly to the Nile River, which over the years had shifted course and was now five miles away. *Twelve thousand years ago.* There was that date again.

Amanda set down her phone and stared out the window, the setting sun turning the bottom of the clouds into a golden fleece. This description of declining skills matched what she had seen at Gobekli Tepe and in the Altamira Cave and when analyzing the Venus of Dolni—advanced technological achievements dating back to the fall of Atlantis, after which the technology regressed and eventually faded.

Meryn leaned across the aisle and interrupted her musings. "I see you're reading up on the pyramids."

"I assume that's what we're going to see."

"Yes and no. I can hardly bring you to Egypt and not show you the last of the Seven Wonders of the Ancient World. But our focus will be on the Sphinx."

Abraham slowly chewed his corned beef sandwich as Madame Radminikov wiped down the counter. This was his second lunch in a row eaten at her butcher shop. He tried to recall if he had eaten in the twenty-four hours since. As he glanced through today's newspaper he came across an article which made him realize he had more important things to focus on. He closed his eyes, weighing his next step. This battle he was fighting, had been fighting his whole life, often seemed like a futile one, like trying to stop the tide with a single sandbag. He had never feared death—he and mortality had become intimate companions during his time in the camps, the contemplation of death being one of the more comforting parts of his daily existence. But he did fear no longer being alive, no longer able to defend his people.

"Madame, I think it may be time to test our Templar friends," he said finally.

"How so?"

He turned today's *Boston Globe* article toward her. "Apparently the Students for Justice in Palestine interrupted a Holocaust Remembrance Day ceremony at Brandeis University yesterday." Celebrated on the 27th of Nisan on the Hebrew calendar, the day generally fell in late April or early May.

Madame Radminikov stopped wiping. "Interrupted? How so?"

He fought to keep his voice steady. "They threw pig's blood onto the stage and spray-painted swastikas on the outside of the building. Many of them were wearing black and white Isis head scarves. Some yelled 'Death to the Jews.'"

She spat. "Swine. Was anyone hurt?"

"Not this time." He put down the sandwich, his appetite gone. "And there shall not *be* a next time." This SJP group had grown increasingly bold over the past decade. It had become nothing more than a front for vicious anti-Semitism, a place where hate-mongers could spew their odious beliefs under the cloak of fighting for Palestinian rights. In truth they did not give a damn about the Palestinians.

"Were they arrested?" she asked.

"Yes. And immediately released. Free speech, they claimed." If the past was any indication, none would receive significant punishment.

She voiced the very question he had been mulling over. "Do you think the Templars will care about something like this?"

"That's why I said this would be a good test. Today SJP and their ilk attack Jewish groups. But it is only a question of time before they turn their attention to Christians and other non-Muslims as well. The Templars will see this. They will see the need to yank this particularly noxious weed out by its roots." He paused. "Or at least I hope so. Else I have misplayed our hand."

This time Mrs. Bean-Brown knocked on the door of Astarte's classroom, her feeble effort barely audible. "I need to see Astarte," she mouthed in a stage whisper as the students settled into their desks after lunch.

Astarte sighed. No doubt this involved Mr. Saint Paul. She already told him everything she knew on Sunday. It was only Wednesday.

On their walk to the main office Mrs. Bean-Brown tried to make small talk, but Astarte gave one-word answers. *Don't act like you're my friend when you're not.* Instead she asked, "Why are you helping Mr. Saint Paul?"

Her nervous eyes swept the hallway to make sure nobody was listening. "Because he is a very important man. And by helping him I can help you." She swallowed. "Help you stay with your new parents."

It was a weak answer, but Astarte let it go. She knew adults often did things because other more powerful adults told them to.

Mrs. Bean-Brown closed the door to the small meeting room they always used when she visited and motioned for Astarte to sit. She felt a cold lump in her stomach and noticed her underarms had begun to sweat.

"Do you have your phone? Mr. Saint Paul wants you to call again."

"Now?"

"Yes, dear, now. Apparently it is very important."

The Gulfstream landed without incident in Cairo, where a driver in a beige Mercedes fought his way through evening traffic from the airport to the suburb of Giza, home to the Pyramids and Sphinx. Amanda longed to explore the area with Cam and Astarte. She made a decision. "You know what, we can skip the Pyramids."

Meryn, seated in the back seat next to her, said, "You may be the first person in history to say that."

"It's just that I know it is getting dark and you want to show me the Sphinx. If we have time we can circle back."

Meryn smiled. "Well, you can't really see the Sphinx without seeing the Pyramids." She pointed. "There they are."

The massive Sphinx rose out of the dessert, backlit by the setting sun, standing guard in front of a row of three massive pyramids. The Sphinx, the largest statue in the world, had been carved from the existing bedrock so that it sat in a depression in the desert floor. At sixty feet tall and almost two hundred fifty feet long, its size took Amanda's breath away. But as large as it was it looked like a kitten lounging in the sun compared to the two largest of the massive pyramids looming over it—the Great Pyramid and the Pyramid of Khafre, each of which stood almost as tall as the Washington Monument.

Even battered by the elements, its nose broken off and its face pockmarked and rutted, the pharaoh-faced Sphinx still evoked a sense of regal majesty. Based on what Amanda had read, the statue's face may originally have been that of a lion but was re-sculpted in his own image by the egotistical Pharaoh Khafre at the same time he built the nearby pyramid named for him. In any event, the statue was either old or *really* old, depending on whom one believed. Amanda had no doubt which way Meryn would be arguing.

As they stepped out of the car and approached the monument, their driver fending off trinket salesmen and beggars, Meryn made her case. "So, either the Sphinx was built at the same time as the Pyramid of Khafre was built, around 2,500 BCE, or it is much older. Dr. Robert Schoch, a geology professor from Boston University, makes the strongest argument for the older dating. He has studied the erosion patterns on the base of the statue and also on the walls enclosing the statue and concluded that only long periods of excessive rainfall could have caused them. We need to go back thousands of years to find a time in Egyptian history when the climate in the Nile Valley matched the erosion patterns." She pointed to a wall of the depression area in which the Sphinx sat, a wall formed when the statue was cut from the bedrock. "There. That's a good example. Those vertical fissures are the result of massive amounts of water pooling on top before running down the side of the rock. That's a different kind of erosion pattern than one gets from wind, which tends to be horizontal."

Amanda peered in the direction Meryn pointed, the area off limits to tourists. "I'm sorry, I can't really make it out."

Meryn smiled. "Young eyes, I suppose."

She motioned to the driver, who Amanda now noticed was carrying a black, hard-shelled case. He set it down and removed a small helicopter-like device with a camera attached. "A drone," Meryn announced, enjoying the look of surprise on her grandniece's face. "I may be old, but I try to embrace technology." She reached down and took hold of a remote control, quickly sending the drone airborne in the fading light. Five minutes later the camera mounted on the drone transmitted a black-and-white image of the erosion patterns to a wireless monitor the driver had flipped open.

Sphinx Enclosure Wall Erosion Patterns

Amanda nodded. "Very impressive." She could picture the rivulets of rainwater flowing down the side of the wall. "How far back in time are we talking for the necessary amount of rainfall?" Amanda asked, though she already suspected what the answer would be.

"Perhaps seven thousand years ago. Before the reign of the Pharaohs."

Amanda did a double-take. "I was certain you were going to say twelve thousand."

Meryn smiled. "I still may." She handed the drone controls to the driver and turned her attention back to Amanda. "The twelve thousand date certainly works—there was plenty of rainfall during that time period as well. But we also need to look at more recent dates, again approximately seven thousand years ago. The problem with more recent dates is that Egyptian society during that time was primitive and unsophisticated. There is no evidence whatsoever that they had the ability to construct something as massive as the Sphinx. So this becomes a process of elimination: The Sphinx predates the age of the Pharaohs, and earlier Egyptians did not have the ability to construct it. I would argue that the Atlantean refugees are the only plausible candidates."

Amanda exhaled and nodded. The argument wasn't ironclad, but it had a certain logical simplicity to it. *Someone* had to build the monstrosity.

"And one more thing: At this time, at a date twelve thousand years ago, the constellation Leo—the lion—would have risen in the eastern sky on the vernal equinox. So the Sphinx would have been looking directly at his celestial twin. That wouldn't have been the case thousands of years later."

Amanda nodded again. "As above, so below," she whispered. That kind of astronomical alignment was precisely the type of thing ancient cultures would have incorporated into their ceremonial structures. She would need to confirm Meryn's assertions when she got home, but assuming her great-aunt's information was accurate, the evidence in support of Atlantis was becoming increasingly compelling. She stared at the Sphinx. *If you could talk, what would you tell me?*

Using the payphone in Madame Radminikov's butcher shop, Abraham phoned Manuel de Real, the Templar Commander. "Are you on a secure line?" he asked by way of introduction. He had arranged for the phone company to maintain the payphone at the butchery just for calls like this.

"Let me give you another number."

Abraham redialed, Madame Radminikov leaning close to listen in. He described the situation with the Students for Justice in Palestine group. "It is only a matter of time before these zealots turn on you Christians as well as us Jews."

"I agree," de Real responded. "I share your concern. What can we do?"

Abraham explained that the SJP leaders regularly met on Wednesday evenings at an apartment in Cambridge. "Usually their entire leadership team is in attendance. In addition, each college in the city sends a representative. So there are perhaps two dozen people in attendance. With many students leaving the city for the summer in the next few weeks, I am guessing that this meeting will be well-attended. It may also be our last chance until next fall. I suggest we pay them a visit."

Amanda had begun to lose track of time. She was pretty sure it was Wednesday evening Egyptian time, which made it early afternoon in Boston. As they drove away from the Giza complex she turned to Meryn. "Where to next?"

"One more site."

"For what it's worth, you've convinced me already." Plus she was getting tired of sleeping on planes.

Her great-aunt smiled. "You'll not want to miss this next stop."

A half-hour later they had taken off yet again, this time the orange glow of the setting sun visible out the left window of the plane. So they were heading north. Amanda wondered whether they were flying to Israel. If so, she guessed even Meryn would be unable to arrange to be whisked through security.

Amanda napped a bit, her dreams haunted again. In this version she was sitting atop the stone, lion-faced Sphinx when suddenly the entire structure collapsed beneath her, sending her downward into a watery, fire-filled abyss; Meryn stood by, smiling and watching calmly as Amanda tumbled. Amanda rubbed her face with her hands, trying to erase the images. It didn't take a therapist to decode this dream.

"We land in ten minutes," Meryn said. "Beirut. Most outposts were along the Atlantic rim, but our traders also traveled to the Mediterranean. One of our outposts was in what today is known as Byblos, a port city just north of Beirut. Historians refer to Byblos as the oldest continuously-occupied city in the world." She smiled. "They only know half the story."

"So there is a group of Atlantean descendants living in Byblos?"

"Nearby. In the mountains around Byblos and Beirut. Much like the Basque in the Pyrenees, they have lived there since before recorded time. Remember the story of Lilith, our sexually aggressive ancestress? She was one of these people, living in the mountains not far from the coast. These people have had many names. But they have lived here for over twelve thousand years."

The wheels of the plane kissed the runway, as if to emphasize Meryn's words. "We know these people today as the Druze."

Amanda assumed a car would meet them on the tarmac. Instead Meryn led her into the Hariri International Airport terminal. "There is someone I want you to meet."

From the modern, airy main arrival area they took an elevator to the third floor and entered a private lounge. Meryn whispered to a hostess who led them to a secluded table against a bank of windows overlooking the runway. Her great-aunt surprised Amanda by ordering a glass of white wine. "We can enjoy a late dinner while we wait for our guests," she said. "I will tell you more about the Druze. Or perhaps you already know their story?" she asked, arching an eyebrow.

"No. I don't think so."

"You've read the Old Testament, yes?"

"Read it but not studied it."

"Well, their story—at least their origins in the area—is told in it. In the Bible they go by another name. The Watchers."

"Aren't they the fallen angels?"

"That is how they are remembered today, yes. But their true story can be gleaned by reading the Book of Enoch."

Amanda knew the Book of Enoch was an ancient Jewish religious text, lost to time until rediscovered in Ethiopia in the late 1700s. The book told the story of Enoch, Noah's great-grandfather. The book was purportedly written by Enoch before the Great Flood, inspired by dreams he had of the upcoming calamity. The Book of Enoch played a critical role in Freemasonry, which was how she and Cam first came to study it. If something was important to the Freemasons, it likely had been important to the Knights Templar as well.

Meryn continued. "The Book of Enoch tells how the Watchers—described as angel-like figures—lived on Mount Hermon and eventually descended to corrupt mankind. Mount Hermon, by the way, is just east of Beirut, where our Atlantean outpost was located. One by one the Watchers taught humans different skills—weaponry, metallurgy, jewelry-making, writing, cosmetics, herbal medicine, astrology, meteorology, astronomy." She paused. "Do these sound familiar?"

"They sound like the different vocations the Atlantean outpost residents were experts in."

"Precisely. Incidentally, one might ask how the teaching of things like medicine and literacy are *corrupting*, but I digress." Meryn sat back in her chair and sipped her wine. "Eventually these Watchers—mostly male but some female, and numbering about two hundred—came down from Mount Hermon and mated with the humans, creating what are described as giant-like offspring."

Amanda saw where this was going. "Didn't you tell me the Atlanteans were over six-feet tall?"

"I did."

"So obviously their offspring would have seemed gigantic to early man."

She nodded. "I believe what happened was the outpost survivors knew their gene pool needed to be expanded. They simply could not survive with such a small community. So they descended from the mountains to procreate with the hunter-gatherer tribes of the area. They must have seemed god-like to the natives due to their advanced culture and technology, not to mention their size."

"And not to mention Lilith's sexual appetite," Amanda laughed. She reflected on Meryn's version of the story. "But in the Bible these Watchers and their offspring are described as evil."

Meryn nodded. "As the saying goes, it depends on who is writing the history. These Atlantean survivors and their technology would have been a threat to the status quo, a challenge to the authority of the leaders who had until that point seemed all-knowing and all-powerful. It is no surprise that those in power would have tried to demonize them. Much as the Church tried to demonize scientists and forward-thinkers during medieval times." She shifted in her seat, lowering her voice to drive home her point. "But at its core, the story is a true one, even if the dates are off. Approximately 12,000 years ago a technologically advanced race of large-statured people living in the mountains of Lebanon descended and interbred with the native population. It says so in the *Bible*," she emphasized.

Amanda pictured the Atlantean survivors living in the mountains, secluded, 'watching' the hunter-gatherers below for perhaps three or four generations before eventually coming to the realization they needed to expand their gene pool. Like visitors throughout history, they offered trinkets and other gifts. Hoping to win the favor of their hosts, they shared their technology, and hoping to impress them, they shared their knowledge of the stars. Meryn's version of the story made sense, especially to those like Amanda who didn't believe in angels and other supernatural beings...

Amanda's thoughts were interrupted by an olive-skinned woman in a long yellow dress gliding toward them, escorted by a bearded, heavy-set man in a dark robe. "Ah, our guests." Meryn clapped lightly and stood. "Amanda, I'd like you to meet the descendants of the Mount Hermon outpost." She smiled. "The descendants of the Watchers."

Cam and Astarte sat in front of the TV watching the Red Sox game and eating fried chicken. Amanda would not have approved of so much fried food. But the only one who might rat them out was Venus, and Cam had bought her silence with a chunk of breast meat.

"Can I have some ice cream for dessert?"

"Only one scoop. Let's not get carried away."

Astarte grinned, her white teeth shining against her almond skin. "You won't believe how much I can get with one scoop."

The reality was the girl burned calories like Cam's SUV drank gas. If she wasn't on the softball field or soccer pitch she was chasing Venus around the yard or trying to best her high score on a dance video game. But Amanda felt strongly that their diet should be a healthy one, and Cam usually complied because of his diabetes.

His cell phone rang. "Cameron, this is Manuel de Real."

Cam wiped his hands and scratched Venus's neck. "Hello, Manuel, thanks for calling back."

Cam had met de Real a year-and-a-half ago when giving a lecture to the local Knights Templar Order. The group understandably was interested in the history of their forbearers, especially Cam's research related to Templar exploration of America and possible plans to create a New Jerusalem in New England. After the lecture Cam and de Real lunched a few times and the Templar Commander invited Cam to join the Order.

"But I'm not even a Christian," Cam had replied. And he definitely did not see the need for a modern-day Crusade.

"Then we will make you an honorary member," de Real had said, clapping his hands once as if sealing the deal by doing so. "You can't object to that, can you?"

Cam had chuckled and accepted the offer with as much grace as he could muster. The ceremony the following weekend had been full of ritual and pomp, Cam dropping to one knee and being 'knighted' with a tap of the sword on either shoulder, followed by de Real draping a Templar-crested medal around Cam's neck and reciting a few sacred-sounding lines in Latin. In English, de Real had then concluded, "Welcome to the Order of the Poor Fellow-Soldiers of Christ and of the Temple of Solomon. You are now my brother." He had pulled Cam to his feet and kissed him on both cheeks, his leather-scented cologne making Cam think of country houses and brandy. Holding Cam's eyes, he purred, "It is often said that the Freemasons are not a secret society so much as a society with secrets. It is the same with us. I have also heard it said that the true measure of a man, first and foremost, is how willing others are to share their secrets with him." He paused. "We, the modern-day Knights Templar, have chosen to share our secrets with you, Cameron Thorne."

The experience had actually been more moving than Cam had expected, which he guessed was the point of the ceremony. There was something about tying oneself to a thousand-year old legacy and its secrets. And de Real's words and ritual only added to the solemnity of the event.

The relationship over the past year had been a symbiotic one. The Templars had helped Cam with his research, giving him access to restricted sources and opening doors otherwise closed to him. His research, in turn, tended to glorify the Templars and their accomplishments, assisting de Real's efforts to increase membership and influence. Cam hoped the relationship would continue—if he was correct, the Templars had been and probably still were caretakers of many of the secrets of Atlantis.

All of this passed through Cam's mind as de Real greeted him. "How is my favorite historian?" he asked, his Portuguese accent smooth and refined.

"I'm fine. Actually, not completely. I had a little incident recently with a guy who I think may be part of the Templars. Military haircut, light blue eyes, black and red cross tattooed on his neck."

There was a slight hesitation on de Real's part. "I think I know the man. What kind of incident?"

Cam left out the faux Astarte abduction; he could always disclose more once he had a better sense of de Real's relationship with Smith, if any. "He came to one of my lectures over the weekend. Wasn't happy about me claiming the Templars were questioning the Church teachings."

"Yes. Some of our brethren are staunch Catholics. To them, questioning the Church is unthinkable."

"But it's common knowledge that the Church excommunicated the Templars for being heretics." Not that Cam wanted to debate the matter.

"Yes, but then in 2007 the Vatican issued an apology. It turns out we were not heretics after all."

"I guess that explains why this guy was upset. Here I was, listing all the heretical things they did."

"You said there was an incident?"

Cam worked his sore jaw, decided it was okay to exaggerate the encounter at the lecture in light of the more violent encounter in his office. "Essentially he threatened me." Cam pushed harder. "So you said you know who he is?"

"Yes. And I will speak to him, explain to him that you are a true friend to our Order." He chuckled. "Even if you do accuse of us of being heretics."

"Thanks."

"But now let me ask you a question, unrelated to all this," de Real said, clearing his throat. "Do you think there is any truth to the rumors that the Templars discovered the Philosopher's Stone?"

This came out of left field, but Cam was used to people asking odd questions about the Templars. He had, in fact, seen many sources alluding to the Templars' ability to turn base metals into gold. It would surely explain their immense and seemingly-instantaneous wealth. "I can't say it's impossible. If you look at a list of the scientists who were said to be experts at transmuting metal into gold, guys like Francis Bacon and John Dee and Nicholas Flamel, they were all members of secret societies like the Freemasons and Rosicrucians. The Templars may have picked this knowledge up in Jerusalem. Why do you ask?"

"One of our members saw something interesting the other night. She's pretty sure she witnessed an older gentleman, a Holocaust survivor, turn metal into gold using a spiral necklace of some sort."

Cam hit the mute button on the television remote. His neck burned. "Did you say spiral necklace?"

"Yes, that is what she heard. Made with some kind of metal not native to this planet. I believe the exact words she heard were 'alien metal.'"

So it wasn't just the Crones who had these necklaces. Cam wondered if Amanda's great-aunt knew there were more. And did she know they possibly could produce gold? Amanda was halfway around the world, but Cam had a free day tomorrow. And once again it seemed like his research on the Templars was intersecting Amanda's exploration of her Atlantean ancestry. "Do you think there's any way I could see this spiral necklace?"

"No," de Real chuckled, "I do not think that is possible. But I can introduce you to the gentleman who possesses it. We are in the process of forming a partnership of sorts with him. As it turns out I am meeting with him tomorrow. I doubt he'd object if I brought a member of our Order who happens to be an attorney. We are, after all, going to be discussing business matters."

Magnuson drove as the Templar Commander, de Real, chatted on the phone in the backseat. They were in de Real's town car, the front and back seats separated by privacy glass.

From Storrow Drive Magnuson crossed the Charles River, their journey taking them out of Boston and into Cambridge. The red bricks and ivy of the world's most famous university rose before them in the twilight, mocking Magnuson and his GED high school equivalency degree. *Well, fuck them.* He could kick their asses, his wife was hotter than most of them would ever see and he wasn't drowning under hundreds of thousands of dollars of student debt.

Just after dinner on a pleasant spring night, the streets of Harvard Square were packed. Packed with liberal pukes wearing backpacks and chinos and t-shirts with geeky wordplays. He was tempted to speed through the intersection and run a few of them down in the crosswalk, sending their lattes and laptops crashing to the pavement. Instead he braked gently and took a deep breath. *Patience.* The night would end with blood on his hands, no need to rush things.

The privacy glass slid open. "I have a message for you from Mr. Thorne," de Real said. "He'd like you to stop threatening him."

Magnuson smiled wryly. "Why doesn't he tell me himself?"

The Templar Commander did not respond. Perhaps he was not used to answering questions from underlings.

"Are the men in place?" de Real asked after a pause.

Magnuson scanned the messages on his phone. Six Templars had joined a half-dozen members of Kidon to form six two-person teams. He and the African Jew, Solomon, had roughed things out after lunch and then de Real and the Kidon leader had made a few small changes and approved the mission. "Teams one through six, all in place." Normally they wouldn't have rushed something like this, but the Palestinian activists' meeting was being held at the Central Square apartment of a female MIT student and it was doubtful that any of them would be armed. Or at least not heavily so. And it was a simple operation. These were college students, after all. Busybodies and idealists, with a random anarchist thrown in, most of them living off of daddy's dough. Nobody with any actual battlefield experience.

From Massachusetts Avenue Magnuson turned onto a side street of tightly-packed Victorian homes. He flashed his lights and an agent who had been saving a parking space pulled out to allow Magnuson to slip in. "That's the house, across the street," he said to de Real. "The apartment is on the first floor. Entrance on the side porch."

"Private?"

"Yes."

"Good. I don't want to target any innocents."

"Three girls live in the apartment. One from MIT and two going to Boston University. All active in SJP. Plus whoever shows up at the meeting. I think anyone coming out that door tonight is fair game."

Out of the shadows a tall, angular man suddenly appeared on the sidewalk next to Magnuson, startling him, his wolf-like eyes peering through the driver's side window. Something about the stare held Magnuson in place. Only when he realized that the eyes resembled his own did he scramble from his seat to open the rear door for the elderly Jew.

Well past midnight Meryn and her Druze friends finally got to the point of their meeting. Uddin, the heavy-set man in the dark robe, was apparently on his way to Boston, his flight from Beirut conveniently delayed to allow for this conversation.

"I don't understand," Meryn said. "If you have the spiral, why do you need Gottlieb?"

The olive-skinned woman weighed her response. A few days ago Meryn had said the Crones did not know each other, did not meet. Obviously this was some kind of exception to that rule. Which, Amanda guessed, meant something of vital importance was transpiring. Amanda studied the woman. Where Meryn exuded warmth and nurturing, Jamila sat stiffly, almost imperiously, her visage unchanging as her large black eyes drank in the scene around her. "We cannot make the spiral function," Jamila said. "We have put our best scientists on the job." She glared at Uddin. "Still the solution escapes us."

Uddin spoke. "We are hoping that this time, finally, Gottlieb will show us his secrets. He is like a chef who shares his recipe but omits a key ingredient." Uddin explained how Abraham had allowed them to examine his mechanical device and had demonstrated how, using their spiral in his device, he could transform bismuth into gold. But the Druze had failed in their attempts to reproduce the process back in Lebanon.

Jamila replied, "We have leverage over him. Why not use it?"

"The problem with leverage such as this is that once you use it, it is gone. We have successfully extorted him by threatening to reveal his secret. But once the secret is revealed, he has no reason to cooperate with us."

Amanda didn't understand what this leverage might be. But she did understand how important it would be for the Atlantean descendants—or for anyone, for that matter—to be able to produce gold. Jamila's next comment jarred her out of her musings. "Once we obtain the secret, we can finally eliminate him."

Meryn shifted uncomfortably in her chair, apparently not ready for Amanda to be privy to this plan. "That will require a vote of the Crones."

Jamila waved the comment away. "We are in agreement." She fixed her eyes on Meryn.

"You do not know that," Meryn countered.

"What the others do not know can not hurt them."

Meryn shook her head. "No. If we are going to take such extreme measures it must be by vote. We need a conclave."

Jamila seethed, her black eyes reflecting the restaurant lights like smoldering charcoal. "Very well. I will instruct the intermediary to make arrangements. Where and when?"

"As senior Crone it is for you to decide. But it should be soon."

Jamila stared at the far wall. "Since Gottlieb is in Boston, that is where we shall meet. We can monitor things from there. Three days hence. Saturday."

"*Assuming* we decide to proceed, it will not be easy," Meryn said. "Gottlieb is surely well-guarded. And we do not exactly have a hit squad at our disposal." She turned to the robed man. "Uddin, when you visit Gottlieb, how is security?"

He bowed his head. "Very tight. It is designed to appear lax, but there are hidden cameras throughout his house and a squad of well-trained ex-soldiers act as armed guards."

Amanda wasn't just going to go along with 'eliminating' someone. She interrupted and asked the obvious question. "Why? Why does he need to be eliminated?"

Meryn responded, though Amanda got the sense she was irritated by the inquiry. And also the sense she might be holding something back. "The Crones have always been women. It has been so for hundreds of generations. Gottlieb's mother died and he claimed the spiral. He refuses to yield to a female relative. I mentioned to you that we lost a family during the Holocaust; I used the word 'lost' in a figurative sense only. We know where Gottlieb is. But he is a rogue, refusing to follow the rules set forth for the outpost families. He brings unnecessary attention to himself and by doing so he puts us all in danger." She smiled sadly and shrugged. "Hopefully he will step aside. But if not he may leave us no choice."

Trey and Solomon sat in a coffee shop in Central Square on a Wednesday evening, his five fingers clasping her three across the table. Lovers killing an hour, sharing a corn muffin. It was their cover and also their reality.

Solomon checked his phone for texts. "People have arrived at the meeting. Fourteen of them. Meeting started a half hour ago, so that's probably everyone." His playful nature had disappeared, replaced by the cold operative. Even his hands had turned cold.

She shifted in her chair, her body alive with adrenaline. She missed it, missed the high and the thrill and even the danger. Not that this was a high-risk operation. But every operation had its dangers; something could always go wrong. "With six teams, that means eight people get off free. Plus the host. Why not expand the operation and go after everyone?" Despite her military experience de Real had not chosen her to plan the operation. Old-boy habits died quickly. But Solomon had shared the plans with her.

"If we do our job with six, the others will get the message. This is meant to be an operation of deterrence, not retribution."

She nodded. Okay then. "You want to head over?" She reached for the backpack at her feet.

"Soon. With a group this large, it will be impossible to hold a meeting of less than an hour."

"Are you saying us Americans are opinionated?"

The playful Solomon appeared for a few seconds. "I'm saying you like to hear yourselves talk, even when you really have nothing to say."

She arched an eyebrow and squeezed his hand. "Maybe if we had better things to do, we wouldn't feel the need to talk so much."

"I will keep that in mind." He checked his texts, then his watch. "Teams are beginning to get into position." He pushed back his chair. "We should do the same."

She popped the last bite of the muffin into her mouth and grabbed the backpack. "Ready. Let's do this."

Walking slowly, bouncing together as lovers did, they wandered toward the meeting site, up one side of the street and down the other, killing some time cuddling on a neighborhood park bench, trying to stay in the shadows as much as possible—even in liberal Cambridge a biracial couple would leave an imprint on some people's minds. Solomon checked his texts every minute or so. The meeting began at 8:00; they had been walking the streets since 8:55; a few minutes before 9:30 he read a text and nodded. "It is time."

They had been designated Team 4, which meant they were responsible for the fourth person to leave the meeting. Trey knew Solomon had been tempted to designate himself as Team 1, but he wanted to observe the first three teams in action before leaving the site himself. A tall young man with a pony tail and goatee loped down the porch steps; Magnuson and one of Solomon's men, both dressed in business suits as if coming from an after-work event, fell in behind and followed him back toward Massachusetts Avenue and the Central Square subway station. Teams 2 and 3—one a pair of male joggers and the other a couple walking a dog—locked onto two women strolling together in the opposite direction.

"We're next," Trey said, knowing her words were not necessary. She shifted the backpack to her left shoulder, where she could use her good right hand to grab what she needed from it. Solomon removed a bottle and a thick cloth from the bag, then replaced the bottle.

"I hope it is a man," Solomon replied. "I prefer not to commit violence against women."

She squeezed his arm. "If it's a woman, I'll handle it."

He nodded and grunted in reply, his eyes resting on hers in a silent thank you.

Solomon got his wish. A swarthy twenty-something man carrying a satchel and smoking a cigarette bounded down the stairs, his eyes alert for danger.

"Good," Solomon breathed. "It is Labban."

They recognized him as one of the ringleaders, a Pakistani attending Northeastern University. Walking briskly, Labban cut through the park Trey and Solomon had been canoodling in only minutes earlier. "Here would be good," Solomon growled.

"Agreed."

Picking up their pace, they began to talk loudly, laughing and haranguing as if they had had a few too many drinks. Skipping now, they closed the distance on their prey. As Labban passed through some shadows on the edge of the park, Trey called out, "Hey, I think you dropped this."

Labban stopped and turned as Trey, squatting, lifted a set of keys from the ground. He scowled and patted at his front pocket, the cigarette hanging from the side of his mouth. "Those are not mine."

She moved forward. "Are you sure? I just saw them fall from your pocket."

Silently Solomon repositioned himself. With a single stride he closed from behind, his right arm circling Labban's neck in a choke hold while his left hand pinned a chloroform-soaked rag over his mouth and nose. Trey leapt forward and kicked Labban's feet out from under him and punched him in the solar plexus. The combination of the chloroform and a spasming diaphragm quickly disabled Labban. Solomon, his grip vice-like, dragged him off the path into an unlit corner of the park and waited for the last of Labban's fight to ebb as the chemical took effect.

Ten seconds later Solomon exhaled and loosened his grip. "Okay." Labban slumped to the ground.

Fumbling inside the backpack, Trey removed a black-handled box-cutter and released the blade to its most shallow setting. As she moved toward Labban, the Pakistani suddenly uncoiled, a metallic object flashing as it slashed through the dim light. "Solomon, look out!" she hissed. "He has a knife."

Solomon had loosened not only his grip but also his attention. As Labban swung the blade toward him, Solomon raised his arm to block the blow. But Labban had timed his attack well, knocking the larger man back. Seeing his captor off-balance, Labban jumped to his feet and spun to make a second attack, the knife this time aimed at Solomon's midsection.

The next few seconds passed in a blur. Trey took two strides and leapt, her legs outstretched. As she soared, she focused on the back of Labban's neck and kicked out, all of her power and energy concentrated on the stem linking the monster's head to his body. She exploded into him, the force of her blow sending him tumbling forward. He landed face-first, the knife skittering away.

Solomon bent over the prone Labban, lifted his head and shoved the chloroform rag back over his mouth and nose. Again Labban's body fell limp, this time apparently for real.

Trey smiled, even as her heart thudded in her chest. "I think you owe me one." Then she noticed the blood running down Solomon's arm. The knife had caught him near the wrist. She reached for him. "That didn't get your vein, did it?"

He closed his hand over the wound. "No. But it is a significant cut. Do you have a bandage?"

At the bottom of her backpack she found the first aid kit and helped him tape the wound. "Quickly," he said, his left hand pressuring the bandage on his right forearm. "We need to hurry. The commotion might bring trouble. Give me the box cutter."

She turned to Labban, then back to Solomon. "No. There's no way you can do this with that cut." She knelt over their prisoner and turned him onto his back.

"Very well." Solomon moved out of the shadows, searching the park. "We are alone. But please hurry."

Nodding, she took a deep breath. She had never done anything like this, anything so ... savage. She was glad it was Labban on the ground in front of her rather than one of the idealistic but misguided college students—he was a true enemy, hatred in his heart for Westerners, no different than the ISIS radicals terrorizing Europe and the Middle East. He carried a student visa rather than a suicide vest, but he was no less dangerous.

Even so, her hand shook as it held the blade. She closed her eyes and pictured the terror of the Paris nightclub massacre, imagined herself and her friends inside. She let out another long breath and gritted her teeth. Might as well do the cross first, it would be easier. Applying medium pressure, she dug the blade about a sixteenth of an inch into the upper part of Labban's right cheek. As if opening a box, she slid the blade along, the blood bubbling and marking the four-inch incision running to his jaw line.

"Good," Solomon said. "Now across. Not too deep."

Her hand still shaking, she completed the cross, going from nose to ear to form a lowercase 't' letter.

"Okay," he urged. "Now the star."

She turned Labban's head to give herself a flat surface, the smell of stale cigarette smoke wafting over her. This time she carved a triangle, the point at the top of his cheekbone. Over it she carved another triangle, this one inverted. Together they formed the Star of David.

Swallowing back her nausea, she pulled away. "What next?"

A voice from deeper in the shadows startled her. She spun, on guard, "I will handle it from here." Out stepped the Holocaust survivor, Abraham, his gray eyes piercing the night. "You two have done well. Go."

Solomon raised his chin. "I would prefer to stay, sir."

Abraham nodded. "Very well. This will not take long." He glanced at his soldier's wound. "Then you will need to take care of that. You know the protocol." From the pocket of his trench coat Abraham removed a sandwich bag and unsealed it. The stench identified it immediately as fresh feces. He slid his right hand into a latex glove and, using his index finger, inserted the waste into each of Labban's nostrils. He then dropped a golf ball–sized wad into Labban's flaccid mouth. Finally Abraham removed what looked to be an MP3 player from another pocket, plugged in a set of headphones, inserted the pods into Labban's ears, pressed play and raised the volume to full. The metallic sound of Hatikva, the Israeli national anthem, filled the quiet of the park. "It is an endless loop," he said by way of explanation.

Trey stared at the sight, transfixed. Then she understood. Five senses. All of them triggered to offer painful reminders to Labban of this night. He would taste and smell the feces for months, long after the foul excretions had been washed from his orifices. Just as he would long hear the anthem, now blaring deep into his subconscious. The pain from the incisions would throb for weeks. And of course the cross and star would scar him for a lifetime, the face he both saw in the mirror and showed to the world a constant reminder of Kidon's retribution.

"But won't the police know who did this, based on the star and the national anthem?" Trey asked.

"Yes," Abraham answered. "And so will Labban's friends." He shook his head sadly. "It does not have to be this way. But nor can we ignore the realities of the world we live in. Animals like this would take our heads, would rape our women, would butcher our children. What we do is infinitesimally less severe." He turned to lead them from the park. "Hopefully it is enough."

Xifeng crouched behind a tree on the far side of the park, her night vision goggles illuminating the strange events in the Cambridge park. Now things were getting interesting. The Gunn woman was apparently out of state, the Sharpie with Xifeng's tracking device transmitting uselessly in their Westford home. That was another problem with Western women—they couldn't be counted on even to keep the same pocketbook for more than a few days.

The dog, on the other hand, kept her collar on. With the Gunn woman away, Xifeng had turned her attention to the husband, Thorne. Through the listening device on the collar Xifeng had overheard a conversation that might end up being the single most important accomplishment of her career. Thorne and a man named Manuel de Real discussed turning metal into gold. She replayed de Real's exact words in her mind: "*One of our members saw something interesting the other night. She's pretty sure she witnessed an older gentleman, a Holocaust survivor, turn metal into gold using a spiral necklace of some sort.*"

After consulting with her handler, she had followed de Real here, tonight. To Cambridge. To a car, seated in the back seat with a tall, elderly man.

Was it possible that in an incredible stroke of luck—or perhaps fate—she had stumbled from Thorne to de Real to Abraham Gottlieb all in one day? Could it really be him, the legend they called the Old Jew, the man who purportedly had the ability to turn lead into gold? Her government had been trying to eliminate him for decades. As the largest gold producer in the world, China was particularly vulnerable to the prospect of a glut of gold. She had been briefed on this matter because she was based in Boston, because her handlers figured someone, somewhere might spot him. Well, it seemed, she was that someone and here was that somewhere.

But what to do know? First, she needed to make sure that this really was the Old Jew. He had begun to amble across the park toward her, his two companions exiting in the other direction. Making a rash decision, she stuffed the goggles into her purse, moved out into an open area of the park, kicked off her shoes and began to perform Taijiquan, a ballet-like stretching exercise that millions of Chinese performed in parks every day. The Old Jew eyed her as he passed, one of her legs extended at right angles to her core. Hopefully he did not know the exercise was traditionally performed in the morning—the Chinese had an expression, "An hour in the morning is worth two at night." As he turned away, his nose and ears and lips and Adam's apple almost grotesque in size, she snapped a couple of pictures with her phone. The light was bad, and the angle not perfect, but with modern enhancement techniques they should be able to determine whether this indeed was the Old Jew. She doubted *Tian* in heaven would endeavor to create two men so ugly.

Grabbing her shoes, she scurried after him at a safe distance. If she could learn where he lived, tonight truly would be a night where fate had smiled upon her. She jumped on her scooter and turned the

corner in time to see him entering the dark sedan. As long as the
sedan stayed off the highway, there was no way she would lose the
trail.

Madame Radminikov lurched to her feet and rushed to greet
Abraham in the hallway as he pushed through the front door of his
Brookline home. He was not surprised to see her anxiety—she was
used to being on these missions, and fussed over the Kidon members
like a mother hen.

"How did it go?" she blurted.

He removed his coat and nodded, noticing the half-eaten tray of
pastries on the table in his kitchen behind her. "Without incident."

"Come, Abraham, I need more details than that. I've been
waiting for hours."

"Very well. Sit." He had no appetite, but he did sip some lemon-
flavored water after scrubbing his hands clean. They sat on either
side of the pastries. He gathered his thoughts. "We successfully ...
marked ... six of the activists. Fortunately one of them was Labban.
I added a few special enhancements for him." The operation was
meant as a deterrent, but for thugs like Labban a bit of retribution
was also justified.

"Were there any glitches?"

"Nothing major. As I said, all six teams completed their
missions."

"How were the Templars to work with?"

He pursed his lips. "Excellent, in fact. Better than could be
expected. Commander de Real provided his best-trained men and
women."

"So they have proven to be useful allies?"

It was a bit premature to reach that conclusion. But it was a good
first step. "My goals tonight were threefold. First, to test our new
allies. As I said, they passed. Second was to, as the expression goes,
get the Templars to put some skin in the game. I want this to become
personal to them, as it is to us."

She nodded. "Getting blood on your hands can make things
personal pretty quickly."

"Yes. And third, I of course wanted to take action against SJP. I believe the proper message has been sent."

There was a fourth goal as well, one Abraham was not prepared to share. He told her only, "I have a meeting tomorrow with de Real. He is bringing a lawyer to advise him, a man named Cameron Thorne who is also an expert on the Templars and their early exploration of America." There were balls in play here that Madame Radminikov knew nothing about—one such ball was this Cameron Thorne. "I had hoped that our relationship with de Real would also bring Thorne into our orbit."

'Hoped' was actually not the right word. 'Needed' was more accurate.

Chapter 7

Amanda and Meryn grabbed a few hours sleep at a furnished apartment owned by Uddin in downtown Beirut. Meryn woke her before the sun rose. "Our driver will be here in twenty minutes." Apparently Atlanteans didn't believe in sleep.

Amanda took a quick shower and put on some clean clothes. She had guessed where their next stop would be, but asked anyway.

"Baalbek," came the one word reply in confirmation. Neither brought up last night's conversation about eliminating Abraham Gottlieb. Amanda would never be part of a plan like that. And she guessed Meryn had sensed her opposition.

They drove northeast into the fertile Bekaa Valley toward the border with Syria. As they moved east, the sky darkened above them in the morning light as if warning them away from the war-torn Syrian border. They again rode in an SUV; this time the driver had an armed companion, both of them supplied by Uddin. Amanda read about Baalbek in the backseat alongside Meryn.

The site itself was ancient, she read, showing signs of habitation going back at least nine thousand years. During Biblical times the Phoenicians built a temple dedicated to their god, Baal. Later the conquering Romans built atop the existing foundation, rededicated the site to their sun god, Jupiter, and renamed the site Heliopolis. But the earlier Phoenician temple may itself have been built upon an even more ancient sacred site. Amanda read aloud to Meryn from the website she had found: *"Long before the Romans conquered the site and built their enormous temple of Jupiter, long even before the Phoenicians constructed a temple to the god Baal, there stood at Baalbek the largest stone block construction found in the entire world."*

Meryn nodded. "This information is accurate. The massive foundation stones predate even the Phoenicians." She pointed as the site rose in the distance, framed by the dark storm clouds. "There. You can see for yourself."

They walked from the vehicle toward the complex, the absence of sun somehow appropriate in light of the dilapidated condition of the temple built to glorify it. The wind messed her hair as Amanda stared at the massive structure. A span of six pillars from the two-thousand-year-old Temple of Jupiter stood atop a foundation itself many thousands of years older. Amanda snapped a picture, knowing the image could not do justice to the super-human scale of the stonework.

Baalbek, Lebanon

She approached the wall, circling around, dwarfed by the foundation stones—six massive blocks, each about the size of a railroad caboose, each weighing (she had read) four hundred tons. "Four hundred tons," she whispered. That was 800,000 pounds. How had ancient man quarried, transported and lifted these into place?

But these 400-ton stones were themselves dwarfed by a triad of blocks that sat atop them. Called the Trilithon, these monstrosities weighed eight hundred tons and approximated the size of a ranch-style home with attached one-car garage. Incredibly, they sat atop the smaller blocks. She took another picture, purposefully including a pair of black-clad, ant-like tourists standing in a gap on the wall to show scale.

Baalbek Trilithon Blocks (second row up)

She stared at the foundation wall. Who had decided to raise these massive 1.6 million pound colossuses fourteen feet in the air? Why not use them as base pieces? And having decided for some reason to raise them, how did they do so? All of this, of course, was exactly what Meryn wanted her to ponder.

As if on cue, her great-aunt appeared by her side. "Believe it or not, there are even larger blocks in the quarry nearby." She showed Amanda an image on her phone. "This is called the Pregnant Lady. A perfect match to the Trilithon stones. She weighs over a thousand tons. Believed to be the largest stone ever quarried."

Baalbek, "Pregnant Lady" Stone

Amanda exhaled. With the house in the background for scale she got a true sense of the enormity of the block. "Why was it not moved to the site?"

Meryn smiled. "I think a better question is how was it possible the other blocks *were* moved?"

Amanda shrugged. Eight hundred tons, one thousand tons—the numbers were so vast she could not relate them to anything. "Could they be rolled over logs?"

"No. Even the hardest cedar would be crushed under their weight."

"Well, someone moved them, somehow."

Meryn continued. "And beyond moving them, they are so precisely cut, and so expertly fit together, that one could not even slide a playing card between the blocks."

Amanda took a deep breath. The Romans had done some amazing things technologically. And this was not the same as the Gobekli Tepe site, indisputably dating back to before the invention of writing and the wheel. She said so.

"I agree. The Romans could have built this foundation. But if so, why did they leave the Pregnant Lady in the quarry? They needed thousands of blocks of stone after putting the Trilithon stones in place."

"Maybe they decided it was too much hassle to move the Pregnant Lady, so they used smaller blocks instead."

Meryn angled her head. "Possibly. But then why not cut the Pregnant Lady into smaller pieces? It is a beautiful stone, already squared and already quarried. And it matches the other foundation stones. The Romans were nothing if not practical."

Amanda shrugged. "I don't know."

"I think you do. It is a simple matter of common sense."

Amanda stared at the ruins. Why waste the enormous block? Then it hit her. "How far away is the quarry?"

"Half a mile."

"And is it out in the open?"

"Now. Only recently was it unearthed. Or re-unearthed."

"So maybe the Romans didn't know about it."

Meryn smiled. "It seems not."

"Which means they probably quarried their stone from another site."

"Go on."

"And if they didn't know about it, and it matches the Trilithon, that means they didn't quarry the Trilithon stones either. Someone else did it. Earlier. With advanced technology."

Meryn nodded. "And the geology backs this up. The weathering on the Trilithon stones is thousands of years more advanced than the Temple of Jupiter additions." The sun broke through, casting beams of light on the cragged Trilithon stones as if to highlight their antiquity. "There is simply no way the Romans built this foundation." She turned away from the ruins, her blue dress swishing as the winds picked up, and called back over her shoulder as she left Amanda to ponder the mystery of the site. "Did I mention that Mount Hermon is just a day's walk from here?"

Mount Hermon. Ancestral homeland of the Druze. Of the Watchers.

Pak pressed his nose against the window of the taxi as the driver navigated his way through Boston. Consulting a tourist map, Pak noted Massachusetts General Hospital, the State House dome, the famous Beacon Hill and Back Bay neighborhoods. Turning his head, he spotted a soaring obelisk, the Bunker Hill Monument. Across the Charles River, filled with sailboats on a breezy spring day, he recognized the famous MIT library dome. In the distance the buildings of Harvard—he desperately wanted a sweatshirt, though he knew he could never wear it in public. Then Fenway Park and parts of the Boston Marathon route. So many things to see in just a fifteen-minute ride. He hoped their meeting would go quickly to allow for some sightseeing, jet-lag be damned.

Uddin had been a pleasant, albeit reticent, travel companion. Now, finally, as they approached their destination not far from Fenway Park, the burly man spoke. "I told you that the gold-making technology has not been perfected. That is not entirely true. It has in fact been perfected here in Boston. Our problem has been in reproducing it in Lebanon."

The taxi stopped on a tree-lined side street in front of a large, three-story, red-brick home with black cast iron fencing surrounding it and thick shrubbery shielding it from the street. The sound of the nearby highway hummed as Uddin and Pak were met on the front walkway by a tall, black-skinned man wearing a windbreaker and blue workpants, the bulge of a firearm evident beneath the waistband. Hidden from the street by the shrubbery, the guard thoroughly searched the visitors before stepping aside. Pak thought the security a bit loose until they then had to pass through an airport-like body scan machine on the front porch, this overseen by another armed security operative.

Other than the security personnel there didn't seem to be anyone on duty. Uddin and Pak stood on the far side of the body-scanner for a few minutes before Uddin shrugged and rang the doorbell. An older, angular man in a three-piece suite, whom Pak assumed was the butler, greeted them. He tried to hide his surprise when Uddin introduced the man as Abraham Gottlieb.

Pak had rehearsed his lines for this moment. "Mr. Gottlieb, it is an honor and a pleasure…" He stopped when his host waved the comment away and spun on his heels.

"Perhaps I should have mentioned that Gottlieb is not much for ceremony," Uddin whispered." Uddin must have told Abraham his plan to share the gold-making secret with the North Koreans. Pak wondered what the Jew had demanded in return.

They followed Gottlieb down a hallway to a door which led to a steep, creaky staircase. Their host flicked on a light, the smell of heating oil wafting over Pak as they descended. They circled around behind the staircase where Gottlieb spun a dial on a steel door set in the concrete wall and ushered them inside an old bank vault with a workbench along the side wall.

Uddin pulled a dark gray, fist-sized stone from a pocket beneath his robes. "Bismuth."

Gottlieb shook his head. "It is not that I don't trust you, Uddin, but I cannot risk putting your sample into my device without examining it first. If it is not pure bismuth, it could damage my electronics." From a drawer beneath the workbench he pulled another stone, similar to Uddin's. "My geologist has certified this sample."

He handed it to Pak. The stone felt cold and heavy in his hand. Pak's heart raced. He had expected something futuristic, with white walls and microscopes and bespectacled scientists in lab coats. He eyed a rusty sink in the corner. Was this really the place where magic took place? He thought of the old Frankenstein movie which sometimes played on Lebanese television.

Gottlieb took the bismuth back from Pak and placed it, along with a metal spiral, in a water-filled box connected to an electrical device. He handed his guests goggles, flicked a switch, counted to eight and flicked the switch a second time. Using a thick pair of gloves and fireplace tongs, he pushed the lid off the box, removed the bismuth and rinsed it in the sink. But it was not bismuth. It had turned coppery in color. Gottlieb dried the sample with a towel and handed the metal, still warm to the touch, to Pak as if offering a cigarette. "You can keep it if you want. It is gold."

Pak would love to have kept it for himself. "Thank you," he stammered. But he knew it had to be tested.

Gottlieb turned to Uddin. "We can try it again with your spiral, if you'd like."

He repeated the process using another chunk of bismuth and the Druze leader's spiral. Same result, Uddin pocketing the second chunk of gold.

Uddin bowed his head. "Thank you for again demonstrating this amazing technology. May I, again, photograph your device?" He pulled out a small camera.

Gottlieb nodded curtly and stepped aside. "Perhaps the problem is that you are not using a pure enough specimen of bismuth. You might want to try to obtain samples from Bolivia, as I do."

Pak stood stoically to the side while Uddin photographed the capacitor. It looked simple enough. He was tempted to photograph it himself; no doubt the Korean engineers could reproduce it. But without the spiral necklace it was worthless. He glanced at the Druze leader. A bear of a man, he could best Pak in a fight. But how hard would it be to snatch the necklace while Uddin slept? Pak shook the thought aside. No reason to risk the operation with anything so rash. At least not yet.

Cam spent the morning at Brandeis, teaching his class and afterward holding office hours. Now, dressed in a dark suit and blue tie, he arrived for a lunchtime meeting at Manuel de Real's posh office in a repurposed granite warehouse building overlooking

Boston Harbor near the city's North End. A polished mahogany sign in an old-style script greeted visitors: 'Global de Real Import-Export, Inc.' That could mean anything, Cam knew. And probably did.

A shapely blond receptionist escorted him to a conference room that looked like the library of a European country estate, dark leather and plush carpeting and the smell of cigar smoke contributing to the sense of old money. He declined a midday cocktail and sat in a leather recliner, peering east out the window at the Atlantic in the direction of de Real's home country of Portugal. Was it possible, in ancient times, that a vast continent had loomed over the mid-Atlantic? If not, a lot of intelligent people were wasting a lot of time on nothing.

And if not, where did these strange spiral necklaces come from? For something supposedly so rare and valuable, somehow three of them had passed through Boston over the past week: Amanda's, Meryn's and now apparently Abraham Gottlieb's.

The door opened, interrupting Cam's musings. Manuel de Real escorted a tall, elderly man with a long face and gray, piercing eyes into the room. Cam swallowed his surprise as he recognized the man with the Holocaust tattoo from his lecture last Friday. Abraham Gottlieb, obviously. Which meant this meeting had probably been Gottlieb's idea all along. A linebacker-sized black man marched into the conference room and frisked Cam before nodding and withdrawing.

"Mr. Thorne sometimes provides legal advice to our group," de Real said by way of introduction.

Gottlieb nodded and offered a perfunctory handshake. "You can dispense with the pretense, Mr. de Real," he said in a thick German accent. "I am familiar with Mr. Thorne and his work. He is here because he is curious about the spiral necklace your underling, I believe her name is Trey, observed this past weekend." Still standing, Gottlieb's expressionless eyes shifted back and forth between Cam and de Real. "I, in turn, have not objected to his presence because I believe he may have knowledge about another similar necklace." Gottlieb then sat down in the lone straight-backed chair in the room. "Now that we have cleared away the pretenses, we can get down to business. I am a busy man, as I am sure are the both of you."

Chuckling, de Real took a seat between Cam and Gottlieb. "You don't like to beat around the bush, do you Abraham?"

"I am too old to beat bushes," he said unsmilingly.

Cam actually appreciated the man's bluntness. He met it in kind. "So does it work? Can these spirals really turn metal into gold?"

Gottlieb took Cam's measure, the hard eyes of a man who had spent a lifetime judging others and who was alive only because of his skill in doing so. "It does. It can."

Cam hadn't expected such a direct response. He didn't really have a follow-up question other than the obvious. "How?"

"That is proprietary, Mr. Thorne. But the fact I have divulged this much shows that I trust you to be careful with this information. It is not something I wish to publicize." He folded his long-fingered hands together in his lap. "But now I have a question for you: Would you be willing to allow me to test the necklace your wife possesses?"

Cam's fingers tingled, as they often did when danger lurked. "How do you know about that?"

Abraham flicked the question aside with a backhanded movement of his hand. "It is enough that I do."

Cam knew he could not agree to such a request. He turned his palms to the ceiling. "I can't make that decision without her. And she is out of the country now." But he would like to have someone with Gottlieb's expertise examine the spiral. "I will ask."

With barely a nod, Gottlieb turned to de Real. "Now, you wished to meet to discuss this arrangement of ours?"

Cam blinked. Why had Gottlieb redirected the conversation? After a few seconds he realized what had just happened. Somehow the old fox had gotten him to admit that Amanda possessed the necklace and also that Amanda was out of the country. Which was probably everything he hoped to learn from Cam today.

Meryn's Gulfstream jet sat on the tarmac in Beirut's broiling midday sun, its air-conditioner cutting the humidity but doing little to reduce the heat inside the aircraft. Amanda wore a pair of cargo shorts, a blouse and some flip-flops, fanning herself with a magazine. Meryn, as always, wore a flowing blue-green dress—no two were exactly alike, but they all served to both bring out the aquamarine of her eyes and convey a sense of watery movement.

"So, where to next?" Amanda asked.

Meryn studied her for a few seconds. "That depends on you," her normal kind smile absent.

"How so?"

"I have shown you everything you need to see. Now I'd like to hear your thoughts. Take your time."

Amanda shifted in her seat, the back of her legs sticking to the leather. For the past three-and-a-half days she had thought of little else beside Atlantis. She reviewed the evidence in her mind. There were the alien-metal spirals themselves, of course. Not to mention the matching, tentacled Frost Valley Petroglyph. But there was so much more. She scrolled through the voluminous mental checklist of additional evidence she had compiled:

1. Plato's dating. His date of Atlantis sinking 11,600 years before present was a dead match with whatever massive calamity ended the last Ice Age. The dating was too specific, and too ancient, to be a coincidence.
2. Eels and butterflies. The migratory and spawning patterns of eels, butterflies and (according to Meryn) birds pointed strongly to the existence of some ancient landmass in the middle of the Atlantic.
3. Native American ruins. The Tikal pyramid carving, depicting an ancient city falling into the ocean due to a volcanic eruption while people escaped by boat, offered compelling evidence that the Atlantis catastrophe was remembered by Native American cultures. And the commonality of black-hatted, broom-riding European and Native American witches pointed to a single source for these ancient crones.
4. Azores geology. Based on Cam's research, the bathymetry around the Azores islands matched Plato's description of the Atlantis topography and size. And the existence of fresh water fossils and beach sand indicated the lands now underwater once crested above the Atlantic, as explained by the geological phenomenon called isostatic rebound.
5. Early maps. European maps from the 14th through 17th centuries, presumably based on ancient maps from the Middle East, all showed a large land mass identified as

Frisland located south of Iceland along the northern Mid-Atlantic Ridge.

6. Linguistics. The antiquity of the Basque language, and that it did not have a common origin with the other Indio-European tongues, indicated the existence of some ancient culture in the Pyrenees Mountains. The word for knife, meaning 'stone that cuts,' proved the Stone Age origin of the language.

7. European Cave art. The sophisticated cave paintings in and around the Pyrenees Mountains spoke to an ancient culture inhabiting the area before the last Ice Age. This culture venerated the bison, as purportedly did the Atlanteans.

8. Venus of Dolni. Like the cave art, the kiln-fired ceramic figurine indicated the presence of a technologically-advanced civilization in Europe dating back tens of thousands of years. And this civilization, like Atlantis, was apparently goddess-worshiping.

9. Sanskrit writings and other ancient sources. Early writings from Sumer, India, Egypt and Phoenicia all told of an ancient, advanced society located in the mid-Atlantic. All used words nearly identical to 'Atlantis' in naming this land.

10. Red Paint burials. In addition to the Red Paint burials Cam had unearthed along the Massachusetts coast dating back to just after the end of the last Ice Age, other ancient Red Paint burials had been found along the Atlantic rim in Mexico, northern Spain, the Orkney Islands and Scandinavia. Since it was unlikely that this distinctive burial custom evolved independently amongst these varied cultures, it was likely this practice originated in an ancient culture common to each. And the technologically-advanced tools and weapons found in these burial sites pointed to a culture far more advanced than the Native American cultures that followed.

11. Gobekli Tepe. The sophistication of the site, built just as the last Ice Age ended and six thousand years before 'civilization' was supposed to have begun, spoke to an ancient advanced society. And the odd technological regression of the site, with each successive addition to the temple complex growing more rudimentary, was consistent with an advanced culture unable to perpetuate itself.

12. The Sphinx. Water damage to the base of the Sphinx predated the age of the Pharaohs (and in fact may date back to the end of the last Ice Age), and earlier Egyptians did not have the ability to construct anything so elaborate.
13. Baalbek. Both the weathering patterns on the massive Trilithon blocks and the fact that other Trilithon-sized blocks were left unused in the quarry indicated that the original construction of the site predated the Roman repurposing of the temple. Pre-Roman cultures did not possess the skills and tools needed to quarry, lift and move the massive blocks of stone.

And it was all held together by the Bible stories, the Old Testament tales of a tribe of large-statured, technologically-advanced 'Watchers' living in isolation on Lebanon's Mount Hermon who eventually came down to breed with the locals, producing oversized offspring. Plus Meryn had hinted at DNA tests that linked the Basques, Druze and other Atlantic Rim peoples together.

This all ran through Amanda's mind in less than a minute, Meryn waiting patiently for her to organize her thoughts. "If you're asking if you've made your case, if you've convinced me that the legends of the ancient Atlantis colony are true, then yes. You've convinced me."

"But?" Meryn had sensed there was more.

"Well, I'm still not sure why it all matters. I mean, it does from a historical perspective—the world should know about this. But why does it matter to you personally, to the other Crones?" She paused. "Why should it matter to me? I'm ... human. Just like everyone else. So what if I have a bit more Atlantean blood in me? Unless you're making the argument that we are some kind of super race, who cares?"

"Not a super race, no." Meryn's blue-green eyes held Amanda. "But history teaches lessons, and we—the descendants of Atlantis— remember those lessons. We know the dangers of a male-dominated society. It destroyed Atlantis, and it threatens to destroy us again today. We are finally in a position today, after hundreds of generations, to restore the Crones to their rightful place as leaders of humanity. That is what we are fighting for." She paused for effect. "It is not a super *race* you belong to, Amanda. It is a super *gender*.

A gender with an awareness, an insight, an innate understanding of how the world should be."

Amanda considered herself a feminist but she didn't go so far as to think of women as a superior version of humanity. Balance, as in all things, was the key. "You are speaking in generalities. What precisely is it you want from me?"

Meryn stared out the window of the plane, as if looking for inspiration from her ancestors atop Mount Hermon. "Last night we briefly discussed Abraham Gottlieb. Almost seventy years have passed and this man"—she almost spit the words—"refuses to step aside. In fact, we have strong reason to believe he is using the necklace for his own personal profit." She paused again. "We want you to retrieve the necklace from him."

This she had not expected. "Me? Why me of all people?"

"Because your Cameron has worked his way into this man's circle." Meryn described the recent alliance between Gottlieb and the Knights Templar. "This is the first time Gottlieb has let his guard down, has allowed any but his close circle of Jewish cohorts to get near to him. This is our best and perhaps only chance."

Amanda turned away, her arms crossing involuntarily in what she knew was a reflection of her discomfort with her great-aunt's proposal. "Even if I could get to him—and I'm hardly qualified to be some kind of operative—why would I agree to this? This Gottlieb has done nothing wrong." She locked eyes with Meryn. "Other than be born with a penis."

Meryn's eyes turned the color of the storm clouds over Baalbek. But the storm passed quickly, her features softening as she took a deep breath and exhaled. "You are mistaken in your assumption. He has done many things wrong—many horrible, hateful, vile things." She poked at her phone, turning the screen toward Amanda. Amanda recoiled at the site of the ugly scars—a cross and a Jewish star— disfiguring the face of the young woman in the image. "This woman is a college student. Her only crime was to join a group supporting Palestinian human rights. For this, Abraham Gottlieb and his group of hateful vigilantes attacked her. And others. They castrated one man. They executed two others. Gottlieb is a powerful, ruthless, cold-blooded oligarch who maims and even kills with the same thoughtless regard as the rest of us swat away mosquitoes. Abraham has made his choice. His allegiance runs to his religion. He does not

care about Atlantis, does not care about the things we care about."
Her voice turned icy. She dropped the phone onto the table between
them. "This, the things in these images, is not the way of Atlantis.
He uses our spiral to fund his evil purposes. He defiles the spiral, and
us with it. This is not our path to a better society."

Amanda was not sure how to respond. "No. I suppose not."

The storm clouds returned to Meryn's blue-green eyes. "You
suppose?"

"No. Of course it is not."

"Then we must do something about it. All of us. Including you."

Before Amanda could respond Meryn stood abruptly and
marched toward the airplane's cockpit. Apparently she was going to
give Amanda time to consider if she really wanted to become a
Crone.

And do all that it entailed.

The call came in on Trey's cell phone while she was shopping
for fresh vegetables for tonight's dinner with Solomon. Her CIA
handler. It was not the time for their weekly call. So this must be
important. "Hold on," she said.

Leaving her shopping cart near the broccoli mister, she trotted
out of the Brighton supermarket into the parking lot. She held her
hand over one ear to block the Commonwealth Avenue street noise
and stood in the shade of a lonely elm to filter the midday sun.
"Okay," she said. "I'm alone." She knew the line was secure.

"We have a situation." Her handler was a woman, from the
sound of her voice a Midwesterner. But they had never met. "We
followed up on your gold-making report. You may be on to
something. Good work."

"Thanks."

"We think Gottlieb may be sharing this gold-making technology
with the Druze. You know who they are?'"

"Yes. I served in the Middle East."

"The Druze, in turn, may be sharing this technology with the
North Koreans."

Odd bedfellows. "Why?"

"Long story, and it doesn't really matter. But, assuming the technology really works, the last thing we want is for the North Koreans to be able to produce an unlimited amount of gold. The only thing keeping them from being the tyrant of Asia is that they have no money. Obviously a golden goose would change that."

"How much could they make? The block I saw was only about the size of a hot dog roll."

"But a chunk of pure gold that size is worth, say, fifty grand. And you said it only took a minute to make. I did the math. That's over twenty billion per year, just using one spiral."

"So what do you want me to do?"

"Ideally, get the spiral necklace. But even that might not be enough. There may be other copies of the necklace floating around. We need to get all of them."

Trey had agreed to go undercover, gather information, do whatever spies did. But she was not a trained operative. "How am I supposed to do that?"

"Stand by for specifics." Her handler paused. "But, Trey, we know about Solomon Massala. You should be prepared to leverage that relationship."

Magnuson was surprised he was not beckoned to Admiral Warner's office until after lunch. He dropped his sandwich, wiped his mouth, grabbed a pad of paper and jogged down the hall.

"Yes, sir."

"Sit down, Magnuson. We've no time for formalities."

His boss looked haggard, distracted. Normally Admiral Warner seemed to be in control, the puppet-master in a world of strings and stages. Today he looked like a man whose strings had become entangled.

Warner continued. "I've just finished a teleconference with our lawyers. New York, Washington, London. The best in the world." He offered a wry smile, matching his crooked bowtie. "Probably cost me twenty grand just for an hour of their time. Bottom line is that this U.N. treaty is ironclad. If there's any evidence of human activity going back more than a hundred years, no project can go forward. Let me repeat that: *any evidence of human activity.* That pretty much shuts down the entire Mid-Atlantic Ridge. No mining, no pipelines, no wind farms." He sighed. "Might as well tell us we can't use power tools."

Magnuson understood the catch here. "But only if someone can prove there was human activity, right?"

Warner slapped his desk with his palm like a judge dropping a gavel. "Yes. That is the key point. As long as Atlantis remains nothing more than a legend, this treaty will do nothing more than gather dust." He took a deep breath. "But Pandora desperately wants to get out of her box. We must not let that happen."

"I'm not sure what you mean by that. By Pandora."

"What I mean is that Thorne's wife was recently spotted at Baalbek. There is no doubt. They are on the trail of Atlantis. *Hot* on the trail."

Magnuson nodded. He didn't know what Baalbek was any more than he did Pandora, but obviously it was important. He repeated his words from yesterday. "Just tell me what to do."

The old man sighed. "I wish it hadn't come to this." He chewed his lip, his head moving slowly side to side. "In your experience with Thorne, is he the type of man who will back down in the face of threats?"

Magnuson considered the question. He didn't want to be put in a position where he might have to abduct the girl, this time for real. "He'll do whatever is necessary to protect his family. But he's got some powerful friends, including Commander de Real. So it's not like we can just push him around."

Admiral Warner stared at the map of Atlantis on the wall. "In business there are casualties, just as in war. The livelihood of thousands of people depends on Warner Industries' survival." He took a deep breath. "Make preparations to take Thorne. He and his wife need to be stopped."

Amanda sat alone in the plane's cabin, its lights dim and its air-conditioner running. Meryn had not returned from the cockpit, leaving Amanda with her thoughts. Should she agree to try to steal the spiral necklace from Abraham Gottlieb? If she did agree, could she succeed? She really wanted to hash this all out with Cam. And not by text or email or even over the phone.

Twenty minutes after she first left, Meryn flowed back into the cabin in her blue-green dress. She stood in front of her grand-niece, almost regal in appearance. "So, have you made your decision? The pilot is awaiting my instructions. He needs to submit a flight plan. And we need that necklace."

Amanda was not sure where else Meryn might be considering flying. But she had made up her mind. "I'd like to go home. I need to discuss this all with Cameron."

Meryn's eyes darkened. "This does not concern him."

"Of course it does. He and I are married. We have a daughter. Whatever happens to me happens to him."

Meryn sighed, her exasperation evident.

"Plus," Amanda continued, "you yourself said you want me to use him to get to Gottlieb. I can't very well do that without his assistance."

"Not true. You could easily fool him, trick him into helping you. For millennia women have manipulated their men."

"Perhaps. But I'll not be one of them."

The two women held each other's eyes for a few seconds until Meryn sighed again.

"Very well. If that is the price for your cooperation, so be it."

Amanda looked away. It suddenly occurred to her that perhaps Meryn was responsible for the fact that cell coverage had been so poor on the Gulfstream, making communication with Cam difficult. "Meryn, I still haven't agreed to help. All I have agreed to do is talk to Cameron about it."

Magnuson cursed under his breath as he strolled from Admiral Warner's office. He was happy to do the admiral's dirty work—that was his job. But things like pressuring an employee to resign and punching a guy in the jaw and even vandalizing an archeological dig were all misdemeanor-type offenses. The worst that could happen to him would be a slap on the wrist. But this—this order by Warner to abduct Thorne—could lead to some serious repercussions. He loved his job. But was he willing to go to jail for it?

Yet he couldn't really turn down a direct order. When a company paid you to do dirty work, they expected you not to mind getting your hands soiled.

He stopped in his office only long enough to grab his rucksack and jacket. Jumping into his Lexus SUV, he raced ten miles north on Route 93, exiting into downtown Manchester. Wheeling through the familiar, dreary streets of his old neighborhood, he cut down the narrow driveway of a clapboard apartment building and stopped in front of a cinder-block garage he rented for a hundred bucks a month, cash. He unlocked the door and tore the canvas off his Harley Fat Boy. He rarely rode anymore—he'd told his wife he had sold the bike. Wearing an old German military-style helmet with goggles, he sped north toward the White Mountains. Pushing eighty he flew along, the wind in his face and the smell of spring filling his nostrils. Someday he would get his pilot's license—until then, tearing across the asphalt on his windshield-less bike would have to do.

Somehow the engine roar quieted his senses, allowed him to think. It was a simple problem: Admiral Warner wanted Thorne silenced; Magnuson did not want to risk going to jail by doing so. The problem had no obvious solution so Magnuson fell back on one of the few sage pieces of advice his father had ever given him: If you're playing cards, and you've got a shitty hand, best thing to do is turn over the table. So how could he turn over the table here?

The answer came to him as he watched an eagle circle high above. *I'm not the only predator in this forest.* There were others who wanted things from Thorne. Others who wanted him silenced. Grinning, the wind forcing his lips back in what he imagined was a grotesque clown smile, Magnuson turned the throttle and watched the needle touch ninety. Admiral Warner didn't care *who* did the silencing, only that it be done.

Chapter 8

Amanda and Meryn took off from Beirut just before midnight on Thursday. Fleeing the sun, but not quite able to outrace it, they landed eleven hours later in Boston just as dawn broke.

Cam and Astarte had tracked the flight on Astarte's phone. They watched the Gulfstream taxi toward the near-empty international terminal against a blue-black sky.

"I've missed Mum," she said matter-of-factly.

Cam feigned insult. "What, you don't like my cooking?"

She rolled her eyes. "Peanut butter crackers and sliced cucumber is not cooking, Dad."

The truth was Cam had missed her also. The four days apart marked their longest separation. More to the point, so much had happened this week—it would take the entire weekend just to catch up on each other's adventures. And to make what Cam sensed would be an important decision. He replayed the conversation with Manuel de Real in his mind; the Templar Commander had pulled him aside after yesterday's lunch meeting with Abraham Gottlieb.

"You are, I assume, going to allow Gottlieb to examine this spiral of yours, yes?"

"I'm not sure. It's not mine, it's Amanda's."

The Templar had smiled sardonically. "Please, Cameron, let's not hide behind a woman's skirts. If you believe it is the wise thing, I'm sure you can convince your wife to go along."

Cam had lowered his voice in case any of Gottlieb's men were nearby. He let the chauvinism pass; when dealing with the leader of an order tracing its roots to a medieval male fighting force, one had to expect a certain amount of backwardness. "That's just it. I'm not sure it is the wise thing."

"Careful, Cameron," de Real had warned. "You do not want to make an enemy of Abraham Gottlieb. If he wants to see your necklace, I strongly suggest your response should be to ask when and where."

Despite the threat, Cam wasn't sure Amanda would see it the same way. In fact, he was pretty sure she would not.

Amanda lay on the bed—*her* bed—staring at the ceiling, her mind racing. Cam snored quietly next to her, his naked body atop a tangle of sheets. They had put Astarte on the bus and then fallen into bed like a couple of panting teenagers. Leaning over, she kissed him lightly on the cheek and breathed in his scent. So much had changed in the past four days. But not *everything*. Her body still trembled at his touch, her heart still raced at his smile.

She would have liked to lounge the rest of the morning away, maybe awaken Cam for another frolic. But the world had other plans for them.

After showering she threw on a pair of jeans and sweatshirt, Venus shadowing her around the house as she had done continuously since her return. She'd take an hour to go through mail and return a couple of phone calls. Then she would awaken Cameron. They had some decisions to make.

He wandered into the kitchen twenty minutes later. "I just had an amazing dream," he grinned, his hair sticking up at odd angles. "Nice to have you home."

She stood to embrace him. "Funny, I had the same dream."

After checking his blood sugar he poured himself some juice and opened a breakfast bar. "I want to hear all about your trip." They had exchanged dozens of texts but managed only a couple of short conversations. "I feel like you've been gone a month."

Using the photos on her phone as a guide, she spent the next hour taking him through her journey.

"So," he asked, "here's the obvious question. You buying this Atlantis stuff?"

She nodded. "I am. There's so much evidence. But it's the Plato thing that clinches it for me. He has the *exact* date. How could that be a coincidence?"

His smile conveyed his response: They didn't believe in coincidence when it came to their research. "So what happens next?" he asked.

She took a deep breath. "It turns out there's more to being a Crone than just passing down the family secrets." She explained Meryn's request that Amanda help steal Gottlieb's necklace. "They really despise the man. But I don't know how Meryn expects us to get in there. I mean, we can't just call him and ask to see his necklace."

Cam surprised her by not reacting right away. He stared out the window, his eyes tracking the flight of a blue heron over the lake but his mind clearly elsewhere. After a few seconds he said, "For someone who doesn't believe in coincidences, I have one for you. Meryn wants you to steal Abraham's necklace. Well, Abraham wants to test *your* necklace. In fact, he pretty much is insisting on it. So this might not be as hard as you think."

This changed things. Until now Amanda had believed there was no way even to get close to Abraham. "If we go there, he might end up keeping them both."

"Fair point."

"Which perhaps wouldn't be the worst thing. This necklace may be more hassle than it's worth." They discussed the possible risks and benefits of meeting with the Kidon leader. "Honestly," Amanda said, scratching Venus' neck, "from what I've heard of this Abraham I don't see any way we are going to just walk out of his house with his necklace."

"Agreed. He's about as cunning as anyone I've ever met. But worst case scenario is we learn more about your necklace by letting him test it. So maybe it's worth it. I'll make the call."

She smiled wryly. "Actually, worst case scenario is we go in there and never come out."

Barricaded inside the safe room of her suburban Boston home with her husband at work at his accounting firm, Xifeng pressed the transmitting device to her ear and listened as the Gunn woman and her husband discussed the spiral necklaces. This necklace must be the key to the Old Jew's ability to turn rock into gold. And it turned out there was more than one of these magic spirals. That doubled her chances to steal one.

Xifeng had called in sick today—her job as a booking agent for a local function hall offered her both flexible hours and the excuse to get out of the house when needed. If Abraham Gottlieb was going to open his house to strangers, she needed to be there. She quickly emailed a report to her handler, asking for permission to observe the meeting. He would surely give it. Not only was the possible glut of gold a threat to the Chinese economy, but her handler had explained that it was crucial that the North Koreans not get their hands on the gold-producing technology. The North Koreans had long been a puppet state of China, but lately the puppet—in the person of Kim Jong-un—had begun to tug back on his strings. For now Beijing could control its erratic ally by withholding financial aid. But an influx of gold could, and would, quickly change that.

The email came back immediately, approving her request. But observation would only be a preliminary step. At some point her government would need to examine a spiral, test it, determine whether it could indeed be used to product gold. Yes it might be risky. But why else had she spent the past seven years living among the foul-smelling, small-minded Americans?

Standing on the back deck overlooking the lake while a light morning mist fell, Cam dialed the number on the card Abraham Gottlieb had given him. From his years as an attorney he was used to the rhythm and pace of these calls—a receptionist would answer, who would feed the call to a secretary, who would then ask her boss if he or she wanted to take the call. Often it would be a full minute before the connection was made. Cam, still wearing his sweatpants, was therefore surprised when Gottlieb answered on the first ring.

"Hello, Mr. Thorne."

"Oh. Hello." He cleared his throat. "Um, we'd like to take you up on your offer to examine Amanda's spiral."

"A wise decision. Can you be here in an hour?"

"Today? Now?"

"Yes. I am an old man. And the mystery of these spiral necklaces has baffled me for a lifetime." He gave Cam an address in Brookline. "I will expect you shortly."

Trey rode the subway into downtown Boston, dreading her lunch with Solomon during his forty-minute high school lunch break. She had wanted to tell him the truth last night. But she had also wanted one last night with him. So she had traded truth for wine, deadening her guilt with alcohol and savoring the touch of his hands, the taste of his lips, the flow of his energy into her when they made love. Her head throbbed from the wine, but not nearly as badly as her heart ached.

They met at a sub shop in the Mission Hill section of Boston, not far from Northeastern University. She arrived first and found a booth in the back. Five minutes later he ambled toward her, powerful yet graceful, holding an elaborate origami green-stemmed red rose in his outstretched hand. He grinned. "No thorns. Just like you."

She stood and forced a smile. "Oh, I have thorns all right."

He stopped mid-stride, sensing her trepidation. "The poet Maya Angelou says that the thorn from the bush one has nourished and pruned pricks most deeply." He angled his head. "Why do I get the sense I am about to bleed?"

The fact that he read her so quickly and accurately only heightened her misery. Where would she find another like him? Six days they had been together. A blink of an eye, really. Yet when someone touches your soul like no one ever has, it feels like a lifetime. She took a deep breath. "Please sit." She grasped his hand across the table and took a deep breath. "I have not been totally honest with you." Speaking quickly, almost without breathing, she spilled out the truth, explaining that she was a Homeland Security operative assigned to perform surveillance on the Templars. "And then they asked me to spy on Kidon also," she blurted, her eyes misting. "But I swear to God that my feelings for you are real." She closed her eyes and hung her head, dreading the next ten seconds of her life. She could live with the pain of losing him—she had brought it on herself. But he had done nothing to deserve such duplicitous treatment.

Of all the things she expected, of all things she feared, a long, rumbling cascade of laughter from Solomon was last on the list. He took her hand and kissed it gently. "Did you think I did not know this already, Trey?" He chuckled again.

Despite herself, she grinned, his laughter infectious. "But, how could you know?"

"I am an intelligence officer, it is what I do. And what else would you, an ex-soldier, be doing with the Templars?" He spread his arms. "You are hardly a religious zealot, after all. And Abraham has a vast network of sources we can turn to. It was not difficult to learn your mission."

"And you're not upset?"

He shrugged. "Why should I be? You are working for your government, for your people. Just as I am. It is no more complicated than that." He reached over and brushed her tears away. "No, enough of this. I am a hungry man. A man," he said, lowering his voice, "who was up most of the night making love to a beautiful woman. I need food."

She grinned. "Yes. Something hardy to replace all the blood you've lost from those nasty thorns."

"You want me to go without you?" Cam asked. He had just described his conversation with Abraham Gottlieb to Amanda.

She tossed her dirty clothes from her suitcase into a laundry basket in the master bedroom closet. "Fat bloody chance. I want to meet the old coot myself. I can be ready in ten." She turned away, then turned back. "So we're agreed." They had spent the morning going back and forth on this. "We're not really going to try to steal his spiral."

"Agreed." He smiled. "At least not today. Today is just reconnaissance."

Ninety minutes after first talking to Gottlieb, and after swinging by the safe deposit box to retrieve the spiral necklace, Cam and Amanda pulled into a parking space on a quiet side street off Beacon Street near the Boston-Brookline border not far from Fenway Park. Amanda studied the ornate brick Tudor homes through the mist as she tucked the necklace into her handbag. "What an oasis. Look at all the ivy and cast iron. This could be a college campus rather than the inner city."

"Tons of money in this area. I think a lot of Boston University professors live here. Plus doctors at Beth Israel. Maybe some Red Sox execs."

"And apparently one old eccentric Atlantis descendant," she said. "If what Meryn said is true, a *nasty* old eccentric."

Cam took a deep breath. He wasn't sure he wanted to bring Amanda into Abraham's orbit. "Sure I can't talk you into waiting in the car? Like you said, he's nasty."

"We went over this. He's nasty to his enemies, to anti-Semites. That's not us."

Cam chewed his lip. "No, we just want to steal his golden goose. No reason for him to get angry about that."

She took his arm. "Not today we don't. Come on." They strode toward the cast iron gate in front of Gottlieb's brick home.

For the second time today the old man surprised Cam, this time by meeting them along the slate walkway. Tall and angular, with a prominent Adam's apple, he bowed politely as the mist moistened his dark suit. "Mr. Thorne. Ms. Gunn." He rested his blue-grey eyes on Amanda. "I believe we may be distant cousins."

She studied him. "I believe we are *all* distant cousins, if one goes back far enough."

"I suppose that is so. But our particular branch of the human family tree is unique in that we possess the ancient spirals." He turned. "Please follow me."

He led them through the mahogany front door, waving away a dark-skinned man in a blue suit who apparently wanted to search them. "No need, Solomon. They are here today only to satisfy their curiosity. At a later time they may come with nefarious intent." He said this unsmilingly, as if he knew that at some point every person he met in life would want to do him harm. Cam and Amanda shared a nervous glance.

Gottlieb pushed open a door under the main stairwell, pulled a string to illuminate a single bulb and descended a set of creaky wooden stairs, his body angled sideways to avoid knocking his head. The smell of heating oil and wet basement wafted up the stairs. "No doubt you are curious as to whether the stories are true. Can these spirals really turn base metals into gold? And if so, can your spiral also do so?" He continued, not pausing for them to respond. "I, too, am curious. That is why I have invited you here."

On the far side of the basement Gottlieb stopped in front of a massive bank vault door. Using his body as a shield to block their view, he spun the dial back and forth and shouldered his way in. Cam paused at the door, unsure whether it was wise for them to step into a locked bank vault with their host. "I'll go," he said. "You stay out here."

"I've come this far," she whispered, pushing past him, "I'll not miss this."

Gottlieb handed them both a pair of goggles and held out his hand. "The spiral, if you please."

Amanda hesitated, and in response the old man retrieved his own spiral from a liquid-filled white marble box sitting on a work bench, dried the artifact on his suit coat sleeve and handed it to her. "A trade. Mine for yours. Temporary, of course."

Nodding, she completed the exchange. He studied her spiral with a jeweler's loupe he pulled from his pants pocket as Cam noted the fire extinguishers on the walls and the battery-like object attached to a thick power cord atop the workbench. After a few seconds the old man nodded. "It appears to be authentic. Let us test it."

He pulled a fist-sized dark gray stone from the workbench drawer and handed it to Cam. "Bismuth," he said. "A base metal similar to lead. This chunk is worth perhaps seventy dollars." He dropped the bismuth into the marble container. "The container is filled with distilled water." He placed Amanda's spiral onto a soap-dish-like shelf inside the marble box (submerging it in the distilled water), put the lid on the box and donned a pair of thick fireplace gloves. "The spiral, being an alien compound, somehow weakens the bonds between the bismuth's protons and its nucleus. Given the proper electric charge, the protons are sheared away, transmuting the bismuth into another base metal entirely. When precisely four protons are removed from the bismuth, the resultant base metal is gold."

Without further preamble he flicked a switch and counted to eight in his thick German accent. As steam rose from the marble container Abraham removed the lid, reached in and withdrew the bismuth with a pair of fireplace tongs. He rinsed the sample under water at a utility sink in the corner. Cam and Amanda edged closer. A grayish residue tinged the water as it pooled in the bottom of the sink before draining, probably impurities from the old basement pipes. There was no denying the newly-transformed copper color of the bismuth. Abraham dried the sample with his glove and handed it to Amanda as if it were no more valuable than a piece of fruit. "This belongs to you now. Go have it tested. You will find that it is solid gold."

She stammered. "You're giving it to me? A block of solid gold? For nothing?"

He eyed her, the goggles magnifying his cold gray eyes. "No. Not for nothing. I have a favor to ask. I would like you to set up a meeting with the Crones. I am an old man with no family. I do not wish my cousins to be my enemies. I would like to think we can come to some kind of mutually satisfactory resolution of our differences."

The call came in on Amanda's cell phone even before they had arrived back in Westford from their visit with Abraham Gottlieb.

"Hi Meryn," Amanda said as Cam merged onto Route 128 from Route 93 in Woburn.

"What do you think you are doing?" her great-aunt demanded.

Amanda tilted her head and turned off the radio. She also pressed the speaker button so Cam could hear. "I'm sorry, what?"

"Meeting with Abraham Gottlieb. Don't try to deny it."

She had never heard Meryn's tone so harsh. "Why would I try to deny it? You *asked* me to meet with him, remember?"

"No. I asked you to steal his spiral, not socialize with the beast."

Cam caught her eye and shrugged, making a face conveying his confusion. "And how did you expect us to do that?" Amanda replied. "By just waltzing in past his armed guards? This was a reconnaissance trip. Now we know the home's layout and even where he keeps the spiral. Plus we know his technology works—he used my spiral to turn bismuth into gold."

Meryn exhaled. "The gold is not important. We need the man neutered, not coddled."

Amanda considered whether to convey his message. She couldn't really not do so, no matter what Meryn's reaction. "He wants to meet with the Crones. He used the phrase 'mutually satisfactory resolution of differences.'"

Her great-aunt's tone turned even icier. "You told him we are meeting?"

"No, I said nothing of the sort. But he seemed to know about it already."

Meryn exhaled again. "Very well. I suppose he watches us just as we watch him." She seemed to consult someone in the background. "I think a meeting might be arranged. I will contact you with the details."

Amanda hung up. "Odd. Quite odd."

"She seemed angry."

"Or perhaps frightened. She has almost an irrational hatred of this Abraham Gottlieb. I wouldn't want to invite him home for dinner, but he was hardly the devil incarnate I expected."

"What about those pictures you saw, of the college girl's face? Not to mention the castration and the murders."

Amanda nodded. "Yes, there is that. Beastly, as Meryn would say. But I didn't sense any … evil, I guess. No warmth, but no evil either." She paused. "It was weird, that's all."

"Yeah, well, people said Charles Manson was charming. So who knows?"

They drove in silence. Cam broke it. "Stupid question, but he gave your spiral back, right?"

"Yes."

"Do you think we have time for a stop?" He pointed at the Burlington Mall ahead. "I know a jeweler who has a kiosk in there. He could take a look at this stone and tell us if it really is gold."

She checked her watch. Astarte didn't get off the bus for another ninety minutes. "Let's do it. I'll grab us some sandwiches in the food court."

Cam exited and parked. Twenty minutes later they met back at the SUV. "So, are we rich?" Amanda asked.

Cam smiled wryly and shook his head. "Solid gold, with just a few impurities." He tossed the chunk into the air and caught it one-handed. "Six pounds. Worth maybe fifty grand after it's been refined. That explains why someone tried to steal the spiral from us."

A shiver washed over her. She felt like she did after seeing a rainbow or watching a puppy play or witnessing a great magic trick. Of all the evidence Meryn had presented in favor of Atlantis, nothing spoke quite so loudly as the ability—apparently passed down through hundreds of generations of Abraham's family—to turn a hunk of rock into gold. It was the thing of fairy tales, yet she had seen it with her own eyes. She couldn't help but grin.

"What's so funny?"

"Not funny, just amazing. It's almost like we witnessed a miracle." She handed Cam his sandwich. "That'll be ten thousand dollars please."

He placed the gold piece into her palm, his fingers brushing against hers. "Keep the change."

The call came in from Meryn as Amanda played cribbage with Astarte while Cam washed the dinner dishes. "Sorry, love, I need to take this." The girl seemed out of sorts again—hopefully it was just because Amanda had been traveling. "I'll be quick like a bunny."

Meryn didn't waste time with small talk. "The Crones arrive tonight."

"So soon?"

"This is the twenty-first century. Forty-eight hours is plenty of time."

"I suppose so." Especially if they all had private planes like Meryn. And apparently this would be a big deal—according to Meryn the Crones rarely if ever met as a group.

"We will meet with Abraham tomorrow morning and then make our decision following that. Tell him to be at Belcourt Castle in Newport, Rhode Island at eleven o'clock. I trust he can find it without directions. And you should be there as well, Amanda."

She had expected as much. "Okay."

"You may voice your opinions, but you will not have a vote." A pause. "And of course your husband is not welcome. It is bad enough that even one man will be attending the conclave."

Amanda bit back a retort. "I understand."

She hung up and relayed the information to Cam.

"Okay, I'll call Abraham. I wonder why they're meeting in Newport."

"Belcourt Castle is one of those mansions from the late 1800s. I suppose if you're going to have a conclave, that's as good a spot as any to do it. Large, private and luxurious. And it seems the Crones have plenty of money."

"Yeah, well, they've had thousands of years to save up."

Chapter 9

Abraham awoke early, before the sun rose, as he often did. When he had purchased the old brick mansion he had chosen for himself a small bedroom on the third floor—an old servant's bedroom—because it looked out over the Charles River and in the spring and summer he could see the sun rising on the northeast horizon, glistening on the waterway in the purple light of dawn. He was not a religious man, not after everything he had witnessed, but he did find the daily sunrise to be an almost magical experience, bringing the promise and possibility of a day never lived before and never to be lived again.

Today had more promise and possibility than most.

He had not expected the Crones to agree to meet with him. They wanted him dead, he knew. And in some ways the feeling was mutual. The Atlantis descendants were a threat to the Jewish people, both because of what they knew and what they represented. He could to some degree control the extent of their knowledge. But as to what they represented to radical groups around the globe—this was something no man could control. It was only a matter of time before some madman used the example of Atlantis as a basis for racial cleansing. It was Atlantis, after all, upon which Hitler modeled his dream of an Aryan master race. As long as the light of Atlantis shone, it stood as a shining beacon to despots with dreams of racial hegemony. And in that game the Jews always lost.

He turned his thoughts back to today. The Crones must want something else from him, beyond merely his death, otherwise they would not have agreed to meet. Perhaps today they hoped to have both. He shrugged. One day, probably in the near future, he would watch his last sunrise.

Madame Radminikov arrived shortly before seven, insisting on fixing him a hearty breakfast. "This is an important meeting. You'll need your strength." He forced down a dry bagel and some orange juice while he read the morning papers. Another ISIS attack. They were growing bolder, stronger, more brazen. They were a cancer that had spread throughout the body of the planet. It would take a heavy, virulent dose of treatment to eradicate the disease. And an entire new approach to radical Islam by the Western democracies to make sure the malady did not return.

At eight he folded his papers, gathered his briefcase and exited the house to greet his team gathered in the front circular driveway. Four vehicles and a dozen men and women stood waiting, their breaths visible on an abnormally cool May morning. He nodded a greeting. They had been briefed the night before so there was no need to go over things again. "I will ride with Madame Radminikov, Mr. Clevinsky, Barnabus and Solomon." He was not normally a sentimental man, but this was not a normal day. These people constituted his inner circle, his most trusted advisers and cohorts.

As close as he had to family.

Xifeng drove south toward Rhode Island. She hadn't had much time to make a plan. But she was confident she could gain access to the mansion.

An hour after leaving her home she drove through the old mill town of Fall River and crossed the bridge from the mainland onto Aquidneck Island. She steeled herself for what she was about to see: From what she had read about Newport, it marked the height of American decadence and capitalistic depravity. Titans of industry, exploiting the common citizens, amassed unspeakable fortunes in the late 1800s in industries such as steel, oil, railroads and banking. They then trumpeted this wealth by building mansions along Newport's Bellevue Avenue, monuments to debauchery and waste. They referred to these sixty-room edifices as 'cottages,' as if roughing it with ten bathrooms was the price one paid for a summer getaway from the city.

Xifeng located Belcourt Castle near the end of the grand boulevard. She circled the block a few times and found a service driveway. From the road she watched a couple of workers park their cars, both of them wearing a white shirt and black slacks. After changing into matching garb from the suitcase full of clothes she had wedged into the passenger seat, Xifeng turned onto the drive and parked next to the other workers. Ad-libbing as best she could, she had filled her back seat with white table linens, draping them over hangers and covering them with dry-cleaning plastic. She trudged toward the service entrance, a half-dozen hangers in each hand. An Asian woman delivering laundry to a mansion—what could be less suspicious than that?

Amanda gave her name to the guard stationed outside the looming cast iron gate blocking the entrance to Belcourt Castle. As he checked it and also her car model and license plate against a list, she studied the edifice beyond, bathed in the morning light. She had read about it last night. Built by a bachelor heir to the Belmont banking fortune—known today for the Belmont Stakes horserace—the mansion contained sixty rooms and would cost approximately eighty million dollars to construct today. She thought of the chunk of gold Abraham Gottlieb had handed her and did the arithmetic in her head. Sixteen hundred chunks would do the trick. Just a chunk a minute for an entire day.

She drove slowly through the gate—the massive arched windows and deeply pitched mansard roof immediately struck her as something one would find in a French hunting lodge, not surprising given its builder was a playboy horseman. She had no doubt the interior would feature dark wood and heavy stone. This was a home built for a man. Odd that the Crones had chosen it as a meeting place.

Amanda parked and strolled under an arched entryway into an enclosed courtyard dotted with sculptures, fountains and a few round tables and chairs. Meryn spotted her and glided over, resplendent as always in a blue-green layered dress. "Hello, darling." She took Amanda's arm. "I'll introduce you around. Many of the others are breakfasting in their rooms."

A half hour later they gathered in a windowless, mahogany-paneled dining room on the first floor. A pair of antique crystal chandeliers the size of Christmas trees hung suspended over either end of a round, ornately-carved cherry table. A score of red-cushioned, high-backed, Victorian-era chairs surrounded the table. A collection of medieval armor and weaponry adorned the walls and display cabinets, the metallic surfaces reflecting the flames of a massive fire crackling in a stone-cobbled fireplace the size of a small car. The opulent castle and circular table and glistening armor and dark-walled room brought Amanda back to childhood stories of King Arthur and his Knights of the Roundtable.

The twenty-two Crones—two from each of the eleven remaining families, not including Abraham's—sat around the table. Apprentices like Amanda sat behind their oracles in chairs less grand. Amanda studied the women. Older, of course. A multitude of skin tones, though Caucasian predominated. Most in long dresses. And all wearing their necklaces, each spiral pulsating softly in concert with its host. These were the women who linked the present to a secret past, the women chosen to bridge the thousands of years lost to history. Amanda felt a flutter in her stomach, both excited and daunted at being chosen to be a part of the group. She studied them further. Most had been distant and cold when Meryn introduced her—like they were worried about a country bumpkin cousin, unschooled in the ways of high society, embarrassing them at a fancy function. She had hoped for a warmer reception. But she understood the occasion was a somber one. The matter of dealing with Abraham was a serious one, and Amanda herself served as a living reminder of the recent death of a fellow Crone.

Amanda checked her watch—ten-thirty, a half-hour before Abraham was scheduled to arrive. Jamila alone remained standing as the others took their seats. She nodded to a middle-aged woman in the corner of the room who gave a signal, immediately emptying the room of white-shirted staffers—all women—who had been serving beverages. "Welcome, sisters," Jamila said, her chin raised. She again wore a long yellow dress, this one belted with a cape that hung from its shoulders. "Thank you for gathering on such short notice. We have urgent business that cannot wait until our next conclave."

A banging at the main door interrupted her words. As heads turned the tall figure of Abraham Gottlieb pushed past the middle-aged staff woman. "I believe I am that urgent business," he proclaimed.

Jamila glared at him. "Allow him to pass," she said icily.

He entered the room, a broad-shouldered woman about sixty years old in his wake.

"*She* is not allowed," Jamila proclaimed.

Abraham stopped and spread his arms. "This is Madame Radminikov. She is my apprentice. I believe every Crone is allowed an apprentice, no?"

Without waiting for a reply Abraham loped toward the round table. Madame Radminikov remained standing near the door. "Fellow Atlanteans," he said, showing his yellowed teeth. Most of the spirals had darkened, matching the mood of the room. "It is good to have the chance to settle our differences. First things first." He loosened his necktie and unbuttoned his top shirt button to reveal his own spiral, pulsating slowly against the grayish skin beneath his Adam's apple. He circled the table, showing the necklace to all. "In case any of you doubt my bloodline."

"We do not doubt your bloodline," Meryn said. "But we reject your claim to wear the spiral."

"Yes," he nodded. "That, succinctly, is the crux of the matter. The reason I am here." He paused, studying the chandelier near him, his head angled to one side. "A beautiful piece of workmanship," he said, more to himself than to the others. "I believe this is original to the home."

"What of it?" Jamila demanded.

He shook his head. "You are correct, it is of no matter." He reached high toward a hidden switch along the central metal stem, using almost all of his Lincoln-like height. "But unless anyone objects, I would like to turn the brightness down. My old eyes have become very light sensitive."

Jamila shrugged his request away. "Fine. Then sit down. Have your say. And then leave."

"I will stand, thank you," he said, remaining at one side of the table beneath the chandelier.

He gestured toward Madame Radminikov. "There is no need for Plan B," he said pointedly. She nodded and left the room. Apparently Abraham had some kind of back-up plan in the event the Crones did not allow him to speak. Amanda exhaled, glad not to know what Plan B might have entailed. She was not quite sure what to expect from these people.

Turning back to the Crones, he said, "I will make a gesture of peace." Theatrically he unclasped his gold chain and tossed his spiral necklace onto the wooden table, the bouncing of the spiral the only sound in the room. "I know you do not want me to have this. More to the point, you believe that my using this spiral to produce gold somehow puts the Atlantis descendants in danger."

Meryn replied. "It is reckless. And worse still you are using the spiral to fund your horrid, hateful vigilantism."

"Incorrect on both points," he responded calmly. "In fact, my use of the gold is far more benign than yours." He turned to Jamila. "Do you have with you the piece of gold I produced for your agent, Mr. Uddin?"

She nodded. "I do."

"And perhaps you would share with the other Crones what you planned to do with this technology once I taught it to you."

Jamila set her jaw. "This is not about me, Abraham. This is about you and your fitness to serve as your family Crone."

"I have been accused of using the technology for selfish gain. It is you, Jamila, who is guilty of this crime. You plan to share my technology with the North Koreans in exchange for military cooperation. According to my sources, together you plan to ally with the Iranians. Collectively you will then attack Israel." *What was this?* "The Druze will supply the gold, the North Koreans the nuclear capability and the Iranians the base of operations and fighting force." He smiled sadly. "I know of your prophecy, of how in the year 2021 you *believe* the Druze are destined to sweep across the Middle East and rule from Jerusalem. The ability to produce gold would allow this prophecy to be fulfilled. You would have the homeland your people have long yearned for." He glared. "At the expense of millions of lives."

The other Crones watched the exchange like fans at a sporting event, leaving Abraham and Jamila to do battle. "You are lying," Jamila said. "Lying to cover up your own crimes."

"Not so." He dropped his phone onto the middle of the table, the screen displaying a video of an Asian man speaking into the camera. "This is Pak Chol-su. He is an agent of the Democratic People's Republic of Korea, more commonly known as North Korea. My team questioned him under the control of a truth serum. If you listen, he will verify what I have just told you."

In the silence of waiting for the video to begin Amanda noticed a faint hissing noise, seemingly coming from the chandelier. She shrugged it away. Perhaps just the hum of one of the light bulbs...

The drugged-up voice of the Korean interrupted her thoughts, confirming the plan as Abraham had outlined it. Amanda eyed her great-aunt, who seemed shocked by news of the Druze alliance with two of the world's most hated regimes. The alliance made sense, at least on paper. The Iranians had long wanted to wipe Israel off the map; the North Koreans, isolated and its citizens starving, yearned for hard currency; and the Druze, without a homeland throughout their history, dreamed of seeing the prophecy that they would rule become a reality. But of course it would mean war in the Middle East.

"Why should we believe you?" Meryn asked, making at least a show of supporting her sister Crone. She pointed her chin at the phone. "This man could be a stooge."

Abraham shrugged. "Honestly, I care not whether you believe me. I am merely explaining the reasons for what I am about to do."

Meryn responded to Abraham. "And what is it you are about to do?"

Amanda again heard the low hiss in the silence that followed. And this time she also noticed the faint smell of rotting cabbage. A wave of fear washed over her. Reflexively she stood, ready to flee.

Abraham noticed her reaction and focused his wolf-like eyes on her. His words froze her. "The doors are locked from the outside, Ms. Gunn. So please take your seat." He addressed the group. "The young have superior hearing and senses of smell than we older folks. I believe Ms. Gunn understands exactly what I am about to do."

With Amanda in Newport at the Crone conclave, this was a perfect chance for Cam and Astarte to head down to the park. He'd throw her some batting practice, then she could work on her pitching, and they'd end the morning at IHOP with a massive plate of pancakes.

He shook her gently awake just after ten. When she buried her head in the pillow he sent Venus in to do the job. When even Venus failed he knew there was a problem.

"What's wrong, honey?"

"I'm tired."

She was normally full of energy. "I thought we could head down to the park and then grab pancakes."

She burrowed deeper. "I don't feel like it."

The last few weeks had seen her moody and withdrawn. She was eleven. Was she already transitioning to the difficult teenage years? "Are you sure there's nothing wrong?"

"Yes. I just want to sleep."

Not sure what else to do he shrugged and walked out. But Venus stayed and twenty minutes later he heard the faint sound of sobbing. This time when he checked on her she buried her head against his shoulder, her body convulsing as she sobbed.

"What is it, Astarte?" He had never seen her like this. She rarely cried, much less uncontrollably.

"Promise … you … won't … be … mad," she said between sobs.

"I promise. Just tell me."

She took a deep breath and pulled away. Her dark hair, wet with tears, masked her face. She wiped her nose on her pajama sleeve. "I've been … spying … on you and Mum…"

The sobs came again, but eventually the story flowed out with her tears. Cam let her finish, holding her, saving his questions for the end, his anger building as the story unfolded. What kind of sick person preyed on the insecurities and vulnerability of an orphan? Were there no sick babies to torment?

But he knew this went deeper than mere cruelty. This was a calculated plan, one that demanded a calculated response.

Abraham repeated his words. "As I said, Ms. Gunn understands exactly." He gestured toward the chandelier. That the meeting was being held at Belcourt Castle, previously owned by a Kidon supporter, was a lucky break. As was the fact that it was a cool morning, necessitating a warming fire. But as the saying went, luck favored the bold. "My home in Boston, like this one, was built in the 1890s. And like this my dining room features a crystal chandelier. When these homes were built electricity was the newest fad. But it was also unreliable—"

"Get to the point," Meryn interrupted, uncertainty on her face.

Abraham nodded at his adversary, enjoying controlling the room after years of Crone hostility. "Very well, Madam Eneko. The point is that these antique chandeliers are wired for electricity but also piped for gas as a backup. Ms. Gunn noticed the sound and smell of natural gas filling the room."

Two dozen eyes shifted immediately to the open flame in the fireplace. Meryn voiced their collective thoughts. "Turn it off, Abraham, or you will kill us all."

He grinned. "Precisely." He imagined their thoughts, searching for an escape route or a way to turn off the gas flow. "As I said, the doors are locked from the outside, guarded by my men. The staff has been safely evacuated. And don't bother to try your cell phones—the signals are being blocked. This room being originally built as horse stables, there are no windows. As for the gas flow, I don't believe any of you is tall enough to reach the valve. I suppose you could try to overpower me and climb upon a chair, but the explosion could occur at any second." He held up a cigarette lighter. If they rushed him he would simply ignite the lighter. "And it will take even an old man like me only a microsecond to spark a flame."

Meryn set her jaw. "You would die with the rest of us, Abraham. I don't believe you have the courage."

She had no idea. "Try me," he said icily.

"How much time do we have?" Ms. Gunn asked.

Abraham felt a pang of guilt. She would be an unfortunate piece of collateral damage. In his short interaction with her she reminded him of a younger Madame Radminikov—principled, fair, intelligent, caring. In short, a worthy successor to the ideals of Atlantis. In evaluating people, Abraham used a simple litmus test: How would he or she have acted during the Holocaust? The evil, of course, actively participated. The vast majority of society simply went along, taking the path of least resistance. But they too were evil to a degree because, as Elie Wiesel pointed out, passivity always favored the oppressor. The truly heroic—people like Oskar Schindler and Irena Sandler and Marie and Emile Taquet—actively resisted. Ms. Gunn, he sensed, would have been among the resisters. As he looked around the room he did not see any others. In fact, during the Holocaust none of the Atlantean families had used their wealth or influence to assist the victims.

He refocused and responded to the question. "I don't know how much time, honestly. It depends, I suppose, on the air currents. It's a large room and the gas flow is slow, but clearly at some point the gas will waft close enough to the open flame and ignite." He spread his arms. "Perhaps you should all gather on one side of the room and blow."

"This is madness, Abraham," Meryn said, her courage waning as the seconds passed. "End it now. Tell us what you want."

Now, finally, they were getting somewhere. He honestly did not care which way this went. He was an old man, long since ready to die. Madame Radminikov, safely outside the room, would continue in his place. What mattered now was the deal he could cut with the Crones. A good enough deal and he'd turn off the gas. Not good enough—or not fast enough—and he'd let the room blow, all memories and vestiges of Atlantis blown away with it. That, in reality, was probably the better course. As long as the memory of Atlantis lived, the threat that some Hitlerian tyrant would model a quest for racial purity upon it existed. Likewise, the threat existed that someone would trace one of the Atlantean outposts back to the Black Sea city of Atil and do the same DNA testing Abraham had done. The DNA testing would indicate that the modern-day Jews of Israel were not actually the descendants of the Biblical Abraham. Rather, they were descendants of the Khazars, converters to Judaism during the Dark Ages of Europe. It didn't take a genius to figure out how that would change world opinion on Israel's right to a Jewish homeland in and around Jerusalem. The Druze understood all this perfectly, and had been making increasingly-burdensome demands on him in recent years. Extortion. *Share the gold-making technology or we will leak the DNA information.* And now they were allied with the Iranians in an effort to take the Holy Land. All this must end. Would end.

These thoughts passed through his head in a matter of a few seconds. It was, after all, an analysis he had conducted in his mind hundreds of times. He took a deep breath. "Here, then, is what I want. What I demand. First, Jamila, you and the Druze will end this ill-conceived alliance with the North Koreans and Iranians."

A few Crones murmured their assent. "Acceptable," one called out. "Yes," said a second.

Jamila slapped the table. "No." She lifted her chin. 'The Druze need a homeland—why should the Jews have one and not us? You can murder us all in this room, but the alliance will survive."

"Not for long." He shook his head. He could smell the gas now. How much longer did they have? One of the Crones had found a pair of billows and was blowing air away from the fireplace; others had joined her, using a wall painting to fan the gas away. Three of the younger woman had hoisted a chair and were about to try to bludgeon their way through the thick entry door. Eyeing Jamila, he said, "Did you really think I would allow you to pass the gold-making technology on to the North Koreans?"

"It is too late to stop us. Our scientists will soon replicate your capacitor."

Abraham allowed himself another smile. He was prepared to die. But he was pleased he would be able to share this, one of his most elaborate and well-conceived stratagems, before he passed on. "I seriously doubt that."

"Why is that?" Jamila replied.

"Because it is a hoax, a scam, a parlor trick."

Jamila's brow furrowed. She had lost some of her imperious stature. "But our people witnessed it on multiple occasions." She pulled the chunk of gold from her lap. "And we had this tested. Solid gold."

Ms. Gunn weighed in as well. "As did I." She showed her gold piece to the group.

"Yes. Both of you are holding pieces of gold. And both of these pieces came out of my capacitor, seemingly converted from bismuth. But what evidence do you have that the original stone was in fact bismuth?" He paused, scanning the room. "You were all blinded by your greed. It never occurred to you, or to anyone else for that matter, that I would willingly give away chunks of gold worth fifty thousand dollars each."

Ms. Gunn understood first. "So it was gold all along. You just painted it gray and then, during the electrical reaction, the paint washed away." Almost to herself, she added. "That's what we saw in the sink when you rinsed the sample. Residue from the paint. We thought it was staining from the old pipes."

Abraham nodded, impressed by her acumen. "You saw what you wanted to see. Just as others went away convinced I had the ability to produce gold. The technology does, in fact exist—but it takes a nuclear reaction to convert base metals to gold, not a silly spiral necklace."

"So why bother?" Meryn asked.

"Do you really fail to understand?" He shook his head; he had expected the Crones to be more savvy than this. "How else was I to get a meeting with all of you? How else was I to convince you of my power and influence? It is my apparent ability to make gold that opened doors for me around the world. And that brought you all here today." His voice dropped. "All together in one room."

He moved on, the gas smell getting stronger. A few of the Crones were throwing coffee and tea on the fire, trying to extinguish it. But the flame was a massive one, hissing but otherwise barely responding to their efforts. He turned back to Jamila. "Needless to say, the North Koreans will end this alliance when they learn you have duped them about your gold-making abilities. But I want to make sure nothing like this happens again. Which leads to my second demand: Jamila, you will step down. The Druze will elect a new Crone and this body a new leader."

Meryn objected. "You cannot tell us what to do."

"We can debate the matter further, but my sense is others in the room are getting anxious."

"Yes, give him what he wants," a voice called from in front of the fireplace. "Give up, Jamila."

Jamila slammed her chunk of gold down onto the table and stormed off into a corner of the room.

Abraham nodded, pleased he was making headway. "I am not done yet. Third, you will accept Madame Radminikov as a Crone, as an equal member."

"Agreed," rang out. "Accepted."

"And, finally," he said, clasping his hands together, "all of you will give up your spiral necklaces. They will be destroyed. All of them."

This silenced the room, the hiss of the gas now audible to all. Meryn managed a response. "But why? These have been passed down for twelve thousand years."

"I have my reasons." Without the spirals nobody would ever be able conclusively to prove the existence of Atlantis. Which meant nobody would ever see the need to do DNA testing on the Khazar gravesites in the Black Sea area. That, in the end, would be his life's greatest accomplishment—ensuring the preservation of the Israeli state for the Jewish people. He shrugged. "Discuss it amongst yourselves. Take your time."

Another voice from the fireplace area. "We don't have time." A Crone tossed her spiral onto the table. "Not worth dying for." A half-dozen others followed.

"Stop," Meryn implored. She stood and glared at Abraham. "This is not the way of the Crones."

"Nor is an alliance with countries like Iran and North Korea," he replied. "Yet that doesn't seem to bother you."

Ms. Gunn surprised him by reaching out and grasping Meryn's arm. "He's right. The spirals are not worth dying for, Aunt Meryn."

Meryn turned on her with a sudden, ferocious intensity. "Don't touch me!" she screeched. "Stupid girl. This doesn't concern you."

"Wait. What?" Ms. Gunn teetered in her chair, her porcelain pale face turning ashen.

Amanda didn't understand. Why had Meryn turned on her, insulted her? She pulled her hand away. "Why doesn't this concern me?" None of this made sense.

Meryn ignored the question, her focus instead on Abraham. "You will never defeat us," she said. "We are united. The blood of Atlantis runs thick through our veins."

But the Crones were anything but united. A chorus of voices called out, agreeing to his terms. "Turn off the gas!"

Abraham held Meryn's eyes. "It is hypocrisy that runs through your veins. Answer the young woman's question. Tell her how you've been using her."

"This doesn't concern her, as I said." Meryn spoke with disdain, Amanda unable to comprehend what she had done wrong.

Amanda raised her voice. "What do you mean, using me?"

Meryn's eyes flashed. "We don't have time for this. But if you must know, I needed you to get to Abraham. I knew he was allying himself with the Templars. You offered a chance to infiltrate his inner circle."

Amanda blinked, fighting back a wave of nausea. "So this has all been a lie? You're not my great-aunt?"

Meryn snorted. "Of course not. You're nothing but a foolish girl, a commoner from a broken family who happens to be married to someone associated with the Templars."

Abraham understood immediately, even if the Gunn woman's look of confused hurt indicated she did not. Meryn had been using Ms. Gunn to get to Abraham, no doubt telling her all sorts of lies and making all sorts of promises. Abraham nodded. Well-played by Meryn, luring him from his bunker. But coldly so. Abraham, an orphan himself, understood the despair Ms. Gunn must be feeling. She had believed she had finally found her family. Instead she had been played, sacrificed as a pawn in a larger game by those who cared nothing for her.

With sudden clarity Abraham realized he could not trust Meryn or Jamila or any of the Crones. They were ruthless and cowardly, more concerned with maintaining their privileged status than in fighting for the utopian ideals of Atlantis. The way Meryn had used Ms. Gunn proved that. As did their obsession with eliminating him.

He sighed. The deal they had just agreed to was illusory. They would never abide by its terms once they were safely out of the room. And he had no way to force them into doing so. Admiral Warner, at least, was a man of honor. Abraham could count on him to keep his word: If Abraham eliminated the Crones, Warner promised he would continue his support of Kidon. It was a small price for Warner to pay to save his company, but at least he could be trusted to pay it.

Abraham made an instantaneous decision. "Ms. Gunn, please leave the room." It would be a final benevolent act in a lifetime in which it seemed like even his most unselfish gestures resulted in pain and suffering. She was innocent. And if she were lucky, Warner would assume she had died with the rest of the Crones.

She looked at him funny, all color gone from her face. "Why?"

He held up the lighter. "Please, I implore you. Do so immediately. And even then your life will be in danger." He spoke directly into a transmitter on his lapel to Madame Radminikov. "Ms. Gunn will be exiting the room. Only her."

A few other Crones edged toward the door with her. He half expected Jamila to be one of them, trying to skulk away like the coward she was. But she was sulking in the far corner. "Only her," Abraham repeated. "Only the righteous." He held the lighter high, his thumb on the trigger, freezing the Crones from rushing the exit.

As the door closed behind Ms. Gunn, Abraham reached his free hand into his left breast pocket and caressed the old black and white photograph he kept of his parents and younger sister. "I am sorry. But Atlantis dies here, now. Only Ms. Gunn shall know the truth of our lost homeland. It will be up to her to choose the proper path, to determine when and if the secrets of Atlantis shall be revealed." He took a deep breath. "Shema Yisrael," he mouthed in prayer.

He stood tall, ready to snap the lighter to life, knowing it would end his. And all the others in the room.

Meryn watched as Abraham lifted his lighter toward the gas-spewing chandelier. Things were spiraling, both literally and figuratively, out of control. *The future of Atlantis left in the hands of that contemptible, man-loving twit, Amanda?* No. All her planning, all her machinations—everything would be lost at the flick of an old man's thumb.

Atlantis must not end like this. Not again, not at the hand of a man who knew nothing but violence. She knew what she must do.

Her hand moved with superhuman speed, lifting the revolver into the air as if guided by the Goddess herself. Meryn took a second to admire the steadiness of her arm, to note the way the lights of the chandelier played off the metal barrel of the gun, to perceive the look of surprise and then fear on Abraham's face.

Her index finger pressured the handgun trigger, the barrel pointed directly at the old Jew's heart. No hesitation. Nothing could stop her now, nothing could prevent her from saving Atlantis. The collective consciousness of five hundred generations guided her, giving her strength and fortitude. The world moved in slow motion, the trigger moving micro-millimeters at a time. But steadily so, toward its inevitable result.

The trigger snapped, releasing the hammer. *It's over, Abraham.* But he had somehow matched her pace. As her bullet fired so too did the flame of his lighter.

The sound of her gunshot never registered, swallowed as it was by the roar of his explosion. Meryn's last thought was the coldly sobering realization that Abraham's hand was being guided by the collective consciousness of his ancestors as well.

Admiral Warner had called Magnuson into work mid-morning on Saturday. His boss looked a lot less frazzled than he had Thursday afternoon, though his desk remained unusually cluttered. The Admiral normally preferred a shipshape bridge.

"Sit, Magnuson. Would you like some coffee or a pastry?"

"No thanks, sir." Magnuson made it a point never to eat with his boss, feeling it presumptuous to engage in any kind of social activity with his superior.

Warner tugged at his bowtie. "It turns out that Gottlieb may be doing our dirty work for us."

"How so?"

"I won't go into why, but he has his own reasons for wanting to keep Atlantis secret. He's meeting with the surviving families today. It may be one of those meetings where everyone goes down with the ship."

"Including Cameron Thorne?" Magnuson was hoping Gottlieb would take care of Thorne, sparing Magnuson from doing so.

"No. That will be a loose end you will have to tie up." Warner shifted in his seat, his eyes glancing at the large map of Atlantis on his wall, and pursed his lips. "We are close to wiping out all memories of the lost continent. Assuming Gottlieb does as I suspect, Thorne will be the last remaining threat to Warner Industries."

Magnuson nodded. "Understood."

"In fact, I just received a call. From the girl." He shook his head. "She's actually an excellent source of information, very sharp. Well worth the small fortune I am paying to bribe her social worker. But the news is not good. Apparently Thorne has discovered more evidence of Atlantis. He has been working at a site in southern New Hampshire called America's Stonehenge. According to the girl, there is something about the site that conclusively proves the existence of Atlantis."

"What?"

Admiral Warner spread his hands. "I don't know. But Thorne is an excellent researcher. And he is well-connected. I think we have to treat this seriously. More than ever, we need to stop him. How quickly can you have a team together?"

Magnuson sat up. "This afternoon."

"I was hoping you'd say that."

The dark-skinned man named Solomon took Amanda by the elbow and rushed her away from the mansion's dining room, through the main entryway and to the far end of the driveway. "Quickly," he said, his eyes registering the spiral swinging from the chain around her neck.

Dazed by the morning events, she allowed herself to be pulled along. Was Abraham really about to blow up the room and all the Crones in it? And did Amanda really care? Apparently Great-aunt Meryn was neither her aunt nor the least bit great. Wicked would be a better word, playing on Amanda's loneliness and vulnerability. Meryn had called her a 'commoner,' implying that this was about bloodlines and DNA after all. Which made Meryn and the other Crones racists on top of everything else. But that didn't mean Meryn should die. Suffer, perhaps. And the others were presumably innocent, excepting it seemed Jamila and her unholy alliance.

"Wait," she breathed, resisting. "We can't let them all die." She called out to the staff members assembled behind a carriage house. "Someone turn off the gas main. Quickly!"

A man in blue coveralls nodded and raced away. What else could they do? She turned back toward the mansion, began to move toward it. If she could open the door, vent the room...

Solomon reached out and with a vice-like grip clenched her arm. "I am sorry, no. It is too dangerous."

"But we need to stop him." She held his eyes. "Please."

Solomon met her gaze, his eyes large and sad. He shook his head. "There is no stopping Abraham Gottlieb, I am afraid."

The ground shook, throwing Amanda to the ground as a thunderclap put an exclamation mark to his words.

Even as the explosion echoed in Xifeng's ears she was running toward the mansion. It would be now, during the chaos and confusion, that truths would reveal themselves.

It hadn't taken long for her to figure out what the Old Jew was planning—word had spread quickly through the panicked staff members that he was threatening to blow the mansion up. But she also knew things were rarely as they seemed when it came to Abraham Gottlieb. This all might be an elaborate ruse. Either way, her government needed to know as much as possible about this gold-making technology. From what she had seen just walking around the mansion, there were more than just a few of these spiral necklaces.

A gaping, flaming hole had replaced the side of the mansion where the dining room once stood as smoke billowed skyward, obscuring the upper floors. But somehow the explosion was contained, limited to one wing of the mansion, likely because the old gas pipes didn't extend beyond the kitchen and dining areas. Xifeng sprinted to the undamaged far end of the sprawling edifice, pushed through a side door and climbed a back staircase to the second floor. Doubling back, she headed to the front of the home. From there, looking down through what she guessed would be the burnt-out remains of the ceiling above the dining room, she hoped to be able to assess the situation.

At some point the fire would be put out. She would wait. And she would not leave without a spiral necklace.

Amanda hit the send button on her phone and looked up in time to see an Asian woman running through the ashy debris toward the burning mansion. Something about her features caught Amanda's eye. *The woman who had borrowed her phone.* And then her fluid, graceful movements made everything come together. *The burglar.*

Without thinking Amanda followed, tracking the woman as she ascended to the second floor. Was it possible she was working with Abraham? But if so, why run back into the building? Could she be an agent of the Crones? If so, she had failed in whatever her mission might have been.

Amanda took the back staircase two at a time, the footsteps ahead of her beckoning, her own ash-covered shoes leaving footprints on the carpet. *Footprints.* A sudden realization hit her: Meryn had delivered the spiral to Amanda using the remote control drone. That's why there had been no footprints. She pushed the insight away. It didn't matter anymore—it had all been a lie anyway.

Smoke wafted through the mansion, but this wing of the building was otherwise undamaged. Sirens rang in the distance; the thick walls of the mansion muffled the panicked voices of the staff gathered safely in the driveway. She shivered at the thought of the Crones caught inside the explosion. Such a needless massacre. Even Meryn, coldhearted and ruthless as she had been, didn't deserve this. Perhaps they had been right in trying to eliminate Abraham.

As the wail of a siren ebbed, Amanda realized the sound of footsteps had not followed in its wake. Had the Asian woman stopped? Following a long corridor lined with antique tapestries and ceramic pieces, their timeless elegance standing in sharp contrast to the carnage and destruction below, Amanda loped along. She felt a bit like the dog chasing the mail truck—what did she hope to accomplish once she caught the woman? Get answers, for one thing.

Cam smiled across the kitchen table at Astarte. Her cell phone sat between them. "Wow," he said, "you are an excellent actress. You sounded really scared and nervous."

She took a deep breath. "I *was* scared and nervous."

"Do you think he believed you?"

She nodded. "Yes. He acted the same as he always does. I don't think Mr. Saint Paul thinks kids are very smart."

Cam had listened to the entire conversation. He agreed with her. Saint Paul—whoever he was—seemed to buy the America's Stonehenge story. Now it was up to Cam to parlay the ploy to his advantage. A woman claiming to be a descendant from ancient Atlantis had pulled a gun on Amanda in a supermarket parking lot. A thug calling himself Smith had sucker-punched Cam and threatened to kidnap Astarte. Another scumbag calling himself Saint Paul had blackmailed Astarte into spying for him. A black-clad gymnast had tried to steal Amanda's spiral. A group of fake Native Americans had destroyed a Red Paint burial site. Cam wasn't sure these people were working in concert, but everything seemed related in some way to the necklace and to Atlantis.

As if on cue, Cam's phone lit up with an incoming message. Amanda. Her words froze him. *Can't talk but I'm OK. Abraham blew up mansion, killing self and Crones. Awful. He let me go but warned we are in danger. Meryn not really my aunt. Gold-making just a trick. Take Astarte to safety. Hurry. Love you both.*

Cam stared at the words. A cold, heavy tightness constricted his chest, making it hard to fill his lungs. He sucked for air. What the hell was going on? At least Amanda was okay. For now. But her words were clear: It was time to get to safety.

Cam clenched his fists. It was also time to find some answers. He had had enough of people threatening his family.

Xifeng sensed her pursuer more than saw or heard her. On a hunch she checked the tracking device inside her purse. *The Gunn woman.* Still carrying her Sharpie.

Moving soundlessly, Xifeng slipped behind a floor-length curtain draping French doors leading to an outside balcony. Peering through she saw the Gunn woman approach. In a stroke of incredible fortune, her spiral necklace hung from her neck, glowing maroon and bobbing in concert with her gait. Why forage through the vestiges of an inferno when the prize dangled only feet away? Her grandmother's words screamed to her: *When luck enters your home, give her a seat.*

Xifeng didn't hesitate. Using the curtain as a shroud, she leapt at her prey, knocking her to the ground and covering her with the drapery. The curtain rod tumbled with them, clanking against the floor. As if in response the smoke alarm in a nearby room began to shriek, adding its voice to the others, the wailing muffling the sounds of their struggle. They wrestled on the thick carpet, the Gunn woman surprisingly strong and agile. Xifeng rode her like a bronco, twisting the curtain around her limbs and keeping her head in the dark. Disorientation was her best weapon—it would cause panic and eventually shortness of breath, weakening her quarry. Periodically she delivered short, sharp blows, using her elbows and knees.

Twenty seconds passed, Xifeng careful to stay on top. The resistance began to ebb. Freeing her right hand while holding firm with her left, she looped a corner of the curtain around the Gunn woman's neck. Rolling onto her back, her shrouded opponent's back now lying atop her, Xifeng twisted the fabric and hissed: "One more twist and I crush your windpipe. Stop struggling if you want to live." To prove her point she gave a half-twist.

A gurgle escaped the Gunn woman's throat, ending her resistance.

Xifeng shifted to her hands and knees and ripped the necklace from her quarry's pale, thin neck. She bound her arms and legs with a curtain sash, stuffed one of her socks into her mouth and dragged the writhing body into an empty bedroom. Remembering a laundry room she had seen earlier in the morning, she retrieved a wheeled laundry cart and hoisted it up the stairs. A cacophony of alarms now shrieked inside the mansion, muffling the sirens of rescue personnel arriving outside. Xifeng didn't have much time.

She dragged the Gunn woman onto the bed, placed the laundry cart next to the bed and tumbled her into it, the weight of her body thumping against the floor. She threw a pair of pillows over the body, then grabbed a blue and white Ming Dynasty urn from the fireplace mantle and dropped it in atop the pillows. If anyone approached her they would think her merely a thief. And if she made it free the vase would make a nice addition to her living room.

Before making her escape, she paused. Should she bother with the Gunn woman? She had the spiral. But the woman had seen her. And there might be more about the spiral Xifeng could learn. Leaving her behind could be the type of thing that would be second-guessed in Beijing.

Leah Radminikov paced outside the mansion as firefighters rushed in, her eyes pooling with tears. This was not right, not the Jewish way. Abraham had gone too far this time. It was one thing to punish the guilty. But it was not justifiable to kill the innocent. That was a decision only for God, not for man.

Solomon took her by the elbow. "We should go, Madame," he said.

"Go where?"

"Away. There will be questions. Many questions. It is best to keep the story simple. Abraham set off an explosion. All are dead, presumably. There is no reason for your involvement to be noted in any way."

She thought about the innocent victims, incinerated. "But I had no involvement." She had no idea what Abraham was planning. He had told her he was going to threaten the Crones, to intimidate them. But not this, not a slaughter.

"I know you did not. None of us knew." He pushed her toward the back of the mansion, away from the commotion and chaos. "This way."

She followed, still dazed, trying to make sense of the morning's events. Had Abraham really been at the center of a suicide bombing? She never would have believed he could be so ... vicious. Calculating, yes. Cruel even. But a taker of innocent lives? No, never. Then it occurred to her: In his mind they were not innocent. There must be more to this, more to the Crones and their activities that he had not shared with her. She lifted her chin, the thought giving her strength...

Solomon stopped midstride, interrupting her thoughts. "What is it?" she asked.

He squinted at a woman pushing a laundry cart through the rear parking lot, away from the mansion. "Odd to be walking calmly away from a burning building."

"That's what we are doing," she replied.

"Exactly. And we have something to hide." He pulled Leah behind a service van and observed the woman. "Asian. And there is something very heavy in that cart; I can see it dragging almost on the ground."

"Is she stealing something?"

"Could be." He jotted down the license plate number of a Volkswagen Golf before peering out again. "Or some*one*. I'm fairly certain I just saw a movement in the cart."

Amanda coughed herself awake, confused that darkness shrouded her even as she opened her eyes. A flood of memories washed over her—the curtain, the struggle, the choke, losing consciousness. Panic replaced confusion. She gasped, trying to fill her lungs, but she breathed in the sock and gagged. Thrashing, fear replaced panic. *Calm down, or you'll choke to death.*

She forced herself to breathe through her nose, the edge of the drapery fluttering against her nostril but allowing some air to pass. Slow and easy. She filled her lungs.

What now?

Bouncing along, Amanda tried to get her bearings. The sound of sirens close by indicated they were still near the mansion. Good. And the cool air of the day penetrating her bondage and the steady hum of wheels told her they were likely on a driveway. Probably heading to a vehicle, so not much time. Wriggling, something heavy pinning her legs, she struggled to free a hand to reach for her phone tucked in her blazer's breast pocket, fearing her captor had taken it. *There.* She rubbed at it with her forefinger, trying to catch the edge and slide the phone upwards. Stretching and straining, while at the same time remembering to keep her breathing even, she worked her pocket. Millimeter by millimeter the phone shifted until finally she grasped it between thumb and forefinger. But then whatever she was riding in stopped.

Working in the dark, she unlocked the screen using her thumbprint. Through the curtain fabric the screen glowed faintly in front of her. She tapped at what she was pretty sure was the message app. Cam was her last message so he should be at the top of her contacts list. She touched what she thought was his name. At the bottom of the screen her cursor blinked. Or at least she thought it did. She touched the screen to activate what she hoped was the keyboard. The sound of a key fob unlocked a car door. She was running out of time.

A trunk popped and she wheeled forward. *Now or never.* She jabbed at the screen and pressed send.

Air flooded Amanda's face as the curtain was lifted off her. The Asian woman stood over her, a gun pointed at her face. She reached in and snatched the cell phone. "Get in the trunk," she said calmly. "And don't try anything stupid. Nobody will hear the gunshot over the sound of the sirens."

The message from Amanda arrived on Cam's phone, as mystifying as it was disturbing. *So sorry.*

He stared at it, waiting for something more, a follow-up or elaboration. He dialed Amanda's number—straight to voicemail. Sorry for what? "Maybe it's a typo," he said aloud. Was the word actually 'worry'? That made more sense. Was she telling him not to worry? But then what was the first word?

Pacing around the kitchen, growing more frantic as no follow-up message arrived, he stared at the screen, allowing his eyes to blur, trying to find a pattern in the letters. But nothing. Was it some kind of clue? Perhaps a code? The word 'code' rang a distant bell. "That's it," he hissed.

Using his own phone, he typed the letters 'SOS' and watched, not breathing, as the phone immediately autocorrected his spelling. The words '*So sorry*' stared up at him. "Shit." He dropped into a kitchen chair. Amanda had typed 'SOS' as her message, probably hurriedly or surreptitiously. But what could he possibly do to help her from a hundred miles away?

Admiral Warner took the call on a private line that only a few people in the world knew. He spun his desk chair so that he could look at the Atlantis map on the wall as they spoke. "Yes, Mr. Ambassador."

"A new development." Warner concentrated, having difficulty understanding the thick Asian accent. "We have Gunn woman, along with spiral."

Warner exhaled. Slowly the loose ends in this kerfuffle were being tied up. Abraham Gottlieb had taken care of the Crones, effectively wiping out the Atlantean families. Magnuson had cleaned up the Red Paint burial site. With Gottlieb himself dead and the spirals destroyed, the silliness of this gold-making operation would finally be put to rest, placating the Chinese. All that remained was Thorne and this new proof of Atlantis at the America's Stonehenge site. "Excellent."

"We retain spiral. No more talk of gold-making." Warner knew high gold prices were crucial to the economic well-being of China, the world's largest producer. "But what do we do with woman?"

Magnuson should be able to handle Thorne. But it never hurt to have an insurance policy. "Hold her for now. But be prepared to make it look like she died in the explosion."

Cam continued pacing his living room, stopping to scribble a list of names on a legal pad at the kitchen counter. Meryn. Abraham Gottlieb. Smith, or whatever his name was. Saint Paul. Miguel de Real. The night burglar. Amanda was in trouble and he had no idea where she was or who was threatening her. But he had to assume it related back to Atlantis and one of the names on his list. With the Crones and apparently Abraham Gottlieb now dead, the only players left in this game were Smith, Saint Paul, the burglar and de Real. Only de Real might be a friend. The others, some of them perhaps working together, clearly were not.

He dialed the Templar Commander's cell. "I need your help." Less than twenty minutes had passed since Amanda's text. He explained the morning events as best he understood them.

"Wait, Abraham Gottlieb is dead? And all the Crones also?"

Cam exhaled. "I believe so, yes."

"How horrible. And your wife was there?"

"Yes. But she got out. She texted me. But now I think they have her, whoever 'they' is."

"The place must be crawling with police. Shouldn't you call them rather than me?"

Cam had weighed that possibility. "That's the problem. They're going to be focusing on the scene, as they should. All I have from Amanda is a cryptic text. By the time they follow up it'll be too late. I will call them and ask them to keep a lookout for her, but I doubt much will come of it."

The Templar let out a long breath, the air whistling through his teeth. "Yes, I agree. The police would be a dead end. I have an agent in Newport, a woman, ex-military, very capable. We have been assisting Kidon in some of their operations. I will contact her and order her to try to find Amanda."

It wasn't much, but it was better than nothing. "Thanks, Miguel."

"I just wish I could do more."

The call came in on Trey's cell phone less than a half hour after the explosion at Belcourt Castle. Trey had been hanging out in the parking lot, not really part of the Kidon security team but sort of tagging along in case she was needed. She and Solomon had reserved a room in a bed and breakfast for the night. "I look forward to exploring a mansion," he had said in his serious way. *Exploring.* It turned out that he had the first five and last three letters correct, but the 'r' ended up being really a 'd.' After the conflagration Trey had rushed toward the building, she and Solomon and even Madame Radminikov hoping to rescue any survivors. But the explosion had been massive, incinerating the entire wing of the mansion. Nobody could have survived it. Fortunately the staff had all moved to a safe distance. Brushing her hair aside with her three fingers, the smell of soot on her hand, she answered de Real's call.

"Trey, are you okay?"

"I'm fine. But what a disaster this is." She had seen explosions like this in Iraq. So many innocent people killed. For nothing. "From what I hear Gottlieb filled the place with natural gas and then set it off."

"Who knows what goes through a man's head at times like this?" de Real replied. "But there is something I must ask you to do. I just received a call from Cameron Thorne. Have you seen his wife, Amanda Gunn?"

"I think I saw her briefly." Solomon had pointed her out. "Abraham let her out for some reason. After the explosion someone said she went running back into the building."

"Well, Thorne believes she has been abducted. Can you try to find her?"

The Lexus SUV pulled into Cam's driveway at four o'clock, more than four agonizing hours after he first received Amanda's SOS text. The time had flown by in a whirlwind, Cam planning and strategizing as best he could. Including driving to America's Stonehenge to prepare the site for what he anticipated would be their upcoming visit. To say he had a plan to save Amanda would be a stretch. But he was still in the fight, still had a puncher's chance.

He let out a long breath as he watched Smith and a couple of sidekicks in black leather jackets march down his driveway. An older man wearing a bowtie remained in the front passenger seat. Saint Paul, Cam guessed—not many people in Cam's universe wore bowties. Astarte and Venus were safely hidden at Cam's cousin Brendan's house. But Amanda was presumably locked in some room somewhere. For now the only thing he could do for her was act his part.

An angry fist pounded on the door. Cam was glad he had not kept Venus with him—these guys didn't look like the type to offer her a milk bone. He opened the door and stepped back, recalling Smith's quick hands. "I see you brought friends this time."

"Yeah, well, this time I came for more than your computer. Time to go for a little ride."

"What if I say no?"

Smith shrugged, his eyes steady and unflinching. This kind of thing was what he did, and he knew he did it well. "You can say no, you can say yes. Doesn't matter either way."

"Where to?" Cam didn't want to appear overanxious.

"Listen, Thorne, I'm not on the witness stand. And I'm not one of your college students. Let's go. And hand over your phone."

"Just tell me if you have Amanda."

Smith stared at him, smirking.

Cam tried another approach. "We just adopted a girl. You know. Astarte. Do what you want to me, but the girls needs a mother."

Smith's face remained inscrutable. "Stop fucking around. Let's go."

Cam exhaled, tossed his phone to Smith and grabbed his backpack.

"What's in there?"

Cam opened it to reveal a water bottle, a high luminescence flashlight Amanda had given him as a gift, a measuring tape, bug spray and a notebook of pencil drawings and calculations he had scribbled out just before Smith's arrival. "I assume we're going to America's Stonehenge."

Smith eyed him sideways. "How'd you know that?"

Cam shook his head and pushed by him, out the door. "Why else would you be here?" He gestured with his chin to the bow-tied man in the front passenger seat. "And why else would you bring *him*?"

Pak Chol-su awoke in a sunlit room, his face bathed in sweat and his mouth dry as sawdust. A digital clock flashed 4:38 on a night table next to him. He had no idea where he was. He focused on a pad of paper next to the clock: "Marriott," read the letterhead. He was back in his hotel?

The memories came back slowly but quickly intensified. The old man's brick house. Going to the basement. Watching him convert bismuth into gold. The black-skinned man jumping from the shadows and covering his mouth with a rag. Awakening in a chair in a dulled, dreamlike state. Being asked questions in front of a video camera. Wanting to lie, to protect and serve his country, to honor Supreme Leader—but being powerless to resist whatever truth serum coursed through his veins. *Oh shit.*

He was in trouble. He swallowed, the taste of his saliva vile and bitter. He had told them about Supreme Leader's plan. Everything. The plan was ruined. And so was he. That's why they had returned him to his hotel: They had extracted all the information they needed from him. Stumbling, he found his way to the bathroom sink and splashed water on his face. He stared at his face in the mirror, his eyes bloodshot and afraid.

Should he defect? The South Koreans surely had a consulate in Boston; they would be thrilled to have a diplomat turn against their rivals. The image staring back at him in the mirror shook his head slowly. If only it were that simple. Pak knew what happened to the families of defectors—torture, followed by prison camp. He had heard stories of life in the prison coal mines, with captives descending into underground caverns from which they never reappeared. An existence of darkness and cold and starvation, where the strong overpowered the weak for the privilege of eating rodents. His parents wouldn't last the summer. And that assumed they survived the torture.

But if he returned to North Korea that would surely be his fate instead of theirs. What else could he hope for? Supreme Leader had crafted an inspired plan. And Pak had ruined it. Were it not for Pak the North Koreans would soon be awash in gold, its troops part of an alliance marching to take control of the Middle East...

Suddenly something the old man said popped into his head. Was it a dream, or was it real? The memory was clear, the words unmistakable, spoken when they thought Pak was unconscious. Gottlieb had said, "The Druze will have a lot of explaining to do once the North Koreans realize the technology does not work."

That was it. The details didn't matter—the technology didn't work. Pak's mind raced. He could rewrite the narrative. *He* could be the one to expose the treachery, the one to protect Supreme Leader from being duped and losing face. He'd need to fill in some gaps and change some of the details, but the bottom line was the same. He could be the hero rather than the scapegoat.

For now all that was important was that he be the first to expose the subterfuge.

Breaking all protocol, and not giving a damn about it, he used his phone to remotely log onto his work computer in Beirut. Typing as quickly as he could on his phone, but choosing his words carefully, he sent an email to the private address Supreme Leader had given him. It was six in the morning in Pyongyang; Supreme Leader would see the message soon. The meat of the message, after the requisite preliminary niceties, read: *After infiltrating the residence of Abraham Gottlieb, I have ascertained that the gold-making technology does not work. It is a ruse. The Druze have been lying to us. I do not know if the Americans are part of this deception.*

He hit the send button. Less was more. The fewer details he gave the easier it would be to manipulate the story.

Exhaling, he returned to the bathroom and washed up. Again consulting the face in the mirror, Pak wondered if there was anything else he could be doing. He and Uddin had taken adjacent rooms at the Marriott in Copley Square. Uddin had, apparently, disappeared—not surprising given that he had been sent to America to obtain the gold-making technology. Pak walked to the window and peered outside, barely able to make out the brick row houses below in the dimming light of an overcast day. Far to his right, nearly blocked by the corner of the building, the lights of a ballpark shone in the late afternoon dusk. Could that really be Fenway Park?

Pak allowed himself a smile. If he was going to spend the rest of his life in a prison camp, before he did so he would treat himself to a hot dog and a Red Sox game. Maybe also a sweatshirt and a beer.

His phone buzzed, startling him. Had Pyongyang responded so quickly? The message flashed at him. *You are to be commended for exposing this subterfuge, Pak Chol-su. Your service to your country is needed now more than ever...*

Pak sighed and sat on the edge of the bed, reading further. There would be no hot dogs tonight.

Cam knew he was playing a long shot. He had deduced that Smith and his bow-tied boss were intent on suppressing any evidence of Atlantis. Only because they believed Cam had new evidence were they keeping Cam, and probably also Amanda, alive. Once he showed his cards they would have no need for either of them. Cam needed to buy time, and during that time figure out a way to gain the upper hand on his adversaries.

All this passed through his mind as they walked to the Lexus SUV parked in Cam's driveway. The bow-tied man stepped from the passenger seat and nodded at Cam. Nearing seventy, he stood erect despite a sizeable paunch, his eyes hard and his gray hair short and neat. The yellow bowtie featured a series of small blue battleships, matching his blue blazer. "Thank you for joining us, Mr. Thorne," he said, his hand extended. "I am Bartholomew Warner."

Cam recognized the name. A Navy admiral. Warner Industries. Things started to come together in Cam's mind. He knew from his work at a Boston law firm that Warner Industries specialized in underwater industrial projects in the Atlantic. Would evidence of Atlantis somehow be bad for business? It would explain a lot of what had occurred over the past week. At least with the Crones and Gottlieb and the Templars there were moral issues at stake. With this guy it was, apparently, just about the money.

But this was all conjecture. What was almost certain was that Warner/Saint Paul had been tormenting Astarte. He likely held Amanda's fate in his hands. He had destroyed the Red Paint People burial site. And that was just the stuff Cam knew. Cam needed to change the dynamic, to throw his adversary off balance. He strode up to the older man and, not breaking stride, threw a short right hook, burying his fist deep into Warner's protruding midsection. *For Astarte.* An 'oomph' sound, wet with saliva, erupted from Warner's mouth as he dropped to a knee.

Smith rushed to his boss as his two henchmen grabbed Cam on either side, awaiting instructions. His face red with anger, Smith said, "Stupid move, Thorne." He raised a fist as his men held Cam in place. Cam braced. Punishing Warner would be worth whatever came next. What kind of asshole preys on the emotions of an orphan girl?

"Stop." The word froze Smith. Warner lifted a hand, still on his knee. "Not here, Magnuson. Put him in the car. But search him first for any weapons. Including his pack."

The men did so before shoving Cam into the back seat. Warner, after a few minutes of recovery, climbed in on the other side. The two henchmen squished into the third row while Smith, whose real name apparently was Magnuson, locked the doors and put the vehicle into reverse. Cam decided to continue his game, still intent on changing the dynamic. He turned to the older man. "The punch was for Saint Paul." He filled his mouth with saliva. "This is for you." He spat, a thin spray covering Warner's cheek as he turned away reflexively.

"That's it, Thorne," Magnuson barked. He nodded in the rearview mirror and the thug behind Cam jabbed a sharp fist into the nape of Cam's neck. His head snapped forward and his extremities went numb; white pinpricks of light danced in the periphery of his vision. *Shit, that hurt.* He blinked and tried to catch his breath, his fingers and toes beginning to tingle back to life. He wasn't sure how long he wanted to trade blows with these guys. But it felt good to be fighting back. Not that it would help Amanda much. He allowed himself a few seconds to think about her, to wonder where she was and how she was being treated. Then he refocused on the present. That was the best way he could help her.

Cam's attacks on Warner had, indeed, unnerved his adversary. Clearly the ex-admiral and current business titan was not used to being punched and spat on. Anger seethed from his pores, his blue eyes dark and narrow as he glared at Cam. He removed a handkerchief from his breast pocket and wiped his face. He had let the first blow pass, but not the spew. In a low, measured voice he said, "Thorne, you do something like that again and I'll feed your wife to my hounds."

Cam arched his neck, hiding a small smile. Warner had just confirmed he had Amanda. And of course he couldn't feed her to his dogs if she were already dead. "Yeah. You're good at picking on women. Little girls too. How many kids did you napalm in Vietnam? Maybe raped a couple babies along the way?"

Warner's jaw pulsed. This was not going as the admiral had scripted the meeting, which was Cam's goal. He tried to regain control, addressing Cam as he would an ensign. "*We* are going to America's Stonehenge. *You* are going to explain to me how and why this site offers proof of Atlantis. *I* am then going to decide your fate and the fate of your family." He gestured with his thumb toward the back seat. "Either way, *they* are going to teach you some manners. Am I *clear*?"

Cam pushed his lips into a wry smile. "I'm not sure what incentive I have. Sounds like you have some nasty plans for me and my family whether I cooperate or not."

Magnuson interjected before his boss could respond. This, too, pleased Cam—he had gotten under the underling's skin as well. "Oh, you'll cooperate, Thorne. Trust me on that."

They rode north in silence, fighting heavy traffic, the SUV crossing back into New Hampshire—Cam had avoided the congestion earlier in the day by taking back roads. He used the time to review the plan in his head. When he saw a highway exit sign for America's Stonehenge, he broke the silence, continuing his ploy of trying to keep his adversaries off balance. "The megalithic yard," he said, incongruously.

"What?" Warner replied.

"32.64 inches. 2.72 feet."

"What about it?"

"It is a unit of measurement. Used in Atlantis. I thought you were some kind of an expert."

"I know what it is," Warner blustered. "I *am* an expert. But what about it? Why did you mention it?"

Cam did not want to play his cards too early; time was his best ally. "It's okay to admit you don't know what it is. Know what it *really* is."

"Don't be ridiculous. I've been studying the megalithic yard since you were in diapers. It's the unit of measurement used to build megalithic sites all over the British Isles," he said, the term megalithic referring to ancient sites built with massive stones. "Stonehenge. Carnac. Avebury. Hundreds of others. All built using the same unit of measurement."

Cam nodded. "And that unit of measurement originated on Atlantis. Passed down to Stone Age Europeans by Atlantean survivors." He smiled. "Or perhaps not. Perhaps it was just adopted by some early carpenter or stone mason and it spread throughout the British Isles through trade and travel."

"No. The megalithic yard originated on Atlantis. I am certain."

It struck Cam that the admiral must be torn. In order for the megalithic yard to have originated on Atlantis, there first had to *be* an Atlantis. So Warner was a believer, apparently a passionate one. But he apparently also had been taking drastic measures to keep knowledge of the lost landmass suppressed. He was like a vegetarian butcher, his personal beliefs in direct conflict with his pecuniary wellbeing. "But you have no evidence," Cam countered. "Again, it could just be an early European adaptation. In order to tie the megalithic yard to Atlantis you need a site outside of the British Isles."

Warner's eyes widened, a droplet of saliva visible on his bottom lip. "That's what this is all about. America's Stonehenge," he breathed. "You've found evidence of the megalithic yard in New Hampshire?"

Cam smiled. The SUV turned onto a side road. They were minutes away. Time to see if his ploy would fool the admiral. "Evidence? I wouldn't call it evidence. I'd call it ironclad proof."

Amanda had no idea how much time had passed. It seemed like she had been cramped in the trunk for a few hours, driving on country roads, bound and hooded. They had stopped once, her captor allowing her some fresh air and a couple of sips of water, but otherwise Amanda had been left, literally, in the dark.

Now the car came to a stop again. An electronic garage door hummed and the car pulled forward again down a slight slope. The engine stopped and the trunk popped. The Asian woman spoke matter-of-factly but with the assuredness of someone who had been trained for just this type of situation. "You are my captive. I will treat you humanely as long as you do not try to escape. If you do try to escape or make noise or otherwise cause a disruption I will take a scalpel and remove your nipples." She paused. "If necessary I will then do the same to your clitoris."

A cold fear caused Amanda's body to recoil and curl reflexively. If she planned to rebel, she'd better make damn sure she was successful.

The woman untied her feet and, standing behind her, pulled off her hood. She helped Amanda from the trunk and led her, Amanda walking stiffly, hands still tied, to a low door cut into the cement wall of the garage. She unlocked the door, flicked a light switch and pushed Amanda into a room with food, bottled water and other supplies piled on shelves along the walls and a pair of cots on the floor. A curtain in the corner shrouded a sink and what Amanda guessed was a toilet. Some kind of safe room.

"What's your name?" Amanda asked, trying to learn more about her captor.

The woman ignored her, instead flipping open a folding chair. "Sit." She tied Amanda's hands behind the back of the chair and clipped the chair to a vertical bar of the metal shelving. "I do not have much time," the woman said matter-of-factly. "Which means you do not have much time either."

She walked around in front of Amanda. "You borrowed my phone," Amanda declared, trying to stall.

"Yes. You were kind that day. I will try to return the favor. But as I said, I do not have much time. My kindness will not last long." She pulled the spiral necklace from a satchel. "How does this work?"

Amanda took a deep breath. She knew now that it did not. But that was probably not the answer her captor wanted. She played a hunch and decided on the truth. "It doesn't. The whole thing was a trick. I know that's not the answer you want to hear, but it's the truth."

For the first time the woman's plain face revealed her emotions. "That is ridiculous. The Old Jew has been producing gold with his spiral for years."

"No, he's been fooling people for years." Amanda explained the ruse. "It cost him hundreds of thousands of dollars. Apparently it was worth it to him."

"I don't believe you."

Amanda shrugged. "Think about it. Why hasn't anyone else been able to replicate it? The Druze have been trying, probably others also."

The Asian woman stared at a point well beyond the cement wall of the bunker. She made some kind of decision. More to herself than to Amanda, she said, "It does not matter whether I believe you or not. My government must know the truth. And for that there is only one certain method." She removed a syringe and a sealed bottle from a locked safe on one of the shelves. "I am sorry, but this will hurt."

Magnuson turned into the America's Stonehenge driveway well after six o'clock, the traffic almost doubling the normal drive time. Dark clouds had moved in, accompanied by a brisk wind. A locked gate greeted them. Cam was glad to see it—he did not want to put others in danger.

"Don't suppose you have a key, Thorne?" Magnuson asked, unlocking Cam's door.

Cam stepped out, a henchman following him outside. "No, but I know the combo." He often came at sunrise to view the equinox and solstice sunrise alignments, so the owner had given him the combination. He pulled the gate open and the SUV rolled through.

They left Cam in the vehicle while Magnuson and his two men loaded gear from a roof cargo carrier into backpacks. Cam couldn't see exactly what they had, but clearly they were preparing to spend a good amount of time in the woods. Which was fine with Cam: Time was one of his few allies. He again wondered about Amanda. Warner was savvy enough to understand she was worth more to him alive than dead. At least for now. And, ruthless as he was, he didn't seem the type to inflict pain just for the fun of it.

It was almost seven-thirty when they began the hike from the parking lot along the trail to the ceremonial site on the hill in the center of the complex. What little daylight remained was being filtered out by the clouds and canopy of trees. Cam was glad for the coming darkness. What he was going to try to sell would not withstand the light of day.

Amanda swallowed as her captor filled the syringe and readied the needle. She didn't guess the Chinese spy agency wasted much time teaching the finer points of bedside manner.

Without warning the woman stabbed the needle into Amanda's shoulder, sending a cold fluid into Amanda's bloodstream. "Ouch," she reacted. Involuntarily her body recoiled, her muscles tensing and her heart racing. What if her captor gave her too high a dose? What if she had an allergic reaction? These types of drugs were normally administered by a doctor, not a spy. Her head whipped around, searching for some weapon or escape route.

The Asian woman stood back, out of reach, studying her watch. "Resistance is futile."

Amanda thrashed for another few seconds, then suddenly everything turned warm, like three glasses of wine on an empty stomach. "Resistance is futile," she repeated, giggling. "I've heard that before. On *Star Trek*. I miss that show." Why was she rambling? "I liked Geordi. He was blind." She giggled again. "With the way he sees and the way you look, it's a perfect match…"

The drugs. Was she talking or merely thinking? She tried to focus. But instead she felt herself falling, spinning downward, spiraling, spiraling, spiraling…

"Yes, spiraling," said the voice from far away. "Tell me about the spiral."

Trey and Solomon parked at the far end of a cul-de-sac in the northern Boston suburb of Woburn just as many families were finishing dinner. Trey had been able to run the license plate Solomon noted in Newport. Eventually they traced it to the Woburn address, though not before hitting a few dead ends along the way. Whoever registered the car did not want to be tracked.

Trey pointed to a yellow Colonial with black shutters and trim. "That's it. The American dream."

Solomon studied it somberly. "Perhaps for Amanda, a nightmare." Madame Radminikov, mortified at the massacre in Newport, had instructed him to accompany Trey and do all she could to make sure nobody else was hurt.

Trey took his hand and tried to stroll by casually. "A couple of lights on." The house was owned by Gerald and Xifeng Chang. He was Chinese-American, born here; she an immigrant. No children. They bought the house seven years ago. According to the building records available online, they had built a safe room in the basement off the garage when they moved in. Nothing else noteworthy. "If they have her, she'd be in the safe room."

"Yes," Solomon said. He snorted. "Where I grew up the safe room was a hole in the woods covered with twigs and vines."

"Where I grew up, or maybe it was *when* I grew up, we didn't need safe rooms."

They passed the home and circled back. "You know what?" Trey said. "I'm just going to be bold." She dug around in her satchel and found a clipboard and legal pad. She wrote up a petition in longhand calling for removing restrictions on cell phone towers, added a dozen signatures using a couple of different pens and marched to the Chang's front door. "Nothing is more American than community activism." She smiled. "And nothing provokes activism in America quite like dropped cell phone calls."

Magnuson studied Thorne as they followed him along the muddy path through the woods in the fading light. He was up to something, Magnuson could feel it. But he had no idea what. One thing was certain: No way could he make a run for it. Magnuson and his men—burly, bearded Rejean and wiry Yves, the ubiquitous cigarette wedged in the corner of his mouth—were armed and well-equipped, including night vision goggles and gear to spend the night in the woods if necessary. Thorne knew he was overmatched. Magnuson guessed whatever game Thorne was playing was one of subterfuge.

Either way, having him alone in the woods like this was a blessing. Especially at night. It was why Magnuson had not detoured out of traffic and had dawdled in the parking lot unloading their equipment. There hadn't been time for Magnuson to turn Abraham Gottlieb and his group against Thorne. But if Thorne simply disappeared there would be little to tie it back to Magnuson and Admiral Warner. And with Thorne's wife presumably killed with the other Crones there'd be nobody left to expose Atlantis. Then Magnuson could get back to his normal routine of policing Warner Industries.

Thorne had stopped at a small stone chamber near the bottom of a low rise. Warner stood with him; Magnuson edged closer while his two men hung back, their eyes scanning the woods, their hands buried in their pockets against the cool evening air. A pair of parallel stone walls snaked up the slope along a path from the chamber. "If I explain my research to you, you'll let Amanda go? And leave us alone?"

Warner nodded. "You have my word."

Magnuson wasn't sure Thorne believed him—who would?—but Thorne didn't really have a choice. Thorne's shoulders slumped as he pointed to a three-foot high stone standing upright along the wall, shaped like a pyramid with its top cut off and notched into a shallow bowl. "Essentially this whole complex is a calendar in stone." He pointed up the hill. Other than in the deepest parts of the woods, the snow had melted and left spring mud in its place. "If you stand at the center up there and look out to the horizon you'll see dozens of vertical standing stones like this. They mark various astronomical events. Solstices, equinoxes, cross-quarter days. At sunrise and sunset the sun will sit right on top of these upright stones, like a golf ball on a tee."

Admiral Warner wiped his nose with the back of his hand, his face red from the exertion of the short hike. "Are the alignments exact?" Something about the way Admiral Warner asked the question told Magnuson it was a test.

Thorne shook his head. "No. In fact, all of them are off by about two degrees. And all in the same direction. So the golf balls actually sit on the edge of the tees."

Warner raised an eyebrow. "Oh?"

"That's what allows us to date this complex. Over time the orbit of the earth shifts, or wobbles. But going back in time at some point, the alignments would have been perfect. We shouldn't expect them to be the same today. If they were perfect today, that would disprove an ancient origin."

"So how far back do you need to go to make the alignments work?" Warner asked.

Cam bit his lip. "There are two possible dates. Four thousand years ago is the first. That's what most historians believe. But also twelve thousand years ago."

It seemed to Magnuson that Thorne's answer intrigued the admiral. "Twelve thousand," Warner repeated. "Do you think this site relates to Atlantis?"

Thorne shrugged. "That's your expertise, not mine." He continued, "Notice this wall, right next to the standing stone." He stepped over the wall and into the underbrush. "The tall standing stone marks this spot as important. Look how these stones veer off the wall and make a spiral shape."

Warner squinted. To Magnuson it just looked like a pile of rocks, even after he shined his flashlight on them. But Thorne walked around the cluster, pointing out some rounded edges and a circular divot area in the middle of the so-called spiral. The admiral nodded. "Yes, I see that. What of it?"

"I don't need to tell you that spirals were sacred to Atlantis."

Warner studied the cluster. His next statement did not surprise Magnuson: His boss often challenged underlings by trying to bully them. Lifting his chin, Warner said, "You have a reputation as an accomplished researcher, Mr. Thorne. And I know you are a trained attorney. I would hope you can present a more compelling case than a round pile of rocks. From everything I've read, this site is nothing more than the ruins of a Colonial farm."

Thorne turned and gave the admiral a wry look. "Look, you dragged me up here. I don't really care if you believe me or not."

"I suggest you should care. Lives hang in the balance, Mr. Thorne."

Thorne swallowed and took a second to gather his thoughts. He took a deep breath. "I'm just showing you stuff as we see it. The really compelling evidence is at the ceremonial center of the complex. But context is also important. There are lots of spirals here, all located near important standing stones. Almost as if to highlight them, like we underline or capitalize things today." He paused. "And I don't think Colonial farmers wasted time making spirals."

The explanation seemed to satisfy Warner. Magnuson knew Warner loved this history stuff. Magnuson just wanted Thorne to tell his story so they could do what needed to be done and get out of here.

Thorne turned now and faced the chamber that marked the end of the double stone wall. He removed a tape measure from his bag, climbed over the wall and maneuvered his way down a slick stone slope. He measured the opening leading into the chamber interior. "Thirty-two and a half inches high, maybe a smidge more," he called out. "Sixteen and a quarter inches wide. Sound familiar?"

Admiral Warner angled his head. "Are you certain?"

"You just watched me measure. Come see for yourself."

Magnuson helped Warner edge his way down to within a few feet of the chamber. Thorne stepped aside, one hand holding the tape in place.

"I'll be damned," the admiral said. Warner gazed up the hill toward the main portion of the site. "Is the whole complex built using the same unit of measurement?"

Thorne nodded. "The whole thing. Built using the megalithic yard."

Cam exhaled. Warner had bought it.

He was glad it was dark, glad the entrance to the chamber was fairly inaccessible to the older Warner so he couldn't see Cam fudging the measurements a bit. Not much, just a half inch or so. Cam had spent an hour at the site today, identifying chambers featuring dimensions which approximated the 32.64-inch megalithic yard measurement. Some worked, most didn't. Again, the cover of darkness would help his ruse.

As would controlling his guests. He lectured, using the lesson to cover up for the fact they were not stopping to measure other non-compliant features at the site. "It's one thing to show that all the megalithic sites in the British Isles were built using the megalithic yard. That sort of makes sense, given that ancient people traded and traveled in that area. There was probably one group of priests responsible for building the religious shrines. Who knows, maybe they all trained together at some school or something, sort of like the Druids did during the time of King Arthur." He led the group up the slope and deeper into the complex, picking his way carefully, not wanting to use his flashlight until absolutely necessary. He wondered about Amanda but quickly pushed the thought aside. "But to have the same unit of measurement here, thousands of miles away and across the Atlantic—how do we explain that?"

He let the answer hang, waiting for Warner to provide it. The obvious answer, of course, was that Europeans four or five thousands of years ago came across the Atlantic to build this site. That, in fact, was what Cam believed had occurred. But most people did not believe in early transatlantic travel. Including, probably, Warner— other than travel by the ancient Atlanteans.

Warner took a deep breath, the exertion of the climb obviously affecting him. "It must be that the ancient people who built this site had similar origins to the people who built the megalithic sites of Britain," he said.

Cam nodded. "There can be no other explanation." He smiled. "Other than ancient aliens, of course."

Warner glared at him. "Don't be ridiculous." He was a serious man, and Atlantis to him was serious business. No room in his world for UFOs. Which again was fine with Cam. "If what you're saying about the megalithic yard here is true, then the conclusion is unavoidable."

Cam decided the time was right to push his advantage. He stopped and removed his pack. "I was going to save this for last, but I'll show it to you now." He reached into his pack, Magnuson hovering close by to make sure Cam didn't pull out a weapon. Instead he pulled out a grey stone the size and shape of a dessert plate. An elephant figure had been carved onto the face of the stone. "This was what got me really focused on this site. This artifact was found here, just a few months ago."

Elephant Carving, Burrows Cave, Illinois

Cam allowed the admiral to study the carving. The stone had been found not in New Hampshire but in a cave in Illinois. What mattered was that the carving looked ancient. And, more importantly, it depicted an animal not native to North America.

"This was found here?" breathed Warner.

Cam nodded. "In a stone niche," he lied, "protected from the elements. But geologists believe it is thousands of years old." He paused. "At least."

He watched the admiral's eyes flutter as his brain raced. "But elephants are not native to America."

"Not today. But they were twelve thousand years ago," Cam replied simply. "They died out at the end of the last Ice Age."

Cam let the comment hang as they continued hiking. It was a question of simple logic: Primitive man could not have built such an elaborate complex, but whoever built it knew about elephants, which had been extinct in America for 12,000 years...

In silence they reached the crest of the hill. Cam found an opening in the chain link fence that protected the ceremonial structures at the center of the site from vandals. He led them inside, searching for those structures he had identified as exhibiting dimensions consistent with the megalithic yard. "This chamber here is one of the most important chambers in the entire site," he fibbed. There was nothing particularly noteworthy about this edifice. "And note the height." He unfolded his tape measure. "Forty-nine inches. Exactly one-and-a-half megalithic yards." He stepped back. "Would a Colonial farmer use these dimensions?"

Warner stared for a long time at the stone structure, as if by concentrating he could see its ancient inhabitants. After a few dozen seconds he turned to Cam. "Continue."

Winding his way between and around the cluster of stone chambers, Cam led them to the center of the ceremonial complex. A large, flat, trapezoidal stone about the size of a bumper-pool table sat on four stubby legs. The Sacrificial Table. A half-inch-wide channel had been carved around the border of the stone approximately three inches in from the stone's edge. The stone was used for sacrifice—perhaps human sacrifice—in ancient times, the channel used to divert the blood away.

Sacrificial Table, America's Stonehenge, NH

Cam explained all this to Warner. What he didn't explain was that some historians believed the ancient seafaring Phoenicians constructed America's Stonehenge approximately 2,000 BCE. The early Phoenicians, part of the Canaanite peoples, were known child-sacrificers. Cam ignored all this and instead focused on the possibility of Atlantean origin. "Did the Atlanteans engage in human sacrifices?" he asked.

Warner nodded. "Yes. Of their enemies."

Cam exhaled, pleased at the response. He was scoring some points, but sensed he was still losing the match. He eyeballed the Sacrificial Stone. He had spent half his time this afternoon measuring the table. In the end he chose to focus his measurements on the channel as it gave him leeway to measure to its inner edge, its center or its outer edge. He pulled out his tape measure. "Since the blood flowed through the channel, the channel was considered the most holy part of the table," he lied. "So that is where whoever built this would have applied their sacred geometry, using the megalithic yard." He laid the tape measure down widthwise, at the point he had mentally marked as matching the desired dimensions. His heart raced. *This had better work.* The whole ruse would fall apart if the Sacrificial Table measurements weren't exact. He stretched the tape and forced himself to look—

He exhaled, swallowing a grin. Center of groove to center of groove, exactly 49 inches. "Again," he announced, "we have the sacred unit of measurement of 1.5 megalithic yards." Emboldened, he turned the tape measure in the other direction, angling the tape slightly. As he expected, just off, 66.5 inches rather than 66. He jostled the tape a bit. "And the length is exactly two megalithic yards, just under 66 inches."

He stuffed the tape back into his bag. "So, I don't know who built this complex. But whoever it was, they worshiped spirals and knew about elephants. And they used the same megalithic yard first used on Atlantis and later used at the megalithic sites all over the British Isles."

Warner stared at the Sacrificial Table, rocking back and forth as if trying to get his land legs back. He spoke more to himself than to the others, a mix of wonder and disbelief in his voice. "I've been trying to prove Atlantis all these years. And the proof was right here, in my backyard, the whole time."

Somehow Pyongyang had tracked the location of the spiral to a house in the Boston suburb of Woburn. Pak understood his mission, and the reason for it: Steal the spiral back, before the Chinese realized it was worthless. Then Supreme Leader, using his expert negotiation skills, would barter the useless technology back to Beijing. It would not be as profitable a deal as the original one with the Druze, but, as he had heard the Americans say, half a loaf of bread was better than nothing. And the Chinese would be content, in the end, knowing that nobody was out there flooding the market with manufactured gold.

So, yes, Pak understood the mission. He just didn't understand how he was supposed to accomplish it. Not to mention somehow get out alive.

He took a taxi from the city to Woburn, a thirty-minute drive, amazed at the size of homes and abundance of restaurants and shopping areas. He checked his watch—past eight o'clock. By this time in North Korea everyone would be home, before the electricity went off for the night. Here, it seemed, people were just heading out. And so many service establishments—did nobody in this country wash their own car or paint their own house or cut their own hair or even brew their own coffee? This Woburn, he decided, must be where the wealthiest Americans lived. But mostly he focused on how he was going to retrieve the spiral.

The taxi pulled up in front of a sprawling Colonial home—Pak figured there were three or even four bedrooms inside—on a cul-de-sac full of equally impressive estates. "You want me to wait?" the cabbie asked.

Pak handed over fifty dollars—enough hard currency to live like a celebrity for a month in North Korea—and shook his head. "No, thank you. But tell me. Do most Americans lock their doors at night?"

Warner's own words echoed in his ears. *The proof was right here, in my backyard, the whole time.* He sighed, his entire being crying out against what he must do. Marveling at the majesty of the site, he stood on the raised knoll that served as a viewing area above the Sacrificial Table, just as the ancients must have stood thousands of years ago as they watched their priests make human offerings to their gods. It had been here all along. He had searched the world for evidence of Atlantis and here it was, twenty miles from home. What an idiot, a blind fool, he had been.

Magnuson looked up at him expectantly, his two soldiers standing on either side of Thorne. Thorne was a good man, sharp and intuitive—in another time he would have hired him to work for Warner Industries. But that ship had long sailed.

Warner stepped down from the knoll. He lifted his chin and squared his shoulders. A good officer knew that sometimes he must make difficult decisions, issue difficult orders. "Ready the explosives. Destroy the site."

Cam was not surprised by Admiral Warner's orders—he had expected them, in fact. But hearing the cold words spoken aloud jarred him into action. As the smaller of the two henchmen, Yves, reached around to remove his pack, Cam made his move. *Now.* Spinning, Cam dropped his shoulder into Yves, knocking him backward over a low stone wall. Like a rabbit in a warren, Cam scrambled into the labyrinth of chambers and walls that comprised the ceremonial center of the complex.

"He's running," a voice called. A gunshot answered, the bullet ringing off a stone near Cam's ear. *Shit.* These guys were playing for keeps. Cam ducked and zigged, finally skidding into the blackened mouth of what he knew to be the site's largest stone structure, the T-shaped Oracle Chamber. Based on what Amanda had experienced with Meryn and the other Atlantis Crones and oracles, he wasn't sure if the name portended good fortune or bad.

He only had a few seconds. His assumption was that Magnuson and the two henchmen would pursue, leaving Warner to place the explosives around the Sacrificial Table. The chamber was dark, its stone floors slick with humidity. Cam navigated his way down the stem of the T, repeating the dry run he had made earlier in the day, finding his way through memory and touch. At the end of the stem, where the chamber broke off in two different directions, Cam felt along the wall for a void. There. A small recess, not much larger than a high school locker. Cam wriggled in. Still working in the dark, he stilled himself enough to perceive a faint waft of fresh air entering along one wall of the niche.

He placed his mouth against the opening through which the air flowed. Lowering his voice, he spoke. "This is an emergency. I am at America's Stonehenge in North Salem. I am being held captive. Please send help."

Cam held his breath. This was his only chance. A second or two passed, then Admiral Warner's angry bellow. "Magnuson, this way! He's doubled back. I can hear him calling the police. He must have had a second phone. He's here, near the Sacrificial Stone."

From the far end of the chamber Cam heard Magnuson's response. "Nobody carries two phones. You two go. I'll stay here. Hurry."

Cam sighed in relief. His trick had worked, barely. The Oracle Chamber was built hidden into the embankment adjacent to the Sacrificial Table. A priest, during religious ceremonies, could crawl into the niche and project his voice through a stone speaking tube out to the Sacrificial Table, just as Cam had just done. The effect would be that it sounded like the gods were speaking through the voice of the person being sacrificed.

He had improved his odds, from three against one to one-on-one. But Magnuson was armed and trained. Still not a fair fight. A heavy footstep echoed through the chamber as if to emphasize that point.

Trey and Solomon had retreated to the end of the subdivision to formulate a plan. When Trey had asked for Gerald's wife's signature on the petition, Gerald had claimed she was not home. Trey didn't buy it—he seemed flustered and nervous. And Trey had noticed a woman's purse and keys sitting on a small table near the front door. In fact, she had snatched the keys while Solomon distracted him.

"Why not call for backup?" Solomon asked.

She shook her head. "They want this operation to be off the books if possible. This is sensitive—the Chinese don't like it when we take out their agents. So if we can claim plausible deniability, that's the preferred way to go."

Solomon smiled sadly. "In other words, we are on our own. And if things go bad, it is your fault."

"Exactly."

"We used to do something in Israel when we needed to take out these safe rooms. Instead of trying to get in, we would try to lure them out."

"How?"

He smiled. "I will show you. Drive me to the drug store. There is one around the corner."

Fifteen minutes later they returned to the cul-de-sac. "You wait here," he said. "Keep watch." Solomon took his bag of newly-purchased supplies and snuck around behind the house. After a few minutes he peeked out from behind the garage and motioned Trey over. Together they crouched in a wooded area behind the home. Solomon showed a small keypad; with a single finger he slowly and dramatically pushed a red button. Instantly a loud, piercing siren began to sound from an area near the rear of the home.

Trey plugged her ears. "What is that?"

"A simple alarm," he said. "But watch."

Within a few minutes Gerald appeared on the rear deck, flashlight in hand, inspecting his back yard. As soon as Solomon saw him he pushed the red button, turning off the siren. When the Asian man reentered the house, Solomon turned the alarm back on. Other neighborhood lights went on, and at one point a neighbor yelled at Gerald to end the racket. This went on for ten or fifteen minutes, Gerald and the siren engaged in an endless two-step.

"I don't get it," Trey said after five or six repetitions, her ears ringing.

"Just wait."

"What?"

He mouthed something to her. She tried to focus on his enunciation, but instead she saw the lips that had kissed her breasts, the tongue that had probed her mouth, the teeth that had nibbled at her shoulder and her... *Enough.* She blinked away the memories. "You're going to have to buy me a drink later to dull my senses."

His face contorted. "I have no desire to dull any of your senses, Trey."

Gerald stepped through the sliding door again, saving her from responding. This time when the siren went silent he threw up his hands and marched back inside. A few minutes later Xifeng, clad in black, glided onto the back deck. "Now we are making progress," Solomon said.

Solomon pushed the button, sounding the alarm again. "Okay," he said directly into her ear. "My guess is that this noise is driving her crazy—"

"It's driving *me* crazy," she interrupted. This sound was so loud she no longer cared about his tongue or his teeth or his lips.

He continued. "Plus the neighbors are complaining and all this is drawing attention to her which she desperately wants to avoid. On top of that she will want to show her husband what a stooge he is." He grinned. "Some things, I believe, are universal to all cultures."

Sure enough, Xifeng marched across her lawn, toward the woods, her flashlight searching for the irritating siren. Trey crouched and patted Solomon on the thigh. "Nice work. I'll take it from here." She edged deeper into the woods, away from the noise. "Just please turn off that goddamn alarm."

Cam wriggled out of the niche and retreated deeper into the chamber, to one end of the cross of the T. The chamber had two entrances, at the base of the T, where Cam and now Magnuson had entered, and at the end of the opposite stem of the T from where he now hid. Above his head there was a narrow opening, a hole in the ceiling to vent smoke or allow fresh air. Earlier today he had been able to climb through it.

"I know you're in here, Thorne," Magnuson called. Their voices would not—other than through the speaking tube in the niche—escape the underground chamber and carry out to the ceremonial area and Sacrificial Table. "I'm glad it's just you and me. Come out, come out, wherever you are."

At first Cam was surprised not to see the beam of a flashlight. Then he realized Magnuson would be using night vision goggles, giving him the advantage of sight in the dark. Cam pulled his own flashlight from his bag and wedged it into his waistband, his heart thumping like a drum in the silence of the underground cavern. Nothing he had rehearsed earlier had prepared him for being hunted down by a trained operative.

"Thorne, stop screwing around. I've got a gun and you've got no place to run." The chamber was not very large, each stem of the T measuring about fifteen feet. The well-trained Magnuson moved cautiously but steadily along. "Trust me, you don't want to piss me off."

Cam found a foot brace and lifted himself, groping for the opening in the ceiling. *There.* His hand found the void. Excitedly his fingers explored the space for a handhold, his knuckles scratching against the stones. He began to hoist himself upward. Magnuson's footsteps echoed. *Shit.* Magnuson would be at the T in mere seconds. It would take Cam longer than that to wriggle out, and he didn't want to be hanging there like a slab of meat when Magnuson arrived. He was running out of options. He lowered himself to the ground.

Desperate, Cam felt around inside the wall and withdrew an apple-sized stone. Holding his breath, he dropped and crouched, waiting until Magnuson's silhouette emerged at the cross in the T. Cam had played high school baseball and had a good throwing arm. But he knew he only had one chance at this. He did a quick calculation: Magnuson was probably a couple inches under six feet, likely slightly hunched in the chamber. Target point should be forehead. So aim should be five-and-a-half-feet. Just over Cam's eye level.

A slight scratching sound on the ground announced Magnuson's arrival. Cam's eyes, now used to the dark, discerned a figure perhaps ten feet in front of him. Silently Cam stood, wound and threw, sailing the stone at what he hoped would be Magnuson's head. A split-second passed, during which Cam expected to hear the thud and groan of a successful shot. But nothing. A split-second later came the reason: The throw cracked off a stone wall at the far end of the chamber, echoing like a gunshot. Cam had missed his one chance.

Magnuson spun toward the noise, away from Cam. In that instant Cam realized his advantage. As Magnuson quickly processed what had happened, he turned back toward Cam, back toward where he deduced the throw had originated. Cam was ready. Flashlight outstretched, he flicked the light on full strength, aiming the concentrated beam straight into Magnuson's night vision goggles. The bright light overwhelmed the goggles, disabling them and momentarily blinding Magnuson. Cam lifted his flashlight and swung down, catching his adversary on the side of his head above the ear. Magnuson crumpled to the ground.

Cam exhaled. That felt good. But already he heard more footsteps rushing his way.

With help from Solomon—the Asian women being deceptively strong—Trey bound and gagged Xifeng and tied her to a tree. With her three-fingered hand, she held up the keys she had lifted. It was the first time she could remember where she hadn't made an effort to hide the deformity. "Now," she said, ears still ringing, "this is how this is going to work. You are going to tell me which key opens the safe room door. I am going to rescue Ms. Gunn. Solomon is going to stand guard over you while I do so. This is an easy plan. Very difficult to mess up. Am I clear?"

The woman spat on the ground. "I have diplomatic immunity. I demand to be brought to the Chinese consulate."

Trey had anticipated such a response. "When the authorities arrive you can explain all that to them. But we don't know anything about diplomacy. In fact, we are downright undiplomatic." She took the siren, held it up to Xifeng's left ear and pushed the test button. The alarm shrieked, its impact on Xifeng's eardrum wobbling her, only the ropes of her bondage keeping her from falling to the ground. Trey circled her captive and held the siren against her other ear. "One can survive quite nicely with damaged hearing in one ear. But losing both ears, that can be a real handicap." She raised an eyebrow.

Xifeng swallowed and nodded. "Okay, okay. It is the orange key. But the woman is drugged. I cannot vouch for her condition."

"Well, you better hope she's okay." Trey removed the orange key from the ring and handed the rest to Solomon. "You might need this if you have to get in the house." She began to walk toward the garage.

"Wait," Solomon said. He turned to Xifeng, the whites of his eyes shining in the night. "I have personal reasons for not wanting anything to happen to this woman," he said, glancing at Trey. "So if there is a booby-trap, or an alarm, or if anything else bad should happen, I will hold you personally responsible." He lowered his voice. "And I will not waste time on your eardrums."

It was hardly a love poem, but in its own way it put a bounce in Trey's step.

Without checking on Magnuson's well-being, his own and Amanda's being of far more importance, Cam slipped off his adversary's night vision goggles and pocketed the handgun Magnuson had been brandishing. He peered through the goggles and tossed them aside; the flashlight had disabled the display. He fished around in Magnuson's pockets and found his car keys—at some point Cam would need an escape vehicle. Hopefully. Cam also retrieved his own phone and, upon consideration, took Magnuson's as well. The most recent text flashed on his screen, an exchange between Magnuson and his two henchmen, Rejean and Yves. Cam composed a quick message and hit send: *Thorne escaped. Yves stay with Warner. Rejean come help me.*

Cam maneuvered back down the long arm of the chamber, making the counterintuitive decision to head straight toward where Rejean would be entering. The element of surprise remained his best weapon. Plus, earlier in the afternoon he had stashed a can of pepper spray Amanda sometimes carried in a niche at this end of the chamber. He retrieved the spray, flicked off his flashlight and waited. A shuffle of feet announced Rejean's arrival. "Magnuson, you in there?"

The massive henchman filled the chamber entryway, silhouetted against the moonlit sky. Unlike Magnuson, he wasn't wearing his night vision goggles, so that strategy would not work a second time. Cam hugged a wall and steadied his breathing. Rejean entered cautiously. "Magnuson?"

Cam preferred not to use the gun. He had never shot someone. And it would bring Yves and Warner running. But he would do what he had to do. As Rejean stepped deeper into the chamber Cam again swung the flashlight, once more aiming for the area between ear and forehead. But this time he misjudged.

The blow was a glancing one, knocking Rejean off his feet but not unconscious. The burly man staggered but recovered and, on his hands and knees, charged at Cam. Cam had lost the advantage of having his adversary backlit; they were both now in the pitch black. Rejean buried his shoulder into Cam's midsection like a linebacker, vaulting Cam back and into the chamber's stone wall. Pain shot through Cam's torso, his entire body going numb and the air whooshing from his lungs. He slid to the ground.

But the blow to the head had disoriented his adversary as well. Both men gasped in the blackened chamber. A flash of moonlight against metal announced that Rejean had brandished his gun. Cam guessed he would not want to shoot in a darkened cave and risk the bullet ricocheting back at him, but if he managed to locate his flashlight and illuminate Cam, Cam would be a dead man.

The sight of the gun sparked a surge of adrenaline in Cam. Reaching up, he sprayed the pepper spray in the direction of Rejean's heavy breathing. The man bellowed in pain, the spray burning his face and eyes. Cam shuddered at what the angry bear of a man would do to him if he caught him.

Stumbling to his feet, Cam lumbered deeper into the chamber. The gasping, cursing, coughing Rejean pursued. This time at the T Cam turned left, toward the second egress. And toward the prone, barely visible body of Magnuson. He stepped over. An idea hit him.

Cam dropped to his knees. With labored movements, his ribs throbbing, Cam spread Magnuson's body lengthwise, across the chamber floor. Meanwhile, Rejean lurched forward, audible but not visible in the blackened cavern, somehow blindly sensing his prey. Cam could actually smell the onion-scented coughs of his pursuer in the close quarters.

Cam stood, Magnuson prone at his feet and the heat of his pursuer wafting over him. *Now or never.* He slapped the rock wall. Reacting to the sound, the enraged Rejean lunged. Just before he reached Cam he stumbled over Magnuson's body and crashed to the stone floor. Cam did not hesitate. He leaned in and whipped the flashlight downward, this time catching his adversary squarely in the head. The henchman gurgled and fell silent.

Holy shit, that was close. Cam exhaled and sat gingerly. Using the flashlight on his phone, he found some rope in Magnuson's pack and, working quickly, bound the unconscious men's hands and tied them together back-to-back. It wouldn't hold them for long, but then again Cam hoped to be making a quick exit.

He exhaled. Two down, two to go. But he was running out of tricks.

Xifeng, her ear ringing, shrugged away the inconvenience of being bound to a tree in her back yard. She had everything she wanted from the Gunn woman. Under questioning Xifeng had ascertained that she was telling the truth—the whole gold-making thing had been a ruse. Her government would still want to test the spiral, but she was done with the Gunn woman. In some ways the arrival of the three-fingered woman and her black-skinned friend had saved Xifeng the hassle of ridding herself of her captive.

The black-skinned man's deep voice interrupted her thoughts. "First, call to your husband. I see him standing on the deck. Ask him to bring you a flashlight. English only. No tricks."

She did as instructed. Solomon watched her husband move cautiously toward the woods, swinging a flashlight back and forth. Circling around, Solomon slipped a hand over his mouth, quickly overpowered him and bound him to the tree next to Xifeng. Xifeng rolled her eyes. Gerald was not just a lamb, he was the runt of his litter.

"Good," Solomon said, turning back to her. "Now, where is the spiral?"

"What spiral?"

He nodded, not in agreement but as if in confirmation that she had answered as expected. "You leave me no choice." Removing his phone from his pocket, he placed a call. "Please arrange transport to Tel Aviv. One woman, Asian. An agent of China. Expect us within the hour."

Tel Aviv? She had not foreseen this. Using her pinky, she pressed the alarm button on her watch, alerting her handler to an emergency. "Where are you taking me?" she asked.

Her captor merely smiled.

For the first time tonight a clammy anxiety washed over her. She suppressed a shiver. The Americans would be careful not to do anything to threaten relations with China. But the Israelis had no relations whatsoever with her country. And therefore nothing to protect. And their ruthless questioning techniques were legendary. They would suck every ounce of information they could from her. "Do you work for the Israelis?"

"I *am* Israeli," came his simple answer.

She made a quick decision. The spiral was fake. The Old Jew's gold-making was a ruse. Her mission, therefore, had been a success. There was nothing left to fight for. With her chin she motioned toward the garage. "The spiral is in the safe room. Hidden in a box of Cheerios."

With Magnuson and Rejean disabled, Cam felt it safe to venture from the chamber. He had a decision to make: Call for help, or try to end this now by himself. If he called the authorities there was no guarantee Amanda would survive. He knew the layout of America's Stonehenge ceremonial complex, he now wore Rejean's night vision goggles, and he carried Magnuson's revolver. He could be the hunter as much as the hunted.

But his throbbing ribs handicapped him, and he didn't have much time. Warner would be getting skittish. The existence of America's Stonehenge, Can had deduced, threatened the survival of Warner's entire empire. That's why he planned to blow it up. And now his top lieutenant had gone incommunicado. Night had fallen. Warner would want to set his explosives and end this. Quickly.

Cam decided to be bold.

He stepped from the chamber and, skirting the ceremonial complex, made his way to high ground. He was pretty certain Warner and the remaining henchman, Yves, would be focused on setting the explosives in the central area, near the Sacrificial Table, to destroy as much evidence of the megalithic yard as possible. Taking shelter behind a boulder perhaps a hundred feet from where Warner worked, Cam called out, "You can destroy the site, Warner, but it won't do any good. I've downloaded videos of my research on Facebook and You Tube and a bunch of other sites. They go live tonight unless I pull them. So even if you blow everything up, it's all been documented."

Cam saw a movement off to his right, in the shadows. Yves was circling around, not aware Cam had the goggles. Cam guessed he had less than a minute before Yves closed in on him.

Warner replied. "Without the actual site there will be no way to verify your research. I doubt many will believe you. In any event, if you want your wife to survive, I'd advise against posting any videos."

Cam swallowed. He was playing a high-stakes poker game here with Amanda as his ante. "We both know that's a lie. You're going to kill her no matter what I do. People like us don't matter to you. You're like a spoiled rich kid with a new toy. All you care about is that nobody takes it from you."

"New toy?" Cam was glad to hear he had gotten under the man's skin. "Warner Industries employs thousands of people. Real people, with mortgages and medical bills and college tuition to pay. This is no game, Mr. Thorne. We are talking about people's lives." He paused. "And speaking of lives, if you do the right thing, I'll spare yours. And your wife's. This can end right here, right now."

Cam knew he was lying. Cam and Amanda were the only people still alive who knew about Atlantis, who could offer a coherent argument which—coupled with the spirals—could prove its existence.

His internal clock sounded an alarm. Time to move. "I don't trust you, Warner. You leave me no choice. I'm going to the authorities."

This next salvo required precise timing. As far as Warner knew Cam did not have his cell phone; Cam's statement that he would "go" to the authorities rather than call them would confirm this presumption. Cam tossed a grapefruit-sized rock toward the wooded path, in the direction of the parking lot and away from Warner. It rustled the brush and thudded to the ground. After counting to five, he threw another smaller rock as far as he could, in the same direction. A second thud sounded in the distance. If Cam had guessed correctly, Yves would report the noises to Warner, who would order him to pursue Cam back toward the base area.

Cam peered out, through the night vision goggles. He saw nothing for a few seconds. Eyes wide, he searched the night. Ten seconds passed, then twenty. Still nothing. Had Yves not taken the bait? Cam edged away, toward the woods, concerned the henchman might pounce at any second. He pulled the gun from his jacket pocket, felt the cold metal in his sweaty hand. *Shit.* He didn't have a Plan B.

He turned to run into the woods. He needed time to regroup, to figure something out. Amanda's life depended on it. He froze. A movement at the periphery of his sight, at the bottom of the slope leading away from the ceremonial complex. *There.* The thin figure of a man loping away down the trail. Yves. Cam exhaled, a wave of relief washing over him. He allowed himself a smile.

It was now just he and Warner. Good versus evil, truth versus lies. Like some Arthurian legend. With, unfortunately, a damsel in distress.

Trey Blackwell freed Amanda Gunn from the safe room without incident. She had been drugged and was lethargic, but otherwise appeared unharmed.

"Thank you," she breathed, blinking.

"Let's get you home," Trey replied.

A text from Solomon lit up her phone. Scanning the shelves, she spotted a box of Cheerios and quickly found the spiral buried inside like a prize in a Cracker Jacks box. She handed it to Amanda. "This is yours, I believe."

"It's been more trouble than it's worth, I'm afraid." The gray spiral pulsated as Amanda slipped the necklace over her head.

Trey smiled. "I hear you. Come on."

They stepped into the unlit garage, Amanda leaning on Trey for support. A Volkswagen Golf sat in one of the bays, a BMW in the other. The cultured voice of Commander de Real spoke to them from the shadows. "Well done, Sister Trey." He stepped forward, a gun pointed at them. "I will take it from here, thank you."

Trey didn't get it at first. "I'm sorry, what?"

"Ms. Gunn. She will be coming with me. And the spiral as well."

"But you sent me to rescue her."

"Yes. From the Chinese. And you have done so commendably. But there are other issues in play here. Things, as they say, above your pay grade."

Trey clenched her jaw. She hated being condescended to. She was tempted to blurt out that he had no idea about her true pay grade. But obviously that would have done no good. For now she stalled. "I get it. She's the last one alive. The last one who can prove Atlantis."

"Yes. She and Thorne, who may be dead even as we speak."

Amanda swayed against Trey, the drugs along with de Real's words obviously impacting her. "Stay strong," Trey whispered. And to de Real, "But why should you care? What does Atlantis have to do with the Templars?"

"Admiral Warner is correct. The truth of Atlantis causes too many complications. The Templar Order is, at its core, the army of the Church. We are sworn to defend it and to fight its battles. The Church has spent two thousand years convincing its flock that God created Adam and Eve six thousand years ago. How, then, can we explain away an advanced civilization living long before that? And what about all this I hear about Jesus being part of some Merovingian bloodline, with his ancestors being from Atlantis?" He shook his head. "The Vatican has enough problems these days. We cannot have things like Atlantis casting doubt on the Bible and Church teachings." He smiled, shrugging. "And this problem, it now turns out, is so easily solved. Abraham and Admiral Warner have done all the heavy lifting already, killing the Crones and destroying the spirals—"

"But it's a lie," Amanda interrupted. "The story of Adam and Eve is simply not true."

"Yes," he nodded. "The story is a lie. But, as the saying goes, it's our story and we're sticking to it."

"At some point people outgrow their fairy tales."

"Yes. Yes they do. In fact, perhaps the wiser play would be to use the spiral to *prove* Atlantis rather than disprove it. There is much in the true story of Atlantis that undermines another fairy tale: That of the right of modern Jews to rule Israel."

Trey knew where this was going. It was the fear of this revelation that caused Abraham to murder the Crones. "You think Christians should control Jerusalem."

The commander shrugged. "I am a Knight Templar. Of course I think this. That is what we fought the Crusades for." He shrugged a second time. "But I do not need to make this decision now. It is a steak-or-lobster proposition: With the spiral I can suppress Atlantis or promote it, depending on what our needs are." He motioned with his gun toward the Golf. "Trey, put her in the trunk. The keys are in the ignition."

Trey readied herself. A shovel hanging on the wall beside her was almost in reach. She could grab it and swing, perhaps disabling the Templar leader before he reacted—

"Don't try anything stupid," de Real said, apparently reading her thoughts. "I had hoped you would be a loyal soldier. I see I was mistaken." He barked a command and two more Templar soldiers stepped out from behind the BMW where they had been hiding. The commander turned to his men. "Like I said, put the Gunn woman in the trunk. And lock Sister Trey in the safe room. It is time for us to leave."

Cam crouched in the wooded area just beyond the perimeter of the America's Stonehenge ceremonial complex, fighting to breathe without sending needles of pain into his side. He and Admiral Warner were at a standstill. But time was on Warner's side—he was no doubt placing explosives throughout the complex and would soon detonate them. Cam could not let that happen.

He weighed his options. He had Magnuson's gun and a pair of night vision goggles. But it could hardly be called self-defense if he fired the first shot. Cam didn't relish the thought of a lifetime in jail.

He could call the authorities, but it would be at least twenty minutes before they arrived. By then the site would be rubble.

He could charge the admiral, try to overpower and subdue him. But then what? How would that save Amanda?

In the end the best leverage he had over the older man was the same advantage others of his generation had: He was more technologically savvy.

He stood and edged toward the Sacrificial Table, where he guessed Warner was concentrating his explosives. "Hey, Warner," he called. "I'm back."

Something thudded to the ground, Warner apparently dropping an object in surprise at hearing Cam's voice. "I'm listening," he sputtered.

"Good. I've been thinking about something. Warner Industries is going to fail no matter what happens here tonight. I just figured it out. There's a United Nations treaty that bans you from digging or exploring or laying pipelines or doing anything in any underwater area where civilization once existed." He had taken an international law class in law school. "So it's just a matter of time before the U.N. shuts you down."

He had hit a nerve. "Don't patronize me, Thorne. Of course I know that. What do you think the point of all this is? We have been operating in violation of the U.N. treaty for years. But nobody knows because I have been suppressing evidence of Atlantis. As you said, the treaty only applies in areas where civilization once existed." He grunted, apparently placing more charges. "But after tonight nobody will know anything about Atlantis, other than perhaps your little videos which I will make sure are discredited. Without Atlantis, there is no underwater civilization."

Cam tried the soft sell. "I understand your dilemma. I really do. And nobody wants to see all those jobs lost. But can't you and I agree to keep this all quiet? Do we really need to destroy this site?"

Warner guffawed. "Thorne, I did not become a rich man by trusting people like you to keep their mouths shut. The only way for me to ensure the survival of Warner Industries is for me to do as I have always done: Destroy any and all evidence of Atlantis, including this site." He lowered his voice. "And also including anyone who stands in my way. Need I remind you, Thorne, that I have a gun and know how to use it? And that your wife is my captive?"

Cam pressed the stop button on his phone video recorder. Praying he had enough cell coverage, he typed a quick message and sent the video to his cousin Brendan. The file began to transmit, the bars slowly moving across the screen. *Come on.*

A gunshot shattered the night, sending Cam diving to the ground. Warner cackled. "That got your attention! I asked you a question. I expect an answer."

Cam rolled behind a chamber, gasping, his ribs barking in pain. Had his fall interrupted the transmission? He peered at the screen. *Complete.* He exhaled. He had told Brandon to post the video on Facebook if he didn't hear back from Cam within the next ten minutes. Finally some leverage.

Cam pulled himself up and stepped into the opening at the center of the complex. He fought to stand his ground and steady his breathing. Nobody ever got used to being shot at. "Warner," he called, "you have a problem."

The Admiral lifted his firearm. "Odd words from a man standing on the wrong side of a gun."

"Not if that man has just uploaded a video recording of you admitting to intentional violations of an international treaty. Not to mention kidnapping, criminal trespass and assault with a deadly weapon." He shrugged. "The video will be posted on Facebook in ten minutes. I bet it goes viral. Like I said, you have a problem."

Bartholomew Warner stood still, his gun raised, replaying Cameron Thorne's words. Damn the new technology. It seemed as if the young lawyer had entrapped him. Warner cursed under his breath. "Fuck it. This old soldier has some fight in him yet."

He called out. "Okay, Thorne, you have my attention. Seems like it's horse-trading time."

"Free Amanda. And pack up your explosives. If you do that, the video never sees the light of day."

A simple deal. And not a bad one. Part of him, in fact, was relieved at not having to destroy the America's Stonehenge site.

But Thorne wasn't done. "You should know that if anything happens to me or Amanda or Astarte or America's Stonehenge, that video will come out. I guarantee it."

"That's it? A simple deal?"

"Yes. Simple. I just need to speak to Amanda and confirm she's safe. You have eight minutes."

Warner nodded. "I'll make the call now." Later he'd figure out how to deal with Thorne and his wife. For now it was paramount that Thorne's video not air. It would mean jail time for certain, and perhaps bring down the company. He dialed the Chinese ambassador. "It is time to free the Gunn woman," he directed.

The response hit him like a rogue wave on a cold night. Warner swallowed and lowered his voice. "What do you mean you may not have her? What kind of emergency?"

Pak Chol-su crouched behind a bush alongside the garage, listening to the conversation within. The fat man with the beard apparently had taken the Gunn woman and her spiral. That was good news, he supposed—at least the Chinese didn't have it. So there was still hope for Pak. He just needed to stop the man who called himself Commander de Real.

Pak shifted, his knee sore from resting on a jagged rock. Which gave him an idea. He snatched the thin rock and edged around to the front of the garage. Apparently de Real was planning to use the Chinese spy's car, at least temporarily. Standing on his tiptoes, Pak forced the angled stone deep into the opening between the top of the garage door and the door frame. He retreated back to the shadows.

A half-minute later the whir of an electronic door opener sounded. The door began to lift, then quickly jammed as the rock became wedged. The motor coughed once before falling silent. Pak had just bought himself a little time. But he had no idea what he would do with it.

Cam seethed. He wasn't sure whether to believe Admiral Warner or not. In the end it didn't matter. Amanda was still a prisoner. Still probably in danger.

Warner leaned against a stone chamber in a posture unbecoming a naval officer. Cam strode over. "Last chance. Free Amanda."

The admiral shrugged. "I can't. I no longer have her. Apparently … someone else … has taken her. But we can still work this out, I'm certain—"

Cam's frustration boiled over. His balled his right hand into a fist and stepped forward. "This is your fault, Warner." He really did want to pummel the man.

"Wait," the admiral panted, holding one hand up in defense. For the first time Cam saw real fear in his enemy's eyes, apparently in response to the rage evident on Cam's face. "I can give you the address. In Woburn." He sniffled. "She was being held there. She may still be. I just don't know."

Cam nodded, seething. It was his only shot. He grabbed the admiral by the chin, their faces close, Cam smelling the stale fear on Warner's breath. The fetid aroma of the man pushed Cam over the edge, the final insult in a day full of affronts. Cam snapped a short, vicious, right cross into Warner's jaw, the impact of his fist on his enemy's face satisfying him at a near-animalistic level. The admiral toppled slowly to his side, coming to rest semi-prone against the chamber.

Cam leaned over and shoved him the rest of the way to the ground. "Call off your last hound, Warner. And then give me your phone."

Cam raced down the trail toward the parking lot, gasping with every stride from the jostling of his ribs. He had snapped the wires on Warner's detonation devices after obtaining the address from Warner. Warner and his henchmen could find their own way down.

As he ran he phoned his cousin. "Astarte okay?"

"Fine. Kicking my ass in ping pong. What's going on?"

"Trust me, you don't want to know." He fought for breath. "You post that video yet?"

"You told me to wait ten. It's only been seven."

Really? It seemed like an hour had passed. "Hold off. But if anything happens to me, post it right away." He gulped air. "In the meantime, call 911 and get some cops over to America's Stonehenge."

Cutting through the woods to skirt the bottom portion of the trail in case Yves was still lurking about and chose to ignore his stand down orders, Cam stumbled into the parking lot. He collapsed into Magnuson's Lexus and gunned the engine. Woburn was a thirty-minute drive. Which was thirty minutes more time than he had.

Solomon watched from the woods as an Asian man snuck to the front of the garage and wedged something into the door. Who was this and what was he doing? And what was taking Trey so long to return with the Gunn woman?

He turned to the bound Xifeng. "Who else knows about the spiral?"

She shrugged. "At this point it seems like *everyone* knows."

He nodded. She was right. He phoned Madame Radminikov and, in a hushed voice, gave her a quick update. Solomon would mourn the death of Abraham but not miss his myopic leadership. The modern world, quite simply, had passed him by. Madame Radminikov would, he believed, prove to be the superior tactician and, more importantly, visionary. "Who are the other players in this game?" he asked. "Who might be here?"

She responded immediately. "I can only think of one: Commander de Real. Abraham was concerned the Templars were looking to use Atlantis to undermine the Jewish claims to Israel."

"How so?"

"It's complicated. Does he have the spiral?"

"Perhaps."

"You need to stop him. That spiral must not fall into enemy hands."

"Do we need it?"

"I don't think so, no. But we can't leave it with de Real either."

"Can you send back-up?"

"Most of our men are still in Rhode Island. I'm afraid you're on your own."

Solomon nodded and hung up. Ignoring the throbbing from the three-day-old knife wound on his right forearm, he tightened Xifeng's and her husband's restraints and removed all sharp objects from their pockets as he evaluated the situation. Solomon was alone, Trey apparently having been immobilized. And no doubt de Real had operatives with him. The odds were not good.

But who was this Asian man? An Arab saying popped into his head: *The enemy of my enemy is my friend.*

Solomon took a deep breath. Time to make a new friend.

There was no way Amanda was going to get back into the trunk of that car. At least not without a fight. But she and Trey were outnumbered and outgunned.

She caught Trey's eye and flicked her pupils at the safe room door. Trey understood immediately.

"I'm not going to help you, de Real," Trey reiterated, stalling for time. She turned and stepped toward the already-open safe room door. "You're an embarrassment to the Order."

The commander seethed, his face turning red. He was not used to insubordination. "Into the safe room," he ordered, waving his gun. He turned to one of his henchman. "You, put the Gunn woman in the trunk." To the other, he said, "And you, fix that garage door."

Trey loped past Amanda toward the safe room door. As she hit the threshold she turned and issued a blood-curdling scream, pointing at a spot on the far wall. All heads spun, reflexively. Except Amanda's. Instantly she dove through the opening and into the safe room. Trey slammed the door behind her and bolted it.

From the other side of the door de Real offered a deep laugh. "Ah, nicely played! But do you really think I will hesitate to burn this house down?" In a lower voice, he added, "Men, get those gasoline tanks. It may be time for a bonfire."

Amanda swallowed. A safe room like this would be of no use during a fire. They were trapped.

The large black hand locked over Pak's mouth before Pak could so much as finish his swallow. A low voice growled into his ear. "I am not here to harm you. I believe we want the same thing."

Pak sensed the man's strength and bulk. This was the man he had seen at Abraham Gottlieb's home. No way could Pak physically overpower him. He nodded slowly, indicating he understood.

The grip loosened. "Why are you here?" the dark-skinned man asked. "Quickly. There is no time for lies."

Pak trusted his gut. "I must have the spiral."

"Why?"

"To save my life," he answered honestly.

"What will you do with it?"

"Bring it back to North Korea."

"You realize, do you not, that the technology does not work?"

"Yes."

"My name is Solomon. Perhaps I can help you acquire the spiral. But I need your help rescuing the women from the safe room." He loosened his grip and held out his hand. "Do we have a deal?"

'Perhaps' was better than anything else Pak had. He nodded and shook the man's strong, dark hand.

Cam sped south down Route 93 in Magnuson's Lexus SUV, the gas pedal to the floor as he weaved around traffic at speeds in excess of one hundred miles per hour. He had thought about calling the police to try to arrange an escort, but concluded they would never believe his story. He prayed nobody in front of him made a sudden lane change.

He hit the Woburn exit in sixteen minutes and raced, less recklessly, through the suburban streets to a cul-de-sac not far from the highway. The outdoor lights of a yellow Colonial, number seven, beckoned welcomingly. He shook his head. Did he have the right spot? Had Warner lied to him?

He strode to the front door, ready to hit the buzzer. A whistle from his right, toward the garage, froze him. "Cameron, Cameron," came the whisper.

Cam stepped off the steps. Had he imagined it? The call came again, no doubt this time. Cam exhaled. The person knew his name and he hadn't shot him. Given the way things had gone tonight, that made him a friend.

In the dark Cam made out the features of two men, crouched in the shrubbery. A large black hand beckoned him. "Is that Solomon?" he asked.

"Yes. Stay quiet. I just received a text. Amanda and Trey are safe for now, in the safe room off the garage. Commander de Real and his men are inside and are planning to burn the house down. But we have a plan."

"Wait, de Real?"

"Yes."

Cam cursed. Another betrayal. But there was no time to figure out the whys and hows. "Your plan. Tell me."

Solomon explained how Pak had wedged the garage door closed. "The garage is below grade. There are no other doors or windows other than a doorway to the house." He held up a set of car keys. "There is a Volkswagen Golf sedan in the garage with a set of keys in the ignition. But I have locked it from the outside." He shrugged. "So they cannot ram their way out."

"So what's the plan?"

He held up the keys a second time. "The BMW has a remote starter."

Cam nodded. "We could smoke them out. Do it."

The black man swallowed. "It is already done." In the silence that followed Cam heard shouting from inside the garage. Solomon continued. "The trick will be knowing when it is safe to open the door."

Cam huddled with Solomon and the North Korean, Pak, on the side of the garage. Somewhere inside was Amanda. So close. "How long will it take for the carbon monoxide to knock them out?"

"I would say ten minutes," Solomon replied. "But that is just a guess."

"Well, obviously we don't want to kill them. But we can't open the doors too early—I'm assuming they're armed."

"I doubt they'll just sit there and wait," Solomon said.

Before Cam could reply the sound of shattering glass filled the night. Cam and Pak cringed. "My guess is the Golf," Solomon said calmly. "They will try to ram their way out after all. Hopefully it is a steel door. They built a safe room into their home, so they might also have taken extra precautions with their doors."

On cue the garage doors thumped and bowed. Cam waited for a second volley, but none came. He peeked around the corner of the garage. The door featured a long dent but otherwise held. "The air bags must have deployed," said Pak, now next to him. "Many Golfs have standard transmission. If this is one of them, it will be difficult to work the clutch with the bags in the way."

Cam had a thought. "Well, at some point they're coming out. Wait here." He ran to Magnuson's SUV and retrieved the night vision goggles. "These might help."

Pak spoke. "Give me the house keys. I will go in and find the circuit breaker. Once it is dark you will have the advantage with your goggles."

Solomon nodded. "It is a good plan. Also make certain the door from the garage to the house is locked. They would prefer to leave by car, but at some point they will try to escape through the house."

"Then let's hope that door is steel also," Cam said. He added, "I work in real estate. These Colonial homes are all the same." He scratched out the floor plan in the dirt. "The electrical panel will be in the basement, exterior wall, toward the front of the house. Not on the garage side."

Pak stood. "Okay." He raced away.

Cam handed Magnuson's gun to Solomon. "You take this." Somebody should have it who actually was willing to use it.

Another smash of glass. "They are probably hoping to turn off the BMW," Solomon said.

"Can they?"

"Not without the key, no. Or a mechanic who knows how to disable the engine."

"But they could try to ram through the door again, this time with the BMW."

"That is what I would attempt," Solomon said. "But wait." He sent a quick text. "Trey says the BMW is facing out. So if they use it as a ram they will smash the headlights."

"That's our advantage," Cam said. "The dark."

An engine raced, this time the BMW straining against the garage door like a Sumo wrestler. Back and forth the car went, each cycle ending in the car's front end smashing into the door.

"The problem for them is that by racing the engine they are creating more carbon monoxide," Solomon observed.

The door bowed again. "It won't hold much longer," Cam said.

Suddenly the property went dark. "Bingo," Cam said. He adjusted the goggles. A siren in the distance. "Maybe the neighbors called the police."

Solomon nodded. "We don't have much time. I, for one, do not want to have to explain this all to the authorities."

"Me either," said Pak, just returning from killing the power.

"So what do you propose?" Cam asked over the sound of the roaring engine.

Solomon stared at the garage door, straining at its hinges. It wouldn't hold much longer. "That we do the unexpected."

The plan came together quickly. Not much better than a Hail Mary, but Cam had seen plenty of those plays work at the end of football games.

"Ready?" Solomon asked.

Pak nodded and handed the house keys to Cam. Pak stood beneath the rock he had wedged into the garage door frame, a thick block of wood in his hand.

Cam also nodded, a cloth tied around his nose and mouth.

Solomon was on the phone with Trey. "Three, two, one," he counted down, waiting for the BMW to pull back for its next charge. "Now."

Pak knocked the rock aside with the block. At the same instant Cam cupped his hands under the door and lifted. Not much, just a few inches, but enough for de Real to notice a ribbon of light from the outside. "Stop the car. Lift the door," ordered de Real. "We may have knocked the jam free."

A pair of hands grasped the door from inside the garage and hoisted. On cue, as the door raised a foot off the ground, Solomon sprayed ankle-high gunfire into the garage. "I can promise you I won't kill anyone," he had said. "But I might take out some ankles and knees." The hands disappeared, replaced by the sound of shouted curses and scurrying feet.

In the commotion, Cam rolled under the door, pinning himself against a side wall next to the Golf. He stayed low, shielded by the Golf and trying to ignore the pain. The BMW still idled. Frenzied shouts filled the darkness, de Real cursing and his men responding in confused fashion. Through his goggles Cam scanned the room, deducing what had happened in response to Solomon's gunfire: The man who had lifted the door had thrown himself against a side wall while de Real had dived into the Golf and the operative driving the BMW had ducked under the front seat.

Solomon barked a command from outside. "Throw out your weapons and come out with hands up. One at a time."

The muddled voice of Commander de Real responded. "I think not." His words sounded heavy in his mouth. "God is on our side."

"Yes, well, sometimes even God gets outmaneuvered."

In the blackened garage Cam rose quietly to his feet. He circled, creeping, to check on de Real through his goggles. The Templar slowly extricated himself from the Golf's front seat and tried to stand. Instead he flopped to the cement floor and, frustrated, raised himself unsteadily to his hands and knees. He peered toward the front of the garage, gun drawn, moving drunkenly as the carbon monoxide took effect. For Cam it was like watching a neon green alien figure in some video game running at the wrong speed. But the gun was real. Cam stayed low, edging around the garage slowly, quietly, checking on the other two henchmen. Same thing. Disoriented in the dark, dizzied by the poisonous gas, they waved their guns. Cam didn't have much time—the carbon monoxide would soon disorient him as well.

He tiptoed to the back corner of the garage and rapped on the door to the safe room, the sound lost amid the shouting. Tap. Tap-tap. Tap-tap. Just as Solomon had arranged. The door swung open. Through his goggles he saw Amanda's anxious, green face. She never looked better. He reached out, took her hand. "Stay close," he whispered, pushing her hand against his heart.

"Always," she said. She clasped his belt loop, with Trey close behind. Hugging the wall, Cam led them the short distance to the door to the house. He slid the key into the lock and clicked open the deadbolt, the cylinder snapping into place.

A voice. "They're escaping!"

Cam shoved Amanda and Trey through the door. A barrage of gunfire erupted, spraying the walls around him. He dove through, rolled to his knees and shoved the door closed. Amanda flicked the lock. "Let's get the hell out of here," she exclaimed.

Amanda, Cam and Trey pushed out the front door of the suburban Colonial. Sirens approached. Solomon stood guard at the garage, occasionally spraying bullets at the ankles of de Real and his men. The entire neighborhood had lit up in response to the gunshots, the powerless yellow Colonial an island of darkness in the moonless night. Amanda shivered in the cold night air, her body still slowed by the truth serum.

"Like Amanda said, let's get out of here," Cam said. The garage door groaned, the Templars redoubling their efforts to ram their way out. He yelled for Solomon to join them.

They jogged across the front lawn toward the SUV. Amanda slowed, lagging behind. Out of the corner of her eye she saw a movement, a flash. She turned just in time to see Xifeng, airborne, flying at her, her hands clawed and teeth bared like a panther pouncing.

Adrenaline surged through her. Instinctively she ducked, skirting most of the impact but taking a knee to the shoulder. "Cam, help," she shouted. But the sirens and the ramming BMW drowned her voice.

Xifeng rolled to her feet, into a crouched attack position. "Where is the spiral?"

Involuntarily Amanda reached for the spiral nestled under her shirt. Maybe she should just give it up—it had caused nothing but trouble since it first arrived on her front porch. But it was the last tangible proof of Atlantis. And people had died for it. She shook her head. "Go to hell."

Xifeng lept again, this time catching Amanda with a chop to the nose. Blood spurted, pooling in Amanda's mouth. She spat and backed off, unsteady on her feet. She was in good shape, an ex-gymnast who worked out three times a week. She had taken a self-defense class and actually outweighed her assailant. But the drugs made her feel like she was moving underwater. No way could she match the Chinese woman's speed. But her strength should be largely unaffected.

And surprise was on her side.

Amanda turned as if to run but then, without warning, spun and exploded into the smaller woman. They fell together, Amanda twisting and landing atop her. Xifeng writhed, but Amanda pinned the woman's arms with her knees and, using her thumbs, pressed hard on the carotid sinus on the side of the neck just below the jaw. Xifeng scratched at Amanda's eyes, but Amanda buried her head against her assailant's shoulder, shielding herself. Focusing her strength on her thumbs, Amanda dug at the spot, picturing her thumbs pinching the opening, blocking the blood supply through the artery.

Xifeng screeched, her desperation giving her added strength. She reached around Amanda's head and grabbed a handful of hair. The pain was too much. Amanda withdrew her thumbs and rolled away. Xifeng did not hesitate, leaping acrobatically from a prone position back to her feet.

"Give me that necklace," the Asian woman hissed.

Amanda felt her energy ebbing. She had lost her advantage. They eyed each other, circling like a pair of boxers. Xifeng charged again. Acting instinctively, Amanda ducked under the attack. Xifeng landed on her feet and turned to attack again. Amanda knew she had only one more burst in her. Rather than ducking again she charged a second time, their bodies thumping together. This time as they fell Amanda slipped the necklace over her neck. She pulled Xifeng atop her, the woman's back on her chest, just as Xifeng had done to her in the Newport mansion. "You want the necklace," she said. "Well here it is." She looped the chain around Xifeng's neck, pulled it tight and twisted. What her thumbs had started the chain quickly finished. Xifeng coughed and gurgled, her writhing ending.

Cam suddenly appeared. He pulled Xifeng off and dropped next to her, his eyes wide. "Amanda! Are you okay?"

She exhaled, blood still pouring from her nose. Her whole body hurt and the world around her seemed distorted, like a carnival mirror. She handed Cam the necklace, reaching for what she thought was his chest. "Take this bloody thing. I never want to see it again."

Chapter 10

Venus' wet tongue on Amanda's nose woke her as the first rays of daylight filtered into their bedroom. The memory of yesterday's horror show raced through her mind—Meryn betraying her, Abraham blowing up the Crones, the Chinese spy kidnapping her, fighting her way to freedom in the garage, then finally brawling on the front lawn. Not to mention Cam's near-death encounter with Warner and his henchmen at America's Stonehenge. And yet here she was, in her bed, Cam snoring lightly beside her, Astarte in the bedroom across the hall. It was as if none of it had really happened.

That was not true. Her whole body hurt, a sharp reminder that the memories were real. Dried blood crusted inside her nose, her neck ached and the corner of her heart where Meryn had begun to make a home felt empty and raw, as if she had ripped her way out. At least the lethargy from the truth serum had passed. She smiled, recalling how Cam had playfully quizzed her on the car ride home, asking how he compared to ex-lovers. She turned toward Cam, pulled Venus to them and closed her eyes. They had earned the right to sleep in a bit.

An hour later—just past seven o'clock according to her clock— a text dinged on her phone. "Leah Radminikov," she read aloud from the display. What in the world could she want? Actually, Amanda could think of a dozen things. She opened the message. *Can we meet for breakfast? Many things to discuss.*

Amanda kicked the sheets off and shook Cam awake.

"Good morning," he mumbled. "What is it?"

"Time to get up. I think we need to clean up the mess we made yesterday."

Cam had not slept well. His neck throbbed, and he half-expected the doorbell to ring in the middle of the night and police to drag them off for questioning. He and Amanda had, by rough count, been involved in at least a half-dozen felonies: assault, kidnapping, mayhem, firearms violations, destruction of property, auto theft. And that didn't even include Abraham's massacre of the Crones. Yet somehow—apparently through Kidon's influence and because the CIA had taken the attitude that all was well that ended well—their crime spree was being treated no more seriously than a parking meter violation. The lawyer in him recoiled at the lawlessness of it all. But not so much that he felt inclined to go turn himself in.

All this occupied his thoughts as he showered. He had forced himself out the door for a short morning jog, trying to loosen up his body stiff from yesterday's exertions and altercations. He hated to turn the hot water off, but Amanda was right: They needed to clean up the mess they had made.

Twenty minutes later they climbed into Cam's SUV, Astarte and Venus in the backseat. They had picked Astarte up the night before at Brandon's after leaving Woburn but had not discussed anything with her. "So, Astarte, you don't have to worry about Mr. Saint Paul anymore," Cam said. "It turns out that was not even his real name."

"I don't understand," she replied.

"His real name is Warner," Amanda said. "He was trying to stop Dad and me from researching Atlantis. That's why he wanted you to spy on us." She squeezed Cam's knee. "But Dad put an end to it. So nothing more to worry about."

Astarte nodded. "So, is Atlantis real?"

Cam and Amanda exchanged a glance. She gave him a look like she wanted to answer. Which, as the only surviving person privy to the Crones and their secrets, was clearly her prerogative. "It appears so, yes. There were a lot of people—this man Warner being just one of them—who wanted to keep it secret. But I think after yesterday those people have ... changed their minds."

Astarte nodded, pensive. "Sometimes people change their minds because they have no choice. Is that what happened here?"

Amanda laughed. "You could say that, yes."

"Well, I'd like to learn more about Atlantis."

Amanda turned around in the passenger seat. "And I'd be happy to tell you everything I know."

After dropping Astarte and Venus off again at Brandon's house, Cam and Amanda drove toward Boston. On the trip Amanda did a quick Google search.

"Turns out Meryn and the Crones really were all about bloodlines," she said. "The Basques, the Druze, the people of the Canary Islands and Orkney Islands, the Berbers of Morocco— they're all isolated populations, and they all share common DNA and blood types."

"And all these places are along the Atlantic Rim," Cam added. "Atlantis descendants."

"So that song and dance about being a spiritual legacy was just more rubbish. Meryn was a racist, plain and simple."

"Well, then, you're probably better off not being related to her."

Amanda laughed sardonically. "I'm just like Hermione from Harry Potter. Muggle-born."

Cam squeezed her thigh. "Yeah, but it turned out Hermione was magical after all. So like I said, you're probably better off."

Amanda had insisted on choosing the breakfast locale, tired of all the surprises over the past week when other people were setting the agenda. Cam parked around the corner from Sound Bites, a diner in Somerville near Tufts University. They arrived early, grabbed a table in the back corner and sipped tea while waiting for the Jewish butcher. By late morning the restaurant would be packed with college kids, but for now it was just a few locals.

Madame Radminikov marched in five minutes later. Cam was surprised to see Solomon and Trey with her. "Did you know she was bringing them?" he whispered.

"No. I assumed she was coming alone. But I suppose they've earned the right to be here." She smiled and squeezed Cam's hand. "They saved me while you were out playing in the woods."

The three newcomers sat down, the two women heavily. Trey sighed as they exchanged greetings. "I was up most of the night debriefing," she said. Seeing Cam's and Amanda's surprised looks, she continued. "Guess I never told you guys. I work for Homeland Security."

Amanda nodded. She and Cam had figured it was something like that after she turned on de Real.

Trey continued. "Our guys showed up after we left and cleaned up the Woburn scene. Commander de Real and his two men had some carbon monoxide poisoning, but they should recover just in time for their arraignments Monday."

Madame Radminikov added, "I too was up all night. Trying to put out all the brushfires. I think we've convinced the Newport police to label the explosion an accident from a gas leak. But it took just about every favor I could call in." She smiled at Trey. "Plus a phone call from Washington."

Trey offered a tired smile of her own. "As far as my bosses are concerned, none of this ever happened. Abraham is dead. He was acting alone. There's nothing to be gained from a messy investigation."

Solomon waited for eyes to turn to him, his expression serious and unsmiling. Then he broke into a wide grin. "I had a wonderful night's sleep."

"So," Amanda said as the laughter died down, "what is on the agenda for this morning?"

"As I said," Madame Radminikov replied, "we still have a bit of a mess on our hands. And we have some decisions to make." She looked around the table, her soft-spoken manner in contrast to her bulk. "As a group." The comment was an apparent counter to Abraham's secretive, autocratic style. "But first I think I owe it to you to bring you up to speed."

She explained how the authorities had recovered seventeen spirals from the carnage and debris of the explosion. "The rest must have melted or simply vaporized. Amanda, I'd like to keep one and give the rest to you."

"Why me?"

They ordered food before Madame Radminikov replied. "I could hear everything said in the mansion over Abraham's transmitter. Abraham specifically left the future of Atlantis in your hands. It is up to you to decide whether to reconstitute the Crones, whether to continue this tradition of keeping alive the memory of Atlantis." She smiled kindly. "To do that, you'll need the spirals."

"Actually," Trey interrupted, "we found eighteen, not seventeen. We gave one to Pak. It probably will save his life."

Solomon added, "His government will ransom it back to the Chinese." With Xifeng held in Israel, she wouldn't be able to tell the Chinese the spirals don't work. "Later, when it turns out to be nothing but a pulsating piece of meteorite, Kim Jong-un will be able to claim he put one over on China."

Cam leaned forward. "But that will give Kim hard currency."

Trey replied, shrugging. "Some, yes. But doing damage to the Chinese-North Korean relationship is worth the tradeoff. And I'm pretty sure we didn't give the spiral to Pak for free. It won't hurt to have eyes and ears in Pyongyang." She smiled. "Listen to me, now I'm an expert on Asian affairs."

Cam didn't completely understand the deal between the North Koreans and the Druze. "Did the Druze really believe the North Koreans were going to march across Asia?"

Again Trey replied. "Best we can tell, both sides were waiting to call the other's bluff. The North Koreans didn't really believe the Druze could deliver gold-making technology, but they went along with the plan just in case. And more and more it looked like the technology really did exist. And the Druze didn't really believe a sect of Asian Druze were ready to march across Asia, with the help of the Iranians, to help them take Jerusalem. But apparently Kim built an entire village and dressed his people up like Druze and armed them, as if they were ready to go to war—I've seen the pictures, it looked pretty convincing. Again, it was a bizarre plan but too good an opportunity for the Druze not to play it out." She shrugged. "With the North Koreans and the Iranians, you have to assume anything is possible."

As heads nodded Amanda redirected the conversation back to the spirals. "Sorry, but why should I keep the spirals? I'm not even part of the Atlantis families. Plus I barely know anything about the history."

"Actually, with the Crones dead, you probably know more than anyone else alive," Madame Radminikov said. "Meryn did train you." She lowered her eyes shyly. "Abraham's last request of me was that I become the Crone of his branch of the family. If it is okay with you, Amanda, I would like to honor his legacy by doing so."

"Of course," Amanda blurted. She and Cam last night had discussed the butcher's involvement in the mansion conflagration and concluded she knew nothing about it. Apparently the police agreed.

"What about Warner?" Cam asked. "Do the authorities make believe his crimes didn't happen either?"

"Indeed," said Madame Radminikov, placing her hands on the table palms down. "What about him? From what I can gather, he and Abraham were working together. Each had his own reasons for suppressing Atlantis." She paused. "Each, unfortunately, took things too far."

Trey pursed her lips. "What happens to Warner depends on you, Cam," she said, eyes on him.

He sensed something unsaid in her comment. Something disquieting. "What do you mean?"

A voice from Cam's blind side interjected. "She means I am here to make a deal."

Cam spun, recoiling at the sight of Warner standing above him. The admiral looked anything but crisp—clothes wrinkled, unshaven, eyes bloodshot. "What are you doing here?" Cam hissed. He looked past the man, searching for Magnuson or his other henchmen.

Warner held up a hand. "As I said, I am here to make a deal."

"With whom?" Cam asked.

"With you. You are in a position to ruin me, ruin my company. I am willing to make a generous offer to induce you not to do so."

Cam exchanged a quick look with Amanda. "We don't want your money."

"It is not money I am offering." He motioned to an empty chair. "Do you mind if I sit?"

This was the man who had tormented Astarte and caused Amanda to be abducted. "Yes," Cam said, "as a matter of fact, I do. Say what you have to say and then get out of here."

Warner blinked and nodded. He leaned against the back of the empty chair. "We have something in common, Mr. Thorne: We are both historians. In fact, I have been studying the mystery of Atlantis for my entire adult life."

"Where I come from, historians preserve history, not destroy it."

He nodded. "That is a fair criticism. I have been torn between my love for history and my duty to my company. In a perverse way, you have freed me of this dilemma. Until now I had to choose one or the other. Now, thanks to you, I have a chance to choose both."

Cam wasn't tracking. He gave him a quizzical look.

Warner continued. "I have a collection of artifacts that prove the existence of Atlantis. Items my company has uncovered over the years during our underwater exploration, objects I myself have purchased—"

"Bones you have stolen," Cam interjected, thinking about the Red Paint People burial site.

"Yes. Those too. The point is that only a few people in the world have ever seen these artifacts."

"So open a museum," Cam said dismissively.

"That is exactly what I hope to do," he said. "And I want you to be its curator."

Cam exchanged another look with Amanda. She shrugged and gave him a look that said it wouldn't hurt to hear more. But Cam was a long way from wanting anything to do with the industrialist, much less work for him. "Sorry, I have a job."

He shifted his weight. "That actually works out well. This one doesn't begin for another five years. And you would not be working for me. I would give you full control of the museum."

"You want to share your artifacts with the world, but just not yet."

"I have an obligation to my workers, Mr. Thorne." He held Cam's eyes. "I admit I have made some poor decisions, some selfish decisions. But I have always taken very seriously my obligation to the employees of Warner Industries. We employ thousands. If your video were to come out, or if proof of Atlantis were to come out, my company would go bankrupt." He swallowed. "What I am asking for is a five-year grace period. During that time I will work to redirect our projects away from the Atlantic Rim. And our lawyers and lobbyists will work to convince the United Nations to soften some of the language in its underwater treaty."

Cam didn't care about Warner. But the appeal on behalf of his employees resonated. "Why should I trust you?"

"Because at any time you could simply release your video and ruin me. And because I am prepared to turn over all the Atlantis artifacts to you now."

Cam angled his head. He smelled a trap. "But you'd be giving me all the cards. How would you be sure I wouldn't double-cross you?"

Warner's tired blue eyes held Cam's. "Simple. I believe you are one of those rare people whom I can take at his word."

Bartholomew Warner raised himself up to his full height, ran his hand through his hair and tucked in his shirt as soon as he was out of view of the breakfast diner. He hated appearing in public looking anything less than shipshape. But battles were won as often with subterfuge as with firepower.

His limousine waited, live-parked in front of a hydrant. Magnuson, his head bandaged, scurried out to open the door—Warner should have fired him after yesterday's debacle, but he chose instead to keep him on, knowing that shame could be a powerful motivator. Warner slid into the back seat, glancing at the olive-skinned woman beside him. A cast encased her right arm and the side of her face was disfigured by a blistering burn, rivulets of semi-dried blood snaking between islands of curled, blackened skin. But Jamila's coal-black eyes shone with their usual unnatural intensity and she held her chin up in her normal imperious manner. Like Warner, she was a survivor. And a valued ally. But a dangerous one.

"So," she said, the word more command than query.

Warner allowed himself a smile. "As the saying goes, I've lived to fight another day."

"I do not have time for your sayings."

"Yes." He cleared his throat. "Thorne accepted my offer. He believes he has the upper hand now, but it will not last."

"The fool," she spat. She glared at him, holding his eyes until he blinked. Unlike Thorne, Jamila would show Warner no mercy if he crossed her. "And the spirals?" she asked.

"From what I heard, most of them were rescued from the fire. Like you." Apparently she took shelter in a dumbwaiter behind a hidden wall panel. She did not respond so he continued. "The Gunn woman will be taking custody of them."

Her nostrils flared. "A temporary arrangement, I assure you."

"If I may be of assistance, please let me know."

Jamila sniffed and closed her eyes in a long blink, as if shielding her soul from the stupidity around her. "You will be most helpful by staying out of my way." She turned in her seat to fix him again with both eyes. Somehow the nasty wound on her cheek added a layer of gravitas to her words. "I trust I do not need to remind you of our deal, Admiral. You may do what you want to Thorne. But leave the girl and the butcher to me." She spoke the words slowly. "They will lament the day they made an enemy of the Crones of Atlantis."

The End

If you enjoyed *Echoes of Atlantis*, you may want to read the other books featuring Cameron and Amanda in David S. Brody's **Templars in America** series:

Cabal of the Westford Knight
Templars at the Newport Tower (2009)

Set in Boston and Newport, RI, inspired by artifacts evidencing that Scottish explorers and Templar Knights traveled to New England in 1398.

Thief on the Cross
Templar Secrets in America (2011)

Set in the Catskill Mountains of New York, sparked by an ancient Templar codex calling into question fundamental teachings of the Catholic Church.

Powdered Gold
Templars and the American Ark of the Covenant (2013)

Set in Arizona, exploring the secrets and mysteries of both the Ark of the Covenant and a manna-like powdered substance.

The Oath of Nimrod
Giants, MK-Ultra and the Smithsonian Coverup (2014)

Set in Massachusetts and Washington, DC, triggered by the mystery of hundreds of giant human skeletons found buried across North America.

The Isaac Question
Templars and the Secret of the Old Testament (2015)

Set in Massachusetts and Scotland, focusing on ancient stone chambers, the mysterious Druids and a stunning reinterpretation of the Biblical Isaac story.

Available at Amazon,
and as Kindle and Nook eBooks

Author's Note

As is the case with all the books in this series, if the artifact/site/object of art is pictured, it is real. And If I claim it is of a certain age or of a certain provenance or features certain characteristics, that information is correct. Likewise, the historical and literary references are accurate. When, for example, I quote from the Book of Enoch or an ancient Sumerian legend, those quotes are accurate. How I use these artifacts and references to weave a story is, of course, where the fiction takes root.

For inquisitive readers, perhaps curious about some of the specific historical assertions made and evidence presented in this story, more information is available here (in order of appearance in the story):

- The Newport Tower does indeed mark the winter solstice and the thirty-five possible days of Easter with solar-produced light boxes which move across the interior wall of the structure. Images of these phenomena can be viewed on my blog, www.westfordknight.blogspot.com.

- For more information regarding the Newport Tower mortar sample carbon-dating, see *The Hooked X*, by Scott F. Wolter (North Star Press 2009), at page 186.

- Much has been written about the possibility that modern Jews descend from the Khazars, a collection of Turkic clans who settled in the Caucasus and converted to Judaism in the 8th century CE. The 2012 article supporting this assertion can be found here: http://gbe.oxfordjournals.org/content/5/1/61.full. This assertion has been widely discredited for the simple reason that, as there is no record today of actual Khazar DNA, it is physically impossible to determine who is descended from it and who is not.

- There is in fact a "Red Paint People" burial site in Salisbury, Massachusetts. The bones and artifacts pictured in this book are from that site, the so-called Morrill Point dig. The actual bones are not quite as old as I portray them in the story, nor were they preserved by a shell midden. But other Red Paint burial sites do date back to the ages I use in the story. See generally this website for an overview of the Salisbury dig: http://historyofmassachusetts.org/salisbury-massachusetts-history. For a more academic treatment, see *Archeology of Prehistoric Native America: A Treatment,* by Guy E. Gibbon & Kenneth M. Ames (Taylor & Francis 1998), at page 341.

- For an excellent overview of the Druze, their lifestyle and their religious beliefs, see http://www.everyculture.com/multi/Bu-Dr/ Druze.html#ixzz42u8wLHF7. For the assertion that the Druze believe a reincarnated group of Druze in China will return to rule Jerusalem, see http://williamseabrook.livejournal.com/46691.html.

- Two excellent sites for all things Atlantis are these: http:// atlantipedia.ie/samples and http://www.atlantisquest.com.

- For a discussion of eels, butterflies and migratory birds as they relate to Atlantis, see http://atlantisonline.smfforfree2.com/index.php?topic=601.0 ;wap2

- A good overview for the theory that some kind of cataclysmic event circa 11,600 BCE both ended the last Ice Age and destroyed Atlantis can be found in *Magicians of the Gods,* by Graham Hancock (St. Martin's Press 2015). This book also summarizes Dr. Robert Schoch's research regarding erosion patterns on the Sphinx.

- For an overview of the science of converting bismuth and/or lead into gold, see http://www.scientificamerican.com/article/fact-or-fiction-lead-can-be-turned-into-gold

- Information on the UNESCO Convention on the Protection of the Underwater Cultural Heritage can be found on Wikipedia. Due to concerns regarding impacts on the oil and gas industries, the United States has not signed this treaty.

- Basic information on the Venus of Dolni and European Cave Art can be found on Wikipedia.

- Attribution for the following quote found in the text is as follows: https://sacredsites.com/middle_east/lebanon/baalbek.html. *"Long before the Romans conquered the site and built their enormous temple of Jupiter, long even before the Phoenicians constructed a temple to the god Baal, there stood at Baalbek the largest stone block construction found in the entire world."*

- There are some intriguing measurements at the America's Stonehenge site, correlating to the megalithic yard. Work and research on this possible correlation is ongoing.

I have thoroughly enjoyed exploring the possibility of a lost Atlantis colony. Hopefully this novel has provided you with some entertainment and intellectual stimulation as well. Thanks for reading.

Photo/Drawing Credits

Images used in this book are the property of the author, in the public domain, and/or provided courtesy of the following individuals (images listed in order of appearance in the story):

Image of Newport Tower
Courtesy of Richard Lynch

Images of Salisbury "Red Paint People" bones and weapons
Courtesy of Richard Lynch

Image of Hypothetical Atlantis
Courtesy http://www.atlantisquest.com

Image of Gobekli Tepe
Credit, Rolfcosar

Gobekli Tepe Illustration
Credit, http://www.philipcoppens.com/gobekli.html

Image of Baalbeck
Credit, Fouad Awada

Image of Burrows Cave Elephant Carving
Courtesy of Scott Wolter

300

Acknowledgements

Diving down an unexplored rabbit hole and (to mix my animal metaphors) ferreting around there for a few months doing research for a new novel is my idea of a great time. Honestly. Thankfully for me, I have managed to surround myself with fellow researchers who share this passion. Heartfelt thanks for assisting me in my research go out to (in alphabetical order): Alan Butler, Michael Carr, Richard Lynch, Scott MacLauchlan, Wayne MacLean, Dennis Stone. I am grateful to you all. (Please note that inclusion in the above list does not in any way constitute an endorsement of this work or the themes contained herein.)

I also again want to thank my team of readers, those who trudged their way through early versions of this story and offered helpful, insightful comments (listed alphabetically): Allie Brody, Jeff Brody, Spencer Brody, Michael Carr, Jeanne Scott, Richard Scott, Eric Stearns.

For other authors out there looking to navigate their way through the publishing process, I can't speak highly enough about Amy Collins and her team at New Shelves Books—real pros who know the business and are a pleasure to work with.

Lastly, to my wife, Kim: This is my ninth novel, and none of them would have been possible without your guidance, assistance, support and insight. This has been a wild journey, made even more enjoyable by having you by my side.